The Maki

"In short," he said in conclusion, "the man we want must know Americans better than we know ourselves. He ought to be able to touch that inner core, tapping the motivation, pride, and action that's uniquely American."

"Oh Christ!" Charlie Herron groaned. "*That* kind of talk at three in the morning."

But Rich Cuthbert and the others were intrigued. "Okay Pete, let's have it. Who's this genius?"

"Yes, who's the miracle man?" asked Witherspoon.

Stackpole hesitated for a moment, gazed at the imported stained-glass windows as though the name were being borne earthward in a chariot of spun gold, then opened his palms in a gesture of offertory.

"Eddie Quinn," he said.

The silence had the numbing quality of post-collection shock.

Charter Books by Fletcher Knebel

FLETCHER KNEBEL

DARK HORSE

CHARTER BOOKS, NEW YORK

The characters and events in this book
are fictitious, and any resemblance to actual persons
and events is purely coincidental.

This Charter book contains the
complete text of the original hardcover edition.

DARK HORSE

A Charter Book / published by arrangement with
Doubleday & Co., Inc.

PRINTING HISTORY
Doubleday edition published 1972
Charter edition / June 1987

ISBN: 0-441-13785-7

Charter Books are published by The Berkley Publishing Group,
200 Madison Avenue, New York, New York 10016.
PRINTED IN THE UNITED STATES OF AMERICA

To Walter I. Bradbury

DARK HORSE

RESOLVED, That the National Committee be and is hereby authorized and empowered to fill any and all vacancies which may occur by reason of death, declination or otherwise in the ticket nominated by this Convention, and that in voting, in said Committee, the Committee members representing any State, the District of Columbia, Puerto Rico, the Virgin Islands and Guam shall be entitled to cast the same number of votes as said State, the District of Columbia, Puerto Rico, the Virgin Islands and Guam was entitled to cast in the National Convention, or that the National Committee in its judgment may call a National Convention for the purpose of filling such vacancy.

1

Houston, Oct. 13 (AP)—The national committee recessed tonight after failing in five ballots to nominate a suc-
cessor to the late Senator Walter Hudson, the presidential
candidate who died just twenty-two days before the election.

Not yet, not yet, he cautioned himself.

Something was wrong with the electric digital clock on the walnut
table. Instead of a discreet click whenever the new number joined
the march of minutes toward eternity and/or oblivion, the clock
emitted a sound not unlike a weary grunt. Now it grunted again,
apparently opting for oblivion as the ultimate goal, and registered
2:57.

Still too early, thought Pete, even though he felt as if he'd been
cooped up for days in this ridiculously elegant hotel suite.

The spent look of the seven men sprawled over the scarlet velvet
sofas in the marble library testified that this was 2:57 A.M. They
showed signs of wear in their wilted collars and their stubbled jowls
and they tended to snap at one another. Bottles of Chivas Regal
scotch and Tanqueray gin stood half empty on the bar cart. Cigarette
and cigar stubs filled the ornate ash trays, but there was no smoke.
Ah, no one could ever fasten the epithet "smoke-filled room" on the
Celestial suite of the Astroworld Hotel, for the air conditioning, unlike the clock, whirred softly, wafting the odors of tobacco and
sweat into unseen ducts.

The men had been here for hours, ever since the national committee adjourned for the night after the fifth ballot and on the rim of deadlock.

"Wheeler gives me a pain in the ass," said Charlie Herron, the Chicago banker who served as the party's finance chairman. "If he didn't have such a monumental ego, we wouldn't be in this fix."

"Face it," said Ted Witherspoon, the Texas oil operator. His words fell like bricks being dropped one at a time. "Wheeler, Starnes, Graham, all of them ought to be running for county clerk, not President."

A new name lurked beneath Pete Stackpole's tongue, but Pete exercised restraint. Not yet. Still too early to divulge the name. In politics timing was almost as crucial as image. In fact, with perfect timing, people often could be persuaded to transform image into substance, a triumph of psychological alchemy. Let them all grow wearier, thought Pete, until skins itched and Governor Creed Hotchkiss put his shoes back on, realizing at last that his feet stank. Along about 3:30 A.M. Yes, sometime after 3:30 was the time to spring his man.

"At the risk of repeating myself . . ." began Sam Shadowitz.

"Once again," finished Stanley Framingham tartly. The senator from aerospace regarded Shadowitz, a University of Pennsylvania economics professor, as symbolic of three aspects of American life that Framingham viewed with misgivings: academe, the eastern seaboard and Judaism, although not necessarily in that order.

"The point must be stressed, Stan," said Shadowitz without irritation. "Every member on that committee feels he has as much right to the quickie nomination as Wheeler, Starnes or Graham. So we waste time discussing men of the same caliber. And your man, Stan, is more of the same."

Senator Framingham hitched himself sideways on the sofa's scarlet cushion. "Bill Polk has more feel for this country in his little finger than most of us have in our whole body." He scratched his rump as though to punctuate the metaphor.

"Polk can't communicate, Stan," said Rich Cuthbert in the dismissive tone of an older brother. "We all know he's okay in small groups, but the man we pick has to get across to millions in one helluva short time."

"Fat chance," said Charlie Herron sourly. The banker wore a monogrammed shirt with topaz cuff links and he detested disorderly hours. "With less than three weeks to go? The man would have to be a second Eisenhower."

"Of course he won't stand a chance," agreed Cuthbert, "but we've got to think of our candidates all down the line. The least we can do is not burden them with some dolt at the head of the ticket."

Rich Cuthbert, a Michigan publisher, was the party's highly esteemed communicator. He could communicate intimately and persuasively with anyone inside the garden wall of his own predilections.

"Let's go over the list again and try to eliminate the obvious misfits," said Ted Witherspoon. The Texan's life was a harmonious triad of oil, politics and money, and his wife, a congresswoman, had recently consulted a psychiatrist to determine why, among other problems, she loathed her husband.

As they talked on and the clock lumbered toward dawn, fatigue took on the gritty edge of exasperation. In the distance a police siren wailed, a reminder that the have-nots refused to cease their marauding of the night streets and highways merely because the haves were holding a political meeting in the vicinity. Governor Hotchkiss leaned over his magnificent belly and massaged his feet, panting as he did so. It was a good sign for Pete Stackpole. The hour of exhaustion, that darkling hour of decision, was nearing.

"Excuse me for a couple of minutes," said Stackpole. "I need a break."

Pete walked from the marble library and across the corridor, with its Mexican tiled floor and its huge carriage lamps, of the ninth-floor Celestial suite. My God, the place was as big as a hockey rink. Charlie Herron had rented the nine-bedroom extravaganza for $2500 a day—a day!—and invited some of his political cronies to live it up for the duration of the committee's deliberations. Pete walked through his own "Lillian Russell" room, complete with brass and porcelain bed and purple velvet bedspread. He slipped out to the terrace, gripped the iron railing and inhaled deeply.

The air was miasmic. Cicadas droned their metallic lament, the mid-October moon hid behind the sulphurous smog that almost obscured the downtown Houston skyline and across an immense empty parking lot a mushroom of light marked the Houston Astro-dome where the party two months ago had nominated its candidate for President of the United States. The thirty-seventh-and-a-half President in Pete's book. Strictly, the number was either thirty-seven or thirty-eight, depending upon whether Grover Cleveland, who served non-consecutive terms, was counted once or twice. Pete Stack-pole, a politician who prized compromise second only to intrigue and remunerative chores, would always regard the next occupant of the White House as No. 37½.

The party's plight at this moment was as unstable as the presidential arithmetic. The duly nominated candidate, Senator Walter Hudson, had died of a heart attack three days ago in his home on the outmost outskirts of Milwaukee. The site of his demise was understandable, since everyone who counted in the party, being white, lived in outmost outskirts. But Hudson's timing was deemed by the faithful to be as negligent as his heart tissue. He died only twenty-two days before the election in which he had a slim but fighting chance. Since Houston was the city of his birth, his widow, Marsha, decided to fly the body south for interment not far from the Astrodome, scene of the candidate's glory hour.

Under party rules the 162-member national committee, composed of the committeeman, committeewoman and state chairman of each state and territory, was charged with electing a replacement for the late nominee. It was empowered to do this either via a new convention or by its own balloting. Leaders promptly ruled out another costly convention at this late hour. A few of them wanted to elevate the vice-presidential candidate, Shelby Ewing, to the top position, and pick a new Vice-President, but the committee's general counsel publicly decreed that such shuffling would violate the sense of the empowering resolution. Those who favored Ewing's promotion could not generate sufficient enthusiasm to overturn the counsel's ruling. Ewing's personality, spanning the spectrum from bland to drab, was not the kind to inspire crusades.

So, with only nineteen days left before the election, the committee's job narrowed to a single task, the selection of a new presidential nominee by its own vote.

Since most members were coming to Houston for the funeral anyway, it was decided to hold the committee meeting in the Astro-world Hotel, only a Texas-sized parking lot removed from the Astro-dome. Members had watched the remains of Senator Hudson being lowered into the earth that morning, reserved the afternoon for meditation, prayer, whisky and maneuvering, then begun the meeting at 8 o'clock at night in the Astroworld's grand ballroom.

It was taken for granted that the quickie October replacement for Senator Hudson could not win the election. For one thing, Hudson himself had been trailing. For another, the party's outgoing President in the White House was even less beloved now than when he squeaked into office eight years before. He had refrained from indicating a personal choice to the national committee, undoubtedly because his wishes would have been ignored. The new candidate would be hard-pressed for campaign funds, Hudson already having spent $25,000,000 in a vain effort to catch his rival in the polls. Both parties this year had elected not to take advantage of the public financing of presidential campaigns available from tax revenues. If the public route was selected, a candidate could not spend more than $20,400,000. Financial experts believed they could raise considerably more from private sources. Now, however, with Hudson's death, his party's wealthy contributors were in no mood to throw bad money after bad trying to elect a quickie candidate, a cause they considered as lost as that of trying to halt inflation.

Despite these obstacles, a few men eagerly sought the nomination, largely as a means of self-advertising for future political quests or current law firm business. With the three members of the national committee from each state casting as many votes as the state had cast in the August national convention, and with 668 votes, a majority, needed to nominate, the fifth ballot yielded these numbers: Wheeler 341, Graham 298, Starnes 210. The remaining votes were scattered among a dozen men and two women. Since no aspirant stirred the kind of passions or deals that get a bandwagon rolling, the party faced its first deadlock since the smoke-filled room of 1920 when haggard bosses finally settled on an Ohio newspaperman, Warren G. Harding, an event which paid lasting tribute to the durability of journalism and the nation. Both had, in a manner of speaking, survived.

The party's predicament, Pete Stackpole realized, was compounded by the nature of the opposition. The other creaking vehicle of the rusty system had nominated Governor Hugh G. Pinholster of Connecticut, a fifty-year-old Methodist widely mistaken for a rebel Catholic in many urban centers. Pinholster had an Irish mien, an emphatically sunny disposition, even more solutions than the nation had problems and a murky appeal for the powerless of America —youth, blacks, Puerto Ricans, Chicanos, women, consumers, children and college administrators. For the outraged, the outlawed and the outdone, he was the with-it candidate. He reeked with the garments of dissent despite his impeccable establishment background. His daughter, Peg, shared a Chicago South Side pad with a black militant. His son, Hughie, missed graduation ceremonies at Amherst because he was serving a ninety-day jail sentence for smoking marijuana outside the bus station. The governor carried on a mild flirtation with various revolutionary intellectuals. He wore bushy sideburns, vivid shirts and a wide belt with a brass buckle in the form of a dolphin. Pinholster and his wife slept on a water bed, contributed to Common Cause, read the underground press, skied in the French Alps and were profiled in *New York* Magazine as Hartford's leading exponents of radical chic. On all counts, including the potent eighteen-to-twenty-five-year-old vote, Pinholster appeared formidable for the first Tuesday in November.

Pete Stackpole breathed deeply again and peered across the expanse of pavement toward the Astrodome. He sniffed the familiar acrid scent of hovering exhaust fumes on the nearby expressway, an odor that reminded him once again of the name he would soon propose to the men in the marble library. They might snicker at first, but in the end they would, he hoped, recognize the clarity of his vision.

Stackpole, a lean, febrile, disenchanted man, rapidly rehearsed the salient points of his pitch. Since the new nominee would have no hope of defeating Pinholster on such short notice, he should at least serve several lesser functions. He should present a pleasing personality to the public so that the head of the ticket in no way embarrassed the party's candidates for Congress and state, county and municipal offices. He should symbolize the emerging profile of the party's following in this time of shifting allegiances. He should be, that is, a white suburban or outer-city man of modest or middle income who belonged to one of the ethnic groups, notably Italian, Irish, Polish, Hungarian, who were moving into the party's WASPish orbit after collapse of the rival coalition put together years ago by Franklin D. Roosevelt.

The candidate also should rally those who were fed up with the ragged armies of dissent and who hungered for return to the work-and-prosper ethic that once illumined every star and stripe of Old Glory. These were the people who longed to recharge their loins and lungs with the old American missionary fervor and to be revitalized into the nation that once cheered Teddy Roosevelt's Great White Fleet as the warships sailed the world on their errand of peaceful menace.

The party needed a man who held a key to the nation's buried psyche, a man who could rekindle millions of nostalgic campfires in the souls of the Elks, the Moose, the AFL-CIO, the Knights of Columbus, the Sons of Italy, the Patrolmen's Benevolent Association, American Legion, National Conference of Christians Without Jews, Green Bay Packers and the American College of Surgeons. The nineteen-day presidential candidate should be able to accomplish all this, not in the pursuit of victory, but to refine and polish the party's image for future campaigns.

Pete Stackpole had that man, or at least he would profess to have him. Of course, Pete had other, more intricate reasons for advancing the name of his candidate, but these were of no concern to the national committee or the nation at this time.

Compared with the other men in the Celestial suite, Pete had little power. He was not even a member of the national committee, unlike Ted Witherspoon of Texas, Charlie Herron of Illinois, Rich Cuthbert of Michigan, Senator Framingham of California, Sam Shadowitz of Pennsylvania or Governor Hotchkiss of Ohio. Yet if these six men could be persuaded to back Stackpole's man on the next ballot, they would forge a vote-heavy power wedge that could nominate him. And the six would pay attention to Pete Stackpole because he was the busiest mercenary in the party. Pete had a hound's nose for hidden fiscal burrows where still another hundred grand could be found for TV shows in the critical closing hours of campaigns for senator or governor. Pete had uncovered some long green for Senator Framingham in his last campaign and more recently had done the same thing for Governor Hotchkiss. Every party regular knew, and many were obligated to, Pete Stackpole of New Jersey, a man esteemed as an astute craftsman unblemished by the psychological scars that disfigure those who agonize over such matters as the quality of justice and medicine in the United States, the death rattle of the cities or the building of bigger and better doomsday machines. A sharp, facile operator, Pete.

He ran his fingers through his sparse blond hair, tightened his resolve, took a last breath of the carbonaceous air and strolled from the terrace back to the marble library with its immense bookcases for which the management had ordered "563 feet of books" from a wholesaler of literary wares.

Little had changed but time, Pete noted. Witherspoon was speaking as though at graveside, Cuthbert was yawning and stretching and Governor Hotchkiss labored to fit a shoe over his swollen foot. Stackpole slipped into the circle, waited patiently for many minutes, then slowly maneuvered the discussion toward his hidden objective. Once he got the floor, Stackpole put his argument concisely but with dramatic plotting designed to draw his audience into a web of suspense.

"In short," he said in conclusion, "the man we want must know Americans better than we know ourselves. He ought to be able to touch that inner core, tapping the motivation, pride and action that's uniquely American."

"Oh Christ!" Charlie Herron groaned. "That kind of talk at three-thirty in the morning."

But Rich Cuthbert and the others were intrigued. "Okay, Pete, let's have it," said Cuthbert in the tone of a parent determined to humor the child against the best interests of both. "Who's this genius?"

"Yes, who's the miracle man?" asked Witherspoon.

Stackpole hesitated for a moment, gazed at the imported stained-glass windows as though the name were being borne earthward in a

chariot of spun gold, then opened his palms in a gesture of offertory.

"Eddie Quinn," he said.

The silence had the numbing quality of post-collision shock.
Twelve seconds passed before the clock grunted solemnly.

"Who?" asked Ted Witherspoon in a voice gutted by outrage.

"Edward Nicholas Quinn."

"And just who the hell is *he*?" asked Charlie Herron. The banker
seemed deeply offended, as though someone without money had just
asked to borrow some.

"Eddie Quinn," said Stackpole without a blink, "is a member of
the funeral delegation from New Jersey."

"Oh, that Ed Quinn," said Senator Framingham who prided himself on wide contacts within the party. "You mean the highway
man?"

"Right. Eddie Quinn can touch us where we live faster and surer
than any man I know."

"And just where is that?" asked Shadowitz.

"In our cars and trucks out on the expressways."

This time the silence lasted a small eternity.

"Look, Pete," complained Rich Cuthbert, suppressing another
yawn, "is this some kind of inside New Jersey joke or what? I mean,
for God's sake, this isn't the hour for it."

"No, I'm very serious." Pete was about to say "dead serious," but
hastily throttled the phrase as inappropriate to both the hour and
the state of the party. "The average American, the guy we want voting for us in this election and the ones to come, puts twenty thousand miles a year on his car. His suburban wife spends three point
seven hours a day in the family wagon." He extracted a sheaf of
notes from his shirt pocket. "I could give you a raft of statistics. According to the Gallup Poll, eighty-one per cent of Americans drive to
work. Think how much the motorist owes the bank for his wheels."
He glanced at Banker Herron. "How much gas and oil he buys, how
many hospitals and cemeteries he fills up, how many miles he travels,
how many Holiday Inns he keeps in business, the number of Howard
Johnson meals he buys. As I say, I could go on for a week on passen-

ger cars alone. Now you throw in all the pick-ups and big trucks, take a look at more than two million members of the Teamsters Union, then add all the campers and trailers. . . ."

"Okay, okay," broke in Witherspoon, "but what's this got to do with picking a candidate for President?"

"Everything," said Pete. He rushed into it now, pleased that thus far no one had laughed. His timing had been excellent. Exhaustion bred levity only in its early stages. "Eddie Quinn is a man who understands the American voter in terms of his hidden love—his automobile. Eddie has a whole mystique about it. Listen, men, the guy is eloquent on the subject. Cal Coolidge said the business of America is business. Untrue, says Eddie. The business of America is movement, everlasting wheeled transport out on the highways."

Pete Stackpole hurried on, weaving a vivid tapestry of flashing Comets, rearing Mustangs, vaulting Javelins, predatory Barracudas, billions of roadside hamburgers and hot dogs, gas stations, lubrication pits, teamsters and auto workers, towering insurance companies, spark-plug suppliers, battery manufacturers, the Indianapolis 500, Detroit and Flint, long files of mobile homes snaking into the western sunset, the thrum of tires on wet pavements and the shining glory of Akron, hunters in campers streaming into the Rockies on chill autumn days, the famous Ford Foundation showering its benefices throughout the world, the golden ballads of the highway as strummed on the country music guitars of Nashville, the whole wide, beautiful sweep of American industry from the steel mills of Gary to the chic model studios of New York where heavenly bosoms brushed the dazzling chrome of a Buick or a Dodge—and all of it devoted to hurtling motorists and truckers back and forth across this great, God-kissed continent.

When Pete paused, out of breath and imagery, Rich Cuthbert, a son of Detroit and the prince of communicators, asked his question in a low, incredulous voice.

"What does Eddie Quinn do for a living?"

"He is one of the commissioners," said Stackpole, "of the New Jersey Turnpike Authority."

"Holy God," said Herron. "Couldn't he even make chairman?"

But Stackpole, feverish and ardent now, was not to be deflected.

Eddie Quinn served on the party's state committee, had been a one-term congressman and earlier the mayor of Metuchen, New Jersey. He was a handsome, virile man, brimming with warmth and charm. He had two grown sons, had been separated from his wife for some years. He was an Elk, a Knight of Columbus, a gratifying orator, a former Seton Hall baseball player, a certified square and the author of a book: *Miracle of Wheels: A Study of Metropolitan Expressways in the United States.* He did not drink or smoke. If Eddie had a vulnerable characteristic, it was his fondness for women.

"But properly angled, a seeming liability like that could be an asset," said Pete. "It's significant that in his two runs for Congress—he got wiped out the second time under the Johnson landslide—Quinn averaged fifty-five per cent of the female vote."

Charlie Herron tugged at his shirtsleeves, still surprisingly fresh despite the long hours. Ted Witherspoon frowned as he considered this new development. The clock grunted.

"What's your big interest in Quinn?" asked Sam Shadowitz. "If I know you, Pete, you've got something else cooking. Am I right?"

Pete deplored the question. He had hoped it would not be asked so early in his venture. Several deceptive cover stories he had pondered lacked plausibility for old pros such as the men around him. When in doubt, honesty became a viable refuge.

"Sure. We're thinking of grooming Eddie Quinn for governor of New Jersey next year. This presidential campaign would give him a lot of publicity. But you can say much the same about almost every name mentioned here tonight. If a man is to be ruled out because he has his eye on some other office, we might as well quit right now and go to bed."

Governor Hotchkiss nodded. "That's fair enough. . . . What's so special about your man? I mean, why are you thinking about him for governor?"

"Eddie made a big hit in our state a couple of years ago," said Pete, "when a bunch of radical kids tried to tie up the Turnpike. Eddie went down personally and directed operations. He got traffic flowing again inside a half hour. He also got off a line that's still being quoted: 'There is no right of anybody, anywhere, any time to block a public highway.'"

"A paraphrase of the old Coolidge quote in the Boston police strike," said Shadowitz. "Yes, I remember the man now."

"That's right," said Framingham. "I might say I've met Quinn several times. He makes a very attractive appearance. Big, solid, affable type."

Stackpole sensed a freshening of interest. "That Coolidge quote tells something about Eddie. He's a quick study. Actually, he'd never heard the remark, but Phil Liccardo, the PR man for the Turnpike, mentioned it while he and Eddie were driving to the spot where the long-hairs were blocking traffic. Eddie didn't say anything then, but an hour later he got off the quote while talking to newspapermen. He isn't a glib fellow, but he absorbs everything that's said or done awful fast. Good quality for the kind of quickie candidate we're about to pick."

"But, hell, Pete," protested Cuthbert, "the man's unknown outside your state."

Senator Framingham shrugged. "Of course, we're going to lose anyway, known or unknown candidate."

"Yes," agreed Shadowitz. "This whole thing is an exercise in futility."

"But TV can cure some of the problem with overnight visibility," said Stackpole. He leaned forward and ticked off items on his fingers. "Let's face some facts, men. We want the ethnic vote that we've never had. Well, Eddie Quinn is half Irish and half Polish. We want the average guy and his wife on election day. Well, Quinn speaks their language. He's smart politically, but he's also a bowling alley, tavern and street-corner guy by nature. We want to attract those outer-city people who live along the highways in trailers, motels, garden apartments and the small-home developments that spring up overnight. Well, Quinn's our man again. That's where he lives."

"Just where does he live, by the way?" asked Witherspoon.

"In Room Nineteen of the Buccaneer Motor Lodge near New Brunswick."

"My God." Governor Hotchkiss reacted as though he were being asked to nominate a fugitive from justice.

After a moment of brooding silence, Stackpole said quietly: "Now let me ask a question. Just who the hell else is there that we can agree on?"

Again silence, this time prolonged.

"Quinn interests me," said Framingham finally. "We've gone through about fifty names tonight without making any progress. I know this one sounds far-out at first. Still, I wonder. . . ."

Stackpole bored in swiftly. "Just do me the favor of talking to Eddie. Let me get him over here so you can see for yourself. You'll be impressed. He handles himself well. There's something about Eddie that people take to at once. . . . And another thing. If we pull a surprise like this, the candidate will get an awful lot of free TV time and newsprint."

Shadowitz bobbed his head. "Shock-value stuff. Right, Rich?"

Rich Cuthbert agreed. "As a publisher, I can tell you that a new, surprise face is worth a lot of mileage."

The men pondered as they lolled back on the antique Spanish sofas. Above the fireplace gilded cherubs looked down on the wine red wall-to-wall carpeting overlaid with a hand-made Persian rug. A hum of traffic could be heard on ever-restless Interstate 610 and in the low, flat fields near the Astrodome oil pumps labored through the early hours.

"Where was Quinn born?" asked Herron. The banker groped for trail marks in the uncharted biographical wilds of a man with no apparent pedigree.

"Actually Eddie was born in the back seat of a Model A Ford while his father was driving his mother to a hospital in New Brunswick, New Jersey." Pete stood up. "I know this next will sound farfetched, but so help me, gentlemen, it's been checked out."

He paused and looked at the blur of lined, spent faces.

"Eddie Quinn was born at the spot that some years later became the tollgate . . . at Exit Nine . . . of the New Jersey Turnpike."

Again silence, this time fretful, as the kingmakers bent on selecting a possible thirty-seventh-and-a-half President of the United States, shifted their vantage points to accommodate this new, thin beacon of hope.

"And where," asked Ted Witherspoon, "is this Quinn right at the moment?"

2

Right at the moment Eddie Quinn was with, or more specifically enfolded with Congresswoman Kate Witherspoon, wife of Theodore, in a room of the Apollo Motel on Highway 59, several miles distant from the hotel in which the kingmakers labored.

Kate Witherspoon was moaning blissfully under the ministrations of Eddie Quinn and was slowly tuning herself to yet another pitch of joy. The laving of her right ear by Eddie's tongue, a minor movement orchestrated to the more stately symphony of the pelvic region, aroused sweet torment. A less imaginative person might compare the sensation to that produced by a doctor probing for wax with a swab stick. Not Kate. Her ear canal quivered deliciously and sent jubilant telegrams racing from one sensory outpost to another. But what astounded Kate was not so much the state of gentle madness that possessed them both, but its duration. Except for a brief intermission for watering and chatting, the copulatory union had been in progress for three hours, during which two mighty convulsions, registering six on the Richter scale, had shaken her body in the kind of transport that provokes acid debate in some women's liberation sects.

As for Eddie, this long tangle of muscles, limbs and flesh that alternately crushed and caressed her, Kate could only regard him with wonderment. He seemed to be powered by some lofty rapture that at once transformed her body into a shrine and Eddie into an unflagging celebrant. Never in her life had her various crevices, extremities, protrusions, recesses, mounds and orifices been accorded such minute and rapt attention by a male. She and Eddie were lathered in perspiration and awash in seminal fluids. At times she was seized by fright, persuaded that she was locked in the embrace of a madman who would throttle her in a final paroxysm of ardor. But Eddie, alerted by the sudden feel of goose pimples on her arms, would calm her with a whispered banality: "Easy does it, baby," or "Slow down, Kate, we've got all night." At other times she drifted into fantasies. She was being swept from shore into a vast, tepid sea where distant gulls wheeled and cried in banks of mist. Once, when upon command she lay on her stomach, her back became a flower garden that Eddie mulched with moist kisses. Again, in spirited transport, Kate had the feeling of being trampled up and down her spine by thousands of tiny ski boots.

Compared with her husband, Ted Witherspoon, whose increasingly sporadic bouts of *amour* were spastic affairs roughly equivalent to a penny's worth of time on a parking meter, Eddie Quinn was a marvel of continuity. She responded with tremendous bursts of energy, arching, thrusting and at times clawing wildly at his back. Eddie paused occasionally, smiling at her from his ruddy, rugged face, but soon renewed his devotions like a priest gliding about the altar from one worshipful task to another. He was patently uninterested in terminating the services, and so the three hours passed without one of those shuddering upheavals by which the male signals that the moment of the little death is upon him.

At last Kate Witherspoon had had enough. The once rippling muscles now felt like a ton of lead on top of her and she knew that she could not bear another single swoop or tangential tremor. She pressed her palms against his chest and said, "Please." He promptly raised himself and fell away, leaving Kate with a sudden luxury of solitude between her thighs. Eddie and Kate swiveled side by side, risking the purplish contusions of sheet burns, and looked into each other's eyes with unfeigned affection and respect.

"I'll be damned," said Eddie, using a phrase he'd sometimes employed in fifty-one similar circumstances in his life, but always with sincerity, for he hungered for women with an obsession, however transitory, that often confounded him.

"My God," said Kate. She noted that his eyes were brown and unflickering in their gaze. "Are you always like that?"

The question, he sensed, carried pitfalls for the unwary. He smiled, still looking into her eyes, and replied: "Are you?"

She laughed lightly. "Very seldom." They both sighed and turned on their backs and gazed at the ceiling, an expanse of off-white beaverboard. Cars droned on the highway. A fly, frantically seeking an exit in the folds of the heavy, pulled drapes, buzzed in frustration. A band of light marched from the bathroom where the door had been left ajar.

"Be a lamb, Eddie," she said, suddenly practical, "and get us a towel."

Eager for wider movement than that afforded by a mattress, he heaved himself out of bed and did her bidding. They used the towel, content to be sharing without touching for a change, and then Kate threw it across the room. The long bath towel fell on the writing desk, enswathing the telephone. Eddie turned to the bedside table and inspected his wrist watch. Its luminous dial glowed in the gloom.

"Four-ten," he said. "I hope you don't have to leave yet."

"Not for days if I feel like it." She laughed, a throaty, pleasurable sound. "Oh, don't be scared. I just mean that Ted and I have an understanding. My time's my own. It has to be, with me in Congress and Ted shuttling between Dallas and Washington. Anyway, I have nothing to do with the committee, and Ted's at some all-night meeting of men who think they're kingmakers."

Eddie yawned. "Yeah, I heard about it. A good friend of mine, Pete Stackpole, is sitting in. You know Pete?"

"Sure. Doesn't everyone? . . . How old are you, Eddie?"

"Forty-six."

"I'll be there soon. Not that I mind. I thought I'd die when I hit forty, but now it suits me. I pretend less and enjoy more. Do I have to get dressed? Please say no."

"Of course not. What fool would put clothes on a figure like yours when he didn't have to?" This clothes thing, Eddie knew, had something to do with money and class. The women he met in bars and offices preferred, as a rule, to make love in the dark under a sheet, whereas the rich ones who dabbled in tennis, charities and causes were forever prancing about bare-assed. At first female naked-

ness had embarrassed him, but now he reveled in it. "You're beautiful, Kate." He feasted with his eyes on her long body, the plush
breasts and the damp, black hair flung about the pillow. Kate had
class and the stamp of money. She was frank, practical, a politician.
Eddie thought he understood her. And sex aside, he liked her.

She eased from the bed, found her Gucci leather shoulder bag on
the writing desk, fumbled out a cigarette. After lighting, she studied
him through the stream of smoke. He lay with his feet crossed and
his hands behind his head, a crucifix of ruddy flesh with tussocks
of brown hair on the main shaft and pleasant creases about his
eyes. Though retracted, his antenna maintained a posture of relaxed
vigilance like a sentry who senses that another skirmish, while not
probable, is nevertheless possible.

"You're good to look at yourself, Eddie." A trifle overweight perhaps, she thought. "The only thing I don't like is your hair." She
touched his head. "Why not let it grow down your neck and curl
around your ears some?"

"Because I'm a square, that's why. Always have been."

"Some square. Eddie Quinn, you idiot, you're the most sensual
man I ever met." She sat on the edge of the bed and balanced an
ash tray on her knee. The room's furnishings were plastic white. Ordinarily she would have loathed the décor, but now she felt as
though she were afloat in a sea of cream.

"Who picked up whom tonight?" she asked.

They had met casually a year earlier at a Washington fund-raising
dinner. Tonight they found each other along the buffet table, between the curried shrimps and the pantied lamb chops, at a mam-
moth party staged by the Oklahoma state chairman at the Shamrock
Hilton. The Oklahoma chairman, who had fetched a large flock of
buoyant mourners to the funeral by chartered jet, liked to lavish
food, drink and music on anyone in even a remote position to preserve the oil-depletion allowance as one of the ramparts of the republic. Eddie and Kate, after carrying their plates to a table for two, discovered mutual interests beyond those of politics.

"I definitely did the picking up," he said now with a confident,
but by no means conquering, smile. The chivalrous comment was
not quite true, he told himself. Actually he was tired and had in-

tended to go to bed early, but Kate had hoisted signals, a glance, a word, a lift of the eyebrows.

"I'd heard the music in the Continental room," said Kate. "It had a good beat, I said, and did you like to dance?"

"And I said, 'Let's go.'"

"You're an easy dancer, Eddie. Then I had two stingers while you drank ginger ale, and I felt fine, and then I said why didn't we go someplace else for a nightcap."

"And I said how about a drive?"

"A drive, yet!" Kate laughed. "Then I startled you by saying that if you meant a nightcap at your place, well, I accepted. . . . I didn't say so, but I have to be careful in Dallas and Washington. And it gets dull, all politics and no play."

"I liked you for not playing games." But Eddie had not been surprised. The first signal, two hours earlier, had forecast the possible dénouement. Eddie never pressed. He knew by long experience that love seldom prospered under pressure. His kind of women, the ones he liked best, the beautiful Kates, made their decision when and if they were ready. "Anyway, I'll take the blame for everything."

"Blame? . . . Honey." She leaned over and kissed him. She felt wrapped in contentment and tenderness, yet in the distance, she could hear the faint tread of the little ski boots again. As though to guard against invasion before the home troops were properly rested, she said with an edge of reproach: "Eddie, do you realize we hardly know a thing about each other?"

"I think we know a lot that matters."

"No, be serious. *That*, yes. But who we are and where we want to go and what we think. You know, the things down under."

"Oh." Eddie was not enthusiastic. Belly to belly, yes, but psyche to psyche, hmm. "Where would we start?"

"With you. For instance, what makes you tick."

"Well, let's see now."

Her flecked green eyes shone with a schoolgirl intensity, and Eddie saw her need for reassurance. He suspected she wanted to be told that the vehicles colliding at the clover leaf of desire were roughly similar models with a common destination, but Eddie knew better. She, he sensed, was a Mercedes 280 while he was an old Mack semi.

They shared neither chassis nor terminal. No way. He gazed at her with fond and genuine regret.

"Do you know one that Johnny Cash sings?" he asked. " 'There Ain't No Easy Run.' "

Kate's eyes glazed in non-recognition. She shook her head. She smelled richly feminine.

"Great song. To the gear-jammers of America. The title's the message, and it's right."

"Is Johnny Cash your favorite singer?" She felt ripples of apprehension. She scoured her memory in vain for a single friend who listened to Johnny Cash. Her constituents, yes. But in her set, her non-political friends, country music was not the in thing, except for laughs. Kate inhaled and let the smoke flood through her nostrils.

"Not especially. It's just what the song says. You wanted to know what I think about life. Well, baby, there ain't no easy run."

She surveyed him as if for the first time in the dim light from the bathroom doorway. A frown of concentration creased Eddie's forehead. The musk of mingled human juices filled the motel room, overhanging the wide bed like a jungled canopy. Kate wondered if Eddie always ordered super-king-sized beds for single occupancy. She tried again.

"No, there isn't. But what else? You must believe more than that?"

"Yes, a thing or two." Eddie shifted position, uncrossed his legs. Her insistence made him uncomfortable. "I was an altar boy once, but I guess I'm not a religious guy any more. But sometimes, when I think of space and the planets, all those light-years, I wonder. There must be some power out there. Anyway, the unknown scares me when I think about it almost as much as when I was a kid. The only thing I'm really sure about is this." He placed a hand gently on her hip. "A man and a woman. It gets so strong sometimes, I feel like yelling a prayer to the skies. I used to think that the habit of making love in dark rooms was okay, but now if I had my way, we'd all do it on a high cliff overlooking the sea, in bright sunlight."

"That's lovely, Eddie." Her apprehension receded somewhat. "But, darling, that's all about bed. What are you like when you're walking around with your clothes on?"

Eddie turned toward her and grinned. "Persistent, huh? Well, you know what? Everything else outside is a game. Mostly you play it by the rules of whatever country you live in. Oh sure, you can try to play it for making a buck or for doing good, if that's your kick, but in the end, it's all like seaweed. Nothing ever comes of it. You go out as confused as you came in."

"You confused? You don't act it."

"Hell, Kate, I play the game and I enjoy it, don't get me wrong. For one thing, I'm convinced the big guys in this country have got too much and the little guys too little, and the liberals who do all the bullshitting haven't changed things much. I don't like those endless, crazy wars either. I'm in politics and I work at it. In fact, I've got big ideas about running for governor and trying to correct a few things. But deep inside me, well, it's still a game."

"Are you lonely, Eddie?"

"Here with you, no. But outside, sure. You know when I really feel at home outside is when I'm driving my old Impala, zinging along some thruway, staying in my own lane, watching the nuts cutting in and out, feeling that sudden slap of wind when a trailer rig passes me. I know how the truckers feel. I drove a van for Mayflower my first two years out of college. Best time of my life."

"Maybe you like the sense of mastery that all that horsepower gives you, Eddie. You know what the psychologists say about cars. People who are frustrated by civilization can work out their aggressions on the highway. We can feel powerful behind a couple of tons of metal."

"Yeah," he said lazily. "I've heard all that. Maybe it's true. But I'll tell you something else that's true. This country's future is hitched to the automobile. There's no escape. The car is our way of life. That's why these so-called revolutionaries are full of crap. Turn the country over to Jerry Rubin or Eldridge Cleaver or the Berrigan brothers, and what have you got? Just a different bunch of guys sitting around Washington while the rest of us car jockeys go racing along the interstates. Sure, we can change who gets what, but we can't change the way we live. Three point four hours a day in the old bucket seat is the average, I think, outside the cities. That's where we live, right behind the power steering." He paused. "So enough about me. How about you, Kate?"

She stubbed out her cigarette and lay down beside him. "That you're too simplistic, Eddie. Life's more complicated than sex and cars. I believe in making love like you, but I believe it's better when it stems from love and when it extends to flowers and trees and all the things that spring from the soil. I feel depressed sometimes in that car-world you like so much. And I think we foul up our lives too. Look at Ted and me if you want to see a God-awful mess. Everything's a mess, the country, the party. Why, even the national committee can't find a man to nominate because everybody's so scared and confused they don't know what the people want any more."

Kate sighed. "Still, we have to try. Politics isn't just a game. It's serious business. A couple of things bug me about our party. For one, a lot of leaders act as if the party's some kind of exclusive club. We ought to open the doors wide, welcome everyone into it and be responsive to the needs of all classes. For another, we ought to take the lead in preserving the good earth. Did you know that just to support one person in America, we have to extract from the earth and process twenty-five tons of material every year? It's incredible. We ought to be treating the earth as our home, not some big treasure vault to be plundered."

"I'd buy that."

"We'll have to, or our grandchildren will inherit a withered, exhausted old planet with all its juices gone. . . . Anyway, Eddie, it's not so simple." Kate fell silent.

"You sleepy?"

"Surprise. No. . . . And, Eddie, I feel terrific."

"I have nothing to do and all day to do it in."

"Me too."

"Mmm." The Mercedes 280 and the Mack semi might not share destinations, he thought, but the clover leaf of desire was nicely banked and landscaped. Maybe when he returned to work, he ought to make a pitch for more flower beds at the interchanges of the Turnpike. Eddie drew Kate to him.

"I may need help this time," he whispered.

"Baby." She ministered to him even as he had ministered unto her and soon the wide bed throbbed with a steady rhythm and Kate

Witherspoon could hear the growing cadence of the ski boots again. Kate was no more religious than Eddie professed to be, but soon she saw herself as a fellow communicant at the altar of longing, an acolyte at the celebration of the mystery. Why passion inspired holy images in her mind, Kate did not know, but invariably she thought of the sixteenth-century cathedrals that towered from the brown, dry soil of Mexico.

They came down the long, dark aisle together, past the garish, somber saints and virgins, past the empty pews gaping upward at the great gilt vault of the cathedral. They clasped each other in a vise transfigured into grace as the minutes fled and their limbs grew taut and desperate. Once Eddie groaned like an overburdened traveler. But on they went, the nave just out of reach, the altar a seeming mirage. She lay, she knelt, she flung herself on top of him, all in a rushing quest to grasp the ungraspable. Sweat poured from them, sealing them in shared frenzy.

It's near madness, thought Kate, and chanted hymns echoed in the vault above.

She's wonderful, thought Eddie, and I adore her, right now, anyway, every compartment, latch and vent of her.

Far away, in the mist of spires, Kate heard bells chime.

It was the telephone, its sound muffled by the towel that Kate had thrown. They ignored the shrouded ring, still a far clamor of tower bells in Kate's ears. The phone continued to sound its summons.

"The hell with it," said Eddie.

But the phone kept on, each trill another rent in the chapel of desire. Their rhythm ceased. Kate brushed petulantly at the hair falling over her eyes. Eddie moved away.

"Of all the damn times," said Kate. "The sun isn't even up yet."

"Almost." Eddie peered at his luminous wrist watch on the bed-side table. "It's five-thirty."

He lifted himself carefully over Kate, swayed across the floor and plucked the towel off the telephone.

"I hope it's not one of your sons." Kate instinctively drew a sheet over her from the tangled clump at the foot of the bed.

"Hello." Eddie feigned sleepiness. "Oh, Pete . . . for Christ's sake, man . . . yeah, I've got a chair." Eddie dutifully pulled a chair beneath his rump. "Okay, shoot."

It was five minutes before Eddie spoke again. Kate smoked one cigarette and lit another.

"You've got to be crazy," said Eddie at last. He listened some more. "Well, sure, I'll come over. . . . No, don't send any goddamn limo for me. I'll get a cab. . . . Ten minutes. I need five here to dress and shave. Okay. Good-by."

He rose slowly from his chair and turned toward Kate. He folded his arms and stared, not so much at her as over and through her. He's a little overpadded, she thought. He ought to get some other kind of exercise.

"That was Pete Stackpole," he said.

"I guessed. What does he want at this ungodly hour?"

"They're still meeting over at the Astroworld. They want to talk to me."

"You! About what?"

But he was already in the bathroom amid sounds of running water. She heard the drill of the shower, toweling noises, then the whir of an electric razor. When Eddie returned, he lighted a low lamp on the writing desk and pulled on a pair of green-and-white striped shorts.

"Oh yes. You can take my wheels." Eddie sounded as though he had just met himself returning from a long voyage and wasn't yet sure whether he recognized himself. He glanced distractedly about the room for a moment, then dialed the front desk and ordered a taxi. He opened a dresser drawer and took out a clean shirt.

"Mind telling me what's up?"

"Look, Kate," he said as he put on the shirt, "I guess you'll have to get back to the Shamrock on your own. I'll take the cab. You take my Hertz Galaxie when you're ready. The keys are on the desk." He placed them by the phone. "Leave the car with the doorman. I'll pick it up later."

"I thought . . ."

"Yeah, so did I. But things have changed." He zipped up his trousers, came over to the bed and kissed her. His face was smooth and smelled of woodsy shaving lotion.

"You won't be back?" She was growing annoyed.

"Not right away, I guess. You see, I still don't believe it, but those characters over at the Astroworld want to talk to me about . . . well, about maybe nominating me."

She choked on a mouthful of smoke and began to cough. He thumped her back.

"For President?" she asked weakly.

"For President. . . . I know, the whole world's gone nuts." He pulled on his jacket. "I'll call you this afternoon."

At the door he turned.

"See what I mean? There's only one thing that matters. The rest is all a crazy game. . . . You're great, Kate. God bless."

The door clicked shut. She lay quietly for a moment, her thoughts tumbling from a moldering cathedral down a long green slope to a crowded expressway. Then, impelled by an urge to flee, she slid from the bed. She had to bathe, untangle her hair, find her clothes. In the dim light from the desk lamp, she saw two dark, limp objects on the floor.

Then she realized. She ran to the door, cracked it open and peered out. She was too late. He had left.

Eddie Quinn had gone to his rendezvous with destiny with no socks on.

None of the five hundred newsmen, electronic communicators, photographers and newsweekly writers covering the Houston committee meeting cared about the movements of Eddie Quinn that October dawn, but had one of them followed Eddie by whim or hunch, he would have tailed a Houston taxicab from the Apollo Motel on Highway 59 to Interstate 610 and thence to the Astroworld Hotel, a distance of less than three miles.

The cab pulled to the rear of the nine-story structure, halting near a tradesmen's ramp beside an overflowing laundry cart. Eddie paid and tipped the driver and, following Pete's instructions, walked to an outside, glass-enclosed elevator where a guard waited. The guard requested identification, inspected Eddie's driver's license, then opened the elevator door with a key, unlocked the mechanism at the panel and pushed the button. Eddie watched the early sun brushing the distant Houston skyline as they rose silently to the ninth-floor Celestial suite.

Eddie crossed the crimson carpet, heard his heels snap against the tiled corridor floor and was admitted to the marble library shortly before 6 A.M.

He left alone at 9:52 A.M., retracing his route to the rear parking area where an Imperial, hired by Rich Cuthbert, awaited him. The chauffeur, who did not know his passenger's identity, drove Eddie back to the Apollo.

After Eddie's departure, the seven kingmakers in the Celestial suite took a short break, then rearranged themselves while Pete Stackpole nervously sipped coffee from a mug and glanced at the drained men about him.

"Well?"

Rich Cuthbert yawned and stretched out his legs. "I say, why not go with him? Socks or no socks. I like him. He's not the most knowledgeable man in the world, but he's smart and he'll learn fast. Of course, he looks more like a high scorer in a bowling league than a President, but as you say, Pete, maybe that's just what we want now. My hunch is that if the country sees him on the tube, there'll be millions of Eddies and their wives who'd identify with him right off."

"We've got a money problem with or without Quinn," said Charlie Herron. The finance chairman's patrician features showed the strain of the all-night conference, but his monogrammed shirt remained remarkably tidy. "Money's very skittish right now, especially our kind of money." The Celestial suite's host made a gathering gesture as though to indicate that those in the room employed a less offensive currency than that which became wrinkled and soiled as it passed through the lands of supermarket checkers, gas-station attendants, bookies, whores and pentecostal preachers. "The money men don't think our candidate will stand a chance. On the other hand we've got a million eight left in the kitty for the rest of the campaign. That ought to be enough to give Ewing and Quinn or whoever a few whirls on the networks."

"You're not committing yourself, Charlie," said Stackpole. "The question is, what about Quinn?"

"My main thought is that I'm a damned fool for staying up all night trying to pick some candidate who can't win anyway." Herron rubbed at his eyes. "But Quinn? He's a risk, but if we can keep him in rein, he might be all right. Middle-class values, flag decals, car buff, respect for American traditions, no truck with those smart-ass kids who pop pills and quote Mao. Quinn might help the ticket. I'm just warning that he can't expect any new money. One point eight from now until November 2."

"Gentlemen, let's face one fact squarely in the eyes," said Creed Hotchkiss. The Ohio governor had a tendency to invest abstractions with human features. He was also miffed that not once in this long night and morning had anyone in the room suggested him as the compromise candidate. "We're not going to win with Quinn. You can't make a nobody into somebody in three short weeks, not even with the magic of television."

"But, hell, Creed, nobody's talking about winning at this stage," said Sam Shadowitz. "Even Hudson, with all his exposure, was running behind—thanks in part to our friend up in Washington." The economist tilted his head in a vaguely northern direction. "The main thing is to finish out the kind of campaign that will bring us in a good chunk of the Congress. I think Quinn's safe, the kind who'll play ball with us."

"I wouldn't be too sure about that," Ted Witherspoon countered. "He's not our kind and we still don't know an awful lot about him. Our talk with him was mostly generalities. What we're doing is taking him on Pete Stackpole's word, by and large."

"But Ted, look at the time factor," said Shadowitz. "If we can't agree on someone damn soon, the committee might ballot all day without a break. If we let this thing run too long, the country will laugh the party off the boards. With Quinn we've at least got a surprise element that will make the voters sit up and take notice."

"I'll admit that's a good point." The more emphatic Ted Witherspoon became, the more heavily his words fell. His bricks had turned to paving blocks. "I do have one strong reservation about Quinn— the woman thing."

Pete Stackpole was ready for this one. He pulled a well-fingered sheet of paper from his shirt pocket. "I'll read the figures again. In his first race for Congress, Eddie polled fifty-seven per cent of the female vote. The next time, even losing in the Johnson landslide, Eddie still got fifty-three per cent of the women's vote. Eddie was honest with us. Sure, he likes women. I imagine he's laid a few here and there recently. The job of turnpike commissioner isn't too taxing. But don't forget, the women like Eddie too. And I don't buy the idea that his separation is a handicap. Twenty years ago, yes. Now, no. It shows he's his own man." Stackpole hurried on, realizing belatedly that independence was not a quality highly prized in this room. "I've watched a lot of women meet Eddie for the first time and there's something about him that hooks them. What, I don't know. I'm no psychologist. But believe me, if we nominate Eddie Quinn, the women's vote is going to be a real sleeper."

Shadowitz cleared his throat. "An apt word in the circumstances," he said. Only Rich Cuthbert laughed. "You're right about the separation, Pete. All the strict Catholics will empathize with Quinn for separating and not divorcing. He adheres to the rules of the Church. He isn't devout, but he does go to Mass now and then. And a lot of non-Catholics will understand a man who plays the game with no complaints even when the deal isn't to his liking. . . . As for gossip about Quinn and women, well, that's great. It'll get him known ten times as fast." Shadowitz paused and scanned his colleagues with his best professional look, the one that forecast the imminent delivery of a dictum on a tablet of stone. "Remember, we don't want a man so straight he bores us to death. We want his *U.S. News & World Report* on the coffee table all right, but we'd like to think there's a copy of *Playboy* at his bedside."

Rich Cuthbert toyed with a leather tassel on his hand-tooled loafers. "You've got something there, Sam. This Quinn fellow is solid, but if you'll pardon an old-fashioned expression, he has a twinkle of mischief in his eye."

"Yes," agreed Stan Framingham. "I got to thinking that Quinn might do fairly well back home in Orange County." The senator gazed up at the high stained-glass windows with a puzzled look. "Strange things are happening in Orange County. We've got a high density of Birchers, but also a lot of those wife-swapping clubs, and I sometimes wonder how much they overlap."

"Also, I noted in a report," said Shadowitz, "that you've got one of the highest veneral-disease rates in the country."

"Thank you, Sam." Framingham favored the professor with one of those murderously bland looks employed by the club-admissions chairman when confronting a new member he wishes he had black-balled. The senator had nothing against Jews. He just thought they belonged in the other party.

Rich Cuthbert stood up and stretched.

"I vote to settle on Quinn and view it as a trial run for the future," he said. "We all know he can't win, but he gives us a chance to see how the country accepts an authentic mid-America type, speaking psychologically, not geographically. We're always nominating men born into or joined to the establishment. Eddie's the kind of guy you could meet at the corner tavern. Let's try him."

Unanimous though not spirited agreement was reached a half-hour later, just fifty-five minutes before the national committee was scheduled to reconvene at noon for the sixth roll call in balloting for nomination of a President of the United States.

Pete Stackpole telephoned the news to Eddie Quinn and enjoined the New Jersey Turnpike Commissioner to stay in his Apollo Motel room and block all incoming calls at the switchboard save those from Stackpole.

"Why?" asked Eddie.

"We've got a lot of dealing to do with the committee, and I'd just as soon nobody's in a position to check back with you. . . . Relax, Eddie. Take a nap or watch the box."

Eddie climbed back into bed, but strangely, as he propped up the pillows, misted with the lingering fragrances of Kate Witherspoon, he felt less elation than irritation. The zany opulence of the Celestial suite had stunned him. He had met the party's Witherspoons, Cuthberts and Herrons fleetingly at political gatherings, but never before had he spent four hours with the urbane, propertied movers and shakers and taken in the full flavor of their attitudes and customs. Those men at the Astroworld were not his kind. Except for Pete, a T-bird type, they were all Continentals or Fleetwood Broughams. That was not his world. Eddie Quinn was strictly a Mack semi man.

3

The party of manifest destiny, Southampton, Cartier's, the Emancipation Proclamation, Abercrombie & Fitch, Bar Harbor, the Puritan ethic, Grosse Pointe, the protective tariff, *The Saturday Evening Post*, normalcy, Palm Springs, Pebble Beach, the full dinner pail, Mark Cross, the Main Line, preventive detention, Sutton Place and the southern strategy nominated Edward Nicholas Quinn on the seventh ballot.

On the same October Thursday the Houston Oilers toiled in practice in the nearby Astrodome, the American balance-of-payments deficit soared to a twenty-year high, three more corporations decided to flee New York City and a man in Boston died of mercury poisoning after eating codfish cakes.

In the gilt-draped grand ballroom of the Astroworld Hotel, scene of the national committee's deliberations, members milled and churned like passengers suddenly aware that the sinking ship has insufficient lifeboats. Some groped about in shock, while others stood by their chairs and cheered feebly, whether out of frustration, relief or remorse could not be determined immediately by the army of communicators who far outnumbered the politicans in the hall.

Surrounded by newsmen and sweating profusely despite the steady seventy-two-degree temperature, Pete Stackpole opined that the committee had reached a wise, fateful decision and said the candidate, whose whereabouts he refused to disclose, would appear in the grand ballroom at 8 P.M. for his acceptance speech.

In NBC's cubicle in the wide corridor outside the hall, a familiar, wry voice told the network's audience that the party had launched history's most precarious voyage into the unknown since Columbus set sail from Spain.

In the Hideaway cocktail lounge of the Shamrock, Congresswoman Kate Witherspoon, buttery with languor, wondered how the candidate would pick up his rental Galaxie and whether he was still sockless. The canal of Kate's right ear tingled pleasantly, fresh yet vulnerable as though newly dredged. Her cathedral had collapsed, but she could still see its undamaged spire touching a fragment of cloud high above a green slope.

Clinging wearily to the back of his chair in the ballroom, his sleep-famished muscles aching for a massage, Rich Cuthbert recalled the dawn scene in the Celestial suite and Eddie Quinn's poise and tranquillity under questioning. When Ted Witherspoon asked him if he had ever committed an act for which he could have been charged by the police if apprehended, Eddie replied: "Only the usual American offenses, speeding and adultery."

In his fifth-floor room of the Astroworld, Governor Jerome Wheeler, best known of the spurned aspirants for the nomination, vomited in the toilet bowl.

All over America less stricken men and women hurriedly reappraised personal situations in light of the unexpected decision in Houston. Prices gyrated in the final half-hour on the New York Stock Exchange, led upward by motors and oils and downward by rails and maritimes. Tax-exempt expressway bonds surged to new highs for the year. At Seton Hall, Quinn's alma mater, the president, suffering from a post-riot ulcer, tore up his resignation and resolved to face the future with manly courage.

In Bee Branch, Arkansas, Frank (Hunk) Janiszewski, elderly uncle of Eddie, decided to bundle up his lengthy correspondence with the Social Security people and mail it to Eddie. In dispute was $4.88 a month claimed by Hunk as his due under the law.

Lunching at Caesar's Palace in Las Vegas, Jimmy the Greek sat with pencil poised over an envelope resting beside the fruit salad. He wrote Pinholster 1 to 8, Quinn 7 to 1, brooded a moment over life's uncertainties, crossed out the figures, and made it Pinholster 1 to 10, Quinn 9 to 1.

In a brick bungalow with an American flag decal on the living-room window, Mrs. Mabel Probst Quinn of Metuchen, New Jersey, who intended to file for an $80-a-month increase in maintenance allowance, changed her mind when she saw the television cables snaking across her lawn through a clump of newsmen, one of whom stumbled into the pachysandra bed. Mabel, rushing to the bathroom to remove the curlers from her hair, boosted the figure to $180 a month, then realized with a jolt that she probably would have to vote for Eddie, the bastard, out of fiscal self-interest.

In Shreveport, Louisiana, a buxom waitress in a motel coffee shop stood transfixed before a television set as she recalled the long, padded, ruddy-faced man with whom she shared a motel bed during the convention of the International Bridge, Tunnel & Turnpike Association two years earlier. She jingled the coins in the pocket of her white smock and thought: "Holy Mother, I made it with a candidate for President."

That scene, in widely varying versions, was repeated half a hundred times across the land. In an eighteen-room stone mansion in Minneapolis, a slim matron with chicly tousled gray hair sat on a sofa, her small, pedicured feet pointing toward the TV console. She rattled the ice in her highball glass and thought of Eddie Quinn that night in the rose guest room when Art was away. The encounter was graven forever in memory. Afterward she had limped into the library in search of a fortifying bourbon and returned to tell Eddie that she planned to submit his name as America's lone entry in the next sexual Olympics. In the law office of Jefferson, Goldstein, Antonelli & Smidlak on Chicago's LaSalle Street, a libidinous but chronically unsatisfied secretary switched off her transistor radio, buried her head in her arms and sobbed into the typewriter. The weekend with Eddie Quinn at the Drake stood out as one of the few oases in the trackless Sahara of her life.

In a shadowed welfare office in Atlanta, Margot Hicks, a black social worker, heard the name "Eddie Quinn" with a start. At first she could not believe it was the same man, but as additional details poured from the radio, she knew there could be no mistake. As the gates of memory swung open, she could see Eddie Quinn standing beside her high stool at the singles bar on Third Avenue in Manhattan. Was it five years ago? Six? She knew it was before she changed her hair style from straightened to Afro. He had been the first and last white man she had ever slept with and even now, with the weekend at the New Yorker Hotel blurred in memory, she could recall her sharply ambivalent feelings. He had been sweet, alternately gentle and powerful, always considerate, but also condescending and full of random, unknowing opinions that often stabbed her. When they parted, Margot, appeased but wounded and sad, told him: "I guess you're just about the nicest white racist I know, Eddie." He looked as though she had slapped him, and he left unsettled and bewildered. So now Eddie Quinn was a candidate for President. Not a bad dude for a white man. Well, damn me. Margot sighed and picked up the next case folder.

On a high hill overlooking the Pacific Ocean at Santa Barbara, California, R Daniel Fenelli ("R for nothing and not followed by a period, please") was sitting in his spacious, sun-washed office in the Center for the Study of Democratic Institutions, a think spa for men and women who loved heavy thought, light cocktail chatter and medium-rare filet mignon. R Danny was an ebullient, airy, gregarious man who knew most of the intellectuals in the country and almost as many of the choice bars. He had been a musician, newspaperman, movie producer, investment analyst and sensitivity trainer. He had also been Eddie Quinn's roommate at Seton Hall, and when Quinn's nomination rattled off his desk radio, R Danny burst from his office and went scudding about the Center, flinging open doors and overwhelming his colleagues with the news. "Eddie Quinn," he shouted. "They nominated Stud Quinn. Nicest meathead I ever knew. And hey, know what? He's queer for asphalt."

In general the first reaction to Eddie Quinn's nomination was one of incredulity mingled with levity as though a ground crew sergeant had just been recommended for promotion to chief of staff of the Air Force. People saw Eddie in a king-for-a-day role and quickly prepared to share some of the fun with him.

As a sample, all work stopped in the gloomy, marble-floored Empire Motors Building in Detroit the moment the tube carried news that Utah's three committee members had voted for Quinn, thus clinching his nomination. Instant carnival enveloped the Vatican of automobiles. Paper airplanes sailed, whisky bottles sprang onto desks, junior executives embraced their secretaries and the chief counsel proclaimed this the greatest day for mobile mankind since the German, Karl Benz, built the first vehicle with an internal combusion engine in 1885. President Albert Kunsler stood beneath the radiant oil portrait of Alfred P. Sloan, Jr., and clinked glasses with Fred Billings, E.M.'s unofficial vice-president in charge of politics and lobbying.

"He hasn't a chance," said Billings, "but it'll be sweet music to listen to a man who loves the highways. I'd like to see Nader's face right now."

"You know Pete Stackpole," said Kunsler. "Shouldn't we call him and offer his candidate some money?"

Billings shook his head. "No, we put enough into Hudson's campaign. We'd just be throwing it away."

Kunsler looked downcast, a man sorrowing over the lack of affinity between sentiment and cash.

In Montgomery, Alabama, where the stars and bars flew above the venerable state capitol, a stocky man switched off his portable television set and glared at the vanishing dot of light. His eyes burned with the rage of ages. "Highways, God and mother!" he exclaimed to the circle of rapt white faces about him. "Wait'll I dare him to stand in the schoolhouse door and count all the nigrah kids getting off those buses."

This analysis, silently applauded by the circle's nodding heads, failed to assess Eddie Quinn for the 1970s man he was. Highways, sí, God and mother, maybe. While true that Eddie attended Mass occasionally, his feeling about God was less a belief in His presence than a wonderment over the emptiness of space and spirit, a vacuum to be threaded by lonely acts of driving and copulation. As for motherhood, Eddie would shy from unequivocal endorsement of that institution.

The mother hood in question, Mrs. Annabelle Janiszewski Quinn Getz, primed herself for interviews by staring into the mirror as she powdered her prominent cheek bones and penciled light green shadow on her eyelids. She wore jangling charm bracelets, a trinket for each journey and pinnacle of life, a lemon pants suit and white sandals. She strode purposefully to the doorway of her ten-by-thirty trailer residence, pausing only to place the lid on the sugar jar as she passed through the spotless kitchen.

She stepped outside to face seven media men, one of them with microphone and electronic backpack, who were sweating dolorously in the humid air of the Crestview Haven Mobile Home Park just off Interstate 4, south of Orlando, Florida. There was no crest and no view, and concrete piles locked most of the trailers into immobility, but only carping critics would dispute the park's right to call itself a haven. Spanish moss festooned the live oaks, autumn flowers bloomed in russets and golds in neat rows beside the long, boxlike dwellings and contented, gray-haired folk lounged in metal camp chairs. The only sound was the popping of motorbikes on which residents ventured into the suspect outer world of crime, mistrust, real estate taxes and children.

"Mrs. Quinn?" asked the communicator with the backpack.

The woman before him flashed one of those quick smiles that briefly terrorize the landscape like a flare in nighttime battle. Jarred by a whiplash of memory, the TV reporter recalled his own mother and suffered simultaneous urges to wipe his feet, clean up his room and stuff himself with an unwanted third helping of creamed chipped beef.

"Mrs. Getz," she corrected. Her voice split the dank air like an admonishing finger. "I'm Edward Quinn's mother, but after Mr. Quinn died, I married Mr. Getz who also passed away. I'm just a widow living peacefully here in Crestview Haven."

"What do you think of your son's nomination?"

"Well, I'm surprised like everyone else." She studied her pride of bracelets as though it might yield a clue. "But I never had any doubts about Edward. We were strict with him as a child. Edward always did what he was told. He wiped the dishes and cut the grass and we gave him an allowance of thirty-five cents a week, fifty cents when he went to high school. We sacrificed to send Edward to college. He worked part time too. Edward never gave us trouble of any kind."

"Would you describe it as a loving home?" asked the TV man. In memory, he was now feverishly hiding a deck of playing cards, adorned with nude models, behind the Encyclopaedia Britannica as he heard his mother's decisive tread on the stairs.

"Loving?" Mrs. Getz looked as if she had been asked to define psoriasis. "Well, certainly Edward received all the love we could give him. He was an only child, you know. I nursed him through a bad case of mumps, three weeks I think it was. Of course, some years I worked down to the diner, so Edward had to make do on his own."

"Does he contribute to your support?"

"No. I don't ask Edward for money. Mr. Getz left me fixed comfortable enough. My needs aren't many, and since Edward's separation, what with the maintenance, he has his own obligations. Edward and I are friendly, but not all that close since his separation, which is a thing I do not approve of. Of course, that's his business. I'm just stating my opinion, it's a free country. . . . But if I needed funds, naturally Edward would provide. He never shirks what he considers his duty."

"Do you think he'd make a good President?" The questioner from the Miami *Herald* felt as though he were participating in some grand charade.

Mrs. Getz frowned and patted her blue-rinsed silver hair with a profound discord of bracelets. "Well, they say he doesn't have much chance. I wouldn't know about that. I'm not much for politics myself. But Edward always done a good job of anything he tackled. He's a disciplined man. He doesn't drink or smoke. Like I said, I think early training pays off, in the White House or anywhere else."

"Do you think it's strange that the nomination went to a middle-America type like your son?"

"I don't like that term," she snapped. "It was cooked up by those highbrow writers who're always looking down their nose at ordinary people. I'm Polish and proud of it and Edward's half Polish and half Irish and I guess he's proud of both." She pondered a moment. "But it is strange to see Eddie mixing with those rich fellows they say were the main ones who picked him and which I saw interviewed on television just now. He never cared for moneyed people and I'd be

surprised if he went along with all their ideas. Edward's a plain man
and he'll speak for plain people unless he's changed, which I doubt."

"You mean you'd look for some kind of break between Mr. Quinn
and the party leaders?"

"I don't know about that. That's politics, which I have nothing to
do with. I just wonder how Edward will get along with them, that's
all."

After a few more minutes, during which the chief disclosure was
that Eddie sucked his thumb until he was six, the television newsman who had opened the interview closed it with a "Thank you, Mrs.
Quinn."

"Getz," she replied coldly.

The communicator, leading his colleagues down the gravel road
between the rows of shiny, giant shoe boxes, felt a dull ache at the
base of his neck similar to the one which used to afflict him every
afternoon when he came home from school and wiped his feet on
the black rubber mat with the word, "Welcome" in dingy white letters.

Hugh Gregory Pinholster, the candidate of non-violent reforma-
tion, sat with his strategists in campaign headquarters, located in a
low building of the federal style on Jackson Place, Washington,
D.C. Windows of his third-floor offices overlooked the lawns, flower
beds and shrubs of Lafayette Square, the President's park, historic
marshaling yards for pickets by day and muggers and homosexuals by
night. A neck's crane to the right stood the White House, sheltered
amid great trees where hidden loudspeakers gave off a mournful,
whining sound designed to keep the starlings away. Pinholster campaign staffers listened to the White House as they might to a police
whistle or ambulance siren. To their ears, the old order, besieged by
the tribes of loving disruption, gave vent to its grief in shrill lamenta-
tion.

Hugh Pinholster, darling of the new order, hunched forward on a
studio couch. He wore an orange polo shirt and emerald green
sports jacket, the casual uniform of a candidate ready to spring onto
color television at a moment's notice. Actually, his forehead bore
traces of make-up from a recent appearance. Thus far he had at-

tacked, among other things, unresponsive bureaucracy, the FBI and the military-industrial complex and had espoused free abortions, participatory democracy and people's parks. Above and below his rugged jaw, he was the true liberated man of politics, purged of the prejudices which poison the average white American, but not yet certain which of his own could be revealed to the public without damage to his ambitions.

"Eddie Quinn!" Pinholster lifted the name like a toast. "Whenever that party gets into trouble, it sinks back to the lowest common denominator."

"We'll win in a walk," said Jeff Smithers, the campaign manager. His lagoon of sable hair lapped at his collar. He had a habit of crinkling his nose as though constantly sampling the terrain for establishment spoor.

"I'm gonna say one thing right now in this rap," said Martha Gandy, the new co-chairman of the party. She was an abundant black woman from the Bedford-Stuyvesant in Brooklyn. "No overconfidence. . . . They nominated themselves a white male of middle America. They's millions more Eddie Quinns where this one come from and they all going to be voting for Eddie on election day." She swept the room with a glare. "No overconfidence."

"Good advice, Martha," said Hutch Boyington III, Harvard's ambassador to the Pinholster campaign. He was a tall, gnarled anthropologist whose roots clung to the Battle of Bunker Hill and whose sap surged through every conceivable limb of the tree of knowledge. He was a wit, a gossip and a put-down artist who had served three Presidents in varying degrees of disloyalty.

"The men who hand-picked Eddie Quinn," he said, "knew precisely what they were doing, a charge that we can't often level at the opposition. Examine their candidate. He is not a city man, nor a man of the town or prairie, but one of those vague outer-city fellows who spends his life in shopping centers, cars, skating rinks and Ramada Inn restaurants. He's a highway official. My God, they claim he was born on one. He's separated from his wife, a severance not drastic enough to alienate the wives of his fellow Elks, but enough to lend him a certain cachet. He has no fixed abode—I hear he lives in some motel called the Buccaneer Motor Lodge—and no fixed ideas.

That means he will be the vassal of such twelfth-century knights er-
rant as Ted Witherspoon, Rich Cuthbert and Charlie Herron. While
I can't see Quinn winning, Martha's right. We should take nothing
for granted."

"Right on!" exclaimed Teegee (for Thelma Gower) Churchill.
Teegee, a philosophy major from Mount Holyoke with a master's in
sociology at Columbia, had joined the campaign staff only this week
to serve as liaison with the under-thirty tribes. She wore green patches
on her jeans in the shape of peace symbols and signs of the zodiac.
She peered out from the blond temple of her hair like a fugitive reluctant to leave sanctuary. She was proud that she had thrice out-
witted pigdom when others were busted, thus preserving her police
record in a virginal state uncharacteristic of her other belongings.

"This country," she said, "is ass-deep in Eddie Quinns."

Jeff Smithers, struck by an idea, glanced at Teegee with new interest. The talk went on, weighing Pinholster's prospects against the
new competition. Pedro Suárez, the Chicano leader, believed that
the only Mexican-American votes Quinn would get were those of a
few truck and bus drivers. Bill Amory, from the uncommon hierarchy
of Common Cause, thought the Quinn choice symbolized the poverty of the conservative WASP establishment. Seymour Wick, the
money man who had been having a hard time of it recently, said liberal wallets should loosen up now that a Pinholster victory appeared
certain. On balance, despite the warnings against complacency, the
strategists rated the Quinn nomination as Pinholster's best campaign break since the revelation that the late Senator Hudson's law
firm earned a fat retainer from a conglomerate guilty of polluting several creeks and the Bay of Fundy in manufacture of pinball machines, earth movers and flavored douches.

When the session ended, Jeff Smithers beckoned Teegee Churchill to a window. October leaves skipped along Pennsylvania Avenue and a black limousine turned into the west gate of the White
House. A bearded youth on the sidewalk turned toward the vehicle
and thrust one rigid finger skyward.

"How long you been with us, Teegee?" asked Smithers. "Only two
days, isn't it?"

"Right." She drew the word slowly across her larynx. "It's wonderful to hang in here with Hugh and Hutch and everyone."

"Many of your friends know you've joined up with us?" Smithers' nose crinkled as he scanned her.

"Nobody yet," she said. "I don't tell my business unless I have to."

"I've got a plan that might interest you. A political campaign is like a battle. What you need to outwit the enemy is solid intelligence from inside his own camp. Of course, I don't expect much opposition from Quinn, but we want to play it for a runaway vote for Hugh. So, I was thinking. Suppose a smart, attractive young lady from our side were to infiltrate the inner circle of the Quinn people and . . ."

"You want me to be a spy?" asked Teegee in a vibrant whisper.

"Exactly." Smithers's nostrils quivered again. "We'd work out a code and you'd report to me by telephone. We'd pay you maybe $200 a week, plus all expenses, whatever you needed."

"Well, I don't know. I'm really up, working so close to Governor Pinholster whom I adore. And being with you and Hutch and all. It wouldn't be the same. . . . And how would I get into Quinn headquarters? I don't type or anything."

"A smart, pretty girl who'll work for nothing can move into any campaign." His eyes traced the slim figure within the jeans and the soiled, turtle-neck sweater. "I think for the Quinn people, though, it might be better to wear a dress."

"It could be fun, I guess. Mata Hari in Square City. Look, Jeff, could I think it over tonight? I'm sharing a pad with this ec major who's working for Ralph Nader this semester, and, well, I just moved in with him. Could I let you know in the morning?"

"Sure, Teegee." He patted her arm. "Just remember that you'd do more for Hugh Pinholster in a couple of days at Quinn headquarters than you could do in the remaining nineteen days of the campaign around here."

Two hundred twenty miles north, in a hushed office of the New York *Times*, a man with a brooding, emaciated face removed a cigarette from his mouth and placed it carefully beside his typewriter. He stared for a moment at the blank sheet of copy paper, briefly measured his awesome responsibilities within the Kingdom and the Power, then slowly began to type.

Lead Ed.

EDDIE WHO?

In the bright, artificial daylight of the Astroworld ballroom in Houston, insulated by a miracle of spiritual engineering from the gray twilight settling over the rest of the American Empire, a great political party yesterday faced its duty to the nation—and turned away.

It turned from proven leaders, from men of ability and talent, from several men of extraordinary vision. Instead it reached into the grab bag of mediocrity and pulled out someone named Edward Nicholas Quinn.

Future historians may mark the precise time, 2:48 P.M. EDT, when tens of millions of Americans in the torn and bleeding cities, in the isolated, fear-ridden suburbs and along the befouled, dying rivers looked up from their television sets and asked in voices bleak with despair: "Eddie who?"

Were this a bygone era, there might have been a hundred laughs in the travesty played out in living color across a parking lot from the Astrodome's lifeless turf. . . .

4

Eddie was munching a ham-and-cheese on rye and watching television in his motel room when the screen pictured the Utah national committeeman, a florid man with a pronounced lisp, delivering the state's votes to Quinn, thus escorting Eddie past the majority mark and into the footnotes of history.

The first impact was electric. He, Eddie Quinn, an old trucker turned politician, named to run for President when his highest ambition had been a long-shot try for governor. Nominated by a major party! Less than a hundred men in the history of the country had rated that honor. Sure, his chances were slim, but . . . nominated! They said any American boy could aspire to the White House. He'd always thought that line was a crock, but now? Well, he could hope. One thing was sure. He had a better chance to make it now than anyone in America except Hugh Pinholster.

But then, after a few moments, the elation began to ebb away. For one thing, he felt ragged. He'd been without sleep for more than thirty hours and the carnal tryst with Kate had sapped him. In his impoverished state, the whole President business had an air of unreality. The real world included the weekly poker game at the K. of C. hall which he'd miss tonight. His real world was this ham-and-cheese on rye. The motel restaurant had sent him the sandwich minus mustard and plus a lifeless leaf of lettuce that had turned brown at the edges.

Eddie's spirits had been sagging for some time before the nomination. The chief cause of his low morale was the juiceless national

committee scene as relayed by network cameras stationed inside the
Astroworld's ballroom. The members, who had but recently buried
Senator Hudson, now acted as though they had been summoned to
another funeral on the wrong side of the tracks. Enthusiasm for
Quinn, or anyone else, ran riotless. Faces appearing on the screen
looked sullen, bored or merely hung-over. If a politician exuded moderate cheer, he often tended to be flippant at the same time. News-
casters combined gravity and irreverence in their tone, and as time
went on, Eddie began to resent being caricatured as a second-hand
national joke. At one point, he shoved a thumb toward the tube
and shouted: "Up yours, too."

The miniature nature of the proceedings, compared to the party's
huge August convention, also irritated Eddie. Instead of 2700 delegates and alternates in constant turmoil, the committee numbered
but 162 persons. Instead of 50,000 roaring spectators in the Astrodome, now only a few hundred party officials and hacks hovered on
the fringe of the seated committee. In place of a press corps of several
thousand, now fewer than 500 newsmen and cameramen covered
the balloting. It was, for Eddie, a mini-convention nominating a
mini-candidate for a mini-campaign and the thought lowered him
into a small depression.

Utah's vote should have recharged him. Instead, after the brief
geyser of elation, the nomination wafted Eddie, drained and sleepless as he was, into twin fantasies, one fading swiftly into the other.
The first Eddie Quinn mounted the ramp of a campaign jet and
waved farewell to a million frenzied partisans gathered on the mac-
adam below him. He rose to cloudless skies, flashed in and out of
dozens of shining stadiums, showered wisdom and hope over slum
and mansion. The contrails of his jet miraculously turned arid lands
into velvet pastures, halted warring armies, brought fresh parks and
tinkling pools to hot, wasted tenements and, finally, the jet swooped
to a landing in a valley grove of the United Nations where Eddie's
healing words beckoned humanity to everlasting peace and amity.

A second Eddie Quinn mingled with the throng in the grove,
then climbed into an old Mack semitrailer and rolled away on a six-
lane expressway. Posted at intervals of several hundred yards stood
fifty-two women of all sizes and shapes and a few colors. As Eddie

roared past, each woman leaped into the rear of the truck with a happy smile and a graceful bound. They all chattered gaily in the rear while Kate Witherspoon, the last in, arranged herself on the cab seat and began digging into a dashboard compartment for a cigarette. A picnic spirit buoyed the ladies and none of them fell to quarreling with her new acquaintants.

Erasing the Mack semi and its unworldly cargo (in real life several of the women had been shrewish, others dull or morose and some guilt-ridden) with a shake of his head, the candidate walked to the center of the room, faced the large wall mirror above the writing desk, folded his arms, studied himself and said:

"Eddie, I'll be goddamned."

The oath reminded him again of the denigrating circumstances of his nomination and of the patronizing attitude of the leaders who picked him. Depression became annoyance, then flowered into anger. He wanted to lash out at someone. Instead he kicked the wastebasket.

The phone rang. When he answered, the switchboard operator sounded breathlessly unhinged. "Oh, congratulations, Mr. Quinn. . . . I know I'm not supposed to put calls through, but this one is from the White House in Washington."

"Okay, Beatrice." It was pleasant to be treated respectfully. "I'll take it."

"Congratulations." The voice known to millions rang with the usual self-assurance of an empty hall. "They tell me the committee made a wise choice. Of course, in this kind of short, uphill race, there's no danger of peaking too early. You wade in on the offensive and stay in there slugging, just like the late Vince Lombardi."

"Thank you, Mr. President. It was nice of you to call."

"I wanted to be the first to congratulate you." The tone implied that the other pallbearers would be along in a jiffy. "The main job is to prevent a landslide for that jerk in the orange shirts. If he winds up with what he interprets as a mandate, we'll be headed for a national disaster."

"I'll try, Mr. President."

"I know you will. Perhaps we can arrange a meeting after you're squared away. In the meantime, good luck. Good-by."

"Good-by, Mr. President." For a corpse, Eddie felt surprisingly hostile.

He mused for a moment as he finished his sandwich, then informed Beatrice that he was open for all calls, but try to screen out the nuts and cranks, please.

"All right, Mr. Quinn." She giggled. "I feel like I ought to call you something more important."

"How about Commissioner? I'm a Turnpike official, you know."

She sounded delighted to escalate his title and Eddie had always rather liked it himself.

Pete Stackpole phoned promptly and showered him with excited, heartfelt congratulations. Pete called him "Eddie" and disgorged a full schedule that left the candidate choiceless as to details. "Give you more time to think about strategy," said Pete helpfully. Eddie was to meet again with the kingmakers in the Celestial suite at 6 P.M., then go before the national committee and TV cameras at 8 P.M. for a short acceptance speech. A group would play his favorite song, "There Ain't No Easy Run." No need to worry about the speech. Rich Cuthbert's best ghost writer would dash it off. Then he would fly with party leaders by chartered jet to Washington where he had reservations at the Manger Hay-Adams. Eddie would take over Senator Hudson's campaign headquarters on Connecticut Avenue tomorrow morning and hold a press conference. No problem about the press. Eddie's response to anticipated questions would be worked up by the campaign staff.

"Anything you can think of I've overlooked?" asked Pete.

"Yeah," said Eddie acidly, "have somebody buy me four shirts, two white and two blue, seventeen-thirty-fours."

"Right. . . . Is something wrong, Eddie? You don't sound overjoyed."

"For a guy who's supposed to be a commander, I'm taking a helluva lot of orders."

"Come on, Mr. Candidate." Pete was quickly placating. "We're just trying to take the heat off you. . . . And Eddie, don't drive over in that rental car of yours. I'm sending one of the official limos. . . . And, hey man, wear your socks this time."

The lift provided by Beatrice's celebrity-struck voice vaporized. Ed-

die eyed the wastebasket again. Someone in the next room had the
television set turned high and Eddie caught snatches of the commentary through the wall. Quinn was six-feet-one, weighed 184
pounds. . . . Separated from Mabel Probst Quinn who told interviewers she would nevertheless vote for him . . . has two sons, Eddie,
Jr., an appliance salesman, and Al, manager of a bowling alley. . . .
Views on domestic issues, foreign policy, party platform, cloudy. The
word "platform" caught Eddie like a sneak blow to the stomach.
Good God, he had never read the thing.

He heard a knock. Eddie threw sheets and spread over the heavily traveled bed, still redolent with Kate's perfume and exudations,
and opened the door.

He faced a tall, hatless man wearing a look of benign authority
somewhat like a process server or a meter reader. The stranger was
neatly dressed. He had a green pin in his lapel and he carried a black,
oblong box with protruding antenna.

"Commissioner Quinn? I'm Jim Flannery, head of your Secret
Service detail. Congratulations, sir. I wanted to introduce myself as
soon as possible."

"Come in. Come in." Eddie shook hands and ushered the agent
into the room. Flannery placed his walkie-talkie on a chair and surveyed the room with a professional eye, taking in but not lingering
on, the rumpled bed.

"Your phone is going to be ringing off the hook, so I'll make this
short." Flannery's smile was cordial if tentative. "All you have to
know right now is that we're outside, four of us for starters. You're
under our protection and we're ready to do any little chores for you
that don't interfere with our first business, security."

"Are you always . . . around?" Eddie already knew the answer.
Privilege, he was fast learning, carried its own unwalled prisons.

"Yes, but you'll get used to it. We try to be as invisible as possible."

Eddie flinched, thinking of Kate's certain reaction last night had
he hinted of a rendezvous under the looming shadows of government agents.

Flannery, for his part, measured his man, seeking to estimate how much mutual trust might burgeon eventually. He needed some right now.

"Look, Mr. Commissioner. I'd like to ask a favor of you. We're supposed to be on station, ready to take you over the second you're nominated. But, well, frankly, we were caught off guard. Then somebody goofed and we got the wrong Edward Quinn, a rancher in a room over at the Stardust Motel. He and his girl were zonked. Anyway, we wasted a few minutes before we found you."

Eddie, grateful to be placed in a position where he could be magnanimous, waved the error aside. "Don't give it another thought, Jim. As far as anyone will ever know, you had already arrived when Utah put me over."

Flannery looked relieved. "I appreciate that. Not that I mind personally, but it would give the Service a black eye. . . ."

"It's already filed in the forget-it folder." Then Eddie thought of Kate and his rental car. "Speaking of favors, I'd like one too. Naturally, I had no idea I'd be nominated, and a friend of mine drove my rental Galaxie over to the Shamrock Hilton. Somebody ought to return the car to Hertz. They're giving me wheels—a Mark IV, I guess."

"No problem. All we need is the plate number and the friend's name."

Eddie hesitated. "Well, you see, Jim . . . Let me level with you. As you probably know, I'm separated, and this friend . . ."

"No problem, sir—ever," Flannery cut in. "Anything of that kind is strictly between you and me. Same with Oscar, Dave and Bill whom you'll meet later. We don't talk. We don't write memoirs. We're your men, first and last."

"But you report to your chief in Washington."

"Never on personal business. Relax, sir. In the Service, we all wear zippers on our yaps."

Eddie placed a hand on Flannery's shoulder. "Thanks, Jim. We'll get along fine. My friend's name is Kate Witherspoon. I think she left the Galaxie with the doorman at the Shamrock."

Flannery evinced no flicker of recognition at a name well known in Washington. "I'll have Oscar Baker handle it right away."

Eddie felt rapport growing. "Could Baker do me another favor?"

"Sure. Name it."

"Well, I'd like a dozen roses sent to Mrs. Witherspoon at the Shamrock." Eddie took a twenty from his wallet and scribbled a few words on a sheet of motel stationery. "He can put that on the card. . . . I hope this doesn't go beyond Secret Service rules."

Flannery shook his head. "If our man's mind is easy, our job's easier. I should know. Some of the errands I've run . . ." He picked up his walkie-talkie. "I'll be outside when you're ready to move." The message of his wide smile needed no decoding: If you cover for me and I cover for you, together we can beat the system.

Eddie could hear Flannery speaking on his walkie-talkie on the portico. "Houston central, this is Osprey One. We have locked onto Eagle. Repeat, we have Eagle now. All secure." Eddie began to feel better. Eagle Quinn, huh? How about that! This Flannery was a solid eight-laner. Probably a former altar boy like himself.

After several hours of hectic phone calls, Eddie dressed in his good blue suit and traveled to the Astroworld in a limousine, but not the Lincoln Continental Pete Stackpole sent for him. Instead he rode in a bulletproof blue Electra 225, body reinforced with armor plate, custom-built for the Secret Service and, Eddie discovered through questioning, driven from Washington to serve the party's new nominee, whoever he might be. Eddie sat in the rear, flanked by Flannery and Agent Oscar Baker. Two more SS men, one of them the driver, occupied the front seat. A square of Houston motorcycle patrolmen boxed the vehicle. Eddie, savoring this first taste of pomp and privilege, waved at gawking motorists. By the time the brigade halted beneath the hotel's canopy with a fine belching of motors and exhaust fumes, Eddie felt at home.

Pete Stackpole greeted him in the lobby with a big hello and in league with the agents elbowed a path for Eddie through a mass of curious spectators, many of whom treated the candidate as though he were a famous comedian whose smash routine always laid them in the aisles. Eddie's emotional thermometer dropped a degree. In the top-floor Celestial suite, the agents took up stations under the carriage lamps in the ornate corridor, while Pete hustled Eddie into the same marble library where Eddie had spent four post-dawn hours. Eddie noted only a few differences in the opulent room with its twenty-foot ceiling, black marble coffee table, scarlet sofas and gilded cherubs romping with a gilded nude above the fireplace. The electric clock, apparently repaired, had stopped grunting, the men who clustered around him, offering moist handshakes, were freshly shaved and shirted, and Rich Cuthbert was missing. The newspaper publisher, it was explained, was busy overseeing his ghost writer's work on the acceptance speech. Eddie's thermometer registered a further drop, and when Ted Witherspoon began to talk, Eddie felt shadows of his mini-depression again.

"So we all feel, Eddie," said Witherspoon in his ponderous way, "that there must be a team effort if we're going to pull this thing off with dignity and with profit to the party. Our main concern is the state and local tickets. If some miracle or fluke occurs, and you get elected, fine. But our realistic job is to mount the kind of wind-up campaign that will bring us House and Senate gains, plenty of governors, state legislatures and county courthouses. And for that, Eddie, we need your co-operation."

"I'll do my best."

"Of course you will," said Senator Framingham. "We just want to make sure we all understand one another on what has to be done. Charlie, why don't you give Eddie the money picture?"

"Yes," said Herron. "There's one point eight million left in the campaign pot, Eddie, and it would be foolish to expect any more contributions of any size. So we want the maximum return on our money." The banker favored Eddie with one of those cheerful, apologetic smiles that signal forthcoming denial of the mortage application. "Now, as the vice-presidential candidate, Governor Ewing is our seasoned campaigner, heading that congressional team that's touring the country. It just makes good sense, speaking in dollar terms, to put our major investment in Ewing's team." Herron consulted the back of a golf-score card. Eddie felt like an expired due bill. "I just jotted a few figures here. We can put you on several network shows and still leave a million three for Governor Ewing's team and general staff expenses."

Senator Framingham reached out and patted Eddie's knee. "Naturally, you'll get a great deal of free exposure, like your acceptance speech tonight and tomorrow's press conference. The networks will cover those as news."

"Okay," said Eddie. "In a couple of shows, I can put my ideas across. I don't believe in too much talk."

"Good!" Herron beamed. "Actually, we were thinking of slotting you for five, six minutes each show. The rest of the time is being assigned as a general party appeal with senators and governors taking part."

"Oh." Eddie stared at the banker's topaz cuff links and wondered how much they cost. "Well, I'd rather campaign by car anyway, getting out to the people, pressing the flesh, as Lyndon Johnson used to say."

"Just what kind of a campaign do you have in mind?" asked Governor Hotchkiss. Though his hands were folded placidly on his belly, he radiated suspicion.

"I haven't had much time to think, but I'd like to cover the big electoral vote states. I'd go in by jet and then kind of bang around, hitting the shopping centers and highway strips."

Silence fell. The thought of Eddie Quinn flitting about the countryside, pressing strange flesh and saying whatever popped into his mind obviously did not appeal to this group. Hotchkiss, gravely dubious, pursed his lips. Charlie Herron's expression bespoke overdrafts.

"The budget won't stretch for that kind of thing," said the finance chairman. "You'd need advance men, hotel suites, charter jets, motorcades, the works. That costs big numbers, Eddie."

"We might give him three or four single-shot appearances," said Senator Framingham, "say to Chicago, New York, Detroit, L.A."

"That's not where our votes are, Senator," said Eddie. "I'd like to hit the suburbs and those feeder roads off the interstates."

"Let's not get too detailed right now," Pete Stackpole sounded a nervous harmony pitch. "We can work out campaign business over the weekend."

"Yes, I'd like to turn to policy," said Ted Witherspoon. "Specifically, taxes." His jaw muscles twitched as he pronounced the word. "As I understood you this morning, Eddie, you go along with us on taxes. But I think we ought to come into firm agreement. Pinholster has made some sloppy promises about closing what he calls tax loopholes. Nothing could be worse for business confidence right now. Our platform pledges a review of taxes. Now that's promise enough from our side. A review can mean anything. But basically, we're not for radical tax changes. I assume you agree, Eddie?"

"My main idea about taxes is that they're too high," said Eddie noncommittally. He wondered why Kate ever married this pompous-ass little man.

"Good boy," said Witherspoon. "I'm lending you our company's tax expert for the duration. He's brilliant, knows the whole field. I suggest, Eddie, that you check with my man, Durbank, before going into taxes."

"Thanks." Eddie got the message. A new security guard named Durbank would insulate Candidate Quinn from contamination by those who would tamper with the oil-depletion allowance, thus molesting the petroleum industry and the sleep of Ted Witherspoon.

As the kingmakers talked on, hurriedly seeking to cash the I.O.U.s which they assumed Eddie had signed in return for the nomination, Eddie felt less like a candidate than an overdrawn bank account. Herron would lend an expert on the complex banking and insurance laws. Framingham offered a staff member from the Senate Finance Committee to advise on conglomerates and corporate bankruptcies. Shadowitz's specialist would warn against bureaucratic boll weevils, disguised as public-interest champions, within the regulatory agencies.

Eddie had pictured a presidential candidate as a man to whom power rushed as to a magnet. The candidate ordered, commanded and dealt. Instead it was Eddie who was being ordered, commanded and dealt with. By the time they prepared to leave for the grand ballroom and the acceptance speech, Eddie's depression had changed to prickly resentment. He decided he hadn't a friend in the room with the possible exception of Stackpole, and even Pete might have to be placed on probation.

Rich Cuthbert arrived at the last minute and handed Eddie three typewritten pages. "My writer tried to keep it plain and simple," he said as though such a goal magnified the task beyond comprehension. "They're mimeographing it now for the press section."

Eddie glanced at the first paragraph, spotted the words "honor," "gratitude" and "responsibility" and slipped the speech into his jacket pocket. As the men moved toward the door, Ted Witherspoon and Charlie Herron were at Eddie's elbow.

"We gave Rich some ideas for the speech," said Witherspoon. "Your tone should be reassuring. Hudson's death upset the country. Your job is to calm and soothe, give people confidence." He patted Eddie's shoulder. "Easy does it."

"The President urged me to jump in on the attack," said Eddie.

"Poor advice," said Herron. "Your theme is harmony, pulling together. There's nothing basically wrong with the country. It's still sound as a dol— sound as Plymouth Rock. You're the man who'll keep it that way. That's the pitch of Cuthbert's writer and your delivery ought to reflect the text's spirit of stability and good will."

The hands that gripped Eddie's were firm but dismissive, and Eddie recalled the time he had been escorted to the door of the very exclusive Links Club in New York after an uncomfortable lunch with the underwriters of an issue of turnpike bonds.

A few minutes later Eddie stood in a crush of bodies on the platform of the Astroworld's gilded grand ballroom and faced TV cameras and some two thousand people. He was pinioned between Agents Flannery and Baker, who occasionally muttered terse code words to each other behind his back. Near them stood Shelby Ewing, the vice-presidential candidate, who looked about him with an aloof smile, and Mrs. Ewing, who looked put upon. She held clasped hands before her to protect the orchid at her ample bosom. Also in the swaying sandwich of flesh were Eddie's two sons, Eddie, Jr., and Al, who had flown in from Philadelphia and Chicago respectively to lend the old man a family backdrop. Whenever Eddie looked at Al, the young man with the blond mutton chops smiled cynically and shook his head as though to punctuate what he had said earlier: "Jeez, what ass-hole luck!" Eddie, Jr., was impressed but withdrawn. The presence of his sons did little to bolster Eddie's morale, for they had always tended to attribute their father's minor successes to luck and his failures to irremediable character deficiencies.

But Eddie had his anonymous well-wishers. Every few seconds a strange hand would reach out toward Eddie and another feverish voice would say, "Congratulations." In a corner of the hall, a group manning piano, drums and bass viol thumped out the chords of "There Ain't No Easy Run."

They were all locked to the clock in a tight schedule laid down by Pete Stackpole and welded to the word, "prime," an Americanism denoting the best in beef and TV time. They were to launch the oratorical operation precisely at 8 o'clock Houston time, 9 P.M. New York, 7 P.M. Denver and 6 P.M. Los Angeles.

At a signal from Stackpole, the principals moved into position, Mrs. Ewing in the lead, the governor next, followed by the Quinn sons and finally the presidential candidate. As Eddie passed Stackpole, the No. 1 kingmaker cupped his mouth to Eddie's ear.

"Stick to the text, Eddie."

"I thought I might throw in a few ideas of my own."

"No, damn it. Stick to Cuthbert. The text is being handed around now at the press tables." Stackpole gave Eddie a proprietary nudge toward the rostrum.

As they shaped a semicircle before the thicket of microphones, with Eddie in the center, the applause and cheers had a curious muted quality as though the ballroom's soundproofing had been devised to reject such untoward emotions as vexation, glee or anguish. Eddie felt alone. The crowd before him resembled a parking lot at night, every face a white headlight. There were only three or four dark faces visible. Although Eddie didn't know it, his selection already had been denounced by black spokesmen on the verifiable grounds that Edward Nicholas Quinn was another white man nominated by the white man's party.

The principals stood briefly in the glory circle, then retreated to the row of platform seats, leaving the podium to Governor Ewing for his allotted five minutes. Ewing was a solemn man of generous girth who, ever since his August nomination as the running mate, had conducted himself as a kind of political Uriah Heep. He had been all humility, self-sacrifice and subservient dedication.

Now, suddenly, Ewing burst forth as an aggressive leader who would guide the party in the climactic crusade ahead. He made it plain by implication that he was the old, reliable hand and that Quinn was the untried new boy. As Ewing heaved to his peroration, predicting inevitable victory in November, Eddie, glancing to his right, saw Witherspoon, Herron and Cuthbert nodding in smug approval. The sound and sight galled Eddie. He reached into his jacket pocket for the speech of Cuthbert's ghost writer, but when his fingers touched the pages, something within him snapped. Instead of withdrawing the text, he slowly and vengefully crumpled it into a ball.

Eddie's appearance at the lectern provoked the old-style standing ovation and a good-natured cannonade of applause and shouts. After twenty seconds, fearing the noise might abate, Eddie raised his hands for silence. Shorn of the Cuthbert speech, he felt quite at ease now with his juices flowing nicely. He had addressed modest audiences in his races for mayor and congressman and once faced 5408 people during ceremonies saluting the widening of the northern segment of the New Jersey Turnpike to twelve lanes. Eddie gulped only once before beginning.

"Friends on the national committee, guests, fellow Americans," he said into the microphones, "I had a written text, but something happened to it, so I'll just say what I think as I go along."

He heard faint laughter. A newsman at the press bench directly in front of him waved his copy of the Cuthbert speech. Eddie recognized Vince Anderson of the Trenton, New Jersey, Associated Press bureau. Eddie ignored the offer.

"It really doesn't make much difference what I say tonight, because the main idea is to give you people here and all of you voters in the television audience a chance to look me over and size me up. After all, none of you had any more idea yesterday than I did that I would be standing here tonight." This time the laughter was louder and Eddie took heart. "So let me introduce myself. My name is Eddie Quinn and I'm running for gov—for President of the United States. I've been a mayor and a congressman and now I'm a Turnpike commissioner. You just met my two sons. I guess that's enough biography for now.

"I'll tell you about my ideas—uh—policy as the days go by. For me, this short campaign will be a learning process, for I'm not going to imitate my opponent and pretend that I have all the answers. As a matter of fact, the trouble with this country right now is that for the last thirty years too many half-baked answers have been served up in Washington."

A sizable roar sprang from the audience. Eddie, startled, gripped the lectern and stared in disbelief. The idea that a word from him could move two thousand people had not occurred to him. Then he realized that thirty years included the last eight, the tenure of the party's own man in the White House, and that the party faithful, unwilling to boo the President directly, were proud of Eddie for opening this substitute escape hatch. Eddie raised his hands for silence. To his surprise, the cheering stopped on cue. For the first time he felt the adrenalin of power, a sensation not unlike that which galvanized him during the hours with Kate Witherspoon.

"I've been wondering, just like you, why this great national committee selected an unknown guy named Eddie Quinn. I think the reason is that this committee, like all of us, is—uh—tired of the old managers, those rich, self-satisfied men who order us around from their executive suites, their fancy country clubs, their boxes at the horse show, their fifty-acre estates, their big foundations and their expensive, elite universities."

Now a hush descended on the hall as though another funeral cortege were about to pass down the aisle.

"This committee," said Eddie on a rising note, "wants a return to the people!"

The weak applause, like hesitant raindrops, told Eddie that the party had not contemplated such a break with its heritage.

"This committee wants a President who comes from the people!"

This evoked a mild response, in volume more Episcopalian than evangelical.

"This committee wants a President who comes from the kind of people who love and respect the stars and stripes of the United States of America!"

Eddie thrust his right arm upward and outward, palm front, fingers spread, in a gesture of aggressive leadership.

The partisan functionaries, at last grasping the theme, filled the ballroom with reasonable thunder. Eddie smiled and let the mild storm run its course.

"That's my kind of people. Our ancestors came from the tenements, the villages and the worn-out soil of the farms of Europe. My own great-grandparents came here from County Mayo in Ireland. On my mother's side, my grandparents came here as humble peasants from Poland. And if you don't think the wedding of my father and mother was a surprise, then you don't know the Irish and the Poles."

Having played this autobiographical footnote for laughs, Eddie was thrown off pace when none developed. His largely WASP auditors, Eddie realized, were not attuned to the finer points of ethnic infighting. He retreated somewhat grimly to his all-American stance.

"All these people came for the better life promised by that torch held high on the Statue of Liberty. They worked hard, they played hard and they fought hard. It was rough going. They filled the unions and the factories, the police forces and the armies, the farms and the cities. We, their sons and daughters, bear such proud names as Quinn, Powansky, Schmidt, Palumbo, Korona, Damaskinos and Matousek. Let me tell you about us.

"We don't belong to exclusive country clubs. Our club is the corner bar or one along the highway strip. My hangout is a tavern in New Brunswick in my home state. I don't drink myself, but I'm there now and then with a ginger ale.

"When we travel, we don't hire expensive suites in the fancy hotels. You'll find us in a nice, comfortable room in one of the chain motels.

"We don't play—uh—squash or tennis and seldom golf. We bowl. I bowl with Melheisen's Pontiac on Tuesday nights.

"We don't play word games or bridge. We play poker. I play in a two-buck-limit game every other Thursday night at the K. of C. hall."

Eddie, extemporizing as he went, decided that he had filled up enough evenings with unproductive pursuits. Besides, he usually devoted most of the remaining nights to women and did not consider that activity worthy of public comment.

"We don't drive Mercedes or Fiats or Ferraris or Triumphs or Porsches. We drive Firebirds and trailers and Darts and second-hand campers and Cutlasses and Plymouth wagons and Toronados. I drive a '68 Impala with 140,000 miles on it. We think American-made cars are okay. We're proud of them and we're proud of our highways, the finest in the world.

"We're not rich, but few of us are dirt poor any more. And let me tell you another thing about us. We work for what we get—and you almost never find any of us on welfare!"

This detonated a spontaneous, rousing burst of approbation. Eddie flushed. He'd forgotten his Arkansas uncle, Hunk Janiszewski, who spent several months on local welfare rolls before settling down on Social Security and veterans' disability pensions.

"We work and we save and we send our kids to college when we can—and believe me, you don't see our kids dropping out, burning the dean's office or yelling dirty words at the police." Another flash of cheers. "We live in nice homes on fifty-foot lots and we move to the suburbs when we can afford it. And what we don't understand is why we're preached at and ridiculed for trying to protect our homes and our neighborhoods, and why nobody in Washington ever thinks of helping *us*.

"The well-off, old-family people call us prejudiced. We say we're human. They call us narrow. We know our hopes are as wide as the country. They call us limited, but we know we're the ones who built America with our sweat and our toil. And we also know that for many years our country has been mismanaged, depleted, corrupted, polluted and almost bankrupted by the country-club set and the front-office crowd."

Eddie paused, his thoughts dwelling delectably on Ted Witherspoon, Charlie Herron and Rich Cuthbert. The hush was again heavy in the hall.

"Well, now it's our turn. It's the turn of the Eddie Quinns, the Powanskys and the Palumbos. I won't make any big fake claims for us, but I'll tell you a couple of things we intend to do. First, we're going to quit treating this party as some kind of exclusive club. We're going to throw the doors wide open, welcome everyone into it and ask them what we can do for them. Second, we're going to be the party that preserves the earth as a good place to live. Did you know that just to support one person one year in America, it takes twenty-five tons of stuff extracted and processed from the earth? Isn't that incredible? Well, we're going to begin treating the earth as our home, not some big warehouse to be plundered.

"I'll make you two promises. One, that I'll do my best. Two, that I'll be honest with you. I appreciate the honor of the nomination, and I need the help of every one of you if we're going to get this country back on the thruway on November 2. And remember, folks, there ain't no easy run. . . . Thank you."

The quality of applause, unlike mercy, was strained. Many partisans stood in shock for the second time that day. They had given their party, the WASP bride, in trial marriage to Eddie Quinn with considerable misgivings. Now to hear the bridegroom extoll his ordinary bloodlines while belittling the patriotic labors of his gracious in-laws was a bit much. After the polite applause, Eddie found himself the focus of as many wary politicians as outright well-wishers.

"That misfired, Eddie," said Ted Witherspoon. He shook his head in reproof. "You better be damn careful from now on about discarding a prepared text. Remember, man, you're running for President."

Rich Cuthbert glared at him. "Thanks a lot," he said bitterly.

Anderson of the Associated Press squirmed through the crowd. "What about the text, Mr. Quinn. Does that stand too or just what's the score?"

"I said what I said, not what was written." Eddie grinned. "What did you think of the text, Vince? Any good?"

"It might win a Pulitzer for platitudes."

"Well, then, why not just kill it?"

Agents Jim Flannery and Oscar Baker, wedging Eddie between them, began moving toward the exit. "Nice speech," whispered Flannery. "About time a candidate laid it on the line like that."

But Pete Stackpole gave Eddie's arm a savage tug. "What the hell got into you, Eddie? That's a fine way to honor your obligations—by crapping in your own nest."

"Who's the candidate?" Eddie suddenly felt in command. "Me or Cuthbert's ghost writer?"

"But to do a thing like that without warning us. . . . All that jazz about executive suites and country clubs. Just who the hell do you think it was who nominated you?"

"A guy from Utah I never met."

"Very funny. Listen, we're going to talk this all out on the plane tonight, and I don't think we'll find Witherspoon, Herron and the rest in a very pleasant mood. Remember one thing. They've got the money."

"Yeah, but remember another, Pete. . . . I've got the nomination."

Stackpole gaped at him as he might at a stranger who had just passed him a dollar bill in change and blandly called it a ten.

Eddie also left the great American public gaping that night. An estimated 60,000,000 people saw and heard his speech on television, partially out of curiosity, chiefly because all three networks displaced regular shows to carry the event live from Houston. While Eddie Quinn promptly became a household word, no expert could be sure what other words the households were applying to him. A fast telephone poll by the Gallup people showed that 32 per cent of those who saw Quinn were favorably impressed, 30 per cent unfavorably impressed and 38 per cent uncertain.

Another public-opinion hustler, polling secretly and expensively for Candidate Pinholster, found that of those who saw Eddie on TV, 30 per cent liked him, a figure close to Gallup's. But Pollster Swensson went further and broke down his responses by age and sex. He found that 40 per cent of the pro-Quinn viewers were voters between eighteen and twenty-five years of age. By sex, 57 per cent were women. Arnold Swensson, pondering the column of figures amassed by his battery of telephone interviewers, noted Eddie's strength among the two groups, youth and women, in which Pinholster had consistently run far ahead of the late Senator Hudson. Before reporting his figures to Pinholster, Swensson called his friend Don Pugh, who served as his betting blind with a Philadelphia bookie.

"What're Joe's odds on Eddie Quinn?"

"Same as Jimmy the Greek's," said Pugh. "One will get you nine."

"Put one thousand on Quinn for me at nine to one."

"A grand, Arnold?"

"Sure. Get a long-shot hunch, bet a bunch."

Congresswoman Kate Witherspoon was not among the female 57 per cent that so intrigued Pollster Swensson. In the Witherspoon suite at the Shamrock in Houston, Kate watched Eddie's performance on television with swiftly telescoping emotions. His symbolic attack on the men who nominated him took her by surprise. She found his pirating of her ideas about ecology and widening the party both amusing and flattering. Why, he had almost parroted her words! But Eddie's blunt way of drawing class distinctions grated on her. As a politician she might admit the validity of Eddie's complaints, but as a woman who had recently shared his bed she wondered if his gratuitous allusions to country clubs, golf, tennis and bridge—Kate's life had once encompassed all four—might be coded, personal zaps. It was almost as if Eddie had ticked off in denigration the very hills, dales and crannies of her body that he had so recently worshiped or pretended to worship. The cathedral's remaining spire crumbled. In a mood of perplexed irritation, Kate took the telephone, called Western Union and dictated:

Edward N. Quinn
Candidate's Party
Houston Intercontinental Airport
YOUR SPEECH PUZZLING. BITING HAND THAT FEEDS YOU IS STRANGE GAME PLAN. CAN'T STAND JOHNNY CASH.

KATE

She had intended to accompany her husband on the charter flight bearing the new candidate to Washington. Now she called the hotel travel desk and booked a seat on a late commercial flight to the capital. Fifteen minutes later, when the roses arrived, Kate inspected the card, "For an American Beauty," thought briefly of trying to halt the telegram, simmered in frustration and finally broke the stems and let the flowers slide into a wastebasket.

Technically, Americans do not vote for a presidential nominee but for a slate of electors in every state. All over the country that night electors pledged to the late Senator Hudson took careful measure of the party's new man, Eddie Quinn. Some liked what they saw, but many did not. In place of the sedate, prosaic, conservative Hudson, they found themselves bound to an unknown highway official who oddly attacked tennis, country clubs and executive suites. On the other hand, in Salt Lake City, a Pinholster elector named Ezekiel H. Thornquest, would have wired congratulations to Eddie were it not for his party and electoral ties. Eddie had named the very symbols of affluence and class that had long annoyed the hard-pressed Thornquest. And as it went with the official electors, so did it go with the voters. By one short speech, Eddie had thrown traditional alignments out of kilter.

A few people decided on direct action. In her ground-floor apartment on Juniper Street in Atlanta, Margot Hicks, the black social worker, saw Eddie Quinn fade from her television screen, then listened to a commentator describing the candidate's schedule, including the flight to Washington. Eddie's crack about people on welfare galled her—another one of those demagogic slurs by a white politician. Still, there was something about Candidate Quinn that fascinated her even as Eddie had that weekend five years ago. What was it? A way of leveling? An openness? A habit of half closing his eyes as though sharing an intimate joke with each person in his audience? A boyish, receptive quality? Margot wasn't sure. All she knew was that she felt she could talk straight to this Eddie Quinn just as she had with the one some years ago. For a long time Margot had been obsessed with an idea. Maybe Eddie . . . On a sudden hunch, Margot Hicks picked up the phone and booked herself on an early morning flight to Washington. Somehow she would get in to see this new, off-beat nominee for President.

A similar decision, though a far more confident one, was made by R Daniel Fenelli, the thinker at the Center for the Study of Democratic Institutions. Eddie's college roommate was at home now in Santa Barbara, California, sipping his first pre-dinner gin and tonic and musing over the spectacle in Houston. R Dan had cooled down since his outburst at the time of the afternoon nomination and he listened attentively to Eddie's acceptance speech. He grasped every nuance and he sensed the uncalculated nature of his old friend's rebellion against the class of men who manipulated the nomination for him. In many ways, Eddie's speech was but an extension of ideas they swapped during Seton Hall bull sessions. R Dan recalled his last talk with Eddie a year ago during a trip East. Eddie was no meathead. No, Eddie was a reasonable guy, more flexible than most, but it had never occurred to that meathead that he could use his brain for something more taxing than highway plans and minor state politics. Eddie Quinn, if he only knew, had the makings of a populist in the old tradition. What Eddie needed right now was some advice from an old friend he could trust. R Dan's thoughts raced as he finished his gin and tonic. Why not? He would fly to Washington tonight.

In Bee Branch, Arkansas, Frank Janiszewski, Eddie's uncle, watched the speech while rocking in the kitchen of his three-room frame house. He thought of the bundle of Social Security letters he intended to mail to Eddie and of the $275 in cash in a metal box in the cupboard, his savings for a vacation trip someday. Why not take the papers to Eddie himself and combine the mission with a sight-seeing tour of Washington, a city he had never seen? In fact, Hunk Janiszewski hadn't journeyed outside Arkansas in ten years. Suddenly excited, the old man lifted himself out of the rocker, found his flashlight and limped along the path to his neighbors', the Archers, who owned both a telephone and an automobile. Two hours later the Archers were driving Frank Janiszewski to Little Rock where he'd board the late night flight to Washington.

In a one-room basement flat on Capitol Hill in Washington, Teegee Churchill, the youngest and newest member of Governor Pinholster's campaign staff, continued to stare at the TV screen after her roommate, the ec major, switched off the program from Houston.

"Wow!" Teegee customarily invested her exclamations with a kind of reverence. She was sitting cross-legged on the rugless floor.

"Whadayuh mean, wow?" asked Hank, the ec major. "Same old rich reactionaries. They just picked up a brand-new errand boy at the tradesman's entrance."

"Unh-unh." Teegee shook her head, a movement triggering the automatic gesture of sweeping the hair back from her eyes. "My intuition tells me no. Eddie Quinn is different. Didn't you hear him put them down, right to their faces?"

"Probably all programmed."

"And his sign," said Teegee. "Didn't you catch his birth date? He's a Gemini."

"So?"

"So I'm going to make a phone call." If Hank was so dense as not to remember that she was an Aries, then there was no sense reminding him.

Teegee walked to the wall phone in the box of a kitchen and dialed the night number of Jeff Smithers, the Pinholster campaign manager.

"Jeff," she said softly when he answered, "this is Teegee. Remember what you asked me this afternoon? About hanging out with the Quinn people? Well, okay. I'll do it."

"Great. Since Quinn's going to use Hudson's old headquarters on Connecticut Avenue, you won't have to move out of town. Check with me soonest, Teegee."

"Yeah . . . bye."

Teegee quietly replaced the phone. Really weird, she thought. She knew Eddie Quinn was a Gemini the moment she saw him on the screen, even before the commentator gave his birth date. And everyone knew that the attraction of a Gemini and an Aries was instantaneous. Maybe it was fate or something.

5

"Just who the hell do you think finances this party, Quinn?" asked Charles Herron. The banker's cold glance swept across Eddie like a prison searchlight.

"I know that as well as you do," said Eddie, noting Herron's switch to his surname. "You didn't get my pitch. I was trying to get across to the working guy, the kind of voter who's ready to swing to us if we'd give him half a chance."

"By attacking us instead of the opposition? . . . Ted, hand me that tape recorder. I want the commissioner to hear his own words." Herron used the title as though Eddie had stolen it.

The dispute had begun even as the chartered jet sprang from the runway at Houston's Intercontinental Airport, had escalated as the plane flew the airways across the southern states. The king-makers, minus Governor Hotchkiss and Sam Shadowitz, who flew home to Ohio and Pennsylvania respectively, were gathered with their new candidate in the forward cabin. Various party bigwigs, newsmen, wives and relatives occupied the rear seats for the night flight to Washington. The plane, over Atlanta now, banked left for the northern leg. Thunderclouds massed in towering shapes, blotting out the stars. Lightning winked in far canyons of the sky and random squawks came from the tape recorder as Herron pressed buttons in his search for the culpable quotation.

". . . tired of the old managers," Eddie's voice boomed out of the box, "those rich, self-satisfied men who order us around from their executive suites, their fancy country clubs, their boxes at the horse show, their fifty-acre estates, their big foundations and their expensive, elite universities."

Herron glared at Eddie as he switched off the sound. "That's not aimed at Pinholster. That snide remark applies to just about every man in this compartment."

"Not quite," said Senator Framingham with a frail laugh. "I don't have a foundation."

"You know what I mean, Stan," said Herron. "And, by God, it applies all the way to me. Same for Ted and Rich." He waved his hand at Witherspoon and Cuthbert. "You threw away a good, sound, punchy text, Quinn, and then you began lashing out at us as though we were the enemy."

Eddie stared back at the finance chairman. Herron's right, he thought. Uncertain of what he was going to say, the words flowed out as if pumped from some hidden source. But he regretted not a syllable.

"You didn't listen to what I said." Eddie tamped down his temper. "You nominated a different character this time, Charlie, and the voters have a right to know who I am and where I come from. You may not understand me, but you can bet your ass that millions of ordinary guys got the message."

"That wasn't all, Eddie," said Witherspoon in his ponderous tone. "You made it sound as if golf, tennis and bridge were luxuries that only people with money could afford. In the first place, that's trivial stuff for an acceptance speech. Second, it isn't true. But even if it were, it amounts to pissing all over the very people who gave you the break."

"Let me ask you something," said Stan Framingham. He spoke as though Eddie were a witness being grilled by a Senate committee. "If you felt this way about us, why didn't you say so this morning up in the Celestial suite?"

"Nobody asked me," said Eddie. His temper rose. "You were too busy making sure you had a safe one in the bag."

"As long as we're going over your impromptu remarks," said Rich Cuthbert, "I might say I didn't like that reference to foreign cars." The publisher and television station owner often drove his Mercedes and he'd just purchased a sporty blue Porsche for his daughter.

"Why not?" Eddie shot back. "Foreign wheels, especially the cheap Volks' and Toyotas, are flooding the market. Detroit sat around on its can for years, refusing to meet the competition and then had to ask the government to bail it out with an import tax."

"It's a question of wage rates." Cuthbert said it reproachfully. Eddie might have been the chief bargainer for the United Auto Workers.

"Partly," said Eddie, "but mostly because the men who run big industry in this country have gotten soft and fat. The Japs and Germans are still hungry, and if we don't start humping soon, they'll own us all before long."

"That's one of those shoot-from-the-hip cracks about a very complex economic problem," said Witherspoon. "It points up why a responsible candidate should be well briefed before he speaks in public."

"Let's get back on the track," said Herron. "We're talking about a point of personal honor. Every man in this cabin went down the line for Quinn. We did it because we felt he would make a good candidate, a credit to the party and what we stand for. Quinn accepted with few questions asked. Then he swaggers out to the microphones and implies to the whole damn country that we're a bunch of rich, old farts who are plundering the country for our own profit."

"Bullshit!" Eddie rose to his feet and stood over the banker. "You picked me because you knew our nominee didn't stand a chance and because you thought I'd be your patsy for three weeks. Then you cut off my water so I can't campaign, and you load me down with a lot of censors, so-called experts, to make sure I don't say anything that might screw up your own interests. Well, let me tell you something, Charlie. . . ."

The plane captain's voice overrode Eddie's, the plane rocked and a bell sounded. "Please fasten your seat belts, folks," said the captain. "We'll have some turbulence while we detour around these thunderheads. Nothing to worry about, but it may be ten minutes before we pick up a smooth ride again over North Carolina."

Eddie swayed back to his seat. Passengers buckled the belts. Ted Witherspoon's jaw muscles began to twitch and Herron stared pointedly out a window. Wing-tip lights flashed in the blackness and a roll of thunder could be heard over the noise of the engines. The cabin door opened. Jim Flannery slid unobtrusively into a seat across the aisle from Eddie. Rich Cuthbert leaned forward as though to pursue the argument, but became aware of the Secret Service agent and slumped back into his seat.

They rode in tight silence for a quarter of an hour until the seat-belt sign snapped off, the captain spoke reassuringly and stars glittered once again. As quietly as he entered, Flannery eased from the cabin and shut the door behind him. The agent's action, a reminder that the U.S. government placed special value on but one life in the plane, had a sobering effect. Eddie noted that the group sensed a subtle change in his stature. He was a man who merited the attentions of the Secret Service, a status reserved for leaders of the republic, assassins and counterfeiters.

Herron looked at Eddie. "As you were saying?" The glance, though tinted with new respect, failed to reveal which category the banker thought Eddie belonged to.

"Now wait a minute." Pete Stackpole had taken little part in the wrangle, but he saw each thrust as a knife aimed obliquely at him. Eddie had nothing to lose but his ego, whereas Pete, the mercenary, stood to lose a career. "If we're not careful, we can blow the whole election right here. . . . Eddie, you can't run a one-man show. You're the party's candidate and you have obligations to the party and to the people who swung the nomination for you. On the other hand, gentlemen, Eddie's our candidate and he deserves to be treated like one. He needs room to maneuver. So let's quit rehashing the speech and start talking about where we go from here."

"My idea is to pile up the biggest vote possible November 2," said Eddie.

"Exactly," said Framingham. "And the way to do that is to pull together. We're not trying to make you a mouthpiece, Eddie. We're trying to help. You need experts. You're going to face a hundred issues, most of them complex and some real crunchers."

"I don't buy that, Senator," said Eddie. "My job is to simplify the issues so that every gear-jammer and waitress in the country can understand. The experts, the legal beagles, the professors come later—after the election."

"That's not the way it works." Framingham spoke patiently. "A for-instance. Suppose, Eddie, you get a question at tomorrow's press conference about your stand on Berex, you know, the proposal to extend government-guaranteed loans to the Berex Corporation. How would you field that one?"

"Berex faces bankruptcy because the Pentagon canceled its fighter contract, right? And twenty or thirty thousand employees are out on the street?"

"That's right."

Eddie thought a moment. "I'd say I'm against bailing out private companies with public money unless it's some public-service industry. On the other hand, those people are out of work through no fault of their own, so the government ought to pay their wages and salaries for a while, maybe six months, until they can find other jobs."

"And leave the stockholders, banks and bond owners holding the bag for half a billion dollars?" Senator Framingham looked like a teacher struggling with a backward pupil. "That would wipe out a lot of investors, Eddie."

"I lost eight hundred bucks once in a company that went broke. Nobody introduced a bill in Congress to pay me back. My tough luck. I'm supposed to be smart enough to pick winners. That's the way the game's played."

"That's shallow thinking, Eddie. The failure of Berex could shake a good part of the economy." Framingham paused, then asked quietly: "Do you know who's sponsoring the bill in the Senate to guarantee additional bank loans to Berex?"

"Sure. You are."

In the silence, Herron and Cuthbert exchanged pained glances. The whistle of the jet engines took on a strident pitch.

"Let me try another issue," said Ted Witherspoon. "Pinholster's talking about closing some tax loopholes. Some left-wing reporter is bound to ask you about the oil-depletion allowance. What position would you take?"

"I might say I'd have to give that one a lot of study. It would be a mistake to give an off-the-cuff answer."

Witherspoon nodded with a pleased smile, his first of the evening.

"But," added Eddie, "I'd also say that basically I favor the same taxes for everybody. No breaks for special groups. I don't like 'em. I never have."

Ted Witherspoon's smile expired. His jaw muscles quivered. Eddie, thinking of the telegram in his pocket, wondered what Kate had done with the roses.

"You might have said that up in the Celestial suite this morning." Witherspoon's complaint was sepulchral. "In four hours, you said not one word about depletion allowances."

"It didn't come up."

"But god damn it, Quinn," said Charlie Herron, "you knew where we stood. You weren't born yesterday."

"Look, I didn't ask for this nomination." Eddie's pent anger tugged for release. "I was over in the Apollo Motel, minding my own business, when I got a call from Pete. So I came over, my ass dragging, and you guys started asking me a lot of questions about America and moral values and kids and drugs and demonstrations and law-and-order. Nobody asked me about Berex or oil."

"We made our bed and now we've got to lie in it," said Rich Cuthbert. "Is that the idea, Eddie?"

"Correction," said Herron. "Pete Stackpole made this bed."

The kingmakers fixed their eyes on the hapless maker of beds, who looked as if he'd prefer to crawl under one.

"Okay, okay," said Pete, "dump the blame on me. But don't forget. When we walk off this plane, we've got to present a solid front. Otherwise, we tear this party wide open and a lot of fine candidates from Maine to Hawaii go down the drain."

"Yes," said Cuthbert, "we have to work this out. On his part, Eddie wants to be his own man. That's understandable. Also it's not bad politics for the head of the ticket to show a little independence." Having forgiven the spurned speech, the publisher sought compassion in turn. "On the other hand, Eddie, you ought to avoid these, well, unnecessary social comments that seem to reflect on us. You owe us that much, certainly. As for the experts, they'll be there to help you. You may not take their recommendations, but as a responsible man, you owe it to yourself to at least listen to them."

"I'll go for that," Eddie replied promptly. "But money talks. I'd like Charlie Herron to tell me just how much campaign dough I'm getting."

"I told you this afternoon," said Herron. "We're allotting $500,000 for two big TV shows in which you'll take part, and the remainder of the one point eight goes for Ewing and his task force."

"No sale," said Eddie. "I'm the Number One candidate, not Ewing. I want the million three. Ewing's group can have the five hundred grand."

"No." Herron said it quietly, impersonally, in the manner of a man long accustomed to rejecting pleas for money. "The decision's been made." A stranger might think some grand, remote tribunal, clothed in robes and righteousness, had handed down an edict.

"Charlie!" Eddie shot back with a rising, mocking inflection. "You know I could walk right through that door and tell the newspapermen that the national finance chairman refuses to give the party's new candidate any campaign money."

"You wouldn't dare."

"Wanna bet?" Eddie stood up and stepped into the aisle. "Just watch me. What's more, I'll tell 'em flat out."

Herron produced a slim, silver case and extracted a cigarette. "Go ahead," he said, without looking at Eddie.

Eddie took several steps toward the compartment door. Stackpole shot from his seat and blocked the aisle. He linked his arm with Eddie's.

"God damn it, enough's enough. Eddie, you sit down. . . . Charlie, Eddie's right. He's the candidate for President and he deserves a decent bankroll."

"Yes," said Framingham. "Charlie, you'll have to loosen up. We could never explain nominating a candidate and then cutting off his water."

"That's right." Cuthbert bid again for compromise. "Eddie's already given his word he'll be more cautious about what he says from now on."

Herron flicked the ash off his cigarette and stared at Eddie.

"No more smart-ass cracks about executive suites?" he asked after a moment.

"I'll think carefully about what I say."

"Okay. Split it. Nine hundred thousand for you and nine for Ewing's group."

Eddie shook his head. "You know that's not fair, Charlie."

Sniffing compromise in the air, Stackpole moved at once to bottle it. "Make it a million one for the top candidate, Charlie. . . . That okay with you, Eddie?"

Quinn nodded.

"Okay," said Herron grudgingly. "One point one for Quinn and point seven for Ewing and his people."

Stackpole rang for the stewardess and the settlement was irrigated in scotch, gin and Eddie's ginger ale. Flying over Virginia, the leaders managed to restore an air of dispassionate purpose to their talk, although Herron did not join in. He appeared to have lost interest in the problems of the candidate. By the time the jet began its let-down for Washington's National Airport, Pete Stackpole was sitting on an aisle arm rest and regaling the others with the story of his negotiations with the three committee members from Utah.

" . . . so I said we had the votes for Quinn, but we wanted Utah to have the honor of putting him over, and Corby says, 'But hell, he never laid eyes on Eddie,' and Grace says, 'Oh, I have, if he's the one who looks like a state trooper.' I said, 'That's our man,' and then Corby wanted to know whether Eddie favored keeping some arsenal out there, and I said, 'Well, look who's backing him, Senator Framingham, and you know Framingham's stand on military bases.' Then Grace said she'd go for Eddie if Utah could get a decent break on inaugural tickets, and I said, 'Grace, honey, when they inaugurate Eddie Quinn, you and your husband can have seats for the parade in the White House pavilion right next to the President's box.' Then Corby, with that funny lisp, says how about his wife . . ."

When the plane landed, the kingmakers bunched around Eddie and moved in a body of unfractured comradeship. They stood at the top of the ramp while photographers' flashbulbs popped and several hundred people pressed close to the plane. Then Stackpole led the way down the steps, leaving the candidate the lone target for the photographers who swore routinely at one another as they jockeyed for position.

Eddie waved to the crowd. He felt fine. He had $1,100,000 to spend and eighteen days in which to do it.

6

Flanked by Agents Jim Flannery and Oscar Baker, who had proved his discretion in the mission of the roses, Eddie swept into campaign headquarters at nine o'clock the next morning. Behind him trailed Pete Stackpole and a brigade of neatly dressed, self-conscious young men, minor aides from the Hudson campaign. Eddie was discovering that every time he took a few steps he became a troop movement. His only solitary voyages were to the bathroom.

He was in good spirits, although still shy of sleep and annoyed with the specialists assigned to him by the kingmakers. The experts, earnest, pedantic men for the most part, breakfasted with him at the Hay-Adams Hotel and managed to spoil the taste of his ham and eggs. They were slated to meet with him again before the press conference. It wasn't so much their clinical attitude that bothered Eddie, but the fact that they owed their fealty to others. Apart from Pete Stackpole, who was still on probation in Eddie's mind, he was a candidate among strangers. He hungered for someone he knew and trusted. He vaguely considered telephoning the mayor of New Brunswick, the New Jersey Turnpike publicity man, Phil Liccardo, or possibly R Dan Fenelli, his old roommate who thought big thoughts out in California. Best of all, Eddie realized, would be Kate Witherspoon. The congresswoman knew her way around Washington, he trusted her despite the wide gap in their life styles and she was beautiful. Then he remembered. That telegram! What got into her? Eddie sighed.

Campaign headquarters, on the fifth floor of the 1140 Building on Connecticut Avenue, was inhabited by a sharply decreased population since the death of Senator Hudson and the subsequent plunge in the party's fortunes. Some twenty speech writers, schedule makers, advance men, flacks, secretaries and typists stood by their desks and applauded as Eddie entered. He noted that special look he had come to accept as routine, a kind of idle, pleased curiosity evoked by any instant celebrity from suicidal rock stars to grandfathers who improbably crossed the Atlantic in twenty-foot sailboats.

"Good morning," said Eddie. "I'd like to introduce our new campaign manager, Mr. Peter D. Stackpole."

Pete grinned happily. While he had fully expected the post, this was the first time Eddie had mentioned it.

"Everybody just keep on doing whatever you're doing until further notice," said Eddie. "Pete and I are going to sit down and try to figure out our next moves. Any and all bright ideas welcomed."

Stackpole led the way down a side corridor, shucking off the escort of self-conscious young men. A door at the end bore a shining new plaque, "Mr. Quinn." Eddie wished he had been consulted. He would have preferred Commissioner Quinn. A glossy rubber plant adorned one side of the doorway, an American flag the other. On facing wooden benches sat a dozen people, one of them a trim, young black woman under a mushroom of hair. Eddie halted and stared.

"Margot!"

He pulled her to her feet and embraced her. "Talk about surprises." Eddie stepped back and looked at her with some apprehension. "You look great, Margot. . . . What brings *you* here?"

"I've got some ideas," she said, "and I . . . I just thought you might need some help."

"Help! You can say that again."

He scanned the other people, sitting like waiting patients in a doctor's office, over the shoulder of Margot Hicks.

"Hey! Whadaya know? . . . Hunk! . . . And R Danny! This is like old home week."

Eddie was overjoyed to spy some old friends at last. He left Margot and began pumping the hand of an elderly man who wore a frayed blue serge suit and carried a brown paper parcel, then slapped the back of the man sitting next to him.

"R Dan, you old egghead . . . meet my uncle, Frank Janiszewski from Bee Branch, Arkansas. . . . Hunk, this is R Dan Fenelli, my old roommate at Seton Hall."

While the men shook hands, Eddie waved Margot Hicks into the circle and made the introductions all over again. Hunk Janiszewski took Margot's outstretched hand as though it might contain a summons.

"Well, let's see now," said Eddie. "I want to talk to all of you. . . ."

"Eddie!" Stackpole gripped Eddie's elbow. "We have a lot of calls to make, you've got the press conference at eleven and. . . ."

"Got to see my old friends," Eddie insisted. "Okay, ladies first. Come on in with me, Margot. See you in a few minutes, R Dan. Then you, Hunk." He turned to the other people on the benches. "I'll try to make time, folks." Stackpole groaned.

Eddie paused at the door. Under dripping blond hair, the face of a girl peered up at him with a beseeching look. The large eyes were pale blue and without innocence.

"Hi. What's your name?"

"Teegee Churchill. I was supposed to be a spy."

"Supposed to be? What kind of a spy?"

"Political. The Pinholster people wanted me to dig out your plans or something. But I'd rather work for you."

"What can you do, Teegee?"

"I can't type or anything. I'm best at relating to people."

"Can you take notes? Organize?"

"Sure." She sang the word softly in two syllables.

Eddie grinned. "Fine. While I'm talking to some old friends, you ask each one of these people out here why they want to see me. Be ready to report in about half an hour. Okay?"

"Right. Terrific, Mr. Quinn."

Agent Baker took up a post in the corridor. Eddie opened the door for Margot Hicks while Stackpole and Flannery pressed close behind. Eddie found himself in a small room, darkly paneled. A plump young woman rose from her seat behind a typewriter. She appeared both efficient and embarrassed.

"This is Joy Peterson," said Stackpole. "She was Senator Hudson's receptionist-secretary."

"Hello, Joy. Want to work for me?"

"I'd be happy to."

"Sold. . . . Is this my office?" Eddie headed toward an inner door. It opened on a larger room, paneled, carpeted in dark brown and fronting on Connecticut Avenue. There were several chairs, a leather sofa and an enormous desk with but three objects on it, the World Almanac, the Congressional Directory and a small metal vase which held a single rose. Eddie speculated again as to whether Kate had liked his flowers. He held the door open for Margot.

Flannery stepped forward. "Sorry, miss, but you'd better leave that handbag out here."

"Oh." Margot and Eddie both looked surprised. She handed Flannery the small, black purse. "You think I'd try to harm this man?"

"No," said Flannery. "Just the routine when we haven't been able to set up the usual security screening."

Stackpole, harried, looked at his wrist watch. "I'll find me an office somewhere. . . . Try to keep it short, Eddie. A half-hour for your friends. Okay?"

Flannery settled in a chair opposite Joy Peterson. Stackpole shrugged and left. In the inner office, Eddie grasped Margot's hands.

"You're looking as good as ever, Margot. I didn't recognize you for a minute in that Afro. Looks great. Real class."

She wore a snug white knit dress, and Eddie thought fleetingly of a hot fudge sundae. Her slight smile hinted both amusement and cynicism. Eddie remembered that this was the woman who could sense his next move before he thought of it.

"Thanks. You look okay yourself." She sank into the couch and draped an arm over a leather cushion. "You scared of me, Eddie?"

"Scared? No, but I was sure surprised to see you."

"You looked like I was a bill collector. Relax. We don't owe each other anything. I know you're hard up for time, so I'll talk fast. When I heard your speech last night, I remembered this idea I've

had and about our time in New York, and I said, why not? Eddie
Quinn's a man who'll listen."

"If you've got a good idea, Margot, you've come to the right place.
I need all I can get."

"Yeah, well, let me ask you a question first, and tell me straight."
She no longer smiled. "How you feel these days about black people?"

Eddie felt himself tense. "I get along with them," he said warily.
"Of course, I don't know too many, a couple of friends at the Turnpike office and a guy who lives next to me at the motel. I think I
got closest to you that weekend."

Margot shook her head. "You didn't learn much about me. You
didn't try. . . . But that's not what I mean. I mean black people in
general. You know, the big problem."

"Oh, that." Eddie frowned. "I think we've got plenty of laws on
the books. Negroes had a lousy deal for hundreds of years. Now it's
up to the black guy to make it just like the Irish and the Jews made
it."

"Yeah. I figured you'd say just that."

"Why?" Eddie bridled. "What the hell's wrong with that?"

"Nothing, Eddie." The knowing little smile flicked on again.
"You don't understand—I caught your welfare crack last night—but
that can't be helped right now. You're honest and open and that
does help. What I'd like to see you do is say just what you believe,
but speak up in the right places."

"What are you getting at?" Again Eddie reminded himself that
this woman was usually a jump or two ahead.

"I mean that you could do yourself and black people a big favor
right now, Eddie, by walking around black neighborhoods, say in
Harlem, Newark and Detroit."

"Just walking?" Eddie was puzzled.

"Yeah, just walkin' and rappin'," said Margot, lapsing into a
drawl. "Anybody asks you what you goin' do for black people if you
get elected, you say nothin', only you going to give everybody a
fair shake. You tell 'em what you believe."

"And what will that do for anybody?"

"Plenty. You see, Eddie, black people are fed up with phony liberal promises, give you this, give you that, and then nothin' hap-

pens that changes much. I know my people, and we all know what white bullshit is. The white politicians talk at us, not with us. What we want is a guy who *acts* like we're his equals. If he walks the streets with us at night, then we know he cares enough to show himself off. He ain't afraid of us."

Eddie shook his head. "Sounds too simple to me, Margot. Just walking the streets?"

"Yeah, just trampin' around." Margot stood up and began to pace the floor. "Like this. 'Hi, man. What's new? I'm Eddie Quinn.' You walk the streets from ten to midnight in maybe three cities. That's six hours maximum out of the eighteen days you got left. Then you sit back and let that street wire hum with the news."

"I don't believe it." Eddie stared at Margot as she walked about. "I saw a poll the other day. Pinholster was getting ninety-one per cent, I think it was, of the black vote."

"Against Hudson." Margot stopped pacing and stood before Eddie's desk. "Against an old man so white he didn't have no shadow. . . . Listen, Eddie, you preached us last night that you weren't the same as those white dudes who picked you. You got to convince black people that they got to join up with the Eddie Quinns and the Poles and the Italians and the rest of the working men to get a fairer shake for everybody at the bottom. And the way to do that is by walking, not talkin' big on TV. We don't trust white words. We look at what a white man does. . . . Eddie, no presidential candidate ever walked through the ghettos at midnight. It would bring a new feeling. You can't understand unless you're black. Just believe me, Eddie, just believe me."

Eddie said nothing and Margot leaned across the desk. "You chicken? What you got to lose?"

"Only what I'm going to lose anyway, I guess."

Margot walked back to the couch. "You see, Eddie, I think I know you." Her voice softened. "You got a prejudice all right— against a race that's black. That's why I called you white racist that night. But when you deal with a black *person*, I don't feel any bad vibes. I feel that, so it must be true. So if you walk the streets with me and some of the brothers and sisters, and you rap with people, well, they'll feel what I feel. That's good, good for everybody, for me, for you, for lots of voters. You not going to solve any problems anyway, so why not make people feel good?"

Eddie grinned. "You make *me* feel good, Margot." He watched her silently for a moment. "Hey, I tell you what." Eddie rose from his chair. "How about joining up with me? You can be an adviser. Pick out some title. I'll get you a salary, enough to carry you here in Washington. What do you say?"

"I already took a three-week leave of absence."

"Always three jumps ahead of me. . . . Let's see how important I am."

Eddie studied the squawk box, flicked a key and said: "Joy, please have somebody hustle a desk for a new staffer. Name of Margot Hicks, H, I, C, K, S. . . . And send in Mr. R Dan Fenelli. He's waiting in the hall."

Eddie put his arm around Margot and walked her to her door. "Don't wander far, Margot. We'll get some people in here for some planning as soon as I learn the ropes around here."

R Dan Fenelli came on with noisy gusto. He was five inches shorter than Eddie, tubby and simmering like a pot about to boil over. Prematurely white eyebrows beneath a mop of black hair gave him a pixie look. He took a boxer's stance and aimed a right at Eddie's chest.

"Meathead!"

"Egghead!"

Eddie grabbed R Dan's fist, yanked him close and thumped his back. The former roommates squandered time swapping affectionate insults and catching up on each other. Eddie learned that R Dan had spent the summer touring France with his wife, sampling most of the wines and making every, but every, restaurant rated two stars or better by the Guide Michelin. Eddie also learned what the Guide Michelin was. R Dan in turn found that Eddie's appetite for women was as robust as ever and that his idea of perfect travel was still four wheels humming along a ribbon of asphalt.

"You could have knocked me over with a Kleenex when I caught that radio bulletin from Houston," said R Dan. "Jesus, I still can't believe it. And when I heard you giving the shaft to Witherspoon, Herron and that crowd, I felt like firing off a rocket. Then I had this big idea—screw the little ones, what?—and I knew you'd at least give me a hearing. Want me to shoot?"

"Fire away. But don't try to con me with any of your radical ideas. I play the center, Dan, not out in left field with you."

"Maybe, maybe not. If I remember our talk last year, I think you kid yourself some, Eddie." Sitting on the leather couch, R Dan kept in constant movement, shifting his legs, pulling off his black-rimmed glasses, twisting a lock of hair. "You have any hope of winning?"

"Of course not. On the other hand, as long as they've marked me for sacrifice, I'd like to get in some good licks before they cut my throat."

"Good, Eddie, I think this system has damn near had it." R Dan raised a palm to stave off interruption. "You don't agree, but man, I've traveled all over the country, and I'm telling you people are scared and bitter. They plain don't trust the government any more. They think Pinholster's a fake. Inflation is killing them. They're suspicious of the military, figuring its size and power will drag us into another Viet Nam or worse. On the other hand, they're afraid we'll have another depression if military spending is cut much. They hate bureaucracy. They think politics is a big power grab by special interests. They see the rich getting richer and the poor just as poor. They can smell and taste the dirty skies and rivers and they're afraid the good American life is going down the drain."

"You make it sound worse than it is, but I can't argue with the mood. I know what you mean."

"All right. Now, since you can't win anyway, why not forget about chasing votes? Zero in on educating the country. They'll listen to you because you're one of them." R Dan paused, then leaned forward. "Shock 'em, Eddie. Make 'em understand. Shock 'em with ridicule. Shock them with exaggeration. Make them think, God damn it. You gave them a taste last night. Now make them realize how the so-called establishment runs this country for its own benefit and how we've got to redistribute wealth and services and opportunities if the country's going to survive."

"You've got the wrong party, R Dan." Eddie felt himself pulling back from his pal as he invariably did when the ideas began to pelt him like hailstones. "And the wrong guy. It's not my bag to go around shocking people."

"The hell it isn't. What do you think you did to that mob in the Astroworld ballroom last night when you opened up on the country-club set? Think a minute, Eddie. You're the first real ethnic guy ever nominated for President by a major party in this country. Okay, there was Kennedy, but he was one of the new Irish aristocrats, a Choate-Harvard boy. You're different, man. The country senses it already. Millions of voters are fed up with that old establishment crowd and ready to listen to you."

"I don't know. Those cracks just slipped out last night. I surprised myself."

"But they were honest." R Dan smacked a palm with his fist. "The sincerity came through. And you were dead right, Eddie, right, right, right."

"What do you mean by shocking people? Give me an example?"

"Okay, take taxes. I'll bet you've already had some heat from Witherspoon and Cuthbert and those boys over taxes. Right? Well, last night on the plane, I was kicking the subject around while I hoisted a few, and here's my thinking."

R Dan talked for ten minutes, splattering his thoughts like careless paint, shifting constantly on the sofa, gesticulating. As Eddie listened, several ideas caught fire. Once he stopped R Dan and told him what Margot Hicks said.

"Maybe my pitch ought to be a fair shake for all."

"Right as rain," said R Dan. "There ought to be an alliance between blacks and Puerto Ricans and all the working stiffs, the Italians, Poles, Hungarians, Czechs, people who all want to make it in the system. As it is, they're fighting for crumbs from the big boys' table. You walk the ghetto at night and you become the symbol of a new shake for the black man. No more phony programs from WASP liberals who are salving their own guilt, but Eddie saying no more bullshit, let's treat one another fairly and the rest is up to you."

Another ten minutes slipped by as R Dan talked. Joy buzzed, said Uncle Janiszewski was getting restless. Stackpole called, reminding Eddie he must meet with the specialists before the press conference. Eddie stalled for more time.

"Danny, I'm hard up for guys like you. I need people around that I know and trust. What are you doing for the next three weeks?"

"Nothing earth-shaking. We're flexible at the Center."

"How about staying on here as an idea man?"

"Why you think I hopped the jet last night? Is that a firm offer?"

"It is. Stackpole will wet his pants when he hears I've signed on a heavy thinker from the Center. Too bad. Like I told him last night, I'm the man who has the nomination."

"Okay, I'll go hunt up a desk."

"No. Stay here. I've got another idea. I want you to listen to my Uncle Hunk."

Frank Janiszewski was a man on a mission. He shot a querulous glance at R Dan as he entered, shuffled to Eddie's desk and deposited his brown paper package.

"Them's letters back and forth with the Social Security," he said. "Must be a couple of pounds of them. They owe me $4.88 more a month, but they won't pay. Damnedest bunch of snot-noses I ever see. I was going to send them to you, Eddie, but I never been to Washington, so I decided to take the airplane and bring them myself."

The old man had a stubble of whiskers in sunken pockets of his cheeks. His Adam's apple bobbed about like a huge, wayward bearing. His shoulders drooped and one leg dragged. But he boasted a fine shock of white hair and a look of guile in his watery eyes.

"How's the leg, Hunk?" asked Eddie.

"Fusses up some in this fall weather," he replied. He turned to Fenelli. "Lost part of the son-of-a-bitchin' shin in ol' Wilson's war and it ain't never been the same since. Come out of it better than my oldest boy, though. They shot him up bad in Roosevelt's war and he spent five years in and out of them vet hospitals."

Hunk sneezed. He pulled a handkerchief from his hip pocket and blew into it with a medley of snorts and wheezes.

"Then they drafted two of my grandsons for Johnson's war and one of them, Joe, he left half his foot somewhere over in one of them rice paddies. I guess the only war where a Janiszewski didn't lose something was ol' Truman's, but they sure drafted the hell outa Bee Branch that time. Took seven boys, I think it was. Two of my nephews from the Quinns went too, but Eddie never had to go to Korea, did you, Eddie?"

"Nope. I spent my time playing baseball for the Fort Myer, Virginia, team. Damn good, too. We only lost two games."

"How old are you, Mr. Janiszewski?" asked R Dan.

"Born in ninety-nine. You figure it out. I don't like to count 'em no more." He blasted his handkerchief again, then folded it carefully before stuffing it into his hip pocket.

"You've lived through a lot of wars," said R Dan. "I take it you're no great friend of the military."

Hunk squinted suspiciously at Fenelli. "Now just one little minute, son. Don't go bunchin' me with all them long-haired kids, paradin' up and down and yellin' hell no, they won't go, like they did during ol' Lyndon's war. Lot of goddamn Communists, if you ask me. No, sir, I honor the flag and the uniform. Only thing is a lot of them slick politicians, like the ones Eddie took down a peg last night, have gone stickin' our nose all around the world in places it don't belong. . . . I don't hold with all that demonstrating. Hell, a lot of white kids gotten just like the niggers, marchin' here, marchin' there, cussin' and carrying signs. The niggers was marchin' again up to Little Rock just last week. I tell you one thing. Any of them demonstration people come down the road to Bee Branch and they gonna get some lead, because I'm going to be sittin' on my porch with the shotgun."

Hunk suddenly stopped. "How come that nigger girl got in here before we did, Eddie?"

"Ladies first," said Eddie. "She's an old friend, Hunk. Margot Hicks. She's going to be one of my advisers."

Hunk digested the information with a grinding of his Adam's apple. "You going to have a . . . nigrah . . . around here?" His success in tidying up the noun was achieved only after an obvious effort of will.

"Sure. Margot's smart. I need all the help I can get."

Hunk pondered with a frown. "I guess everything's changin'." He sighed. "Reminds me of the other night, along around dark. I was sittin' on the porch and this Chevy comes chuggin' along and then sputters and quits right by my mail box. Two nigrah fellows get out and mess around under the hood. Then one of them walks up the path to the house. Neat dressed fellow, tie and all, and he says, 'Mister Janiszewski?' He seen my name on the box. He asks if he can borrow a wrench if I had one. Real nice-spoken nigrah. City fellow from Dee-troit. Well, I give him one from the shed and they tinker around some and get the Chevy goin' again. Then he brings back the wrench and thanks me and says it's a pleasure to find folks in Bee Branch so accommodating. . . . Now you wouldn't find a nigrah like him stompin' around with signs on the highway. If they was more like him, he wouldn't have no trouble."

"You'll get along okay with Margot, Hunk," said Eddie.

"What do you mean by that?"

"I'd like to sign you on for my campaign staff. We need someone like you."

"Oh no you don't." Hunk threw up his hands. "I just brung up the papers to see if you could straighten it out. And to do some sight-seeing." Hunk's garrulous confidence shriveled. "Eddie, you don't want no old man like me around. I ain't even made a crop in ten years."

"Sure I do." Eddie left his chair and perched on a corner of the desk. "Look, Hunk. We're all city people and younger than you. I need somebody who's been around a long time and who lives in a small town and knows what country people are worrying about."

"What would I do?"

"Just listen and speak your mind. If you hear us dreaming up some screwball idea, tell us we're full of crap. Also, Hunk, a lot of wise guys try to con a candidate, especially a new boy like me. I need old pals around who'll level with me."

Uncle Janiszewski eyed Eddie with a shrewd look. "You don't trust them rich guys who put you in, from what you said between the lines last night. Is that it?"

"Now you've got it."

"Well, I guess I could stay for a few days."

"It's a deal." Eddie pressed a key on the intercom. "Joy, send in that young lady with the blond hair, Miss Teegee something. And tell Mr. Stackpole I'll be ready in ten minutes."

Teegee glided into the office and took the chair indicated by

Eddie. She wore a turtle-necked green crocheted dress that ended several inches above her knees. A macramé bag hung from her shoulder.

"Hi!" She said it softly on a breath of wonder. "I'm Teegee Churchill in case you've forgotten, Mr. Quinn."

"Eddie," he corrected. He made the introductions as Teegee favored each man with her most sincere smile. "Now what was that business about being a spy?"

"I said that to catch your attention." She caressed the hair off her forehead. "But it's true. You see, I was working for Governor Pinholster for two days, and Jeff Smithers, the manager, assigned me to infiltrate your headquarters and report back your strategy and stuff. I agreed, but this morning, after thinking more about your speech and all, I decided it wasn't right. Well, spying's okay, but I didn't want to spy on you."

"Why not?" Eddie was enjoying himself.

"Well, like you were honest, sort of, last night, and I admire honesty, so it would be a copout for me not to be straight myself." She looked at Hunk. "Wouldn't it?"

Hunk frowned. His life encompassed no Teegee Churchills.

"What have you got to offer us?" asked Eddie.

"I'd work real hard at anything. That is, if you'll forgive me for the spy stuff, which I didn't do, actually."

"Why Eddie?" asked R Dan. "I'd think Pinholster would be more your style."

"That's funny, Mr. Fenelli. I was thinking that way about you. . . . It's just that I heard Eddie's speech last night and I got excited. You said things differently and you really told off the system, sort of."

Eddie was beginning to realize that his speech had made a similar impression on widely varying types of people.

"I wish I could have seen my father's face when you were talking," added Teegee. "He's in advertising. I don't get along with my parents."

"How old are you, miss?" asked Hunk.

"Twenty-four last April. . . . And that's another good sign. Being an Aries, I knew I could work with a Gemini."

"You believe in all that hocus-pocus?" Hunk was suspicious.

"I don't buy it all, but signs give you a clue. But don't get the idea I'm an astrology nut or something."

"Tell me about yourself," said Eddie.

She told about her home in Westport, Connecticut, college at Mount Holyoke, the master's at Columbia and rooming with the ec major who worked for Ralph Nader. Teegee said the system wasn't working and she wanted to help change it, and she guessed Eddie would make more impact for change than Pinholster would.

"Although," she concluded, "I definitely don't agree with you, Eddie, about automobiles. We've got to have decent public transportation, or we'll all strangle from pollution when the whole landscape's paved over."

Eddie smiled, but made no response. Instead he asked for her report on his visitors waiting outside. Teegee opened a notebook drawn from her bag.

"They're all okay," she said, "but I guess there's only one you or somebody ought to talk to. That's a Mr. Mancini from Baltimore. He's got some ideas on how to line up all the Sons of Italy clubs behind you and also raise campaign funds through a raffle he runs in some of the clubs. He heard your speech and he's fired up. . . . The others? Well, three girls want typing jobs. There's a man with a genealogy on the Quinn family and two old Greek ladies want to volunteer for telephone duty, and one guy has a scheme to recycle cans, and another wants to sell you a big folder with Pinholster's silliest quotes in it, and four women who took an early morning bus from Wilmington, Delaware, want you to address their Holy Name Society." She closed the pad. "I guess that's it."

"Okay, for a spook, you're a good reporter," said Eddie. "You're invited to join the campaign staff. Let's hope Pinholster's loss is our gain. . . . Let's see now." Eddie glanced at his watch, pressed an intercom key. "Joy, tell Pete Stackpole to come in. And find Margot Hicks and have her join us."

When Stackpole arrived a few seconds behind Margot Hicks, he scanned Eddie's friends as he might a band of students who had just seized the proctor's office. He was in his shirtsleeves, tie loosened, and he vibrated with frantic purpose.

"Let's go, Eddie. First the briefing, then drive to the Statler Hilton for the press conference."

"Slow down, Pete," said Eddie. "I want you to meet my new S&T board."

"Your what?" Pete paused just inside the door, hands on hips.

"S and T. Strategy and tactics."

Stackpole honored this obvious joke with a perfunctory smile. "Great, fine, but let's get moving."

"No, I mean it." Eddie pointed to Fenelli. "R Daniel Fenelli, ideas and plans . . . Margot Hicks, black liaison and consumers . . . Teegee Churchill, youth, environment . . . Frank Janiszewski, problems of the elderly, rural, government red tape."

Pete's mouth sagged. His eyes roved the circle, then back to Quinn. "You're not serious?"

"Sure. Good mix. Besides I like them and trust them."

"Eddie, let me talk to you in the next room a minute." Stackpole was exasperated now.

"No secrets. If you've got a beef, let's air it here."

"Christ, Eddie." Stackpole struggled for words. "I mean, I respect these people, but we're running a national campaign for *President of the United States*. We have a first-rate, savvy, old pro staff out there." He motioned with his head. "We can't go up against Pinholster with untried troops. Never work."

"I'm not firing the pros," said Eddie, "but when they unload ideas on me, I want to test them on some friends I trust. I need the thinking of some average Joes."

"This is one hell of a mistake, Eddie."

"Come on, Pete." Eddie threw an arm about Pete's shoulders. "You know and I know that we don't have a chance to win. Take it easy, man. What have we got to lose?"

"A lot of races for Congress and statehouses, that's all."

"You're sure you're not thinking about static from Witherspoon and Cuthbert—and Charlie Herron?"

"Some. Jesus, Eddie, we have to be practical."

"That's just what we're going to be, practical and down-to-earth. You've got to understand, Pete. I feel more comfortable with old friends. I can't suddenly be taken over by strangers. . . . Now, how we doing on time?"

"The press conference starts in forty-five minutes. All networks are covering it live, so we're on camera at eleven."

"Okay then." Eddie slid back into his chair. "Let's skip the experts this morning. Time for them later. The country can hear me straight without prompting. I want to keep this simple."

"You're wrong, Eddie." Stackpole's voice had lost its snap. "This Washington press corps is sharp."

"Could be. But maybe we are too. Anyway, let's just settle back for a few minutes and yak, so you can get to know one another."

The few minutes passed quickly. Teegee shared a chocolate bar with Hunk Janiszewski, listened to his Social Security complaints and explained that the ec major she roomed with was not a woman. Stackpole tried, without success, to fit Fenelli into a familiar ideological slot while Margot and Eddie discussed Atlanta, welfare and Julian Bond.

Joy's voice broke from the squawk box. "The White House is calling, Mr. Quinn."

Eddie winced. After his applauded crack last night about half-baked answers cooked up in Washington, he expected the worst. He took the call and heard the well-known voice, resonant with the battle against anxiety.

"Good morning, Mr. Commissioner. The diplomatic corps wants to get a look at you. It's an unusual request, but it appears you've stirred some interest abroad."

"I'll oblige if I can, Mr. President."

"Fine. The ambassadors are wondering whether you could meet with them tomorrow afternoon at the Pan American Union? I said I'd help put the arm on you. I think it would be a courteous gesture if you can spare the time."

"Sure." Eddie was relieved to be spared a reprimand. "Anything you say."

"Good. Dr. Alvarez, the dean of the corps, will be in touch with your people on the time."

Hanging up after the stilted good-bys, Eddie filled in his staff. "How about that! The ambassadors want to meet me."

"Hey, that's cool," said Teegee. "I had a chance to meet the Yugoslav ambassador last summer, but then I came down with mono."

Eddie stood up. "Time for the press conference. Let's go. I want you all to come along."

As they filed out the door, Eddie drew R Dan aside. "I'm going to ride with that tax idea of yours. I like it. It ought to shake 'em for starters."

"Sure will, but what if you're not asked about taxes?"

"That's your job. I know one reporter who's been assigned to cover me, Anderson of the AP, out of the Trenton bureau. A little guy with specs and jug ears. I'll point him out to you, then you kind of casually suggest it to him."

R Dan looked at his friend with surprise. "Mr. Straight is going devious?"

"The word is 'prepared,' Dan," said Eddie. "You see, yesterday morning, when they called me to the Astroworld, I went without my socks. Today on my way to the press conference, I'm not going without my wits."

7

Eddie and Pete Stackpole rode to the Statler Hilton in a glossy, bronzed Continental Mark IV on loan from a local dealer who also supplied Pinholster with prestige transportation and asked no returns on his patriotic investment save the free advertising and an annual White House dinner invitation for his wife and daughters. The rest of Eddie's instant brain trust followed in an Ambassador SST, while a Secret Service car set the pace ahead and Washington motorcycle police rode flank.

Eddie's mood, stroked by the sleek upholstery and the sound of singing wheels, was as zestful as the morning. The air snapped with the tang of October. Untarnished sunlight played over the plane trees and sparkled on shop windows as the cars rolled the few blocks from 1140 Connecticut Avenue to the hotel at 16th and K streets. When the motorcade halted at the hotel's portico, Eddie stepped out briskly and took several deep breaths, filling his lungs with the good autumn air, scented with a familiar dash of carbon monoxide.

A capacity crowd jammed the presidential hall on the mezzanine floor where hundreds of partisans ringed the seated newsmen. The spectators had been delivered by Stackpole's eager, neat young men, with the tacit understanding that they would cheer the candidate, thus deluding the TV audience into thinking that the press itself hailed Eddie Quinn. Stackpole reckoned the number of newspapermen at five hundred, or almost half the regular Washington daily press corps. Cables snaked about the floor, photographers shoved and cursed, television cameras swung into position and a sweating technician at the podium made last-minute adjustments to the cluster of microphones. Eddie whispered to Fenelli, pointing out AP's Anderson on the front row. The growl of conversation ebbed as Eddie's party inched toward the lectern. Eddie caught the good-humored but slightly deprecating smiles on the faces before him. The mood was festive, expectant, yet derisive. This was to be living theater with the sophisticated audience taking the measure of the new leading man from the sticks. In Washington, as Eddie knew, everything beyond the beltway—from Jersey City to San Diego—was viewed as a strange hinterland populated by lesser peoples valued chiefly for their ability to consume, vote and answer public-opinion polls. Today the Washington pack was primed for sport and mayhem.

Stackpole introduced Eddie as "a new kind of people's candidate who in less than twenty-four hours has caught the imagination of the country. Today he begins an uphill battle that may confound the pundits and the pollsters."

Eddie stepped smartly to the lectern in his freshly pressed russet suit, his wide tan-and-gold figured tie and his invisible armor of pugnacious confidence. It's all a game, he told himself, so play it high and hard. As he scanned the crowd, he glimpsed a familiar feminine figure among the spectators standing near the wall. When he narrowed his focus, he saw Kate Witherspoon emerge as in a developing print. The congresswoman wore a beige pants suit, and her rich, burnished black hair hung loosely to her shoulders. Eddie smiled at her, but Kate apparently did not notice. Head tilted, she was listening closely to the woman beside her. When Eddie faced his questioners, ready for the widely anticipated immolation, he noted a chic, handsome woman sitting in the second row on the aisle. Eddie recognized her as a network commentator. She glanced at him with a private smile, tinted with that peculiar intimacy that he had seen most recently two nights ago on Kate's face as they stood between the curried shrimps and the pantied lamb chops at the Shamrock in Houston. As Eddie gripped the lectern, he felt a fine flow of juices and confidence.

"Before we begin," he nevertheless began, "I want to introduce my board of strategy and tactics." He presented Fenelli, Margot and Uncle Hunk and announced that Stackpole had been named campaign manager. "And finally, a bright, energetic young woman from Westport, Connecticut, Miss Teegee Churchill. By the 'way, Miss Churchill was sent over to my headquarters as an undercover agent from Pinholster's staff, but we converted her in no time at all. That gives you an idea how the wind is blowing. You're free to interview Miss Churchill or other staff members after we finish. . . . Okay, let's go right to the questions. Just tell me your name and affiliation, please, so we can get to know each other."

A dozen hands shot into the air including that of the television star sitting on the aisle. Eddie gave her the nod.

"Sybil Jamieson, CBS. In that remarkable speech last night, Mr. Commissioner, you told the country how you differed from other political leaders. The speech is being interpreted as a rebuke to the same party men who picked you for the nomination. Did you mean it that way?"

"I can't control interpretations, Miss Jamieson." Eddie shot a personal smile toward her. "I tried to give a picture of the kind of leadership we've had for many years. I didn't just mean political management, but all kinds—economic, educational, cultural, you name it. I'm not going to pick out individuals. But as for the men who chose me in Houston, of course I think they showed great wisdom and I'm grateful for the honor."

More hands leaped. Eddie picked out a dignified, elderly newsman sitting midway in the hall.

"Masterson, Baltimore *Sun*. Mr. Candidate. Governor Pinholster is talking about substantial cuts in the military budget. How do you stand on that?"

"I'm not one of those critics of our fine military services," said Eddie, "but generally I agree with the governor. The Pentagon has grown way beyond what's necessary for defense. I think every thoughtful citizen feels that. Now we ought to cut back this giant spending in a sensible way, making sure we don't phase out the arms industry faster than we can absorb workers in civilian employment —or faster than we can persuade the Russians and Chinese to join us."

Rignoti, *Newsweek:* "When and where did you first learn that the party was considering you for the nomination?"

Quinn: "At five thirty-one A.M. yesterday when Pete Stackpole called me. I was in my room at the Apollo Motel in Houston, no commercial intended."

Rignoti: "Were you surprised?"

Quinn: "Sure. Bowled over, in fact. At first I thought they had the wrong man or the wrong number. Of course, now I think it was a brilliant idea."

Haveg, Knight Newspapers: "Mr. Quinn, as a highway official, you've been a booster of automotive transportation. But what about the decline of public carriers and all the pollution, traffic jams and highway fatalities?"

Quinn: "I favor building up our commuter and inter-city bus and rail lines, but I think people who talk about returning to large-scale rail passenger service are dealing in myths—and some of them are outright fakers. We might as well face it. Americans like the convenience of private cars. We're an automobile society and we're going to remain one for our lifetime and our children's too. Our whole country is tied to the car, our work, our play, our socializing, the entire economy. As for traffic congestion, the answer is improved highways and control. It may be necessary to ban cars in certain downtown areas. That's a local judgment. And someday we may have to limit the number of vehicles, maybe by high tag fees for second and third family cars. As for pollution, we do have to work faster to build more efficient engines. I favor higher federal subsidies in this field. But talk about cutting way back on the automobile is a pipe dream and a bad one. I recognize the need for cars, trucks and high-speed highways, and so do most Americans. Don't forget, you're talking to an old truck driver. I rolled an interstate rig for two years."

Bonsteel, Chicago *Sun-Times:* "This goes back a few years, but did you approve of the conviction of Lieutenant Calley?"

Quinn: "Yes. The idea of shooting unarmed civilians, women and children, turns my stomach."

Kramer, Los Angeles *Times:* "Last night you put a lot of stress on your working-class background. Polls at the time showed that a lot of blue-collar people deplored the Calley conviction."

Quinn: "My own opinions aren't shaped by the polls. I'm a free man. If I believe something, I say so. The massacre at My Lai was a savage, brutal act. Now that's all I'll say on that subject."

Benjamin, New York *Times:* "You reported last night that you were fourth-generation Irish and third-generation Polish and said on behalf of many nationalities that now it's their turn. Could you spell out how their leadership would be different from that of the past?"

Quinn: "It's a question of the mood and climate set by the White House and other power sources. Except for Harry Truman and a few others, our national leadership has been dominated by the elitists, the men from the prestige universities, Wall Street lawyers, old WASP families, the rich men's clubs. Now I don't want to knock any group. A lot of these men and women were and are dedicated, patriotic and self-sacrificing. But they set the rules for people they'd never rubbed elbows with and never understood. If it's a question of the economy, they think first of the managers and owners and second of labor. Down at the corner tavern, we worry first about the working guys and second about the big boys. If it's finance, they think of the banker. We think of the depositor. If it's war, their thoughts go to generals and admirals. We think of soldiers and sailors. If it's foreign policy, they think of investments and profits. We think of the common people in other countries like ourselves. I could go on and on, but that's the general idea. As a matter of fact, busing is a perfect example."

Reilly, Boston *Globe:* "How is busing an example, Mr. Commissioner?"

Quinn: "Because the idea of busing school children from one neighborhood to another was dreamed up by people who don't live in those neighborhoods. It's imposed on families in an effort to achieve a racial balance in the schools. Now there's no racial balance whatever in most neighborhoods and there never has been. People congregate there because they want to live and associate with their own kind."

Fredericks, St. Louis *Post-Dispatch:* "Doesn't that view undercut the old dream of the American melting pot and the integrated society?"

Quinn: "No. Americans will integrate in their own good time, how long from now I don't know. But people tend to flock to areas where they feel comfortable with the habits and customs. They change very slowly. A government that doesn't recognize that fact of life is dealing in pipe dreams. The Black Panther knows this just as well as does the Italian-American six blocks away. The law must guarantee equality of job opportunity and movement. People who want racial integration should be free to accomplish it and live it. But those who don't should not be forced into it by their government."

Fredericks: "Do you personally favor racial integration?"

Quinn: "Sure. In the long run, it's the only solution. I have some good black friends, not many, but some. As a kid in Metuchen, I lived next door to a black family. Our yards and kitchens were open to them and vice versa, and the kids ran back and forth. Right now, in the motel where I live near New Brunswick, my neighbor is George Dawson, a black construction worker. We see each other, yak away and sometimes hoist a few at the local bar. He's a boiler-maker man, whisky chased with beer. I stick to my ginger ale. We get along. At least I think so. Maybe George disagrees. Ask him. He'll beat your ear in."

Gregory, NBC: "Apart from your personal likes, doesn't that political stand mean you're writing off the black vote?"

Quinn: "Absolutely not. I want it, which is more than can be said for our party in recent years. Miss Hicks is on the staff to help me get the message across: equality in all things, and no barriers to anybody, but no more phony promises. It's up to the black man now to make it in this country. I want his vote on the basis that we're equal fellow citizens. He can trust me not to double-talk him. A fair shake for everybody. That's my slogan."

Wilbur, Kansas City *Star*: "Does Miss Hicks agree with what you've said?"

Quinn: "I doubt it. She's not a yes-woman. Why don't you ask her later?"

Stanley, Des Moines *Register:* "A news story this morning reports you've never traveled out of the country. Is that true?"

Quinn: "Almost. I've been to Toronto for a highway convention and I once took a cruise ship to Nassau. That's it."

Carpenter, United Press International: "Your mother was quoted yesterday as saying you sucked your thumb until you were six. Any comment?"

Quinn: "Yes. Honor thy father and thy mother, say three Hail Marys and pray that your mother keeps her mouth shut."

Van Duesen, ABC: "Hutchens Boyington, a Pinholster backer, is calling you the hard-hat-and-head candidate. What do you think of that tag?"

Quinn: "I guess that's his way of putting me down. Professor Boyington isn't noted for making generous remarks about people. Well, the hard-hats I know love the American system but don't think much of the men who have been running it. So, yes, I'm proud to be called that kind of hard-hat. As for hard-headed, if that means practical and realistic, well then, I'm that too. I'm certainly not melon-headed like some notables in the opposition."

The press conference galloped along for twenty minutes through the thickets of foreign policy, child-rearing, cities, balance of payments, separation and divorce, Johnny Cash, Turnpike tolls, prison reform, contamination of the seas, the Supreme Court, crime and abortion. Eddie feared the tax question would never be raised. At last the AP reporter from Trenton lifted his hand. Eddie eagerly recognized him.

"Vince Anderson, AP. Mr. Commissioner, I was asked to pose this question by your new brain-truster, Mr. Fenelli." He paused, acknowledging a ripple of laughter among his colleagues. "But since it's a good question, I'll ask it anyway."

When the laughter dissolved, along with the candidate's blush of embarrassment, Eddie tried to recoup. "I salute your frankness, Vince. You trapped me trying to plant a question. I won't pull that again."

"Yes, sir." Anderson paused again, enjoying the spotlight. "Governor Pinholster favors cutting the oil-depletion allowance. What's your position?"

The newsmen tensed, sensing the implication of both the question and Quinn's sponsorship of it. Washington reporters had spotted the trail of oil leaking through the story of Eddie's nomination. The kingmakers included Ted Witherspoon, a Texas oil lawyer, speculator and lobbyist, and Charlie Herron, an Illinois banker who had made a fortune in oil. Rich Cuthbert's connection was more tenuous, but among his newspapers and television stations he did own a petroleum trade weekly. The oil states all backed Quinn in the balloting after Eddie had been placed in nomination by the national committeewoman from Oklahoma, herself the widow of an independent oil operator. Was this Eddie Quinn's pay-off?

"My opponent has failed to see the woods for the trees," said Eddie slowly. "The industry argues that the oil-depletion allowance, amounting to a tax break of about twenty-two per cent on most income from petroleum, is necessary to stimulate exploration for oil. Without it, they claim, the cost of dry holes and quickly exhausted strikes would eat up profits and ruin the industry. The same argument is made by mineral interests which also enjoy depletion allowances. I'm not quarreling with these arguments. I'm not enough of an expert now to challenge the figures.

"But what I say is that if businesses dealing in natural resources deserve a tax break, then the greatest natural resource in this country —human beings—deserve one too. We humans start depleting at about age eighteen. From then on, it's mostly downhill, however enjoyable. Our energies dwindle, our muscles tire, our hearing and eyesight dim. Why, I've even read that beginning in middle age, each of us loses ten thousand brain cells a day. We may live longer these days, but the story of our life, physically and mentally, is one long depletion.

"So, I'm adding a new personal plank to the party platform. If elected President, I propose to ask the Congress—and then use every ounce of my depleting resources to bring a favorable vote—to give every income taxpayer a thirty per cent *human*-depletion allowance. You'd figure the federal tax you owe, then deduct thirty per cent of the total and pay the other seventy per cent. This will, of course, reduce government revenues, but since I'm going to cut back military and other spending, we'll still have a balanced budget. That I promise. I'm fed up with Washington forever spending more than it takes in.

"Now we won't change the oil- and mineral-depletion allowances, but we'll reduce a taxpayer's human-depletion allowance by the amount he takes for oil. If an oil man takes the twenty-two per cent oil-depletion allowance, then he only gets eight per cent human depletion. So he comes out the same as the rest of us, instead of getting the big break he does now. The same goes for dividends from oil corporations that benefit by the oil-depletion allowance. That will be more complicated to work out, but we'll do it.

"So a thirty per cent human-depletion allowance will be the keystone of my tax program. And if I'm elected, and you don't get that thirty per cent break within one year of my inauguration, I invite you to ask your congressman to impeach me."

There was a moment of thunderstruck silence, then hands waved wildly. Eddie pointed to a man in the second row.

"Jacobs, *Wall Street Journal.* Isn't this a way of reducing every individual's taxes by thirty per cent and at the same time sinking the oil and mineral allowances?"

"That's the effect, yes."

"Brainerd, Houston *Post.* Did you clear this with any of the men who met with you yesterday morning in the Celestial suite?"

"No. . . . One last question."

"Heyl, Chicago *Tribune.* Was this your idea?"

"I had some advice, but I named it and it's my tax plank."

"Thank you, Mr. Quinn," shouted Anderson.

The ballroom exploded in noise and movement. A dozen newsmen bolted for the doors. Chairs scraped, TV technicians snarled at people stumbling over their cables, cameras swung like snouted anteaters and the din of undepleted human voices filled the large hall.

Some newspapermen stood and gawked unbelievingly at Eddie as they might at a new animal in the zoo. Eddie, searching the room, saw Kate Witherspoon in a knot of people to his right. Kate, rooted to the spot, stared fixedly at him. They eyed each other for several seconds. Then Eddie saw her smile faintly. Was it cynicism or a mix of doubt and grudging admiration? Eddie couldn't be sure. She quickly turned and was swallowed up in the crowd.

Eddie sought his advisers as Flannery and Baker edged in close, one at each of his shoulders. R Dan grinned at Eddie and made a circle with thumb and forefinger. Margot Hicks, looking flustered, was already engulfed by newsmen as were Teegee Churchill and Hunk Janiszewski. Pete Stackpole looked stricken, eminently eligible for an instant human-depletion allowance. Grabbing Pete's arm, Eddie maneuvered toward an exit through the milling newsmen. He sensed a marked change in atmosphere, less patronizing, fewer laughs, a respectful glance or two.

"You look shell-shocked, Pete," said Eddie. "Buck up, pal."

"Jesus Christ, Eddie," muttered Pete. "I thought I knew you, but this . . ." He broke off, wordless. Maybe he *is* in shock, thought Eddie.

"Let's go, Jim," Eddie told Flannery. "Our buddies can come along later."

"The car's in the back," said the agent.

They walked down a rear flight of stairs to an enclosed ramp where the Lincoln Continental waited with its motorcycle escort. Eddie and Pete slid into the back seat and the car rolled off.

"Human depletion," said Stackpole after a moment. His voice was slack and he shook his head in disbelief.

"What's the matter? You against a tax cut?"

"Eddie, please." Pete spoke like a battered victim whose old friend ignores his bleeding wounds. "Pulling a fast one like that . . . out of the blue . . . no consulting with me, anyone, just zap, and in one minute you gun down the oil-depletion allowance."

Stackpole palmed his thinning straw-colored hair and gazed morosely out the window as he brooded on his predicament. Eddie cuts his backers off at the knees. Eighteen days later Eddie goes down to triumphant defeat, leaving Pete Stackpole . . . where? The party's power brokers would charge Pete with a fatal error in judgment. Never again could he weave through the hidden lanes and byways of the party, doing a favor here, making a profitable contact there, trusting and being trusted. On the other hand, to quit Eddie would be unthinkable. First, the damage was done. Second, to cut out from a candidate twenty-four hours after manipulating the nomination for him would reveal Stackpole as a fool and an incompetent. Third, he genuinely liked Eddie and was surprised at the agility with which Eddie handled himself. The way he turned Anderson's revelation into a plus for himself showed cool thinking under fire. The truth was, thought Stackpole ruefully, that he did not know what to make of Eddie. But one thing was sure. He was locked to this unpredictable, Stackpole-conceived candidate, and he'd better make the best of it.

"That was R Dan's idea," said Eddie, "but I said what I believed."

"Yeah, you sure did. And you also kayoed the guys who made you. You agreed on the plane to take it easy."

"I agreed to be careful about what I said. I am being careful. But I never promised those characters that I'd be the mouthpiece for their private interests."

"Private! Wait'll you see what the market does. And me with a thousand shares of Phoenix Oil."

The market acted like a man with the hives. Quinn's tax-cut proposal, coupled with Pinholster's easy-money stance, made bullish news for everything but oils. With Pinholster vowing to cut the oil-depletion allowance and Quinn, in effect, wiping it out entirely, traders saw a blow to petroleum profits no matter who won the election. Most stocks climbed upward, but petroleums nose-dived, wiping out hundreds of millions of dollars worth of paper assets of oil stockholders.

And within an hour, three of the kingmakers—Cuthbert, Witherspoon and Herron—called to unmuzzle a dazzling variety of expletives at the candidate of their choice, not to say sportive whim. Rich Cuthbert accused Eddie of violating the goddamned spirit, if not the letter, of last night's protocols of peace between makers and made. Ted Witherspoon, planting his words like land mines, likened Eddie's ethical values to those of such superstars of history as Benedict Arnold and Judas Iscariot. Charlie Herron drove straight and profanely to his favorite subject.

"I'm not countersigning checks for a single dollar for you, Quinn," he said. He sounded as if he had rehearsed his lines in a Deepfreeze.

"And without my signature, you've got no money. My God, you not only answered the question, you planted it. You broke your word, you crapped all over us again and you shot down the goddamn oil industry. That's pretty good for one press conference."

"Now Charlie, I didn't break my word." Eddie was thinking fast. "But leave that. . . . If you shut the checkbook, I'm calling in the press and telling them the facts."

"That bluff won't work today," said Herron. "Go ahead. My out is simple. The party's broke. We may have one point eight in the account, but we owe three million to the banks from Hudson's campaign. I've got my out. But you haven't got yours, you son-of-a-bitch. You go blabbing to the press and this party will never nominate you for dog-catcher—let alone governor of New Jersey. Listen, Quinn, you take that half-assed bunch of advisers, including that voodoo bitch from Atlanta and that ridiculous girl bomb-thrower, and get lost with them. One more thing. Tell Pete Stackpole for me —I couldn't raise him on the phone—that either he's an idiot or a Pinholster agent. And that goes for you too."

The sound of the slammed telephone still rang in Eddie's ears when Stackpole burst into the office without knocking. His cheeks were flushed and his eyes glittered.

"Eddie! What do you think just happened?"

"We lost a million," Eddie replied. He relayed Herron's blasphemous farewell to the Quinn campaign.

"Forget it," said Stackpole. "I just got a call from Fred Billings, Empire's political man out in Detroit. He and Al Kunsler of Empire watched your press conference together. They loved what you said about cars. Fred says Kunsler insists they help you even if you are a sure loser. I told Fred, well, we could use a million or so for the campaign. Might as well talk big dough to those boys. Billings didn't even clear his throat. 'I'll have you a million by next Wednesday,' he said. He'll raise it from the auto crowd and their suppliers, five grand here, ten there. When Billings goes into action, money doesn't talk. It just shuts up and surrenders."

"Great news, Pete." Eddie suddenly felt generous and expansive. "Now I can get out and meet the folks. Hey, tell you what. We'll get up a high-speed motorcade and burn up those highways. Drive by night and politick by day."

Pete planted his hands on the desk and leaned toward his candidate. "You know something, Eddie? We may be idiots, as Herron claims, but maybe you're an idiot-genius. I've been in this racket for thirty years and you're the first damned candidate who ever split the oil money from the auto money. They're like Siamese twins. But you split them. You sure as hell did."

Stackpole beamed proudly on his protégé. "And something else, Eddie. I talked to my mother in Morgantown, West Virginia. She's seen you twice now on TV and she says she's got an open mind."

"That's good?"

"Sure is. She usually makes up her mind early. And Anna Lou Stackpole has voted with every presidential winner since Hoover in twenty-eight."

Eddie's smile was as mellow as the autumn noonday sun outside. He was thinking of Margot Hicks and Teegee Churchill and Sybil Jamieson of CBS, beautiful women all, and of that faint, taunting smile of Kate Witherspoon. This promised to be the happiest losing campaign since Ev Dirksen failed to make the marigold the national flower.

8

Kate Witherspoon eyed her husband over the prosciutto and melon, said one thing and thought another. She said that Ted could not possibly dump Eddie Quinn only a day after picking him up off the highway.

She thought of the two figures on a painted music box her father had given her for her sixth birthday. The soldier in a crimson shako and the peasant girl in a billowing yellow dress moved to the tinkling strains of a Victor Herbert waltz. They circled and spun repetitively, always facing each other but never touching. At first Kate lived in hopes that the couple would embrace with the next turn of the key, but it never happened. Young Kate's hope finally dissolved in regret, a kind of sweet melancholy that lasted until the day she backed her tricycle—inadvertently?—into the music box and smashed it.

"Of course I'm not going to dump Quinn publicly," said Ted, "but I'm sure as hell not going to do a thing for him."

Listening to her husband's dry, humorless voice, Kate wondered how many times the toy figures had waltzed through their smiling, remote routine before the box fell apart.

On a surface level she answered him evenly. "You've got to admit that his human-depletion allowance is a shrewd move. Maybe your man is smarter than you thought."

"Demagogic crap." Witherspoon glared at his melon as though it shared culpability with the candidate.

The Witherspoons were lunching late at Washington's Sulgrave

Club, the exclusive women's club near Dupont Circle. Kate had been invited to join by an aunt, a Truitt, who assumed that a female politician of old family would find respite in an atmosphere of ordered propriety. Actually Kate felt the Sulgrave's mood to be as dated as hand-painted china and she seldom used the facilities. Today it was Ted who suggested they lunch here.

Husband and wife faced each other across ivory linen embellished with the club's silver and two glasses of Ted's favorite sauterne, a Chateau d'Yquem. Television and long-distance calls had relayed the initial reaction to Eddie Quinn's press conference: consternation in the oil industry and baffled curiosity among the voters. Few Americans yet knew quite what to make of Candidate Eddie, but the whole country was talking about him.

"It's hard for me to understand how you could quiz Quinn for four hours," said Kate, "and still not know where he stood on the issues."

"We were guilty of a mistake we'd never make in business. Too much faith in Stackpole and not enough personnel detective work."

"Maybe you crowded him too early and too close. As I heard it, you practically ordered everything for him, his speech, his advisers, his schedule."

"But, good God, Kate, think what he owed us! Until yesterday morning, Eddie Quinn was a nobody. . . . Didn't you say you had dinner with him at that Oklahoma bash Wednesday night?"

She nodded, but in her mind she pictured Eddie sitting in the buff at a motel desk while he talked to Pete Stackpole at 5:30 in the morning, and then Eddie, fully clothed, handling a mine-strewn press conference with unexpected poise. Eddie seemed to fit naturally in either scene. What she could not imagine was Eddie lunching here at the Sulgrave.

"Well, how did he impress you," asked Ted, "before his—uh—coronation?"

"I liked him. He seemed bright, easy, straightforward, had a sense of humor. But I had no idea then . . . Now, I don't know what to make of him."

"You're not going to endorse him, of course." It was an order, not a question.

"You're assuming again, Ted." The figures on the music box moved in their separate, ritualized orbit, never touching.

"What does that mean?"

"It means I have to think of my district. Art is making soundings now. He's going to report this evening. I might just say nothing. After all, Quinn is the party's nominee. I just don't know."

"He boots your husband in the ass and you just don't know." Ted dropped into his ponderous tone, and with each leaden word, Kate felt herself shrivel.

"I'm in politics," she said. "You should know. You bought the seat for me."

They were back again to their dead end, the place on the music box where the figures froze and the melody stopped. Ted had urged her into politics four years ago, bankrolled her primary and general election campaigns in Texas' Fifth Congressional District, which included a large slice of Dallas. He assumed, of course, that a Witherspoon vote was never in doubt on any gut issue.

"I've heard that line before somewhere." He drained his wine without looking at her. "I have to go back to Dallas tonight, so I'm going to run out this afternoon and see Susan. Any message?"

She shook her head. "I'm having dinner with her tomorrow night."

Their sixteen-year-old daughter, Susan, was a student at Foxcroft, the fashionable girls' school near Middleburg, Virginia, where proper young ladies learned to ride and to nurture a decorous, unobtrusive guilt over their social and economic advantages. It had been a year since the Witherspoons had gone together to visit their daughter.

"When are you coming back to Dallas?" Ted laid his napkin on the table. The lunch, among other things, was over.

"Probably Monday. I have two hard weeks of campaigning ahead of me."

"No sweat. You'll beat Larson hands down."

"Maybe, but I can't assume anything, dear." She blessed him with a one-upmanship smile and promptly regretted it. The old games had an acrid taste.

On their way out of the dining room, Ted nodded to the head of a Washington brokerage house. The man smiled with the spurious sympathy reserved for those who have just committed an enormous error in judgment. Ted winced. Worse than Eddie Quinn's betrayal was the fact that Ted Witherspoon had become an object of ridicule. The Witherspoons parted near the grandfather clock in the club's foyer on a plane of deadly etiquette.

Kate cabbed to the Rayburn Building on Capitol Hill and walked to her office along wide, marble-walled corridors that were all but deserted. Congress had recessed two weeks earlier to give members time to defend their $42,500 seats against the biennial invasion by uncouth hordes springing from the creeks, sewers and fountains of popular vexation. Kate had dispatched her own staff to Dallas for the duration of the campaign, leaving only Debbie Eicher, a sallow, unhappy girl who salved her wounded psyche with compulsive work habits, to handle the congresswoman's phones and mail. Kate greeted Debbie, told her to screen out all but the most important calls, then retired to her inner office with its uncluttered desk, its shelves laden with reference volumes and its lone photograph, a picture of Susan taking a jump astride Jenny O, her favorite mare. As for those autographed photos of politicians beaming fatuously at one another, a staple in most congressional offices, Kate found them dreary and would have none of them. Instead the one unshelved wall of her office held four Miró prints, bright, zany creations that invariably gave Kate a lift during her rare fits of depression.

She settled into the big leather swivel chair, swung toward the prints and commanded herself to think about the day's No. 1 political problem: Mr. Eddie Quinn. To endorse or not to endorse? To Kate's amusement, but not surprise, she found herself twisting the question into a more personal one: to embrace or not to embrace? Kate smiled at this alteration. In other, younger years, she would have berated herself for shifting mental gears without intent. The younger Kate had been up to her stately eyebrows with shoulds and shalls and musts. But now, thanks in part to an expensive shrink who invested his earnings in real estate and who could subdivide, zone and landscape almost any psychological terrain except his own, Kate had learned to plumb her feelings with a fair degree of honesty. Furthermore, she had coined her own slogan: Heed the need.

Now, adhering to recent custom, she closed her eyes, stretched her legs and relaxed. After a few blank moments she asked herself:

How do I feel about Eddie Quinn? Quick, impulse, flash reaction, no thinking, just the feeling, please. Prompt answer: Good. . . . Okay, Kate, does that feel a little good, medium good or very good? Mmm. Not sure. Medium good, I guess. . . . Okay, do you trust him? Quick, feel, don't think. Answer: Yes. . . . Is Eddie a plus or a minus in your life? He's a plus. . . . Could you imagine getting really involved with Eddie? Yes. . . . Could you imagine living with him? No. . . . Why not? Because he's different, hangs around Elks lodges and bowling alleys, probably used to cut the grass in his T-shirt. Eddie would never, never hang Miró prints in his office. Can't picture him greeting Susan at Foxcroft or reading Nabokov— my God, did Eddie read books? . . . or listening to Casals. . . . There Ain't No Easy Run, ugh. But this is nit-picking. No, it isn't. These are the little beads of water that drip, drip endlessly, a Chinese torture of the spirit. No, that's not right. That's intellectualizing, not feeling. Well? . . . Start again. Sex only this time. Now how do you feel about Eddie? Great. Let the feeling flow down from your shoulders, slowly, all the way down. Now, do you feel a desire for Eddie? Yes. Strong or so-so? Strong. Okay, Kate, heed the need.

She opened her eyes and felt that sure, welling sensation. It was good to know and trust the body's own primer of knowledge without the fancy, tricky script, all swirls and spirals, that the brain fabricated. The body gave no final answers, but it often pointed the way. One denied the body's message at one's peril. The last time she had tried this was three months ago when she asked her feelings to speak to her about her husband. A quarter of an hour later, she knew that she and Ted were finished emotionally. The legal tie of marriage hardly mattered now. It held advantages for both of them in politics and business, but that it would break sometime, one year, three, she had no doubt.

Katherine Truitt Witherspoon bore but occasional banners in the women's liberation movement, yet she regarded herself as a free female. Her own hands, she believed, held her destiny now. She had gained in self-confidence and mental peace in the last year. She was no longer dependent on anyone. She acknowledged her need for a man and for love, yet she was also aware of other demands.

Kate had learned that within this not unbeautiful body of hers there stirred strong, conflicting desires, for love, for influence, for creature comforts, for admiration and for something she called "the impact." She yearned to make a personal impact on society, to mold and change it in some manner so that she could look at her handi-work, as she might at a home she had designed and built, and say, "I did it." She realized that her own pride of accomplishment was just as important, perhaps more so, than the change itself, and for that she made no apology because the feeling, good, bad or indiffer-ent, was part of Kate and to no other person did she owe the fealty that she did to Kate Witherspoon.

And she knew that she would cheat herself, risking misery, if she sacrificed one need for another. She wanted love, desperately some-times, but never at the expense of her designs for wielding influence, making "the impact" or even for the comforts of an urbane life. No love in a hovel for her, and no entanglement with a man who would belittle her "impact," sabotage her desire to join the movers and shakers or try to reduce her to one of those submissive, doll-like creatures who tag after a man and find doubtful solace in his re-flected image. Her husband never consciously tried to do this, yet she found it strange that Ted, after urging her into politics, soon began to denigrate and resent her success even as he profited in business by his connection with a congresswoman. She knew in-tuitively that Ted felt threatened by her, that her growing inde-pendence and decisiveness compromised his concept of his own manhood. That he occasionally fled to the bosoms of more pliant women, she had no doubt. Ted, she had come to believe, was an insecure, compulsive man who hid his inadequacies beneath a brusque, pompous exterior. A heavy piece of furniture on spindly legs, Ted. At times she pitied him, but mostly he bored her.

Eddie Quinn, she sensed, was another breed of cat. Eddie had easy confidence in his sexual powers, and no woman, waitress, club-woman or politician, threatened him. No doubt Eddie derived much of his confidence from his never-articulated, yet always prevailing, assumption that women were not equal beings. He might defer to them, flatter them, work with them or even take them seriously. He might, she guessed, concede that some women were shrewder, more attractive, healthier or more intelligent than he was. But Eddie would never concede that more brains, beauty, compassion and capacity for love added up to a superior being. He was a male with a magic penis and that settled it.

Kate intuitively felt that her reading of Eddie was not far from the truth. Yet the portrait did not repel her. She had no compulsion to crack the male ego, to prove herself superior, to deflate masculine balloons. The fact that Eddie's assumption of male dominance was absurd made little difference to her. His confidence made him easy to be around and no woman had to resort to flattery and games to bolster his ego.

And politically Eddie was intriguing. She knew now that her bitchy telegram was an error. Eddie wasn't downgrading her in his acceptance speech. Kate Witherspoon was probably far from his mind last night. She was convinced of that after watching his press conference today. Eddie was wide open politically. He believed that the manicured, well-tailored men had made a mess of the country recently—and who could deny that?—and Eddie lashed out from his gut. He said what he felt. She understood that now. But further, she guessed that Eddie might welcome ideas from her. Despite his roots, a man who offered the country a "human-depletion allowance" might be persuaded to endorse her birth-control program. For three years she had sponsored a bill to establish 3000 federal population-control clinics throughout the country. It remained locked in committee, largely because of opposition from old-line Catholics and some black leaders. To Kate, birth control made sense despite a recent fall in the birth rate. Without leadership by governments, the human race could spawn itself into one vast, fetid slum. Birth control was Kate's "impact." She would push it with all her energies, always realizing, of course, that the impact was subject to change on short notice.

So she hankered to join Eddie's small circle of advisers. She had no doubt that Eddie would welcome her, but first she had to think of her district. She was not anxious to jeopardize her considerable popularity in the Fifth District, her power base. What was the reaction to Eddie Quinn now in Dallas after two days of saturation by TV, radio and newspapers?

Kate placed a call through Debbie to her Dallas office. Art Rankin came on the line at once.

"Hey!" Art, an eager young politician who served as her administrative assistant, always sounded as though he'd just downed two drinks and sometimes had. "Just getting ready to report in, Kate. Here's the Quinn rundown as I see it. Upper, upper income, thumbs down. Upper, ditto. Middle, some interest. Lower, ready for Eddie. How much detail do you want?"

"All you can give me." Kate pictured Art cradling the phone on his shoulder and puffing a cigarette.

"Okay. With one speech and one press conference, Quinn made Pinholster a present of the whole damn big-money vote down here. Your kind of people were all for Hudson, as you know, Kate, but they're boiling mad at Quinn right now. Incidentally, Ted's name is mud with that crowd. They think he's either a traitor or a fool, maybe both. Stepping down the income ladder, my guess is that Quinn won't get many votes from the $30,000-a-year bracket. They're scared. In the middle incomes, about the same, although there's some interest in Quinn. But below fifteen thou a year, hell, they dig Eddie already. In the Mex neighborhoods, I sense a switch from Pinholster whose eastern, liberal style seems phony to them. More on Chicanos later. Paco's out making the rounds now. As for Negroes, they're not talking. The busing thing put them off, but then Eddie's raising hell with the big bosses and they like that. Blacks are still for Pinholster, we'd have to say.

"If the election were tomorrow, Quinn would lose big here. On the other hand, everybody, but everybody, is talking about him. I haven't heard Pinholster's name mentioned for two days. And another thing. Women tend to like Eddie, and I mean women in all brackets. I don't know what it is, maybe a sex thing.

"One sidelight." There was a pause and Kate could see Art shaking another cigarette out of a pack. She heard the click of his lighter. "A lot of people are talking about that bit between Quinn and the AP reporter. They're sore at the newspaperman—hell, nobody really likes reporters—for exposing Eddie's attempt to plant a question, and they admire Quinn for his quick recovery. I guess the psychology is that they don't mind Eddie trying to put over a fast one like every-one does, but they're happily surprised at his honest admission when he got caught. They're used to politicians who try to wriggle off the hook. Instead Eddie seemed to be saying, hell yes, I tried it and won't do it again, but so what? Small thing, but people look for little character clues like that when they watch the tube."

Kate thought for a moment after Rankin finished his tumbling monologue. "Art, what if I endorsed Quinn?"

"A gamble. Of course, you're tied to Quinn anyway as the party's candidate and because of Ted's role. Still, if you don't endorse, you could always ditch him without trouble later on if he goes sour. . . . Look, Kate, how well do you know this guy? I hear you had dinner with him the other night."

"Your grapevine's working okay, Art. I don't know him well. A lot of impressions, let's say."

"Yeah, well here's my hunch. If this Eddie's sincere, he might turn the party's image inside out. We're the party of the haves, right? Well, for two days this guy has been talking about the have-nots and the almost-haves. Maybe he's just winging it, but if he means it and he makes a pretty good run against Pinholster, he could really switch things around. So you'd better be sure what kind of party you want. . . . Put it this way. Could Congress-woman Kate of the Highland Park and Mill Reef, Antigua, With-erspoons, the Wellesley alumnae, the Dallas Country Club, the Petroleum Club, find happiness in a party run by Eddie Quinn, the corner gas-pumper, the business agent of the Teamsters' local and some old Polack from Arkansas named Hunk Janiszewski?"

"Happiness is hardly the name of the game, baby. My game is victory in the Fifth."

"On that runway, Kate, you're an easy take-off. This guy Larson is making no dent whatsoever. Pinholster would have to carry Dallas County by a superlandslide before you'd get rubbed out. But think-ing of the party, and your future, you better be sure Quinn is head-ing where you want to go."

"I'm thinking of joining his staff," she said.

Silence settled briefly on the line. "Has he asked you?"

"No, but he needs help. I think he'd take mine."

"We'd have to cancel a raft of your campaign dates."

"I could fly down for the last two weekends. Wouldn't that hold us?"

"Yeah, we could manage. But it's a risk. If Quinn runs bad with you on his staff, it could hurt you."

"I'm ready to take the risk, Art." She felt a surge of spirit at having committed herself. "Compared with Hudson, this man is exciting. As for the party, it's due a shakeup. Haven't you said so yourself?"

"Every time I get a chance to beat your ear." He laughed. "Okay, Kate, good luck. If we lose, you can always retire to Antigua and I can go back to selling municipals."

She waited a few minutes after the good-bys, then went to the door and spoke to Debbie, who was on the phone.

"When you finish, Debbie, see if you can reach Mr. Edward Quinn for me. He's at the Hay-Adams."

Debbie swung around, receiver in hand and eyes wide. "That's funny, Mrs. Witherspoon. He's on the line now."

Kate smiled, closed the door and walked rapidly to her desk. "Okay, Debbie, I have it." She waited until she heard the click. "Eddie?"

"Hi, Kate."

"It's telepathy. I just told my girl to call you—and there you were."

"First minute I've had." His voice had a bounce to it. "Listen, Kate, that telegram last night bugged the hell out of me. Then I saw you at the press conference. What happened? I don't understand."

"I was the one who didn't understand, Eddie." Kate was surprised at the tremor in her voice. "I got a crazy idea that your speech was aimed at me. Too much Apollo and not enough sleep, I guess. Do you forgive me?"

"Sure. Accepted, filed and forgotten. Did you get the roses?"

"Yes, Eddie. They were as nice as the card." She wondered when she could tell him that she had let the flowers slip into the waste-basket. "If I'm forgiven, can I ask a favor?"

"It's already granted. What is it?"

"I'd like to join your staff, help with ideas, strategy, speeches, you know, the works."

"Great! Kate, you're wonderful. But are you sure you want to climb aboard with an old trucker? And how about your district?"

"I've been through that. The district's fairly safe."

"Well then, sure. Be up here at the Hay-Adams at ten tomorrow. We're going to bang some ideas around. You made my day, Kate. My luck is running."

"There's a hook, Eddie."

"Okay, sink it in easy."

"I'm the population champion in the House, you know. I'll try to persuade you. That's a fair warning."

"Birth control! I'm in enough trouble with the Church as it is. Why don't dames just swallow the pill and keep quiet about it?"

"It's not that simple. Will you give me ten minutes sometime in the next couple of days to explain?"

He hesitated, and when he spoke, his voice dropped to a lower key. "Kate, that's why I'm calling. I don't want to give us minutes. I want hours. Are you busy tonight?"

"No."

"Well, let's spend it together. How about it?"

Her mind swarmed with the complications. "But, Eddie, all the Secret Service, newspapermen, God knows who else. People know me. I can't just go waltzing through the Hay-Adams lobby like a call girl."

"I have a plan. Are you ready?"

"That depends on what it is." But she knew she would go almost anywhere, through a boiler room, down an alley, if necessary. This man made her feel more together than at any time in ten years.

"Jim Flannery, an okay guy, is head of my SS detail. He has a cabin on the Potomac northeast of Leesburg. My excuse is that I need a good night's sleep away from the pressure. The newspapermen won't follow if I promise to call them in case of an accident or something. . . . Then you come up on your own wheels."

"Flannery will know about us," she protested. But the fact did not seem terribly important.

"I'm sorry, Kate, but he does already. He handled the Galaxie in Houston—and the roses. Jim doesn't talk. It's part of the code." He paused. "Baby, please!"

"My, what a coaxing way you have, Mr. Candidate." She laughed. Her whole body felt alive. "What if I say no?" My God, she thought, here I am teasing him.

"Then I might get smashed for the first time in twenty years and do something nuts like declare war on Texas."

"Oh, Eddie, I'll come. What time and how do I get there?"

"Nine o'clock." He gave directions from Leesburg to the cabin and made her repeat them. "Jim says there's an old wooden gate at the end of the lane. He'll wait for you there."

"So the conspiracy was planned before you called. And you a man who asks the whole country to trust him." She made a tsk-tsk sound. "I'll rent a car. My Texas plates are too well known. . . . At least we'll be the only couple tonight with an official government beard. Until nine, Eddie."

Five minutes later Kate was on her way to the hairdresser's with thoughts of politics, the Texas Fifth District, the impact, Eddie Quinn and a shack on the Potomac. In the cab, she hummed a few bars. She caught herself. There Ain't No Easy Run? My God, Kate, next you'll be bowling with Melheisen's Pontiac.

9

As she stepped from a cab in front of the Manger Hay-Adams at 10:15 the next morning, Kate Witherspoon felt like a million dollars, or $17,000 more than her trust fund administered by the Republic National Bank of Dallas. This October Saturday morning stood cool, clear, spiced with the scents of autumn, and in Lafayette Square across H Street from the hotel, the grass shimmered as the sun burned off the first frost of the season. Kate, who wore a cinnamon pants suit with a looping brass chain slung at her hips, felt that it was a good thing to be a woman, healthy, vibrant and wearing a new outfit, and equally fine to be a politician bent on business. No less pleasant was a snip of memory, the wide Potomac lapping somnolently under a quarter-moon while Eddie Quinn described, in a low, nostalgic voice, how as a boy he used to trap crabs along the Jersey shore with a fishhead, a line and a net.

The usually quiet hotel lobby teemed with people. Kate heard the clack of typewriters and noted that the paneled dining room had been roped off and converted into a press center. Newspapermen and women, many of whom she knew, promptly surrounded her.

"Is it true you're joining the Quinn staff?"

"Yes it is."

"Does that mean you think he can win?"

Kate smiled. "Not yet. We have to be practical. Quinn is up against tremendous odds. Still, we'll do our best—and we have seventeen days left."

"There are rumors that your husband and his friends who put

Quinn over are furious with him about the oil tax issue," said Sybil Jamieson of CBS. "Is that true?"

"Now, Sybil, you know how to reach Ted. Just pick up the phone and call his office in Dallas."

"But how about you?" persisted Miss Jamieson. "Do you favor wiping out the oil allowance with this new human-depletion thing?"

"I think the idea of a human-depletion allowance is very interesting. It might stir up a lot of debate and that's fine. The whole tax system needs revising."

"Vince Anderson of the AP, Mrs. Witherspoon," said the short, intense man with the winglike ears who had sparred with Eddie the day before. "Does your joining the staff mean that Quinn is endorsing your birth-control bill?"

"It means he's a man with an open mind. I'll certainly try to persuade him, but I honestly haven't done more than mention it to him thus far. . . . Now you'll have to let me through. I'm twenty minutes late. I committed a cardinal campaign sin. I overslept."

The pack opened a path for her, but Anderson stayed close to her side as she headed for the elevator. "I'd like to speak to you privately," he said in a low voice.

"About what?" Kate, paying scant attention, did not break stride.

"About a blue Olds, rented from Avis. The D.C. tag number is 751 742."

Kate halted and faced the reporter. "And?" she asked with stressed coolness. The other newsmen began edging in, but Kate held up a hand. "Please. I'm talking to Mr. Anderson."

"Quinn asked the press to let him have a free night," said Anderson. "I made no commitment. I don't play that way. I parked on the road near the turn-off to Flannery's cabin." Kate now recalled spotting a stationary sedan with the lights off. "I saw a blue Olds, driven by a woman, turn in about nine and leave around three-thirty. This morning I checked the plate with motor vehicles. It's an Avis car. At Avis, after a little hassle, I found out the car was rented for the weekend to Katherine Witherspoon."

"My, you do work long hours, Mr. Anderson." Kate spoke as calmly as she could. "Just what do you want from me?"

"I'm a political reporter, Mrs. Witherspoon, not a gossip columnist. If you talked to Mr. Quinn about politics, I have to ask you about it. If it was a social call, I'll forget it."

Kate stared at him, boiling inwardly, as she considered. At last she said: "It was a friendly call. I had no political business with Mr. Quinn last night."

"Fair enough." Anderson managed an embarrassed smile. "So we'll forget it."

"I won't forget it." Kate was raging now. "And I doubt that you will, Mr. Anderson. . . . I imagine you think your little peephole trick is worth something of value to you."

"Does that crack mean what I think it does?"

"Draw your own conclusions." Kate knew it was a mistake to blow her cool, but her temper tugged her along.

"Listen, I make two ninety a week and never took a dime outside my pay check. I said I'd forget it. I keep my word."

"I apologize," said Kate, knowing she did not.

"Okay." The quick flush of indignation still colored his cheeks. "It's not often an overtaxed working lug rates an apology from a woman who married an oil-depletion allowance." He turned and strode back to the pressroom.

Kate simmered as she rode the elevator to the fourth floor. So now she and Eddie might become a front-page scandal? Anderson might not be a gossip columnist, but he had lines to plenty of the breed. Newspapermen belonged to a close-knit fraternity in which choice tidbits about politicians raced about like molecules in a cyclotron. And, to her surprise, she found she cared less for her own reputation than for Eddie's.

A Secret Service agent nodded pleasantly to her as she stepped off the elevator and Jim Flannery greeted her outside the door to the candidate's suite. She was grateful that his "Good morning, Congresswoman" carried no sly reminders that he had helped her into her car beneath a moon-speckled sycamore tree at 3:30 that morning.

She felt a twinge of embarrassment when she entered the sitting room and faced the circle of staffers, but Eddie quickly put her at ease. He threw an arm around her in one of those neuter, bearlike body hugs so favored by male politicians when dealing with a colleague.

"Congresswoman Kate Witherspoon," he said with a small flourish of triumph. "Meet the S and T brain trust. Pete, you know . . . Margot Hicks . . . Teegee Churchill . . . my uncle, Frank Janiszewski . . . R Dan Fenelli . . . and a couple of newcomers this morning, Congressman Joe Kuzyk from Cleveland and Phil Liccardo, our public-relations man. I borrowed him from the Turnpike."

Kate knew Joe Kuzyk slightly. He was a member of the Interstate and Foreign Commerce Committee, a towering Czech serving his third term in the House. A powerful, shaggy, socially awkward man, a former Olympic discus thrower, Kuzyk was known for his attacks on the baleful dominance of conglomerates.

Phil Liccardo, who huddled at a telephone a few feet away from the circle, reminded Kate of a bartender in a smoky night spot. He wore a pink shirt, a wide, flowered tie and black sideburns that swept south of his ear lobes. She noted his agile, restless air and swiveling eyes.

"We're about to get into policy, Kate," said Eddie, offering her a chair. "We've already roughed out part of the schedule. This afternoon I have a session with the ambassadors at the Pan American Union. The auto crowd wants me for a speech at the Detroit Economic Club and I've accepted for Tuesday noon. A week from Monday, a Teamsters' regional convention in L.A. A couple of ghetto walks that Margot will set up, and as many TV panel shows as we can pay for. The rest is all motorcading, starting bright and early Monday."

Eddie stopped pacing, dropped into an armchair and took a swallow of coffee from a cup resting on an end table. "I'm sorry, Kate. Help yourself to coffee from that urn over there. . . . Now, what do I say? R Danny and I agree that we have to hammer away at the big issues. There's no time for detailed blueprints and that's not my style anyway. Our job is to jolt people into thinking, build up some pressure, so that when he becomes President, Pinholster will know damn well what a lot of us want. Okay then, sticking to domestic stuff right now, let's kick it around. What bugs you the most? If you were czar or king, what would you tackle first? Let it fly, anything that crosses your mind. . . . Teegee, you take notes for me."

There was an uneasy silence while they eyed one another like guests bidden to an unfamiliar parlor game. At last Hunk cleared his throat.

"Them bureaucrats," he said, his knobby Adam's apple pumping industriously. "Maybe I shouldn't say nothin'. I never went past sixth grade, but them snotty Social Security people give me a pain. Six months they been stalling me over a measly four-eighty-eight a month. All them form letters. They act like they own the government and I'm just something that louses up their system."

"So what would you do about it, Hunk?" asked Eddie.

"Fire any bastard that ain't polite to people and junk all that red tape. Just on me alone they used up about five hundred bucks in letter-writing time."

"It's hell trying to fire anybody in this government," said Pete Stackpole. "Civil service rules."

"So let's change some rules," said Congressman Kuzyk. "Make arrogance toward a taxpayer cause for dismissal. . . . Hunk's right about red tape. Why not shift to the Canadian system of old-age pensions? Anybody who can prove he's a citizen and over sixty-five walks in and collects his pension. Throw out all that expensive record-keeping, quarters worked, all that hustle. And knock off the Social Security trust fund. Old-age benefits are all paid out of current revenues anyway."

"I like that," said Eddie. "Teegee, make a note for one of Pete's experts to check out the Canadian system."

"I got an idea on red tape, Eddie," added Phil Liccardo from his post by the telephone. "In my home town of Perth Amboy people think Washington is further away than Mongolia. How about a presidential ambassador in every precinct, a guy who'll listen to anybody's beef against the government and get some action if it's merited?"

"Yeah," agreed Margot Hicks. "People don't know where to turn, government's so complicated. It sure would help if they could talk to the President's man."

"Provided they get action," said R Dan Fenelli. "You're talking about presidential ombudsmen now and that's good, but the system would have to be workable, not just a PR gimmick."

Kate felt herself being swept into the discussion. "What if the President himself made it a practice to make surprise visits to some precincts, say once a month, and sit in with his personal representative?" She thought of how remote a President seemed from most of her constituents and how they brought Washington-born problems to her as though she were an envoy to a foreign power. "It would give people the feeling that the top man cares about their concerns and it would give the President a feel of the people. Our Presidents are too insulated."

"Sounds good," said Eddie. He turned to Teegee whose long blond hair brushed her note pad. "Put a star after Phil's idea as amended by Kate." Eddie leaned forward and slapped his knees. "I like this. We're getting into something. Let's keep rolling. Margot, you're next. What bugs you about the government?"

"The people who been runnin' it," she said sourly. She considered a moment. "Oh God, I hardly know where to start. I guess what really turns off black people is some white dude in Washington telling us what's good for niggers. We want a black face behind the mouth that gives us all that free advice."

"What you want is a nigrah President," said Hunk. "My nephew don't qualify."

Hunk's tart comment did not bother Margot. She grinned at him as though they shared a secret, the admission of their mutual prejudice. "Yeah, old man, too bad he ain't. A little black soul wouldn't hurt your nephew or you either. . . . I guess what I'd like is black men and women heading up every program that has to do with black people."

"How about an all-black advisory council to the President?" suggested Teegee.

Eddie shook his head. "I don't like that any more than an all-Italian council or Polish or Puerto Rican. I want it all-American, a fair shake for everybody." He turned to Margot. "Let's do some more thinking about that. I know what you mean, but I'm not sure how to go about it." He swung around to Congressman Kuzyk. "Joe?"

"Break up the goddamn conglomerates," said Kuzyk. "They got

terrific economic power, political too. They operate like independent governments. Kate and I can name you fifty congressmen who are in some big company's pocket. Might as well be on their payroll."

"Sure," said Fenelli. "They still believe in William K. Vanderbilt's slogan of the eighteen-eighties."

"What was that?" asked Eddie.

"When a reporter asked Vanderbilt whether the public shouldn't be consulted about luxury trains, Vanderbilt said: 'The public be damned.'"

"Right," said Kuzyk. "And shut the damn tax loopholes, Eddie. You made a good start yesterday with that human-depletion allowance, but oil isn't the only villain. The rich have a thousand ways of ducking taxes. It's the working guy, the steel worker, the auto mechanic, who pays the freight in this country. We got to get power back to the people, and one way to do it is to crack down through taxes." Joe Kuzyk's craggy face came alive as he warmed to his subject. "Listen, the dollar is king in this country. You're not going to get that fair shake for everybody unless the dollars are sprung out of those tax-free closets. Look how they beat the tax rap—stock options, big expense accounts, real estate depreciation, tax-exempt municipal bonds."

The telephone rang and Phil Liccardo answered while Kuzyk talked on. "You got multi-millionaires who don't pay more than two or three per cent of their income in taxes, while the poor working slob pays twenty-five per cent or better of his wages, when you figure all the taxes—sales, income, real estate. Guys like you and me, Eddie, are patsies for the big boys. It's time we wised up."

"Hey," broke in Phil Liccardo. "I have some news that ties in with what Joe's talking about. Want to hear it?"

"Shoot," said Eddie.

"They're being flooded with messages at headquarters, reactions to Eddie's press conference. So far, the count is six thousand telegrams, about a thousand long-distance calls and a couple of hundred special delivery letters. It's running seven to one in favor of the human-depletion allowance. And a lot of the affirmatives say that Quinn ought to go after the fancy expense accounts and other tax-dodging schemes."

Eddie looked pleased. "Well, what do you know? I guess some-one out there was listening after all."

"And millions more will," said Kuzyk, "if you go after the whole range of loopholes. And why not? The platform pledges a tax review. Well, let's have an honest-to-God one. I tell you, Eddie, it's a damn scandal. Only a very few working people realize what murder the rich get away with. It's up to you to preach the message, lay it out so they can understand."

"Maybe," said Fenelli, "we ought to consider an income-tax program with no deductions at all. None. Deductions only mean a few bucks to the little guy anyway. Besides, Eddie's offering him a thirty per cent reduction right off. Make the big guys pay the rates they're supposed to. Let's say a big operator takes in a million. After his thirty per cent human-depletion allowance and paying the top rate, he'd still have about $650,000 left for pocket money. That's bad?"

"Now wait a minute," cautioned Pete Stackpole. "What you're talking about is a real tax revolution. You're also flirting with political suicide. If Eddie advocates a progressive income tax with no de-ductions, he won't get a single vote from those making over $20,000 a year."

"And if he just gets the rest," said Kuzyk, "he's elected in a land-slide."

"But it doesn't work that way," said Pete. "Big propaganda guns would open up on Eddie. The media would murder him. Every wheel in the country would turn against him. Okay, Eddie's only a long shot, but we do have to think of the rest of the ticket. At least I intend to." Stackpole glared belligerently around the circle as if he were the lone defender of the faith amid a ragged band of heretics.

"I'm just as much a party man as you are, Pete," Kuzyk shot back, "but I want it to serve the average guy for a change, not just the Shaker Heights, Grosse Pointe and Orange County set. Maybe I ought to make my position clear here. I called Eddie yesterday and told him he sounded like Eric Hoffer and thank God for it. He asked me to join the staff. I said I would under one con-dition—that he was absolutely straight about putting ordinary people

in power and not just indulging in windbag talk. He said he meant
it all and I take Eddie at his word. Not in my lifetime has either
party nominated a man who reflects the big majority of workers in
this country. Until Eddie. Our next step is to come up with a program that gets that message across. And taxes is one of the best ways
to do it."

"Right on!" exclaimed Teegee. Her blue eyes shone with the
fervor of a crusader for the proletariat, whose longings she had
divined through one summer of washing dishes at a rustic inn on
Cape Cod. Kuzyk stared at her, blinking solemnly.

"Taxes are one hell of a complicated subject," gloomed Stackpole. He spoke as though the whole burden of the federal revenue
structure rested on his narrow shoulders.

"But they don't have to be," said Eddie cheerily. "That's our
job—to simplify. . . . Okay, we're still thinking out loud. Let's
move on. Kate?"

Kate felt somewhat unnerved. She had pictured Eddie's counselors dipping gingerly into the caldron of social and economic
issues, plucking out an attractive, salable item here and there. But
she was not prepared for Joe Kuzyk's savage frontal assault on
people of means, her kind. She could see her proud aunts and
affluent cousins being hung by their heels while bonds and currency
fluttered from their pockets. She envisioned her own trust fund,
which she considered quite modest by Texas standards, evaporating
to a puddle of coins under Kuzyk's glare, as hot and relentless as the
noonday sun over the Rio Grande. She sensed that everyone in the
room, with the exception of Pete Stackpole, cheered on Joe Kuzyk
and she wondered whether she belonged here after all.

"Well I guess everyone here knows my cause," she said hesitantly.
"I'm here to talk the candidate into endorsing a real federal program
of birth-control clinics. The birth rate has dropped recently, but it
may be only temporary, and even so we're growing like mad. A century from now, unless something is done soon, people will be living
jammed elbow-to-elbow. And if we don't have room to live and
breathe—human beings need space—we'll become as vicious as
rats. These other big problems you talk about are nothing compared
to overpopulation. We'll wind up with a country paved with ocean-

to-ocean people, no land to grow food on and our resources exhausted. It will be an ugly, hungry world for all our grandchildren."

"Well, now, I don't know," said Margot. "Every time I hear a rich white lady like you talking about birth control, I figure what she really means is no more black kids."

"That's not true," said Kate. "Not me anyway. I resent those pictures of huge white families you see in the newspapers. I thought the Kennedys set a terrible example, all the competitive bragging between Rose and her daughter-in-law, Ethel, about who popped the most children. I'm talking numbers, not color. Black families of seven or eight kids trouble me, sure, but no more than white suburbanites pullulating all over the landscape."

"What was the fancy word, Kate?" asked Eddie. He grinned. "Pull-something?"

"Pullulate," said Phil Liccardo. "It means to breed like hell. . . . You'll have Eddie up against the Pope, Kate. But maybe that's okay. My house is Catholic and we use the pill. Two kids and that's it."

"Me and the old woman had seven," said Hunk truculently. "And I don't want no damn bureaucrats telling people in Bee Branch how small their families gotta be. That's all we need, a bunch of bed-snoopers outa Washington."

"Wrong, Hunk," said Fenelli. "You don't need anti-kid cops. The best way to curb population growth is through taxation. Times have changed for Catholics, Hunk. You had seven, but look at the rest of us. Phil says two. I have one, a daughter. Eddie stopped at two. How many do you have, Congressman?"

"Three," said Kuzyk. "Kate's right. And Eddie doesn't have to run against the Pope. Just lead him. The Vatican is always behind the times."

"Make love, not kids," said Teegee and proudly jotted down her *bon mot* in the note pad.

"Okay, we may make some kind of pitch on birth control," said Eddie. "Kate, you get together with R Danny and Margot and work out something practical. If it makes sense, I'll spring it. . . . All right, you're next, Phil."

Liccardo favored repealing the child labor laws and putting teen-agers to work. Stackpole passed. He was the "nuts and bolts" man, he said, and this crew was coming up with enough oddball ideas as it was. Fenelli argued for federal chartering of corporations, with tight anti-pollution and monopoly controls, and with a proviso that every board of directors include at least one member elected by employees and one by consumers. Teegee Churchill set off a lengthy wrangle when she argued that garbage collectors should be paid as much as stockbrokers because they performed stinking work that no one else wanted to do. The session slid past the noon hour. Phil Liccardo ordered sandwiches and beverages from room service and Eddie talked on while he munched a ham-and-cheese on rye. This time the lettuce was crisp and unblemished.

"I think we're getting somewhere," he said. "You know, I got into this thing without having a chance to think much, but the way those characters at the Astroworld tried to maneuver me into running their errands gave me a jolt. I realized I do have strong feelings about this country. Maybe they boil down to this: the average guy in America deserves a lot more of the action. He fights the wars, he builds the highways and bridges and he pays the taxes, but by God, he doesn't own the country, he doesn't run it and he doesn't have a glimmer of what the guys at the top get away with."

Eddie paused for a swallow of ginger ale. "I was kind of surprised yesterday that nobody asked me what books I'd read recently. That's a trap question that slick know-it-all reporters like to spring on guys they consider to be ignorant. Well, I was ready for them. I have read some books in the last year, three of them, all recommended by George Dawson, the black guy who lives next to me. He's a big reader. *The Rich and the Super-Rich* by Lundberg, *The Great Treasury Raid*, a fellow named Stern I think wrote it, and *America, Inc.*, by two men here in Washington. The books gave me a lot of ammunition for what I've been thinking all along, that the rich movers and shakers, like Joe Kuzyk says, always manage to manipulate the Congress for their own benefit and screw the rest of us. We're just consumers who've got to be paid high enough wages so we can buy their products, but we're not allowed power so we can control our own lives. So, when those Caddy and Imperial types in the Astroworld down in Houston . . ."

"Bulletin!" cried Phil Liccardo. He had been talking into the phone in a muffled voice. He stood up and brandished a sheet of paper. "I was just talking to a desk man at the Washington *Post*. Gallup is in with the first match of Quinn versus Pinholster for Sunday papers. The poll was taken yesterday afternoon and this morning, nationwide. He makes it Pinholster 55, Quinn 34 and 11 uncertain."

"About what you'd expect," said Eddie. He downed the last bite of sandwich and brushed his hands, spraying crumbs over the floor.

"Are you kidding, Eddie?" asked Liccardo. "Three days ago nobody ever heard of you and already you've got a third of the vote."

"It's a start," observed Stackpole, "but it doesn't mean much. You gotta figure most of that is an anti-Pinholster vote that would go to any stiff running against him."

"Let's not con ourselves into thinking we have a chance to win," said Eddie. "It would cramp our style. Our job is to lay it on the line, make people think. If we get big ideas about winning, we'll start to hedge, play for voting blocs, straddle. The hell with all that. We're going to run a wide-open, swinging campaign and we're not going to suck up to the American Legion, the NAACP, Wall Street, Chamber of Commerce, B'nai B'rith, you name it."

"Amen," said Fenelli.

"Okay, let's get to foreign policy," said Eddie. "We'll have to speed it up. I'm due at the Pan American Union at three."

Hunk Janiszewski, no longer shy about his grasp of public matters, led off. "If you ask me, first we gotta quit buttin' in all over the world. With a few years off to put in the crops and get patched up in the vets' hospitals, we been fighting ever since I was in knee pants. Let them foreigners kill theyselves off if they want to. We oughta stay home and mind our own business, what we got left of it. Hell, let them A-rabs and Israelites go at it, if they're hankering to, same with them Orientals and Africans."

"It's not that simple," said Fenelli, "but Hunk's on the right track. How about this for openers: no more military aid. From now on, peaceful, economic aid only."

"Yes," said Kate. "It's crazy to peddle arms all over the world.

Every time the shooting starts, you find people killing one another with American or Russian guns."

"I'm against giving anything away," said Hunk, "guns or tractors. Nobody ever gives us stuff. The last thing we got from foreigners was the Statue of Liberty them frogs give us."

"One thing that riles me is war profits," said Joe Kuzyk. "I got a bill in the House, Eddie, that would stop all corporate profits the minute we get into a war. I wish you'd pick it up and back it. There's no justice or morality in people getting fat at home while American boys are being killed abroad. If we ask a young man to offer his life, why shouldn't we ask his old man to sacrifice his wallet?"

"I think you ought to end the draft, Eddie," said Teegee. She brushed the long hair from her temples and gazed at him. "It's always the young men who do the dying, all the beautiful young ones." Her voice sank. "If the old men insist on making war, let them do the dying."

Eddie leaned toward her. "I'm sorry, Teegee. I didn't hear that last part."

"I said if the old men want wars or something, why shouldn't they do the fighting and dying?"

Eddie stared at her for a moment. "Yes, Teegee. Why shouldn't they?"

Pete Stackpole came on strong. "Eddie, I'd like to see you pledge that you'd never send American troops to fight outside the country without a declaration by Congress. Everybody knows the President would respond in a few minutes if missiles were launched against us or if the Russians attacked our bases in Europe. But if the President wants to send troops to intervene in places like Vietnam and the Dominican Republic, he should present his case to Congress first."

"Get rid of those big bombs," said Margot. "I know the Russians and Chinese are tough, but the American President should keep up the heat until they and we agree to ban all those atom and hydrogen bombs."

"Right," said Fenelli. "We banned germ warfare and we can do it with the nukes. The SALT talks were a beginning, but they just nibbled around the edges. Eddie, I'd like to hear you say that if elected you'd go to the UN and urge nuclear disarmament by every-body. People are scared stiff of those terrible weapons."

"I think Hunk is right about foreign aid," said Phil Liccardo. "Man, nobody I know favors giving stuff away, whether arms, goods or money. Why not limit all our grants overseas to our part in inter-national programs like the World Bank or the UN?"

The Quinn strategy and tactics counsel, short on agenda but long on imagination, bobbed and weaved for another half-hour in a generally peaceful direction. If it showed no lack of resolve in bait-ing the dragons of pestilence and bloodshed, it nevertheless exhibited an ambivalence toward that quixotic and demon-ridden world west of Hawaii, south of the Rio Grande and east of the Virgin Islands. Hunk in particular was torn between retreat and advance, charity and penuriousness. He would intrude on no foreigner's terrain, but he would hurl the Soviet Navy out of the Mediterranean. He would seal the coffers of foreign aid, but feed starving families in Bang-ladesh and the high Andes. Had a stranger eavesdropped on the deliberations, he might have detected, in addition to the conflicts of motive, a certain over-all restraint and a paucity of that self-right-eous zeal that once inflamed the American empire in the days of the brothers Dulles. Vietnam, it appeared, was bitter in memory for everyone.

"There are a lot of items we haven't covered here," said Stackpole as time ran out. "For instance, you'll have to bone up on the mone-tary hassle, gold, dollars, francs, marks. A candidate has to know the score on international finance."

"Not one who doesn't expect to get elected," Eddie retorted.

He ended the session with a happy fusillade of orders. Pete Stack-pole was to button down the schedule and wave a wand for more campaign money. Phil Liccardo should bat out a press release on the volume of telegrams. R Danny with the help of Joe Kuzyk would sift today's ideas through a wide-meshed sieve. Eddie told Hunk to take the rest of the afternoon off and watch the last half of the Ohio State-Purdue game-of-the-week on television. Teegee was to come along to the Pan American Union and bring her notebook. Eddie, newly a martinet, barked out exuberant commands. For a man who claims that it's all a game, thought Kate, Eddie certainly played it gladly.

"Kate, let me talk to you a minute." Eddie beckoned her to a corner near a window overlooking Sixteenth Street. He maneuvered so that his back fenced her from view. "I only wanted to say that last night was beautiful. How about dinner tonight? You know, candidate talks to adviser."

"I'd love to, Eddie, but I can't. I promised Susan."

"Let me call you then, so we can talk. About eleven?"

"Eleven's fine. I'll be in the Watergate apartment."

"I thought you said it was a penthouse."

"Well, yes." Why was she suddenly reluctant to use a word that hinted of luxury? She loved the place, especially its night view of the Potomac and the glow of city lights. "Eddie, there was bad news downstairs this morning." She quickly described her encounter with Vince Anderson of the Associated Press.

"Hell, that's not good." Eddie frowned. "But if Vince gave his word, I think he'll keep it. I'll talk to him. . . . I don't like it. We're open targets now, I guess."

"I blew my stack when I shouldn't have," she said.

He squeezed her hand once, hard and fast, and they rejoined the others.

Eddie and Teegee Churchill rode the few blocks to the Pan American Union in the rear of the elegant Continental Mark IV while Jim Flannery and a Secret Service driver occupied the front seat. A Secret Service car and a photographers' flat-bed truck rode ahead and a press bus trailed them, in all a tidy caravan. The gunning engines of the police motorcycle escort delighted Eddie. All for him, Eddie Quinn!

"You got to me, Teegee, when you said it's the young men in war who do the dying for us old bastards."

"Yeah. I wish you'd stand up someday and announce you're going to end the draft forever."

"We live in a world of armies, Teegee. Still, you've given me an idea." Eddie lapsed into silence as they passed the ancient, rococo Old Executive Office Building, once the citadel of both the old War and State Departments, those twins of despair and hope.

"You look tired, Eddie."

"I do?" He answered mechanically, his mind on the diplomats he was about to face.

"Yeah, you ought to relax tonight with some good music or something. . . . I really dig music."

The words floated past him. His mind was elsewhere.

She turned to him. "You're a Gemini. Did you know I'm an Aries?"

The question hung in the air like smoke. He faced her and saw her eyes full upon his. Damn if he understood these young ones. They commanded invitations.

"I suppose you know about Gemini and Aries." Her sky blue eyes dwelled on him.

No, he didn't, but he could guess. A week ago he would have taken her hand and asked her to tell him about signs. Now . . . what? Well, now there was Kate. Not in years had the thought of one woman clouded the living presence of another. A strange development and one not without regrets.

"Teegee, honey, I'm old enough to be your father." He patted her knee which was separated from the hem of her skirt by several inches.

"Age! That applies to babies and old people."

"Maybe you're right. I hope so." Eddie laughed. "I tell you what. A candidate has to be careful where he goes after dark. But tonight, I thought I'd take some of the S and T gang bowling. You come along, will you? It makes me feel good to have you around."

"Same here. Yeah, I'd like that. I only bowled twice in my life."

She settled back, seemingly content, and a few moments later the motorcade halted at the Pan American Union with a gratifying burst of noise and disheveled movement. Photographers poured off the truck, newsmen swarmed out of the press bus and Eddie advanced on the Seventeenth Street Building like a guerrilla leader at the head of ragged, hungry troops.

Dr. Sergio Alvarez Enrique, the serene, plump, olive-skinned ambassador of Colombia and dean of the diplomatic corps, greeted Eddie at the doorway and steered him into the marble-floored foyer. Alvarez spoke a faultless, courtly English as though it were a heritage from another century. Eddie had expected to be impressed and he was not disappointed. He had met but few ambassadors in his life and those more than a decade earlier during his lone term in Congress.

Followed by his noisy army, Eddie was escorted past an exhibit of Bolivian paintings and into the large New Council Room where some hundred men and a few women, ambassadors extraordinary and plenipotentiary, awaited him. Dr. Alvarez introduced Eddie to the State Department's chief of protocol, a lean, jaded former polo player named H. Ambridge Hennicutt. Then Alvarez stationed Eddie near a floor-to-ceiling slab of marble which bore the seal of the Organization of American States. Not far away stood a long, linen-draped table bearing whisky and champagne bottles and a silver bowl of lime-colored punch.

The ambassadors formed a jagged line like patrons queuing up at a box office for tickets to a hit show. The drill, Eddie noted, consisted of Alvarez presenting each envoy to Hennicutt and the protocol chief then handing the man or woman along to Eddie. Hennicutt pronounced each title and name as though doing penance for having been afflicted with citizenship in a country so lacking in civility as to nominate the likes of Eddie Quinn for its top executive officer.

After 107 how-do-you-do's combined with limp to bone-crushing handshakes, Eddie saw Dr. Alvarez step to the council dais and rap smartly with a gavel, signaling for silence.

"Our guest, the Honorable Edward Nicholas Quinn, candidate for President of the United States of America, has graciously consented to favor us with a few words." Alvarez bowed to Eddie. "Commissioner Quinn."

Eddie bowed in turn and faced the shuffling crowd of dark-suited diplomats. He noted a reaction he had seen before, a kind of amused, condescending curiosity, less unfriendly than distant. It reminded him again of the day he lunched at the posh Links Club in New York.

"I assume," said Eddie after his opening amenities, "that you will shortly cable your home offices and give some personal impressions of me, the new candidate, even though my chances of being elected aren't exactly great. Please tell them that, contrary to rumors, I can read and write and speak fair English and that I don't wear a hard hat to diplomatic receptions. Still, I do consider myself a plain, ordinary American and I want to make our voice heard before this campaign is over.

"We ordinary Americans want peace in the world. I guess that sounds trite to you seasoned diplomats who've heard it in many tongues. I don't have any magic formula to make people quit killing one another, but I do have some ideas about new approaches. Today I'd like to tell you about one of them. I can state it simply.

"If I'm elected President, I intend to propose a UN treaty binding all nations not to put any man into a military uniform of his country until he has passed his fiftieth birthday."

Eddie paused. Most of his audience looked at him numbly, but he heard a few snickers from the envoys and a buzz from the newsmen clustered near the doorway.

"If the big powers agree to such a treaty, I'm confident the smaller nations will fall in line, so that few men, anywhere in the world, need fear military service before the age of fifty." Now Eddie saw many smiles, cynical but interested.

"Maybe we can't abolish war, but I contend that older men can fight these modern wars just as well as the young. Men our age can press the missile buttons and man the naval rockets and drive the tanks.

"For centuries now we've been killing off the best of the world's youth in our perpetual wars. Those who don't die come home maimed, blinded, faces, arms and legs shot away. But the old men who send them off to fight sit home in comfortable offices, drink their booze and move pins around on maps. It wasn't always that way, as you know. In the old days, the knights and warlords, the kings and Viking chiefs led men of all ages into battle. If they decided to make war, at least the old leaders had the guts to fight it themselves.

"But today the slogan of the fat old man is: 'Let's our kids and your kids fight.' There's something disgusting about those pictures of war conferences you see these days. You know the kind. Old generals and so-called statesmen, some of them in their seventies, many of them pot-bellied and bald, sit around big tables deciding where the youngsters should kill themselves off next.

"So let's resolve by treaty that the men who dream up the wars do the fighting. Nobody under fifty in a military uniform."

Eddie's fanning glance caught the blanched face of Ambridge Hennicutt. The protocol chief was mopping his forehead with a handkerchief and looking as if he'd like to flee. Near him stood Teegee, gazing up at Eddie in misty gratitude.

"Of course, since I'm forty-six years old, you may think I'm trying to evade the new draft myself. Well, I won't quibble. If you want to make the lowest military service age forty-five, I'll go along. I just like fifty as a nice, round number. . . . So that, honored ambassadors, is my first peace message. Nobody under fifty marching off to war. And while I'm no psychologist, my guess is that if we force the older men to fight their own wars, there will be damn few of them—wars, not old men. Thank you and peace to all."

Newsmen broke for the door, heading for telephones, but a baffled silence immobilized the diplomats. They regarded Eddie with incredulous expressions as though they suspected they had been made the butt of some inside American joke. After a moment Dr. Alvarez, forcing a wounded smile, clapped his hands, setting off a round of applause that made up in brevity what it lacked in vigor. The envoys stood uncertainly for a bit, then moved en masse to the bar, chattering away like schoolboys who have just been lectured by a lunatic. Dr. Alvarez, who had done his homework, fetched Eddie a ginger ale, touched glasses with his own scotch and soda, and said with ineffable neutrality: "Very interesting, Mr. Commissioner." Eddie saw Ambridge Hennicutt march to the bar and throw down a straight shot of scotch.

The Russian ambassador, a big, hearty man who looked like a playground director, bore down on Eddie with a tumbler of vodka. "I know you Irish." He nudged Eddie with his elbow. "I was on a special mission to Ireland last year."

"You're lucky. I've never been to Ireland." Eddie joined Dr. Alvarez and the Russian in clinking glasses. Other diplomats moved in.

"My cable this evening will be light of heart." The Russian zapped Eddie with an eyeball-to-eyeball dose of camaraderie. "I like that. A man becomes bored with the old themes of espionage and perfidy."

"Peace is what we all want," said Eddie, "and I think it's time to try some new angles."

"And sometimes a jest stirs more response than a serious proposal. Is it not so, Mr. Quinn?"

A number of newsmen, notebooks open, had now joined the circle and more diplomats fattened the fringes.

"I hope you're not implying that my proposal was a joke, Mr. Ambassador. I mean every word of it."

The Russian's laugh sounded a single report like the clang of a trash can. "Including those between the lines? . . . I congratulate you, Mr. Quinn. The world deserves a little fun from time to time."

"I'm serious. I don't consider peace a laughing matter."

"Calling men over fifty 'old men' is not a joke?" The Russian beamed conspiratorially at his colleagues. "Very few of us have lived less than fifty years, but you call us old? I'm sure some members of this corps would urge you to consult the gracious ladies of Washington."

"Maybe I should have used the phrase 'middle-aged,'" said Eddie stubbornly. He was nettled now. "But we who plan the wars and order the battles are old compared to the young men we send off to die in them."

The Russian squinted, assessing Eddie anew. His smile faded. "So, we shall be serious. But my friend, if Russia is ever invaded again, all men—sons, fathers, grandfathers—and many women will take up arms to defend their country."

Eddie thought of asking how many Russian grandfathers had marched into Hungary and Czechoslovakia along with the boyish tank crews, but he choked back the retort. "I'm talking about standing armies," he said. "If conscription everywhere were confined to those over fifty, there would be little threat to the Soviet Union or any other country."

"You see, it is difficult to take your plan except as humor. Do you know what day this is?"

When Eddie shook his head, the ambassador said: "In the United States, obviously, it is a day for joking."

"My proposal is no joke, but I am trying to show how ridiculous war is in this age of missiles and H-bombs."

The Russian nodded. "Let us drink to the interesting new idea." They raised their glasses once more.

Eddie lingered for a half-hour, chatting with the envoys, straining to catch the score of bewildering accents. Many diplomats mirrored the reaction of the Soviet ambassador, but a few predicted that Quinn's remarks would touch off stimulating debates. Later, as he moved toward the exit, flanked by Agents Flannery and Baker, Eddie spotted Vince Anderson among the newsmen.

"Come on, Vince. Walk to the car with me."

Anderson fell into step with the candidate.

"How'm I doin', Vince?"

"I don't know how many votes you're making, Eddie, but you sure make page one every time you open your mouth."

"Vince, Kate Witherspoon told me about her talk with you. You intend to write anything about that license tag?"

"No. I gave her my word, but I wish I hadn't. She made a snotty crack."

"That's not like her. Kate's okay, Vince. You probably startled her. She's a good dame. I appreciate your fairness. She did come up to Flannery's cabin, but it was a social visit, not politics."

"I understand. Forget it."

"Vince, give me a buzz about four tomorrow afternoon. I may have a little exclusive for Monday papers."

"That's not necessary."

"You against repaying favors? Or too lazy to work on Sunday?"

"Neither. I'll call you at four."

Outside, the coppery Continental gleamed in the fading autumn sunlight. Eddie caressed a fender and studied the body lines as he might those of a shapely woman.

"How about letting me drive back, Jim?"

Flannery looked unhappy. "It's not a good idea, Eddie. Somebody hits you from the side, even a scratch, and the chief would eat my ass out."

"Come on, Jim. There's no law against it. Only a few blocks—and we've got the escort." Eddie walked around the car and slid into the driver's seat.

Flannery reluctantly climbed in beside him and Eddie motioned Teegee into the rear seat where she sat as the lone, regal passenger. Eddie gunned the motor and the car purred away from the Pan American Union while photographers shoved and cursed as they fought for a good shot of the drive-it-yourself candidate. Behind the wheel, facing the stylish dashboard and sniffing the beloved odor of a new automobile, Eddie felt happy. He was not at all certain where his unorthodox campaign was headed, but it was good to realize that, for once in his life, he would go first class all the way.

10

On a busy Wednesday five days later, the Win-with-Quinn motorcade, now lengthened to six cars, a truck and two press buses, rolled merrily and often tardily through Ohio on Route 22. A wayward political troubador, Eddie might have pleased such disparate prophets as Peter the Hermit, Robin Hood and William Jennings Bryan. Sprinkled by pale October sunshine and braced by a breeze that riffled through the yellowing leaves, the candidate scattered his gospel among wondering crowds in Lancaster and Circleville, then moved out to the southwest.

Eddie's spirits hummed as he watched the bronzed countryside unfold through the windows of the bulletproof Electra 225. The car was tuned, the highway sound, the news good, his health stout, the weather crisp and riding in one of the trailing staff cars was Congresswoman Kate Witherspoon. Had Eddie been given to diagnosis of his feelings, he might have detected a sentiment unknown for the twenty-five years since he courted the corn-haired Mabel Probst. At the time, he knew the feeling as love, a quicksilver emotion inclined to disintegrate under the strains of hair curlers, marriage, low wages, troublesome sons, buxom waitresses, moralizing priests, yard work, dirty dishes, bars, mortgages, poker nights and the human condition. Since love had not disturbed Eddie's agenda during almost a quarter of a century of lusting quests and gamy sexual congress, his unfamiliarity with the symptoms was understandable. As it was, he churned his random thoughts and plotted the filching of another of R Dan Fenelli's proliferating ideas for his next speech in the town of Washington Court House.

Newsmen aboard the two charter buses mirrored Eddie's untroubled mood. Nothing boosts the morale of Washington correspondents so much as venturing forth on the wings of a soaring expense account to cover the campaign of a candidate with no hope of election. With relaxation of such stern professional pressures as those for impartiality, timely copy and punditry, the campaign becomes less of an industry than a lark, and the writer can indulge his yearning for whimsy and satire. At the moment the newspapermen in the lead bus were occupied with an even more diverting chore, writing a new stanza of their running campaign epic, a parody of "There Ain't No Easy Run."

So Eddie come to Circleville, speakin' off the cuff,
And he told them pregnant mommies, two babies is enough.
He gathered all the old men, said Grandpa, grab your gun,
You're goin' in the army where there ain't no easy run.

In Chicago this Wednesday, thirteen days before the election, the weather was far less benign. A chill rain pelted the gusty Loop and drove in slanting sheets along Michigan Avenue, rattling the windows of the venerable Chicago Club. There three men whose mood was as gray as the overcast were conferring in a private dining room. The host was Charles Herron, and his guests were Theodore Witherspoon and Richmond Cuthbert. The Illinois banker had summoned the Texas oil operator and the Michigan publisher to an emergency meeting. Subject: How could the kingmakers rectify their unholy mistake of a week earlier when they plucked Eddie Quinn from obscurity and set him down on the highway to infamy?

For while Eddie and his entourage might view recent developments with blithe and rising spirits, the kingmakers counted each passing day as one of bottomless menace in which their own handpicked candidate caromed back and forth between the four dark walls of folly, demagoguery, ingratitude and knavery. In short, the kingmakers were convinced that Eddie meant what he said about a "fair shake" for everybody—a goal which, if realized, might reduce the heirs of all three men to the status of millionaires or less, a condition they regarded as pauperdom. But what galled them more than the economic pistol Eddie held at their heads was the fact that, in the eyes of the nation and their business peers, they had been duped by a nobody of no fixed address. The kingmakers could look back on this calendar of horrors:

Thursday night. Eddie, newly nominated, assails elitists, executive suites, country-club barons, and promises a new reign of an ethnic proletariat named Quinn, Powansky, Schmidt, Palumbo, Korona, Damaskinos and Matousek.

Friday. Eddie raps old WASP families and rich men's clubs, vows to run the country for the benefit of workingmen, tavern drinkers, soldiers, sailors and "common people." He sharpens his threat by proposing a 30 per cent human-depletion allowance, also sinking the tax advantage on oil and other minerals and embracing the ominous principle of equality under the tax laws.

Saturday. Eddie says he'll confine the military draft to men over fifty if foreign nations will do likewise. This makes Eddie a hero of youth hostels around the world. Mexico City students parade, chanting "Viva Keen," and bouillabaisses of young men and women spill through the streets of Paris, London, Rome and Berlin. Quinn even inspires an abortive demonstration in Moscow. U.S. campuses ignite with pro-Quinn sentiment and polls show a shift away from Pinholster among eighteen-to-twenty-five-year-old voters. If Eddie intended his plan as a playful barb, youth ignores the play, hones the barb and shatters windows in a number of foreign office fortresses. In the bubbling aftermath, in a five-hour speech that runs past midnight in Havana before 200,000 people, the bearded Cuban Prime Minister hails Eddie's draft of *los viejos* and challenges the arthritic statesmen of the world to take Eddie up on it. He says it's the first sensible proposal made by an imperialist in fifteen years. Other monarchs and prime ministers, all past fifty, nervously label Eddie another American babe in the woods whose innocence will wreak irreparable harm on the planet.

Sunday. Eddie, in an exclusive interview with Vincent Anderson of the Associated Press, says he'll send a presidential "ambassador" to all 170,000 U.S. voting precincts and personally travel once a month to hear citizen complaints in the neighborhoods. He will also open his White House doors every Monday morning to hear the grievances of plain people. Jimmy the Greek drops the odds on Eddie from 9 to 1 to 6 to 1.

Monday. Motorcading toward Detroit, Eddie tells a shopping-center crowd outside Pittsburgh that when and if he's elected, a family's first child will rate the usual income tax exemption, but the second child will get no exemption, a third child will draw a $300 tax penalty, a fourth $400 and so on up the scale of taxable fecundity. Eddie says that each year he'll honor at the White House an "ideal" American family—father, mother and two children. When a heckler calls him a godless meddler, Eddie retorts he's running for President not Pope and adds that he'll establish federal birth-control clinics in every county with a bountiful supply of pills, loops, salves, dia-phragms and other boons to romance. Driving off, Eddie tells the heckler: "So long, pal. Make love, not kids."

Monday night. Eddie walks a mile of the Detroit black ghetto from ten to midnight despite the tremors of his Secret Service agents. He makes three "fair shake" talks at street corners, dodges a lemon, a tin can and record album. He hand-wrestles a friendly nineteen-year-old blood and raps with skeptical brothers in a Black Panther storefront. Eddie says he's for justice, order and law in that se-quence. His official escort, confined at first to Margot Hicks, his motel neighbor, George Dawson, and two local black pugilists, swells to several hundred whooping citizens who manage to protect Eddie by routing the white newspapermen and cracking one of R Dan Fenelli's ribs.

Tuesday. In his noon speech to the Detroit Economic Club, Eddie enrages the auto moguls by demanding they trim profits while hold-ing wages steady and boosting productivity to recapture motor markets from the "hungry" Japanese and Europeans. He pledges to tame the cannibalistic conglomerates, backs federal chartering of corporations with worker and consumer members on boards of di-rectors, and says he'll abolish the tax-deductible status of business entertaining.

Eddie says the auto worker has to pay for his own lunch while his boss's repast with a fellow executive is underwritten by the federal government, in the form of lost taxes, to the tune of three martinis, pâté de foie gras, soft-shell crabs à la Maryland, chef's salad with Roquefort dressing, chocolate mousse, brandy and cigars, in all $47.82, including tip. And that, says Eddie, makes "tax-deductible business entertaining the world's most lavish free lunch counter since the days of the old saloon." Newsmen note that several motor barons stalk from the room and that Pete Stackpole pales beneath the beads of perspiration on his forehead. They also note that all of that day's lunches, including Eddie's, are tax-deductible. Later Eddie mails a check for $6.75 to the club.

Tuesday night. In a speech to Cleveland's City Club, Eddie unveils his plan for "returning power to the ordinary people by use of our mightiest weapon—fair taxation." Eddie comes out for a progressive income tax with absolutely no deductions other than the 30 per cent human-depletion allowance open to everyone. He promises to abolish all privileged tax shelters, including that of capital gains, real estate depreciation, foundations, depletion allowances (other than human) and tax-exempt municipal and state bonds. Eddie says his "one tax for all, loopholes for none" program will permit lowering tax rates to a top bracket of 40 per cent or less. "Counting in his human depletion," says Eddie, "the man who rakes in a million a year could keep more than six hundred grand, enough to keep the wife in wigs and Chanel No. 5 and send the kids off to Yale and/or Vassar." Eddie says his simple income levy will enable the government to halve the number of Internal Revenue agents and "unleash 100,000 tax lawyers for some kind of productive work."

Cries of anguish echo through the nation's executive corridors. A chain-store president declares that Eddie is "striking at the foundations," presumably tax-exempt, "of the free-enterprise system." A steel company chairman says that "in the name of a spurious equality, Candidate Quinn would plunge the world's greatest industrial society into depression and chaos." Officials of the American Bar Association solemnly ponder a resolution of lament. The staff director of the Senate's internal security subcommittee dispatches two investigators to smoke out whether Eddie has hidden links with Maoists, Trotskyites or the Vietcong. *The Kingdom and the Power,* in a lead editorial, questions whether Eddie's "refreshing Populist stance is being gutted by naïve and reckless statements about the complex economic fabric of America."

Wednesday morning. Gallup Poll announces new figures, Pinholster 50, Quinn 37, uncertain 13, a gain for Eddie and a loss for Hugh over four days. Hutchens Boyington III, Pinholster's Harvard brain, entreats "liberals who seek real, attainable reform" of the system to beware of the nostrums and elixirs peddled by that patent medicine salesman from New Jersey. The Los Angeles *Times* reveals that Pinholster's private, daily telephone poll, conducted by expert Swensson, shows defection to Quinn by youth, ethnics and women. (The newspaper fails to report that Swensson bets another thousand dollars on Quinn at Jimmy the Greek's latest odds of 5 to 1.)

With this gloomy background, the mood of the three former kingmakers meeting in the Chicago Club that Wednesday was as sour as the taste of the tiny onions in their gibsons. Rich Cuthbert looked hung-over. Ted Witherspoon, fumbling with a black leather dispatch case beneath his chair, snapped at a waiter who offered to take the case to a checkroom. Charlie Herron, brooding as he watched a curtain of rain lash at the window of the private dining nook, shot his starched cuffs with the topaz links.

"What baffles me," mused the banker, "is where Quinn is getting his money. Now he's in Ohio, sashaying down some damn highway, with chartered buses, mimeograph machines, hotel bills, advance men. . . . God knows who's paying for it all. I cut him off Friday, but now I hear a rumor that he's got Detroit auto money. Can that be true, Rich?"

Cuthbert coupled his nod with a bored yawn. Herron wished the Michigan publisher weren't such a damn dilettante. Here they were, the laughingstocks of the financial world, and Cuthbert still seemed to regard the daylight hours, those ordered for commerce, as though they were a nuisance to be suffered through until dusk fell.

"It was true," said Cuthbert. "Billings lined up the Empire executives first and then began putting the lug on the whole auto crowd."

"But no matter what Quinn says about cars, Detroit's in trouble just like the rest of us," said Witherspoon. "Look at the way he shoved it to them at the Economic Club yesterday."

"Right," said Cuthbert. "I reached Billings from my hotel just a few minutes ago. Here's the story. After Quinn's big promotion for highways and cars at that Friday press conference, Billings called Pete Stackpole and promised to raise a million for him. Monday morning he deposited $200,000 to the Quinn campaign account, but he warned Stackpole that money was getting skittish because a lot of donors thought Quinn's blue-sky idea about drafting fifty-year-olds was nutty and irresponsible. Then Quinn goes to Detroit and demands lower auto profits and knocks business entertaining. Last night in Cleveland he says he'll end all tax deductions. That tied it. Billings reached Stackpole someplace in Ohio this morning and chewed his ass out. No more money, he said. The million pledge is off. So when Quinn runs through the $200,000, he's had it."

"Quinn screwed the motor crowd just like he did us," said Witherspoon. "The bastard's an ingrate."

"The worst of it is," said Herron, "that I'm being accused of recklessness for picking Quinn."

Ted Witherspoon and Rich Cuthbert indicated by rueful expressions that Herron was not alone in his plight. "Think about me," said Ted. "I'm taking double heat because my wife turned up as one of Quinn's so-called advisers."

"That I don't understand," said Rich. "How can you permit a fine woman like Kate to get mixed up with that demagogue?"

"You never heard of women's liberation? Besides, we're not exactly close any more."

"Oh?" Herron hesitated a moment, noted that Ted did not appear overly distressed, then said: "A man can always cut off the dollars."

"Forget it," said Ted glumly. "She has her own money from her father."

The waiter appeared with the menu and Herron wrote down the

orders. Cuthbert said that Quinn's attack on deductible business lunches such as this one reminded him of the story from World War II days. Three businessmen were lunching. A said he'd sign for the $15 check since the lunch would only cost his company $7.25 because of the high corporate tax bracket. B said no, he'd pay the tab because his company was paying an excess profits tax. Thus the lunch would cost the head office but $3.10. Hell, argued C, let him pick up the check. Since his company was on a cost-plus-fixed-fee war contract, it would make a buck and a half on the meal.

"Very funny, Rich," said Witherspoon. Neither he nor Herron so much as smiled politely.

"Let's get down to business," said Herron. "How can we fix this guy Quinn's wagon, but good?"

"Well, I've been doing some serious thinking," said Cuthbert as though this possibility might never have occurred to his friends. "Suppose the worst happens and through some freak break, Quinn wins the election. It won't happen, but just suppose. We ought to be prepared for the worst. . . . Well, I come up with the solution in one word." He paused. "Electors."

"Great minds, etc.," said Herron. He leaned forward and his eyelids lowered. "I've been on the same track."

"I see the possibilities," said Witherspoon. Outside oil and money, nothing so fired Ted Witherspoon's imagination as political intrigue.

For these men experienced in the rules of politics, the possibilities did not have to be spelled out. Under the Constitution, the Electoral College, not the voters, elects a President of the United States. On election day, the voters in each state ballot for a slate of electors pledged to a candidate. Later the winning slate votes for a President. Though bound by custom to a candidate, the electors legally can vote for anyone. Occasionally an elector breaks the traces and votes for a candidate other than the man who carried the popular vote in his state. Efforts to abolish or reform the Electoral College system have failed repeatedly in Congress.

Within the party, most electors were selected from the ranks of the faithful at the same time that delegates to the national con-

vention were picked. This year's electors had been named weeks
ago, all pledged to vote for the convention nominee. Alas, Senator
Hudson, the convention's choice, had been called to higher if less
definitive duties. Now only partisan allegiance bound the party's
electors to support Edward Nicholas Quinn, a man selected not in
convention, but by the national committee.

"You know damn well," said Cuthbert, "that plenty of the Quinn
electors are feeling just like we are today."

"And their moral obligation to support Quinn in case he wins
the popular vote is pretty thin," said Herron.

"Hell, it's nonexistent," said Witherspoon.

Cuthbert pulled a sheet of paper from his inner breast pocket
and donned black-rimmed reading glasses. "I had my secretary get
from the national committee a list of all our electors. I ran through
the names on the plane this morning. Outside Michigan, where I
know all of them, I found I knew a couple of dozen scattered
around the country." He tapped the paper. "For instance, in
Missouri, one elector is the biggest minority stockholder in my St.
Louis TV station. Name's Bob Schaffran. Good man, solid. We
understand each other." Cuthbert's quiet smile hinted at a rapport,
surpassing that of blood brothers, rooted in the common soil of
dividends and balance sheets.

Ted Witherspoon's reaction was quick, though his tone was as
ponderous as ever. "Great idea." He turned to Herron. "Charlie, we
ought to spot our friends on that list too. Then if worse comes to
worst, we can help them see the light."

Herron nodded. "I'm with you. We ought to be prepared. No good
in a landslide, of course, but if Quinn won a close one, we probably
could finger enough electors to throw the election to Pinholster."

The men fell silent, each brooding in his own way over the
ignominy of plotting to defeat the very man that they, in a late,
sleepless hour of colossally defective judgment, had foisted on the
national committee. That the beneficiary of their scheme would be
Hugh Pinholster, a man they rated as an erratic lightweight who
toyed with hazardous reformist notions, only deepened their dolor.

"Frankly, I'm not worried about a Quinn victory." Herron turned his gaze from the streaming window which rattled under the on-slaught of the rain. "He's gained some, sure, but most voters on election day just won't buy a wild man like him. Hell, the same people he attracts with his 'soak-the-rich' gambit are put off by his anti-baby pitch and that crap about drafting men over fifty."

The banker paused while he forked up another slice of his Quiche Lorraine. "The real damage being done is Quinn's campaign itself. Every time he comes up with another simplistic idea that has popular appeal, it tends to push Pinholster and a lot of congressional candidates further to the left. Christ, did you see what Shelby Ewing said yesterday?"

The party's vice-presidential candidate, touring California with the well-financed congressional task force, told newsmen that while he could not endorse Quinn's wholesale attack on the tax laws, he did favor "a careful scrutiny of certain tax shelters to determine whether they contribute to the nation's productivity."

"It was fairly mild stuff," said Cuthbert. "It doesn't commit him to anything really."

"That's not the point, Rich," countered Herron. "Shelby's rock-ribbed. You know that. And when even he goes that far, it shows the impact Quinn is having."

Witherspoon, agreeing, recounted suspiciously egalitarian remarks made by several conservative candidates in Texas. Cuthbert conceded the appearance of a few telltale spots on the otherwise healthy epidermis of the party in Michigan.

"It's like smallpox," said Herron. "Pandering for votes that way is contagious. Before you know it, you've got a goddamn epidemic under way. Electing that pinko Pinholster is bad enough, but if the country returns a Congress that's infected with Quinn's disease, brother, watch out!"

"Quinn's got thirteen more days to babble." Cuthbert frowned. "Question is, how do we shut him up? Even if he runs out of money, he can still talk to the press and TV every hour on the hour."

"Every man's vulnerable," argued Herron. "Ordinarily, I don't go for personal snooping, but this is an emergency. I think we ought to hire the best private detective outfit in the country and have it dig up everything possible on Quinn."

"For once I'm ahead of you, Charlie." Witherspoon's glance was one of pride. "I've got a little present here for you."

The oil man reached under his chair and pulled the black leather dispatch case to his lap. He snapped it open and withdrew three sheafs of flimsy green paper. He passed a copy to each of his accomplices.

"I hired the Blue Star Agency here in Chicago on Monday." His brisk, efficient tone waived all compliments to his foresight. "Steve Kipke's the best in the business. It's costing me twenty-four hundred a day, but it's worth it. Steve put ten men on the assignment. . . . This is the first report. Hereafter, I'm to get one a day by phone. Just run through this stuff."

The trio began reading through four pages of closely typed material. Herron sipped nervously at his coffee as his eyes sped through the text. Witherspoon made marginal notes with a pencil.

"God, this isn't just Quinn," said Herron with some awe. "It's his wife, sons, mother and everybody on his campaign staff."

"Right." Witherspoon spoke without lifting his eyes from the page. "I figured time is short and we ought to come up with maximum firepower. Of course, I hope that after reading this, you'll split the cost with me."

"Okay," agreed Herron. "Bill me for a third," said Cuthbert.

"I deleted some material on my wife," added Witherspoon. "Nothing pertinent, really. I hope you don't mind."

Herron and Cuthbert gallantly disavowed any interest in Kate Witherspoon and Cuthbert even hastily turned over the last page to make sure nothing derogatory to the congresswoman remained on the record.

"It looks like Stackpole's in trouble," noted Herron. He pointed to a paragraph on the campaign manager.

Stackpole, Peter D. Heavily in debt after buying oil stocks on margin. Was assured of $200,000 fee from syndicate seeking race track charter in north Jersey, but legislature has failed to act. Borrowed against expected fee from Essex Mercantile Bank in Newark. Has $75,000 signature loan at favored 5.5 per cent. Stackpole in arrears on interest payments.

"We do business with Essex Mercantile," said Herron. "I'll check the list of officers. . . . An interesting item on Quinn, but not very useful." .

Quinn, Edward N. A Turnpike subordinate of Quinn, Jack R. McGowan of Plainfield, N.J., says that on July 17 at 3 A.M., while a passenger in Impala sedan driven by Quinn, stopped by state policeman on New Jersey Turnpike. Trooper clocked Quinn at 93 miles an hour, says McGowan, but released him without charge when Quinn showed credentials as Turnpike commissioner.

Police files Metuchen, N.J., show two citations under Quinn, Edward N. Subject at age 14 arrested with three other white male juveniles on vandalism charge. Subject released in custody of parents. At age 18 subject among patrons of house of prostitution when raided by police. No charges.

"That kid stuff is worthless," said Cuthbert, "and who's going to get excited over speeding?"

"Nobody," agreed Witherpsoon, "but remember, Kipke's only had his men working on this for two days. . . . But read that part with the asterisk. Promising, huh?"

The three men scanned a section on the last page.

*Quinn, Alfred E., 24, son of Edward N. Quinn. Manager of bowling alley, Long Lanes, on Division Street, Chicago. Young Quinn and wife, Irene, 25, are subscribers to underground magazine, *Sincere Swingers,* and hold Box 103 at said publication. Classified ad in June issue read: "Wanted: Inventive under-30 couples, white or black, for eightsome week-ends at apartment of exploring mates. Ideal for those with interest in visual arts. Films. Polaroid stills. No leather. Write Buck & Doe, Box 103." A classified ad in same publication, August issue, read: "Attention Puss & Boots. Do you still want full-reel negative of big July eightsome action? Our library over-stocked. Reply, Buck & Doe, Box 103."

Puss & Boots, holders of Box 28 at *Sincere Swingers,* identified as Connie Rivers, 26, black stenographer, and Elroy Kimble, white insurance adjuster, 27. Interviewed Kimble for $100. Kimble says he and Miss Rivers share interest in "extending human sexual frontiers." For additional $75, viewed reel of July eightsome action on Kimble's projector, but frames involving "Buck & Doe" have been excised. Kimble vague about disposition of said frames. Mentioned that "Buck's" father thought to be prominent public figure and suspects that negative with said frames quite valuable. Swinger code strict about selling visual arts to straights, but Kimble furtive type who needs money.

(Note to client from S.K.: Involvement of Alfred Quinn and wife Irene in sexual orgies is beyond doubt, but also beyond proof unless the negative can be obtained. Our belief is that Kimble already has sold negative to unknown parties and that he will not disclose identity of buyer except at considerable price. Please instruct.)

"Let's get it," said Herron.

"No, Charlie. Leave it alone." Rich Cuthbert looked uneasy. "That's seamy business going after a father because his son is romping around in group sex. Besides, what would we do with the film? Give it an X rating and show it in first-run houses?"

"Think of the leverage we'd have on Quinn," insisted Witherspoon. "Put yourself in Quinn's place when he's told about the negative. Wouldn't you be willing to trade for the film—say take it easy on the tax bit?"

"Maybe. But if I know Eddie, he'd bust the blackmailer in the mouth first. And I wouldn't blame him."

"But he'd have to deal with us," said Herron. "Almost any father would, especially one running for President. . . . Damn it, Rich, I want to nail this bastard to the wall."

"We could be playing for bigger stakes than you think, Rich," said Witherspoon. "Charlie's right about the possibility of a soak-the-rich epidemic. I hate to say it, after helping to nominate him, but Eddie Quinn could turn out to be one of the most dangerous politicians of the century."

"Okay, tell Kipke to go ahead then," said Cuthbert. He dipped into the finger bowl and dried his fingers with his napkin. "But keep my name the hell out of it, Ted. Publishing isn't the same business as oil."

"Don't worry," said Witherspoon. "We don't have to confront Quinn at Broadway and Forty-second at high noon. There are ways."

Cuthbert fussed with the table silver. "Say, why don't we hire some hecklers to dog Quinn's motorcade?"

"Good idea," Herron agreed. "But reverse it. What about getting some crazies, a bunch of far-out kids, to mix with Quinn's crowds and pretend they're supporters."

"That I like," said Ted. "The kind of kids who'll offend the very people Quinn's trying to reach. Listen. How about this? Suppose . . ."

They plotted for another ten minutes, and when they left the club separately at intervals, the three men bore themselves with dignity, confident they had served society well. They had isolated the common threat, committed family treasure to the defense of the commonweal and were preparing, with only modest attention to personal peril, to meet the barbarian at the gates.

Eddie Quinn got the word about the sudden dropout of the automobile industry contributions shortly after arriving in Washington Court House, a town celebrated in political footnotes as that in which Harry M. Daugherty, Attorney General in the Harding administration, destroyed incriminating bank records during the Teapot Dome scandals. Pete Stackpole delayed informing the candidate about the radical change of heart by the motor executives for fear of further inflaming Eddie's already fiery oratory on the normally dreary subject of taxation. Now Pete told Eddie as he sauntered out of Bray's corner news store after buying a paper and possibly grossing five votes by shaking hands with the owner and four customers.

"You had to expect it, Eddie, after your blast at the Economic Club," said Pete, "unless you don't realize yet who makes the big contributions and why."

"I know how the game's played." Eddie showed no great concern. He plowed along the sidewalk, nodding to pedestrians and waving to motorists. "How much longer can we run on the two hundred grand, Pete?"

"Maybe a week like this. That campaign staff back in Washington costs like hell."

"Well, let's see what we can do about it." Eddie crossed the main street and headed for the Fayette County courthouse where a bunting-draped wooden platform, hastily arranged by an advance man, awaited him. To the surprise of Eddie and the troop of staffers, journalists, photographers and nondescript camp followers tagging along behind him, a crowd of perhaps fifteen hundred people had gathered beneath coppery foliage on the courthouse square. Eddie's audiences had been growing perceptibly each day.

The mayor and county chairman welcomed him, but the local congressman, a conservative member of the House Ways and Means Committee, had developed urgent family business in Columbus when informed Eddie would traverse his district.

On the platform, situated near a German 104-mm. gun captured in World War I, Eddie breathed deeply of the clear air. He stood bareheaded under the noon sun and the cobalt sky laced with scudding clouds. It was a time of pumpkins, first chimney smoke, wool sweaters and rosy cheeks.

"I come to Washington Court House with hat in hand," said the hatless candidate after the introductions. His breath misted and drifted away. "I need money—and who doesn't, you may say? Now before you zip up your wallets and hurry back to work, let me tell you a personal story that reveals some of the political facts of life in this country.

"In Chicago, Illinois, there is a very wealthy and influential banker named Charles Herron. He is one of the so-called kingmakers who selected me for the nomination last Thursday morning in Houston. He's also national finance chairman of our party. So you can see he's a man with a lot of clout."

Eddie described his confrontations with Herron over campaign funds in exhaustive detail, including Herron's grudging allotment of $1,100,000 to Eddie on the night plane from Houston to Washington, his angry cancellation of all funds the next day and his threat to deprive Eddie of resources for lesser campaigns—such as dog-catcher —in the future should Eddie disclose the facts. Eddie then recounted the sudden opening and equally sudden closing of the money tap by

Empire Motors' officials. Eddie's ire swelled as he listened to himself describe the iniquities visited on him by the money men. When he reached the climactic perfidy of Billings' phone call to Stackpole this morning, Eddie surprised himself by smiting the lectern so hard that a tack came loose and the red-white-and-blue bunting fell away as if stunned by such malevolence among the lords of finance and industry.

"These are the kind of men who have been running this nation for their own selfish interests," Eddie cried. Anger put a tomato flush on his cheeks and he felt his fluids pumping swiftly through the valves and filters of his heating system. "They don't care about you and me. They don't care about ordinary people. They don't care about the United States of America. All they care about is their own private interests and the terrible power that big money brings to men."

His listeners were attentive now and Eddie could see that sparks from his scattered fire kindled little flames here and there. "These men are cold-blooded and cynical. They want a candidate who's bought and paid for. If a candidate speaks up for a fair shake for everybody, they snap their checkbooks shut and turn their backs on him. Like old Vanderbilt back in the eighteen-eighties, they say the public be damned." Eddie sped along, ticking off villainy after villainy like mileposts on some thruway of avarice.

"So here I am in Washington Court House, broke. My friends, I need money, not big money, but five dollars, two dollars, one dollar from good, concerned people like you. I can guess what you're thinking. Why should I give my hard-earned dollars to this man who has no chance of being elected? But, my friends, that's not true. I'm coming up in the polls and we've got thirteen big days left before the election, thirteen long days and nights to carry the message to the American people—a fair shake for everybody and no more sucker government of the wealthy, by the wealthy and for the wealthy."

Eddie paused, breathing hard, and looked around for his staff. "Kate . . . R Danny . . . Teegee . . . Margot. Grab a hat or shopping bag and circulate out there while the voters of Washington

Court House give their dollars to the first real people's campaign of this century."

Caught unaware, the campaign assistants hesitated. Then Kate Witherspoon, chic in modish fall coat with lynx collar and cuffs, lifted Hunk Janiszewksi's worn felt hat off his head and stepped into the crowd. R Dan Fenelli removed his short-visored cap and held it out to those nearest him. Teegee Churchill emptied the contents of her macramé bag into a pocket of her corduroy jacket and began circulating. Soon all the Quinn staffers, toting a variety of receptacles, were moving through the throng.

Eddie kept up a running patter. "No hundred-dollar bills, folks, are necessary. Ten is wonderful, five is great and for a one-buck picture of George Washington, God bless you. . . . Help me buy just one-half hour on national television so I can tell the whole country what you've just heard. . . . If you'd rather do it by check, send it to the Eddie Quinn Campaign, 1140 Connecticut Avenue, Washington, D.C. . . . We've got the national press with us here, folks, and let's see if they carry the story of old banker-bandit Charlie Herron to everybody from Maine to California. Let's see if they tell the people the truth, that the big-money crowd has yanked the rug from under Eddie Quinn and that we need contributions from all the plain people who, like me, are fed to the teeth with being ordered around and deprived of a fair shake by the country-club set, the fancy expense-account executives, the private plane-and-yacht crowd and the slick oil-and-gas gang who pay less in taxes because you people here in Washington Court House pay more, way more, than your share. Now . . ."

"Settle for two bits, Eddie?" yelled a rough voice. That fetched a friendly laugh.

"Thank you for two bits," Eddie replied. "We'll take nickels and dimes. As a matter of fact, if you think I'm not worth two cents then just drop a penny in the hat. I promise you this, fellow Americans. Whatever you invest in Eddie Quinn, it will be one of the soundest buys of your life because, if I'm elected, we're going to have a fair shake—and that means a thirty per cent human-depletion allowance for every single taxpayer, share and share alike."

He shot his right arm up and out in his favorite campaign gesture.

With thrusting palm and spread fingers, it became the leader's appeal for an advance toward the lush valleys of brighter tomorrows.

As Teegee worked her way over the courthouse lawn, a heavy-set man in work boots and old army jacket said, "Here's a penny for your thoughts." He dropped the coin, then let a five-dollar bill flutter into her bag. "A fin for Quinn," he added.

"A fin for Quinn!" Teegee shouted toward the platform.

"That's right, friends," said Eddie. "If every working man and woman in the country sends a fin for Quinn to campaign headquarters, 1140 Connecticut Avenue, Washington, D.C., we'll chase that rich, special-interest gang down to Brazil, where they belong."

When the crowd began to disperse and Eddie made his adieus to local dignitaries, Phil Liccardo advised that they lunch in town to afford newspapermen time to write and dispatch their stories and let TV crews hire a pool car to drive video tapes to network outlets in Cincinnati. Eddie lunched in Bryant's Restaurant ("Home of Good Roast Beef"), ordering his usual ham-and-cheese on rye, while Pete Stackpole and Kate Witherspoon counted the campaign loot in an office of the First National Bank of Washington Court House.

An hour later the caravan rolled out of town on Route 22, headed for the next speaking stop in Wilmington. Eddie sat with Stackpole in the rear of the Electra 225 while Oscar Baker drove with Flannery beside him. A canvas money bag of the First National Bank rested on the floor between Stackpole's feet.

"How much, Pete?" Eddie was watching the rusty landscape, neat, open fields, corn shocks, patches of flaming woodland and the black soil of southern Ohio.

"A damn good haul for your first pitch in a town that size. Twelve thousand plus."

"You've got to be kidding."

"Well, yeah, partially. To be exact, you collected $2,207.10 from Washington Court House, including five bucks from the bank teller who supervised the counting."

"I thought you said twelve something."

"I did." Stackpole reached into his breast pocket, withdrew his wallet and handed a folded slip to Eddie.

It was a personal check on the Republic National Bank of Dallas, Texas, bearing the printed legend, "Theodore or Katherine Witherspoon, Highland Park, Tex." It was dated October 20, made out to the Eddie Quinn Campaign in the amount of ten thousand dollars and signed by Katherine Witherspoon in a firm, looping script.

"That's a joint account." Eddie felt strangely unsettled.

"It sure as hell is," said Pete, "and I'd like to see Ted's face when the canceled check shows up next month."

"I'll thank her at the next stop." But Eddie felt less gratitude than a sense of somehow diminishing in size. Perhaps if she had given fifty dollars, but ten thousand dollars!

"Please don't say anything to her, Eddie. Kate didn't want me to tell you, but I just couldn't hold it."

"Oh." For some reason he could not fully analyze, this piece of information restored his emotional balance. Kate had signed herself into a fiscal duel with her husband, but had taken pains not to place Eddie under obligation by informing him. She would not play Lady Bountiful handing out goodies to the needy.

"Ten grand and not deductible," said Pete respectfully. "Hell, she'll even have to pay a gift tax on it—or Ted will." The thought of Ted Witherspoon paying the government for the privilege of financing Eddie's attacks on all the nation's Witherspoons appealed to Stackpole's sense of irony. He dug Eddie with his elbow.

"You know something, Eddie? I find I don't miss Ted and Charlie and the rest of those characters a bit. I've been feeding on their crumbs for twenty years. This is one campaign I'm really beginning to enjoy."

"You and me both." But as Eddie stared at the back of Jim Flannery's head, he was reminded of a cabin on the Potomac under a misted quarter-moon. It was good to fight back at the men who picked him, then dumped him, but it was even better to recall Kate, full and yielding, in his arms. What made this a fine campaign was the fact that Kate Witherspoon was aboard.

11

Cresting the snowy linen, half grapefruits nestled in the ice of silver-rimmed glass bowls, hammered warming lids covered the scrambled eggs, butter oozed from English muffins and wisps of steam toiled off the coffee cups. Eddie grinned at Pete Stackpole across the breakfast table the room-service waiter had wheeled into the suite.

"If we can't go first class, we won't go. Right, Pete?"

Thursday, the twelfth day before the election, was beginning with a touch of luxury, for even a people's candidate deserved occasional sybaritic respite from the rigors of the campaign trail. Eddie found his in the Netherland Hilton Hotel in Cincinnati after a rousing night speech to six thousand people who cheered his "fair shake" doctrine as one worthy of trial, at long last, in the great egalitarian republic. He had visited Kate Witherspoon for several hours in her room down the hall, had slept deeply and was now ready and eager to carry the fray once again to the bastions of privilege. At the same time Eddie was conscious of a tender glow unrelated to his anticipation for battle.

"Pete, how many times you been really involved with a woman?"

"That's a helluva question to ask at seven-thirty in the morning." Pete scooped out a neatly severed segment of grapefruit.

The phone, resting on the table at the end of a long, white extension cord, shrilled at Pete's elbow. He answered. "Stackpole. . . . Okay, I'll wait." He explained to Eddie. "For me. Bishop at the White House. It's got to be trouble."

Russell Bishop served as the President's hangman. His noose slipped over the necks of those who reviled presidential policy, misinterpreted orders or merely said something that irked the chief executive. Bishop was a purulent little man, obsequious to those in favor and poisonous to those who were not.

"Hello, Russell. That's all right. We've been up for half an hour." Pete tapped a fork on the table as he listened. "Now, just a minute. You're blowing that all out of proportion. Hell, no, we're not going to apologize. . . . Okay, you do that. Who cares? . . . Listen, Russell, that would come with a lot more grace if the President had endorsed Eddie. As it is, we don't owe him a goddamn thing. And you can quote that in full when you call in the press for your knifing act. One other thing. You tell the man that the next time he has something to say to us, he can call Commissioner Quinn in person." Pete crashed the receiver back on its cradle.

"God, I'd like to give that guy a good kick in the ass. Brazil!"

"What about Brazil?" Eddie asked.

"Remember yesterday in Washington Court House, you said something about chasing the special interests down to Brazil? Well, I guess the wire services carried the story to Latin America. Last night the Brazilian ambassador complained to the White House. Bishop says the President wants you to apologize. You heard what I told him."

"Why the hassle? Everybody knows the big con men used to take it on the lam to Brazil."

"Of course, Eddie. It doesn't amount to a piss in a hurricane. The White House just wants an excuse to slap you in public. Forget it."

"I already have."

Nevertheless candidate and manager spent five minutes trading blackened views of various White House henchmen, thus recharging their spiritual batteries for a combative morning of motorcading to Indianapolis along Interstate 74.

While they finished breakfast, Stackpole skimmed the front page of the Cincinnati *Enquirer* and read the two-column story about Eddie's speech and his fin-for-Quinn appeal.

"Eddie," asked Stackpole suddenly, "have you got something going with Kate Witherspoon?"

Eddie carefully set down his coffee cup. "What makes you ask that?"

"Well, you asked me about affairs before breakfast. And the usual signs. The way she talks to you. Private smiles. You know. Very chummy stuff."

"I like her, Pete. She's a smart one."

"I'm not talking about her brain. Look, Eddie, it's your own business. I'm just interested, that's all."

"Don't worry, Pete. I'm minding the big store."

Descending in the elevator, pondering a weather forecast of rain and still simmering over the Bishop call, Stackpole had a premonition that this might be one of those days. The scene in the lobby confirmed his hunch. A dozen enraged journalists surrounded Phil Liccardo. Those who weren't shouting were talking simultaneously. The publicity chief, resplendent in a hot pink shirt that matched his rising color, struggled to maintain a calm that threatened to shatter any moment.

Stackpole heard ricochets of the volley directed at Liccardo. ". . . worst campaign lash-up since Adlai's in '56 . . . next time you say bags in the lobby at six-thirty A.M, we're going to lynch you. . . . why weren't you down to watch the goddamn operation?" To Stackpole's trained ear, the abuse indicated that the press corps had been inconvenienced in some dark manner relating to luggage. Nothing so offends the sensibilities of campaigning journalists as a threat to personal comfort. Governments may totter, candidates face inglorious defeat, currencies tremble and soup companies race frantically after vanished cans tainted by lethal botulin, but if the newspaperman finds himself properly housed, wined, dined and transported, he will survey civilization's collapsing pillars with equanimity. What inspires him to a demonic theory of current events is having to sleep in a hotel sample room or being forced to lunch at a highway truck stop.

Stackpole pieced the crisis together from several highly willing sources, including Sybil Jamieson, the television celebrity, who demanded that Liccardo either be fired or banished to the Soviet Union as an Intourist guide. It seemed that the newsmen, by Liccardo's decree, had staggered down to the lobby with their

luggage at 6:30 A.M. so that the bags could be stowed away in
the buses preparatory to a smooth take-off of the motorcade at
7:50. Having lost an hour of precious sleep, the corps but recently
discovered that the luggage had been loaded in the wrong vehicle, a
monster bus chartered by a Buffalo chapter of the Eastern Star.
Jammed with aggressively carefree matrons, this bus was en route
south for visits to Abraham Lincoln's Kentucky birthplace and to
Andy Jackson's Hermitage in Tennessee. A police squad car, dispatched to overtake the vehicle, had intercepted it in Covington,
Kentucky, and led it back across the Ohio River bridge to the hotel.
The transport was now disgorging its innocently hijacked cargo. The
Quinn caravan would be delayed a half-hour unless, as Miss
Jamieson acidly pointed out, some Eastern Star satchels mistakenly
found their way into a Quinn bus, in which case she would vote
twice for Pinholster.

When Eddie's caravan finally rolled away from the hotel at
8:25 A.M., snappish tempers gave way to grousing. The muffled sky
shed a steady drizzle and radio weather reports predicted day-long
rains throughout the Midwest. The cars and buses toiled slowly
through Cincinnati streets, not alone because of slippery pavements
but because the promised police escort did not materialize. No one
knew the reason, but all hands assumed that the mayor's unfettered
support for Pinholster had something to do with it. Then, no sooner
did the motorcade hit Interstate 74 and start picking up speed than
a taxicab sped by with blaring horn and slowed down directly in
front of the lead Secret Service car. Hands waved wildly from
windows of the cab. The caravan braked to a halt and out of the
taxi tumbled Teegee Churchill and a tall Viking, the communications expert on loan from the Bell System. Teegee ran through the
rain with a flight bag over one shoulder and her macramé creation
over the other. The specialist lurched behind toting bags in each
hand. They climbed aboard a staff car and the motorcade moved
off again. Later, word spread that Teegee and the Viking had
overslept, although it was unclear whether they had accomplished
the feat together or coincidentally.

In the Buick Electra 225 Jim Flannery tuned the radio to an
all-news station at Eddie's request as they sped through the wet,

rolling hills of southern Indiana. The car's sleek interior was soon awash in the daily tides of world disaster. First came the depressing bulletins and chronicles from the yellow, black, white and brown capitals of erring statecraft, then news of misfortunes along the home front.

"And from Washington, D.C.," said an announcer, "more politics. Hutchens Boyington III, Harvard anthropologist and a top adviser to Hugh Pinholster, said in a speech last night that Candidate Edward N. Quinn 'must be losing ten thousand brain cells an hour.'

"This was an allusion to Quinn's press conference last week when the presidential aspirant said in presenting his human-depletion allowance, that human beings in middle age lose ten thousand brain cells a day.

"Boyington made the remark in criticizing Quinn's plan for ending tax deductions for charitable contributions, a plan Boyington said would destroy the nation's great private universities within a year and 'usher in a Dark Age for American higher education.'"

Eddie grunted his displeasure. "Boyington's an uptown con man. He knows damn well that when the tax rate goes way down after the loopholes are closed, a taxpayer can give his college just as much without it costing him any more."

Stackpole's mind was not on economics. "Boyington loves to kick a candidate who's not going anywhere. Makes him look good when the votes are in."

Rain streaked the car windows as the radio sprayed more bad news.

"In New York," said the announcer, "a coalition of black leaders today denounced Candidate Edward Quinn, terming his 'fair shake for all' program 'a worse shake than ever for black people.'

"The fifteen-member group rapped Quinn for his stand on busing, for his 'baby tax,' for putting white ethnic groups ahead of blacks, Chicanos and Puerto Ricans in his campaign priorities and for 'false hopes' aroused by Quinn in a speech on welfare last night in Cincinnati.

"Quinn told a Cincinnati audience that greatly reduced federal taxes would permit cities to raise more revenue locally and to lure industry back into the cities via tax benefits. He pledged to get the federal government out of the welfare business within four years, but admitted that as of now he did not know how to do it.

"And this report just in from Washington, D.C. The White House has apologized to the government of Brazil for Candidate Eddie Quinn's remark yesterday that if elected he would 'chase that rich, special-interest gang down to Brazil where they belong.'

"A White House spokesman said that offhand comments made by candidates in the heat of a presidential campaign rarely reflect the policy of the U.S. government and that in this case, the White House 'deeply regrets the aspersion.'

"When asked if the U.S. was apologizing for the meaning of the remark or its grammar, the spokesman said the White House had no control over the syntax of presidential aspirants."

Stackpole snorted. "That's a snide crack. It had to be Bishop."

"Sounds like nobody loves us today, Pete." Eddie gazed through the misted windows at brown hillside fields where water gullied the furrows. After a time Stackpole turned to the crossword puzzle in the morning paper and Eddie began jotting in a note pad.

Despite the rain, several hundred people turned out in umbrellas and raincoats to hear Quinn at the first stop, the small Indiana town of Batesville. Eddie, bareheaded and wearing a black slicker, led his troops from the caravan to the town square which had been turned into a combination parking lot and shopping center. Liccardo and Fenelli placed a portable lectern in front of a Kroger grocery and Eddie took his place, facing the parking lot and, across the street, the Batesville Roller Mills ("Definite Feeds for Definite Needs"). To his right the First Bank & Trust Co. provided free information on temperature and time via a blinking sign: forty-two degrees, 10:10 A.M.

"Lots of money in this town," whispered Liccardo in a last-minute briefing. "Factories make household and hospital furniture and caskets."

"All your definite needs, cradle to the grave, huh?" Eddie gripped the lectern and pondered his opening.

At that moment two battered Volkswagen buses swerved into the parking area with a noisy thrashing of gears. Out poured a weird assortment of young people, the men swampy with hair and the women clad in varying styles from scissored, crotch-length blue jeans to quilted skirts that swirled about the ankles. Two men in head-bands and pigtails were bare to the waist. Several women sloshed about barefoot and none wore brassieres. Their one common at-tribute was dirt. Their clothes were long unwashed and their faces unscrubbed. The newcomers carried plastic, all-weather signs bearing such legends as "A Fin for Quinn," "Unisex Tribe Loves Eddie," "Make Love, Not Kids," "Help Eddie Make Amerika Over," "Draft Grandpa," "Gays for Quinn," "Up the Pentagon" and "Satan, Jesus and Quinn."

The two dozen tribesmen fanned along the fringes of the crowd and began shouting encouragement. "Give 'em hell, Eddie. . . . Power to the people! . . . Run the pigs out of Washington."

Most of the crowd turned to watch the demonstrators. Some townspeople glowered at the newcomers, then looked questioningly at Eddie. A rumble of disapproval swept through the rain-pelted gathering and several sign-carriers were jostled. Eddie noted that the Volkswagen buses bore Pennsylvania license plates.

"Those hippies with you?" asked an elderly man in front of Eddie.

Eddie shook his head. He fumbled for an opening line, then shouted: "People of Batesburg" He could feel the sting of rain on his face.

Jim Flannery, at his side, whispered: "Batesville."

"Good people of Batesville," said Eddie quickly. "Pardon that slip. Blame it on this Pennsylvania weather they've sent over to Indiana. We got off on the wrong foot this morning and I apologize not only for being forty minutes late but for demoting the good, progressive city of Batesville to a burg. . . . I see that we have some young visitors with us this morning."

The tribesmen waved their signs as if on cue. "Tell 'em why we love you, Eddie," one yelled.

"I don't know who these young people are," said Eddie. "They're not traveling with us. However, this is a people's crusade, aimed at a fair shake for all Americans, and we welcome everyone who wants to sweep the old establishment, country-club, front-office crowd out of the seats of power. And I mean everyone, young or old, man or woman, white or black, worker or dropout." He wanted to add "clean or dirty," but let it pass unspoken.

The intruders cheered, but only limp applause came from the Batesville citizenry. Eddie hurried through his pitch, compressing his now familiar litany of upper-crust wickedness into less than five minutes. The townspeople listened attentively enough, but when the staff began to pass the hat, the tribesmen strafed Eddie's huckster patter with cacophonous appeals of their own. Worse, three unkempt characters joined the staff and wandered about holding out tin cups. One held a tambourine in one hand and his sign in the other. In the general confusion, which Eddie's spiel failed to dispel, the collection grossed only a few dollars. The crowd dissolved, people hurrying off to seek shelter from the rain.

Stackpole joined Eddie. "It's a plant."

"I know it." Eddie beckoned to Teegee Churchill. She was standing nearby, looking glumly at the two one-dollar bills she had collected. Raindrops trickled off her chin and her long blond hair hung like wet twine.

"Look, Teegee, we suspect these kids are a frame of some kind," said Eddie. "They probably plan to tail us from now on. You hop a ride in one of their buses and find out the score. Then report to me at the next stop, okay?"

"Right." Teegee handed her bills to Stackpole and splashed off toward the Volkswagens. The gypsies were stowing their signs in racks atop the buses and clambering aboard. They ignored a cluster of newsmen attempting to question them.

The motorcade, spraying water, moved back to Interstate 74 and rolled toward the next stop, Greensburg, sixteen miles away. In the Electra 225 Stackpole and Eddie shed their raincoats. Stackpole sneezed, then cursed.

"Greensburg, Greensburg," Eddie rehearsed. "Batesville, Greensburg."

"For Christ's sake, don't do that, Eddie. You'll just get fouled up again."

"Nope. I'll get it straight. Stinking weather, Pete. What's your guess on those drag-ass kids?"

"Bought and paid for. Only question is who did the buying for

Pinholster. Not a bad ploy." Pete spoke with a touch of professional respect. "It's hard to disown somebody who says he's for you. They hexed us but good in Batesburg. Goddamn it, now you've got me saying it. Batesville."

"If we can't shake them, they'll murder us right across Indiana. Explaining doesn't work when people see those oddballs waving their signs and cheering for me."

"Leave 'em to me. I'll handle it somehow. . . . Jim, how about some more news? Let's hear what Pinholster is saying."

Flannery again tuned in the all-news station and the river of human misadventure, flowing as inexorably as a Congo or an Amazon, merged with the drizzle falling on the expressway and flowing rhythmically off the car's windshield wipers.

"Here's an interesting item from Los Angeles," said the announcer in the bright tone affected by couriers of ill tidings. "A newly formed organization of lawyers, named Concerned Attorneys for Pinholster, has accused Candidate Edward Quinn of 'gratuitously insulting' a large segment of the legal profession.

"The committee, spearheaded by Douglas R. Whipple of the prominent Los Angeles firm of Whipple, Bernbaum and Fogarty, contends that Quinn, in a Tuesday night speech in Cleveland, sought to humiliate 'thousands of hard-working members of the bar who are guilty of nothing more heinous than earning an honest living.'

"Quinn told the Cleveland City Club that if his progressive income tax, without any deductions save a 'human-depletion allowance,' were enacted, it would 'unleash 100,000 tax lawyers for some kind of productive work.'

"The implication that tax attorneys are parasites, said the committee, demeans a body of men who have 'made great contributions to society, not only professionally, but as citizens through a wide variety of civic and charitable organizations.' End item."

"Let 'em talk," said Eddie. "The fact is that if we had simple revenue laws, people wouldn't need a tax lawyer. They could figure it out themselves."

"You're telling me," said Pete. "I spent enough time around state legislatures and Congress to know that every time a new tax bill passes, with all the whereases, ifs and buts, they create work for another thousand lawyers."

"I know what you mean, Mr. Stackpole," said Flannery from the front seat. "When my mother-in-law died, she left us six or seven thousand dollars. The lawyers got a third of it before the case was settled."

"Hey, Jim," said Eddie. "You a Quinn man?"

"Sure am, Eddie. And I'll tell you something just between us. I talked to the Pinholster detail last night, and all six of the regulars are voting for you. They say you may not have all the answers, but you're raising the right questions and laying them on the line."

"Add six Secret Service votes," said Stackpole, "and subtract about three hundred in Batesville. Who said what you lose on the merry-go-round you make up on the ferris wheel? It doesn't work out that way."

They turned off on a ramp and drove south to the town of Greensburg, where a weathered aspen grew quixotically out of the clock tower of the Decatur County Courthouse. An advance man had placed the portable lectern at the head of the courthouse's western steps. About five hundred people stood beneath the dripping trees on the courthouse square as Eddie took his stand facing the Bi-N-Save discount store, Hunter Pharmacy, Holthouse Furniture and Minear's ("Since 1865") clothing store.

No sooner did Eddie uncork his oratory than the Volkswagen buses drove up. The motley crew, looking even more disheveled, leaped out, grabbed their signs and fanned through the crowd, hopping, jigging and chanting Eddie's praises. While Eddie fought to retain the attention of the citizenry, Stackpole conferred with Teegee near one of the Volkswagens, parked on the other side of the square near Kirby's Beauty Salon.

"What's the story, Teegee?" Pete sneezed again. The rain had slackened, but the temperature was dropping and the dank air had a chill cut to it. All of Greensburg dripped.

"They're really nice kids," she said, "And they're for Eddie too—in their way. They have a commune near Beaver Falls, Pennsylvania, and yesterday some character who said he worked for Eddie asked them to join up and help Eddie out. So . . ."

"How much is he paying them?"

"I think it's fifty a day and expenses. I mean fifty for all of them."

"Who's in charge?"

"They don't exactly have a leader, but that brother over there seems to be the treasurer, sort of." She pointed to a young man who was standing by a Volkswagen bus, intent on repairing a sign which bore the legend, "Draft Grandpa." He had a handsome profile and his sandy hair was tied in a pony tail, frontiersman style. His chest was bared to the rain save for a wooden peace symbol dangling by a leather thong from his neck. Pete walked over to him.

"Could I talk to you a minute, son? I'm Pete Stackpole, Eddie's campaign manager."

"Sure, Pete. I'm Bill." He flooded Pete with insistent black eyes. His expression was as defenseless as air.

"Can we talk in your bus, out of the rain?"

Bill nodded and led the way in. The interior smelled like decaying fungi. Boots, sweaters, candy wrappers, plastic bags, socks and two guitars accounted for some of the award-winning litter. Bill swept away an oily rag and a sack of Granola natural cereal to make room for Pete, then seated himself across the aisle.

Pete opened. "I take it you want Eddie Quinn to win?"

"Yeah. Eddie's where it's at. We dig him." The deep black eyes concentrated on Pete.

"Well, Bill, you're smart enough to know you're not helping Eddie. I know you're people of integrity and . . ."

"How do you know that, Pete?" The voice was soft despite the abrupt interruption. The black eyes aimed directly at Pete's, blinkless, unwavering.

"Well, maybe I ought to say that I grant you integrity of purpose." The eyes bathed Pete in dark waters.

"You're a bullshitter, Pete."

Stackpole looked away. The dark pools had a hypnotic quality. Pete reached into his pocket for a cigarette.

"You're also uptight," said Bill. "You put out jagged vibes. Not bad, just jagged."

"Look, son, I'm not here for a sensitivity session." Pete welcomed the feel of his rising temper. It made him less uncomfortable. "You say you want Eddie to win. I'm telling you that you're hurting him. People in towns like Batesville and Greensburg don't understand you and your friends."

"You want us to split?" Bill asked it sadly.

"Yes, I do." Pete lit the cigarette. "Whoever it was that asked you to join us wasn't connected with Eddie's campaign. You live in a commune somewhere?"

"We're a family."

"Then I'd like to make a contribution—two hundred bucks—and in return you and the family break off and go home."

"And I thought Eddie meant what he said about a fair shake for everybody." Bill shook his head in sorrow, but the eyes remained steady, fixed on Stackpole. "You're all the same. The system corrupts everyone in it."

"Eddie means what he says. But I'm his manager and I have to be practical. If you people keep dogging us, nobody's going to hear him."

" 'You people,' huh? Kids, blacks, tribes, Chicanos, we're all just 'you people' to you."

Pete kept his silence. Nothing said, nothing lost. Through the misted window he could see Teegee chatting with one of the newsmen who had apparently tired of Eddie's oratory.

Bill thought while he stared. "How much did you say?"

"Two hundred."

"Okay. We'll split." Bill held out his hand.

Pete stripped off ten twenties from his roll. Bill shoved the money carelessly into a front pocket of his jeans and stood up.

"Tell Eddie for us that there's no hope for the system." He did not sound distressed. "A fair shake for everyone, huh? Well, we're somebody too."

Outside the bus Stackpole started to walk away, but Bill laid a hand on his sleeve and turned him gently. "Pete, do yourself a favor. Get it together." The black eyes drilled the target with a marksman's accuracy. "Man, you're so tight you rattle. . . . Peace." They parted.

The meeting was disintegrating. From Eddie's standpoint, it had been a shambles. A local man had swung on one of the tribesmen during Eddie's indictment of the rich, the amplifier failed, the leaking sky dampened interest and the collection grossed but $133.75.

Eddie and Pete climbed back into the candidate's car, dripping water over the upholstery, and settled back for the ride to the third stop, Shelbyville, on the way to Indianapolis. A man rapped on the window and Eddie lowered it by touching a power button on the rear arm rest.

"Jenkins, Indianapolis *News*, Mr. Quinn." He wore a pork-pie rain hat and his spectacles fogged in the drizzle. He handed Eddie a large folded sheet of paper. "That's an ad we're running. The desk wants comment from you."

Eddie unfolded the newspaper-size sheet. Huge black type bellowed at him: A WILD MAN IS LOOSE! Oscar Baker started the motor.

"See me in Shelbyville," said Eddie. "I'll read it on the way."

Eddie and Pete skimmed the advertisement as the motorcade rolled out of town and regained Interstate 74. The ad was a polemic, accusing Eddie of political recklessness on seven counts. Among other things, his plan to abolish all tax deductions would "cripple hospitals, sound the death knell for private universities and destroy the foundations devoted to the care and betterment of humanity," while removing municipal bonds from the tax-exempt status would "bankrupt every major city in the nation." In actuality, Eddie's innocent chimera of "tax equality" would turn into a "nightmare of depression and chaos."

The sponsoring Committee for Political Sanity embraced two hundred names, including disciples of both parties. It read like a roll call of the American establishment, surgeons, clergymen, conglomerate presidents, foundation heads, university chancellors, museum curators, publishers, attorneys, psychiatrists, foreign-policy savants, importers, network executives, utility-board chairmen, sports entrepreneurs, several labor union chiefs and the owner of America's largest thoroughbred racing stable. A footnote said the ad would appear in three hundred newspapers.

"That's a million-dollar ad campaign," said Stackpole. "Somebody's hurting."

"It's all crap." Eddie was indignant. "When the tax rates go down, people with dough will have more of it to give away."

"They're afraid of you, Eddie," said Pete. "In this country, a politician can advocate race equality, political equality, sex equality, generation equality, you name it—but tax equality! Brother, on that track, you're dead."

Rain washed out the Shelbyville ("City of Progress") rally. The brooding overcast dumped water over the town, flooding gutters, streaming off eaves and driving all but a handful of inhabitants under roof. The caravan splashed to a halt on the main street and Eddie ran under a green-and-white metal canopy and then into the Harrison Cafeteria ("Food You'll Like") for a warming cup of coffee. Newsmen swarmed through the door and surrounded him. Dripping raincoats and damp hair failed to short a certain electricity in the air. Eddie sensed more trouble. A dozen reporters spoke at once and Eddie caught the words "pot" and "marijuana."

"Hold it!" he commanded. "One at a time, please."

"Read it to him, Hank," someone shouted.

"Okay. Okay." A tall, slope-shouldered journalist opened his notebook. "I took this off the air coming into town. It's date-lined Greensburg.

"'A campaign adviser to Candidate Edward N. Quinn today advocated establishment of a nationwide chain of government dispensaries to distribute free marijuana to "uptight" middle-aged and elderly Americans.

"'Thelma Gower Churchill, twenty-four-year-old liaison between Candidate Quinn and youth groups and a defector from Governor Hugh Pinholster's campaign staff, disclosed her views in an exclusive UPI interview.

"'Miss Churchill, who said she smoked marijuana occasionally, urged relaxation of laws against possession of the drug and said the federal government ought to give it free to anyone over fifty, the same age group that Candidate Quinn proposes to draft for military service.

"'"Grass is a peaceful thing," she said. "We'd have less violence and turmoil in the world if the men who run it could learn to relax and love one another like many of the young people do."

"'The interview developed when a reporter overheard Miss Churchill talking with members of a group of hippies who joined the Quinn entourage in Indiana this morning. The hippies, who support Quinn, left suddenly following the candidate's speech in Greensburg.'"

"What about it, Eddie?" someone called. "Do you endorse Teegee's plan?"

"What do you think?" he snapped.

"I think it makes sense," said Sybil Jamieson with a brittle little smile. "After all, if you're going to take men over fifty into the army, you might as well fix it so they won't feel a thing."

Eddie leaned across the steam table and said, "Thanks, honey," to the red-haired waitress who handed him a steaming cup of coffee. He settled at a table near a sign which urged: ENJOY ANOTHER CUP OF COFFEE FREE. He spooned up some of the hot liquid and blew long and deliberately on it before swallowing. By the time he swung around to face the pack, he had gotten his thoughts in order.

"You know, one time when I was a young guy driving a van for an interstate moving outfit," he said, "my crew cracked this lady's big mirror during a household job over to Altoona. She started crying—I guess it was some family heirloom—and I felt so sorry for her, I said the company ought to give her the whole job free on account of busting the mirror. Well, it seems she wrote to the home office, quoting what I said, and about a month later I get a call from the president of the outfit, no less. After chewing me out, he said, 'Quinn, if you want my job, you hustle and try to take it away from me. In the meantime, nobody speaks for this goddamn outfit except me.'"

Eddie blew a long, whistling stream over his coffee and took another swallow.

"Meaning that Miss Churchill doesn't speak for you?" asked the tall reporter.

"Nobody does except me. Now, of course, I don't, repeat, do not, favor the government handing out free dope to anybody, under or over fifty, and I don't favor giving away booze, tranquilizers or tobacco, either. If people want to dose themselves, that's their business, so long as they pay for it and don't mess up other people. As for me, I don't smoke, drink or take drugs except maybe an aspirin when I have the flu. So don't go putting out some big story that makes me into a pothead. I got enough troubles."

"Are you going to fire Teegee?"

"No. This is a free country. People have a right to talk." Eddie paused, stirring his coffee. "Of course, I may have a little get-to-gether with Teegee—tell her about that busted mirror, maybe."

Eddie reached under his raincoat and withdrew the folded newspaper ad. He shook out the folds and held up the sheet.

"Now, let's talk about something important," he said. "Mr. Jenkins of the Indianapolis *News* gave me this ad which is about to run in three hundred newspapers, costing the sponsors about a million dollars. You men and women are all working people on pretty tight salaries, so look at those two hundred names and ask yourself, why does a fellow kick in five or six grand for an ad that calls me a wild man just because I say that everybody ought to be treated alike under the tax laws?

"I'll tell you why. Because in this country a candidate can come out for race equality, sex equality, political equality, in fact every kind of fair treatment under the sun except one—equality under the tax laws. If he's for tax equality, the big guns of privilege, some of whom don't pay a nickel a hundred at income tax time, will wheel up and start blasting him. So everyone who reads this ad ought to ask himself this question: What tax benefit that I don't rate is each one of these two hundred men and women getting? I challenge all members of this-called Committee for Political Sanity to make public their tax returns and also list their tax-free municipal bonds. Then we can decide whether the name maybe should be changed to the Committee for Preservation of Special Privilege Tax Loopholes. Another thing. A lot of wheelers and dealers accuse me of running a soak-the-rich campaign. Well, what they've been running for years is a soak-the-little-guy system."

The newspapermen scribbled busily while water dripped from their clothing and ran into puddles on the floor.

"Aren't you trying to set class against class?" asked a young, harried reporter, peering out from under a rain hood.

Eddie drained his coffee and rose from the table. "Is that your question or somebody tell you to ask it?"

"Well, my publisher, I guess, told the desk to have me ask it."

"I thought so. How much do you make a week?"

"Two ten."

"There's your answer. Son, you and I have been taking in the washing and ironing of the big boys for years and years. Time we quit. . . . Okay, let's hit the road to Indianapolis. We're running late—and wet."

Eddie strode to the door, his brown thatch of hair matted from the autumn downpour, his face ruddy and moist and his broad shoulders thrown back. Kate Witherspoon joined him.

"You get A for effort, Eddie, trying to detour that pot story."

He hooked his arm through hers. She was wearing a belted white raincoat, floppy rain hat and white boots. "Come ride with me to Indianapolis, Kate. I need you around."

On the sidewalk under the fluted metal canopy, they found Teegee counting dollar bills into Stackpole's outstretched palm. "I collected fourteen dollars along the street anyway," she said. "Please don't bawl me out, Eddie. Pete already laid a job on me."

"It hurt, Teegee." He threw his arm around her shoulders. "And if I had a chance to win, I probably would have fired you. . . . From now on, you let me do the talking, honey. Okay?"

"I promise." A drop of rain slid off her nose. "But I still think it's a good idea."

The motorcade splashed out of Shelbyville, heading across the damp midriff of Indiana and toward its uncertain destiny. Almost nothing went right during the long, chill, overcast, soggy day and night. About an hour and a half late for the big noon rally at Monument Circle in Indianapolis, Eddie missed the lunchtime crowds and spoke to a bedraggled gathering of not more than 3000 people. Stackpole had counted on a minimum of 10,000, had hoped for 20,000. Heading west on Route 40, the Win-with-Quinners bypassed a scheduled appearance in Plainfield because of a slashing downpour. Detouring to DePauw University at Greencastle for an outdoor speech, Eddie found himself without rain for a change, but facing a brigade of hecklers who insisted on mining Eddie's views on marijuana, sex and transcendental meditation. While Eddie's doctrine of an economic fair shake won mild approval, the students preferred to climb the ladder of values to such loftier rungs as sensory perception, alienation and self-awareness. Also Eddie lost several intellectual points when it became obvious that he thought Hermann Hesse was the mayor of Greencastle. Gratefully back on Route 40 under skies that wept only sporadically, Eddie spoke to a goodly crowd in the city of Brazil. The citizens applauded and opened their wallets, but no sooner did he finish than Eddie was summoned to a motel phone, the White House calling. This time, Stackpole assured him, it was the President.

"We had a time tracking you down," said the President after the quick-frozen salutations. "What town is this you're speaking from?"

"Brazil, Indiana, Mr. President."

"I'd have thought you would have had enough Brazil for one week. . . . Now, Commissioner, I'm going to speak very bluntly to you. I've suffered without complaint through a good many of the outrageous statements you've been making as the nominee of my party, but I've reached the end of my patience. I think you should know what just happened. The Russians broke off indefinitely our very promising talks about the Berlin Wall."

"That's bad news, Mr. President. Can you say why?"

"I sure can." The President was furious. "They quit the talks because of you."

"Me? What did I have to do with it?"

"Your proposal last Friday, that preposterous business about limiting military service to men over fifty, was made on the very day that Premier Ryabchikov was celebrating his own fiftieth birthday. Were you aware of that?"

"No, sir."

"I'm sure you weren't, even though the Russian ambassador, as I understand it, dropped a broad hint for you."

"I don't remember any hint." Eddie stretched his memory. "He just asked me if I knew what day it was and then went on talking."

"Whatever the facts, Premier Ryabchikov took your statement as a direct, personal insult. While he didn't mention the incident in dropping the wall negotiations, we know that's the reason. . . . Now, Commissioner, you may think it's a gas to go skylarking around the country, saying anything that pops into your head, but I'm telling you it's time to knock it off. Your comments on domestic issues are bad enough, but when you make rash sweeps into the area of foreign relations, you can do great damage to this country."

"Maybe the Russians were just looking for an excuse to quit the talks until after the election," said Eddie. "If you want, I'm willing to call the Russian ambassador and explain."

"No!" The word echoed like the volley of a dawn execution. "Under no circumstances. I'm not going to be President much longer, but as long as I am, I'll handle the foreign affairs of the United States of America." Rolling swiftly off his tongue, the title seemed to belong to five or six nations at once.

"Yes, sir."

"It may be too much to ask you, Quinn, to quit talking like somebody hanging around a pool hall . . ."

"Now just a minute, Mr. President."

"Don't interrupt me . . . or the local drugstore, but by God, I insist that when you touch on any issue involving the rest of the world that you start acting like a candidate for President and not some kid running for head of the sophomore class."

"Is that all, Mr. President?" Eddie's boiler gauge had shot as high as the one in the White House.

"No. One final thing. As a lawyer who has handled some complex tax matters in my day, I associate myself completely, if privately, with the statement made today by Doug Whipple's committee. And if Pete Stackpole is standing by your elbow, you can tell him for me that he is managing a goddamn national calamity. . . . That's all. Good-by."

"Good—" But the click at the other end snuffed out need for the final syllable.

Eddie clenched his fists as he turned to Stackpole who was, indeed, standing just outside the phone booth. Eddie stepped out and stood for a moment, breathing heavily and feeling his jaw muscles tremble.

"You look like Ted Witherspoon," said Pete. "Did the man unload on you?"

"Pete, the President wants me to tell you something for him." Eddie spaced his words with elaborate, mock care. "You are managing a goddamn national calamity. . . . Now, let's you and the calamity get the hell out of town."

A half-hour later the caravan sloshed into Terre Haute, the day's western terminus, under cold and dripping skies. Stackpole was now swallowing pills to ward off a cold, Kate Witherspoon had begun to sneeze, Hunk Janiszewski's war-torn rheumatic shin protested the weather, R Dan Fenelli cursed his lost raincoat and Sybil Jamieson threatened to sue the Terre Haute House and the American Hotel Association for indignity to person—having to share a room in the Terre Haute House with an obscure female communicator whose talents had yet to grace a network show.

Eddie barely survived a series of crises soon after shedding his waterlogged shoes in his hotel room. Margot Hicks, brooding over the black leaders' blast at Quinn, wanted to quit the staff and return to Atlanta and only a half-hour of pleading by Eddie, Kate and Pete dissuaded her. Eddie's briefing on Terre Haute and its politics was conducted by a substitute, a young man from the mayor's office, because the scheduled briefer, the party's county chairman, announced several hours before Eddie arrived that he was switching to Pinholster. The evening television news specialized in shots of the larking tribesmen, who looked even dirtier and eerier on film, demonstrating in Batesville and Greensburg. Teegee's plan for free pot for the pot-bellied rated prime coverage, while Eddie's bombing of the two hundred ad sponsors received only footnote attention. Then came word of flooding of electrical connections in the basement of the hall where Eddie was to speak, forcing cancellation of the meeting. Phil Liccardo, investigating, could not determine which climate, meteorological or political, had sabotaged the rally.

Eddie wound up speaking in the hotel lobby to several hundred people. Bathed by television lights and cheered by a band of teen-agers, he plodded doggedly through his pitch, cannonading the ramparts of privilege, smiting financiers at play on their golf courses and squash courts and pledging to cleave the Pentagon into manageable halves.

One half of the Pentagon, he said, would be named the Department of Defense and one half the Department of Offense, and in the Quinn regime, when and if, 75 per cent of the military budget would be spent on Defense and only 25 per cent on Offense. Eddie said this division reflected his basic foreign policy which, "to quote my uncle Hunk, means we're gonna quit buttin' into people's business all over the world."

To climax his day, Eddie developed a sore throat that he medicated with a steaming bath, a cup of hot tea and an aspirin. He felt feverish, weary and discouraged and before he climbed into bed, he called Kate in her room.

"You sound kind of low, Eddie," she said after they chatted for a bit.

"I am. I don't think I'm hacking it, Kate. Nobody's listening—and eleven more days to go.

"Oh, you're not doing so bad. Even with the rain, I saw a dozen women flirting with you from the crowds today. Get a good sleep, Eddie."

"Same to you, baby. I feel better just talking to you."

But as they hung up, Kate sneezed and Eddie coughed and he wished the election were over that night.

12

Arnold Swensson strode into his Manhattan office, 565 Fifth Avenue, on the stroke of 7 o'clock the next morning. The nation's most skillful, secretive and expensive conductor of political polls switched on the lights, hung his coat on a hall tree and pushed a button on the electric coffee-maker. Unlike many early morning toilers in New York that morning, Swensson was eager to begin work.

He was a large, solid man, built as though to provide a model anchor for less stable humans, and his bald head glowed above a fringe of neatly trimmed graying hair. Swensson smiled but rarely, finding life a serious transit which, as far as he knew, afforded but one crossing per person and therefore was not to be taken lightly or frittered away on emotional yo-yos and frisbees. What fascinated him and made his life a monolith of purpose was his belief in the utter predictability of human behavior, including his own.

Swensson had risen an hour earlier with a sense of expectation that quickened as he clicked through his morning routine, tooth brushing and gum massage, mouth wash, shower, shave, dressing, breakfast, page one of the New York *Times,* elimination and the vigorous nine-block walk to the office. His mind dwelled on those two lines, transmuted from neat rows of numbers, that ran toward each other with steady, unbending insistence. He found great beauty in those lines, a mirroring of truth as precise as Ralston Crawford's painting of a long highway bridge in which the railings, converging in perspective, became at last a remote pinpoint.

Swensson had remained flexible and open-minded for a week, but last night he had glimpsed the shape of things to come and he looked forward to the morning with such eagerness that he gladly would have forgone his sleep if that would have speeded events. As it was, he slept soundly and dreamed of a series of geometric designs in gorgeous colors that slid into one another in endless progression approaching the infinite.

Arnold Swensson ran the most sophisticated poll in the world and this October it was at the exclusive service of Governor Hugh Pinholster under high security precautions at a cost of $28,000 a day. This broke down to $14 per interview, for each twenty-four hours. Swensson's organization questioned two thousand people across the nation. All polling was done by telephone, although the results were carefully weighted by a complex formula to account for those voters who had no home phone. One hundred forty interviewers, operating in two shifts of seventy each, manned the phones in little compartments spread along tables in a Lexington Avenue office building in Manhattan. The dialing crews consisted largely of graduate students of the social sciences at New York universities, supplemented by a few housewives and unemployed professional people. They were paid $50 for an eight-hour shift, but most of them were as interested in public-opinion sampling techniques as in the money.

Calls fanned out over the Bell system's WATS (wide area telephone service) lines, affording unlimited long-distance calls at a fixed monthly rental. Every call resulted from a random selection of a phone number by a computer that performed highly complicated calculations, including the allotment of a higher percentage of calls in those area codes located in states with the largest electoral votes. The computer juggled area codes, exchanges and the final four-digit numbers with lightning speed, serving up long lists of random numbers for each operator. Interviewers also followed a booklet of questions designed to reflect the voting population's profile in such items as correct proportion of males and females, heads of households, first-time voters, elderly citizens and, of top importance, those most likely to vote.

The calling began every morning at 10 o'clock and continued until 2 the next morning. While no call entered a home after 11 P.M.

local time, the New York dialers worked until 2 A.M. because of the three-hour time spread to the West Coast. Operators sprinkled calls to time-distant Hawaii and Alaska through the day. Operators wasted two of every three calls because the computer-selected random numbers included phone booths, churches, schools and business establishments. With few exceptions, those reached at home cooperated willingly. They liked being called long-distance, appreciated the thoroughness of the questioning and, above all, relished the thought that their single vote was significant enough to attract the interest of a professional poller.

Dialers filled out coded forms after each interview and supervisors transferred the data to punch cards. Twice a day figures from mechanical tabulators were fed into a computer console. Instantly rows of figures clattered onto a long sheet that leaped convulsively from the electronic typewriter. A bonded security officer folded the sheet, placed it in a thick manila envelope, put the envelope in his inner breast pocket and walked rapidly the five blocks to Swensson's Fifth Avenue office, arriving each morning and evening at 7:15.

This morning Swensson glanced repeatedly at his watch as he awaited arrival of the messenger. He drank coffee, filled his pipe, relighting it several times, and looked out the window without seeing anything. At last, two minutes late at 7:17, the young messenger came into the office and waited while Swensson signed for the delivery. Opening the envelope and unfolding the sheet, which was eighteen inches wide and perhaps six feet in length, Swensson became conscious of his tension. His stomach, that emotional refuse dump, groaned as a new load of cans, bottles, cartons and other sensory discards tumbled about. If he was certain of what he would find, he thought, why so discombobulated?

He scanned the rows of figures with rising excitement, noting a number here and another there as his vision hopped around the sheet. Then, suddenly, a glow suffused his body and the tension drained away. He was right. The figures confirmed his hunch as accurately as if they had been hatched in his own brain. But first, the precaution of a double-check.

He telephoned Fred, his morning supervisor in the Lexington Avenue bucket shop of polling.

"Did you eyeball those key numbers on the dupe, Fred?"

"Yep, they're okay, Arnold. They check out with the input. No problem with the nine-oh-four this morning. All nice and tidy."

"Fine. I'll be over around ten."

Swensson took a large sheet of graph paper from his desk drawer and glanced at the two lines, one red and one blue, that ran across the graph. Consulting numbers on the computer print-out, he used a blue pencil to extend the blue line about half an inch, then duplicated the process with a red pencil and the red line. Finally, using an ordinary lead pencil and ruler, he extended both lines by a series of light dots and wrote down two letters and a number in a corner of the graph: "T N 2."

"Perfect." Swensson breathed the word with awe. He might have been Christopher Columbus, sighting the low, tropical shoreline of Watling Island in the Bahamas, or Hiram Bingham beholding the long-hidden glories of the lost Inca fortress, Machu Picchu, in the Andes of Peru. For all three men, Chris, Hi and Arnie, there was that supreme vault of the human spirit, that vindication of lonely prescience. By God, they had been right!

Swensson glanced at his watch: 7:28. He could call Hugh Pinholster in two minutes and he would use those two minutes planning just how to break the news.

Swensson's relationship with his most recent client had been sealed when he began polling in the Pinholster-Hudson race in late September. A man with Swensson's record and prestige could set his own terms. In the last quarter of a century, he had polled in more than four hundred political contests, including every presidential race and a host of battles for governor, senator and mayor. He had picked wrong only once, missing a run for governor of Missouri largely because the client refused to pay for what Swensson considered to be an adequate sample. His highest error had been 4.7 per cent, his average error 1.2 per cent, but in presidential elections his last pre-voting figures averaged slightly less than 0.4 per cent off the mark. Swensson had polled for such notables as Eisenhower, Kennedy, Johnson and Rockefeller. Although his price was steep, expenses were also lofty and Swensson netted only about three hundred dollars a day profit for himself during the short-lived political-polling season. He made his living from market surveys. In politics, he was a man who worshiped numbers and their meaning for election day.

Swensson insisted on certain rules. He would communicate only with the candidate himself. With Pinholster, he had an arrangement that he would call the governor at 7:30 A.M. each day wherever Pinholster happened to be. The client pledged not to reveal figures except to a few, close, trusted advisers. Under no conditions were poll results to be leaked to the press. Thus, when the Los Angeles *Times* printed Swensson data Wednesday, Swensson had threatened to end his service unless Pinholster tightened his security. The candidate vowed that henceforth he would hold the daily results as inviolate as his campaign promises, a somewhat ambiguous pledge, Swensson thought. Actually, Swensson traced the leak to his own shop and fired the offending assistant supervisor.

Arnold Swensson could so dictate to future Presidents because of all the new high priests in modern America—the diet druids, the sensitivity gurus, Zen Buddhist mystics, Satan cultists, ecology zealots and the chieftains of the youth tribes—none had quite the impact on the course of the republic as the political pollers. And in the temple of public opinion, Swensson was the priest of priests.

After consulting Pinholster's itinerary, Swensson placed his call to the candidate at the Sheraton-Blackstone in Chicago at 7:31. Pinholster's light, breezy voice, fraught with empathy and yet withal, Swensson felt, a trifle untrustworthy, came on the line promptly. They traded their usual, brief amenities.

"Okay, Arnold, shoot. I've got my form here." No one called Swensson "Arnie," although Pinholster had tried it their first day.

"All right, Governor. Going across, make it 1050 under A, 772 under B, 178 under C, 52.5 under D, 38.6 under E, 8.9 under F and plus 1.1 under G."

For Pinholster the figures translated swiftly as follows: Of the 2000 most-likely-to-vote people polled across the nation in the last twenty-four hours, 1050 said they would vote for Pinholster, 772 for Quinn and 178 did not know. Expressed in percentages, Pinholster had 52.5, Quinn 38.6 and 8.9 were undecided. Column G,

Quinn's gain or loss over the previous day's polling, showed a gain of 1.1 per cent.

"Oof." Pinholster emitted a half-whistling sound. "I don't like that one point one gain, Arnold."

"It's not pretty," conceded Swensson. Actually, he thought the number a thing of beauty. No offense to Pinholster, just a question of aesthetics. One day 1.2, another 1.1, another an even 1. The Column G figure had not varied more than 0.2 per cent since the Pinholster-Quinn matching began eight days ago.

"You said you might make a projection today, Arnold." Pinholster's tone struck a tentative note.

"I did. . . . Governor, I regret to tell you this." But within him, Swensson could feel the fires of elation. "The lines cross at T N 2 on your graph."

Except for a faint, extraneous symphony of far voices, silence overtook the line.

"Tuesday, November 2?" asked Pinholster.

"Yes."

"That's election day."

"Yes, I know."

After a long pause, Pinholster said: "Let me get this straight, Arnold. Are you telling me that if things keep rolling as they are, we've got trouble on election day?"

"That's about the size of it." And, thought Swensson, he'd known it last night, deep in his brain and his gut, thus beating the poll by twelve hours. Instead of commiserating with the client, he felt like dashing off a happy paper for the American Statistical Association. "We have to face the fact that we have a trend."

The trend, that ominous and implacable abstraction, had moved as smoothly as a ship on compass heading in calm seas. Starting with thirty per cent of the vote the night of his nomination, Quinn's blue line rose day by day with an average lift of 1.1 per cent every twenty-four hours.

"You actually put the election in doubt then?" It was as though Pinholster had asked which day the world would end.

"Well, of course, we have the variables. You crank in my average error of 0.4 per cent, you look at places like Chicago where the organization can influence your tally on the upside . . ." Swensson never used such words as "steal" or "fix" with clients. "Then you consider Quinn himself. A man given to the, well, bizarre in campaigning might say something deeply offensive to a statistically important bloc, or get into a brawl or perhaps give the impression of mental instability. . . . Let's put it this way. The numbers say doubtful, but with the variables, you look in better shape than Quinn does."

"Any recommendations from the depths?" Pinholster was braving it now, the cool, imperturbable image.

The depth interviews embraced a series of questions asked every fourth person polled. They were intended to probe the voter's psychic caverns for substrata of prejudice, longing and trust.

"Sure," said Swensson. "As I told you earlier in the week, foreign policy is your trump suit. Let's look at Question Six in the depth interviews. 'Suppose another war breaks out in the Middle East, threatening world peace. Which candidate would you rather have in the White House handling the crisis?' Yesterday 56.7 per cent said Pinholster, only 32.1 per cent said Quinn and 11.2 were uncertain. Quinn gains only slightly on this question day by day. You retain a big lead there. So the message is loud and clear."

"I can't understand how I can be so far ahead on the foreign business and still keep dropping over-all."

"It's the old story, Governor. Bread and butter dominate elections and Quinn has the kitchen image."

But it was more than that, Swensson felt. He preferred to stick close to the numbers with clients, but he had his own theories, privately nursed. From the start of the September polling, he had sensed a lack of basic trust in Pinholster. The governor's image was one of deftness, agility, suppleness. Voters liked him, but they did not trust him deep down as they had Eisenhower, for example. Pinholster led the polls because the voters trusted Hudson even less. But with the sudden appearance of Eddie Quinn, the ball game changed radically in the seventh inning. The initial depth interviews indicated that Quinn's two appearances on television projected a picture of independence and integrity of person. People might dispute or even abhor what Eddie said, but they sensed that he was his own man, a solid fellow who would not flutter about in every breeze. In short, people trusted Eddie to be himself. Swensson surmised the second day that Eddie would gain in the poll as people overcame their aversion to the novelty and the shock of what he said. If Swensson were explaining the phenomenon to Charlie Herron, who had financed some of Swensson's polls in the past, he would put it in banker's terms. Eddie was the rough, blunt construction foreman, without funds, credit standing or social acceptance, who comes into the bank unannounced and solicits a large loan to start his own building company. He is turned down, but he returns again and again until the banker, persuaded at last of the applicant's ability and stubborn commitment, extends him a character loan and even urges his own wife to invest money in the new enterprise.

Eddie began his nineteen-day campaign by projecting an image of a good, warm, reliable man of the people, and Swensson believed that a man whose initial impression was appealing only rarely failed to gain as the days went by. So the daily tallies, showing Eddie on a gradual but steady rise, did not surprise Swensson. In fact, he already had wagered two thousand dollars of his own money at attractive long-shot odds. But that was all hunch and theory, and with the client, Swensson stayed glued to the numbers.

"The depths show your clear superiority on foreign issues," said Swensson. "If I were in your shoes, Governor, I'd hit that hard in every speech. Without saying so, I'd make the voters visualize Eddie Quinn at a summit conference with Ryabchikov or conferring with Pompidou or Willy Brandt. Voters will feel uneasy, I think, about pictures like that."

"I agree, Arnold. I sense my strength in that area. I'm going to exploit yesterday's break, the Russians knocking off the talks on the Berlin Wall. Anything else?"

"Yes. I think from now on we ought to get a computer print-out every four hours. It won't cost that much more, let's say seven hundred dollars a day, and then we can get a running check on the trend."

"Okay, do it. And Arnold, call me any time if you spot a change. Flo will put you through wherever I am. . . . Oof, this is hard to take at this hour in the morning."

"Anything can change, Governor. The numbers aren't ordained in heaven." But once they started to flow in a steady current, thought Swensson, only an act of God could guarantee a reversal.

"Oh, one thing, Arnold. Quinn had a bad day yesterday, rain, hippies, a squabble over pot, a crack about a Department of Offense. Do your breakdown figures show any change after, say, nine P.M.?"

"That'll take a minute." Swensson skimmed rows of figures, looking for key numbers. "Let's see. Most of the late numbers are from the West. . . . Well, I can't be definite without more work, but if Quinn hurt himself, it doesn't seem to show up yet. We'll know more later on."

"Okay, then, until seven-thirty tomorrow, unless you have some news."

Swensson labored for two hours over his master charts, then prepared to walk to the Lexington Avenue quarters to watch the beginning of the telephone calls at 10 A.M. He loved the clutter of voices amid the rasp of dialing and the busy beat of the tabulating machines, for he knew that beneath the noise, as though in a subterranean channel, the numbers flowed quietly and steadily at a predictable speed toward a foreseen destination. But first Swensson called his friend, Don Pugh, his betting blind for wagers with the Philadelphia bookie.

"Is Quinn still five to one, Don?"

"Yeah. No change."

"Put another thousand on Quinn then."

"Will do. See you, Arnold." Pugh seldom questioned his friend. In their arrangement, by which Pugh picked up a tenth of the winnings and shared none of the losses, words were superfluous.

After hanging up, Hugh Pinholster sat for several minutes staring at the numbers on his coded form sheet. It is axiomatic that political candidates distrust polls which show them lagging and place great faith in those that depict them running ahead. Yet Pinholster found himself in the tormenting position of reading results of a poll that showed him in front by landslide proportions, but pondering a pollster's projection which had him winning or losing by a whisker eleven days hence.

True, Swensson had an enviable record for accuracy and Pinholster knew that he never made a projection for a client until satisfied that a trend was under way. But how could this be? How could Swensson predict with any certainty that the voters would continue to swing to Eddie Quinn in a fixed percentage day after day? Pinholster found it incredible that the American people actually would come close to electing a man who scattered outrageous remarks around the countryside, who had no qualifications for high office and who offered thin, naïve, simplistic remedies for the most complex of social ailments.

Still, those numbers. Quinn, 38.6 per cent, up 1.1 per cent from yesterday, 2.2 points from Wednesday, 3.2 from Tuesday, 4.4 from Monday, 5.4 from Sunday, 6.6 from Saturday, 7.6 from Friday and 8.6 from Thursday night after Quinn's nomination. The numbers rang through Pinholster's memory. There was something immutable and changeless, and therefore evil, about the progression. If Eddie suddenly proposed today that the State Department be shut down and all foreign policy abolished—and who could guarantee that he would not?—would he still gain 1.1 per cent tomorrow in Swensson's poll?

Not a man given to self-pity, Pinholster nevertheless began to feel sorry for himself now. They were unfair, those ever-growing numbers, a naked, deformed parade, marching straight ahead, oblivious of anything Pinholster might do or say. He walked about the Blackstone living room, gazed down on Michigan Avenue and tried to think out broad strategy for the eleven remaining days before those goddamn red and blue lines met at their unholy rendezvous.

He called Flo Hendricks, already at work in her room, and asked her to locate Eddie Quinn for him. The rival candidate, she said, was in Terre Haute, Indiana, but would move out within an hour. She would try to get him on the line.

It made sense, Pinholster thought as he sipped his second cup of coffee while awaiting the call. The briefing, the film, the numbers. Especially the numbers. Of course, he didn't believe them any more than he believed in the precision of Swensson's prophecy. Still, if there was even the slightest chance that Eddie Quinn might be elected President, then the poor bastard ought to be prepared before "the moon and stars," as Harry Truman had put it, fell on him. The call came through in five minutes.

"Commissioner? This is Hugh Pinholster. Good morning."

"How are you, Governor?"

"Fine. How's it going with you?"

"Lousy." Eddie sounded as though he meant it. "We got rained out yesterday. This morning more water and I'm running a temperature. Well, that's my problem. Your call surprised me. What can I do for you?"

"I thought we might save the government some money and get to meet each other in the bargain. When's your CIA briefing?"

"Monday, I think. Yeah, the director is going to meet us in L.A. Monday."

"Well, why don't we take the briefing together?" asked Pinholster. "It's logical. That way we both hear the same thing and it ought to clear what sticky areas we ought to avoid for the rest of the campaign."

"Where do you want to do this?" Eddie was cautious.

"Where are you Sunday?"

"Lemme think. . . . Oklahoma City, at the Skirvin."

"I'll be in St. Louis where I was supposed to be briefed Sunday afternoon. Why don't I just hop over to Oklahoma City Sunday afternoon and let the director brief us both at once?"

"Well, I'm not sure what's on our schedule."

"Look, Commissioner, I'm not trying to trap you. To be perfectly frank, in addition to the briefing, there are a couple of things I want to talk to you about. From your standpoint, some bad news and some good news, we might say."

Eddie cleared his suffering throat. "Is this like that story of the school principal who calls a father and says I've got some bad news and some good news for you? The bad news is that we've discovered your son is a fag. The good news is that he's just been elected queen of May."

They both laughed, Pinholster countered with a bad-and-good-news story of his own, then said: "Well, both stories might fit, according to your point of view. Why don't you think over the CIA idea and call me back?"

"No," said Eddie. "I think it's okay. Let's do it. How would four o'clock be?"

"Fine. I'll make the arrangements with the Agency, and I'll see you Sunday at four at the Skirvin."

"Okay. Look forward to meeting you, Governor."

"Likewise."

Two hours later Pinholster was addressing a teachers convention at the Conrad Hilton, across the street from the Blackstone, and imploring the delegates to consider "just who you want occupying the White House when war clouds threaten over the China Sea and Arab leaders meet once more to plot the destruction of Israel." Yet every time he paused for breath, it wasn't a handy phrase, but a number, 1.1, that flashed into his mind.

Eddie Quinn was rolling west through southern Illinois in the Electra 225 and listening to the whine of tires on the drying pavement of Interstate 70. His thoughts held no numbers. Instead he pondered his talk for the next stop, the town of Effingham, where he planned to say that, if elected President, he would order every prison warden, administrator and guard under his control to spend a minimum of two months as inmates of other penitentiaries before resuming their duties. And that, Eddie planned to say, would bring needed prison reform quicker than a ton of articles and resolutions.

13

Teegee Churchill placed her hands on her hips and gazed uncomprehendingly at the scene. Sweat dampened her forehead and grime streaked her bare arms. A yellow pencil, thrust behind her ear, protruded through the long hair, now gathered into a workmanlike bun.

"I can't believe it," she said to Joe Kuzyk. "Fourteen . . . fifteen . . . sixteen. Sixteen more!"

She leaned against the congressman. "Hold me, Joe. I don't know whether to laugh or faint."

But Teegee did neither. Instead she and Joe hugged each other and then she stepped forward and directed two uniformed mailmen who had trundled a cart laden with sixteen fat canvas sacks into Quinn headquarters on the fifth floor of 1140 Connecticut Avenue in Washington. It was the third delivery this Saturday, thanks to a special deal worked out by Kuzyk with the capital's postmaster.

"Just pile them behind this desk," Teegee told the postman.

As they heaved the swollen bags off the hand truck, Teegee drank in the scene around her. It was late Saturday afternoon, ten days before the election, and Quinn headquarters was as busy as a Mexican market. Girls shouted, phones rang, shirt-sleeved young men cruised the narrow aisles, file drawers banged, typewriters chattered. In one corner of the large room two men toiled over a balky mimeograph machine. Nearby, a circle of staffers, some sitting on boxes and upturned wastebaskets, huddled in conference. Others in cubicles along the wall consulted books, papers and one another. Tobacco smoke fogged the room and discarded paper cups overflowed trash baskets. The din pulsed in wavelets. More than two hundred people labored in a space designed for sixty working bodies.

Every political campaign, including those starred for defeat, hits a day when the electricity of hope suddenly charges a headquarters and boosts the voltage of the workers. The day is always one of heightened stress and spirits, even for jaded veterans. In novices the day generates heady thrills. This was Teegee's first campaign and only occasionally in her twenty-four years had she experienced a natural high of such altitude.

Joe Kuzyk had returned to Washington Thursday to straighten out an increasingly confused staff at the 1140 Connecticut nerve center. Joe called Eddie and asked for help. Someone close to Eddie had to manage the mail, he said. Letters with money were beginning to flow into headquarters in response to Eddie's "fin-for-Quinn" appeal at Washington Court House, Ohio, Wednesday noon. Already, Joe suspected, volunteers were pilfering cash from envelopes.

Eddie asked Teegee to take on the chore. At first she protested, contending the transfer was punishment for talking to a reporter about marijuana, but Eddie insisted he was promoting, not exiling her. She pleaded lack of interest in money. Time she became practical, argued Eddie. In the end she agreed and flew back to Washington Friday night. She began work early Saturday morning. Now, eight hours later, Teegee was an expert on the receipt, if not the solicitation, of small campaign contributions.

She made swift calculations as she watched the mail handlers unlock the canvas sacks. Two earlier deliveries had brought twenty bags, each of which contained about twelve hundred letters. The average envelope held $3.47 in currency, coins, checks, money orders or stamps. Thus far today's haul netted $83,280 and she estimated the new bags would yield an additional $60,000 or more. Teegee was beginning to love the sight and smell of money.

A dozen young volunteers, recruited from George Washington, Catholic, American and Georgetown universities, went to work on the new fiscal crop. Teegee supervised an orderly routine. Four workers opened envelopes and dumped the contents into a large drop cloth. Others sorted this pile into a number of large wooden boxes, one for letters, another for currency, a third for coins, a fourth for checks and a fifth for miscellaneous items of value.

Three more college volunteers, who had just arrived, hovered over the sorting. Teegee administered her short order security oath.

"Do you promise not to steal anything? If so, raise your right hand and say, 'I do.' If not, split."

The trio raised right hands and repeated the oath.

"Okay, you go to work on the letters," she ordered. "Put the say-nothings in one pile. If you find one that's interesting, like it could be quoted in the press, put it in this box. Any from Eddie's friends or that you think he ought to answer when he has time, put them on the desk here. Free Cokes and coffee over there. Take your time, but work like hell."

Joe Kuzyk, who had been leaning against a file cabinet, walked toward her with his slow, awkward gait. The big Czech moved like a man trying to stride through a bin of ice cream. He threw an arm roughly about her shoulders.

"What do you guess for the day, Teegee?"

"If this load goes like the last two, it ought to check out around $150,000 or something."

"Some haul, huh? And there'll be more tomorrow. I got a deal for special Sunday service."

"How'd you fix that?"

"Hell, honey, I went to bat for the postmaster when the postal clerks were after him on a job rules thing. He owes me. . . . A hundred and fifty grand in one day. Eddie'll like that."

"Wow!" It was a cry from a girl working over the drop cloth. She held up a check. Everyone stopped and looked.

"Three thousand dollars!"

Teegee took the check and studied it with Joe Kuzyk. Made out in neat handwriting to the Quinn Campaign and drawn on a Milwaukee bank, it was a personalized check in the name of Marsha D. Hudson.

"That's Senator Hudson's widow, I think," said Joe. "There has to be a letter with it."

Joe and Teegee joined several students in pawing through the heap of letters, bills and coins on the drop cloth.

"Here it is," said Teegee. She and Joe moved to one side to read the letter, green script on gray-bordered stationery.

Dear Eddie:

I hope you won't mind my using your nick-name, but after following what you've been saying for the past week, I feel that we are political, if not personal, friends.

It's no secret that I differed with my late husband over many social and economic issues in this country. I felt strongly that if something weren't done soon to close the terrible gap between rich and poor, we faced a revolution in America. I still believe that.

Now your "fair shake" program comes along like a fresh wind. While I don't agree with everything you say, I'm for ninety per cent of it and I admire the bold, fearless way you present it— and this from a woman whose capital came largely through the tax loop-holes you talk about.

I'm making this contribution without strings. The only favor I want from you is a promise that you'll keep on saying what you're saying regardless of who tries to stop you. It has desperately needed saying by a major candidate for many, many years. God bless and Godspeed.

Sincerely Yours,
Marsha D. Hudson

"Love that woman," said Teegee. "That's the first check we've had for more than a hundred dollars." She tapped her teeth with the letter. "Listen, Joe. The RBC camera crew will be up here at five to shoot the counting. Why don't I call Mrs. Hudson and see if she'll let us use her letter."

"Good idea. Go to it."

Joe Kuzyk whistled a few bars from an old high school marching song as he lumbered off to make his rounds. The congressman now headed a thriving if frenetic workshop, designed to funnel facts, figures, ideas and solutions to R Dan Fenelli on the campaign trail. There Fenelli put them into expoundable shape for the candidate who promptly gave them a twist of his own that made headlines.

A sample, thought Joe, was a task force proposal to establish a federal Householder's Complaint Agency in Washington which would handle citizen protests against such everyday headaches as

shoddy products, overpriced supermarket goods, faulty cars, dangerous toys and high mortgage rates. As revamped by Eddie in an
Illinois speech yesterday, this became a White House-endorsed picket line. "When I'm President," Eddie had said in Vandalia, "you
send those complaints to the White House. If we think they're
justified after checking, we'll send you some picket signs. For instance, 'President Quinn Protests the First National's Outrageous
Nine Per Cent Charge on Home Loans.' And if it's bad enough,
folks, I'll come out and join your picket line myself."

Or Eddie's bit yesterday at Effingham, Illinois, where he said
every warden and prison guard in the country should be made to
serve two months' time as an anonymous prisoner in another peni-
tentiary before returning to duty in his own prison. That had come
out of Kuzyk's workshop as a closely reasoned proposal for encounter
groups of prison officials and militant inmates, guided by psychologists and aimed at eliminating the worst tensions of prison life without sacrificing security.

With Eddie, God bless him, one never knew. Right now the
circle of young lawyers over in the corner was hammering out a plan
for preservation of the vanishing wild ocean shorelands. Kuzyk would
phone the consensus to Fenelli this evening in time for Eddie's
speech tonight to a convention of conservationists in Springfield,
Missouri. And what would Eddie do with ocean beaches? Joe had
no idea. But whatever he did, Eddie would electrify his audience,
shocking half of it, and steal the morning headlines from Pinholster.

All week long volunteers had flowed into campaign headquarters,
swamping the paid staff of some twenty persons inherited from
Senator Hudson. Most of them were young and many were lawyers
from the big politically oriented Washington firms or senior law
students from nearby universities. Some, trained in the investigating
task forces of Ralph Nader, knew special pits and burrows in the
caves of federal bureaucracy. After he arrived Thursday Kuzyk made
it a point to talk personally for a few minutes to each volunteer and
he sensed that his growing battalion of young attorneys and graduate
students represented a youth trend away from Pinholster. Eddie's
free-swinging, personal campaign style, unfettered by traditional doc-
trinaire chains of Left, Right, liberal or conservative, attracted them

because they believed that Eddie would listen to any idea, no matter how novel or unorthodox.

Joe now headed for the cubicle where two women law students and a young professor of sociology at Howard University labored over a tough question they themselves had put to Kuzyk: What kind of change in the tax laws would halt the exodus of business and industry from the big cities? Unless someone came up with an answer soon, they argued, unemployed blacks might touch off an armed rebellion that would make the riots of the sixties seem like playground exercises by comparison.

But Joe was intercepted en route by a high school messenger boy. Two more volunteers were at the door. They wanted to go to work at once. Would he talk to them?

Joe met the rookie politicians by the water cooler. They were both young, one bearded and wearing jeans and a heavy, wool shirt, the other smooth-shaven with jacket and unmatched trousers. Joe knew the type by the slouch, the air, the mannerisms. He translated mentally: Ivy, WASP, family tree.

"Are you Congressman Kuzyk?" From the beard, a confirming prep school-Ivy league accent.

"Yeah. Looking for work?"

"Yes, sir." For beardless's intonation, add old money.

"We can't pay anything, you know."

"We know that. We want to volunteer." The beard was earnest, wanted to reform a few things, starting with mankind.

"Give me a little background. You first." Joe nodded to beardless.

"We're both Yale Law seniors and we're ready to work through the election. I'm from Chicago. My name's Brock Herron." Jacket tailored, lined with green silk.

"Herron? What does your father do?"

Beardless smiled, defiant confession. "Banking. Charles Herron, same one you're thinking of."

"And you still want to work here after what Eddie's been saying about your old man?"

"I'm here, Congressman." Very cool, hinting that differences with father were old hat, stuff for yawns.

Joe turned to the beard. "How about you?"

"A son of another man you know. My name's Cal Boyington. My father's the Hutchens Boyington with Pinholster." Cold eyes. Nothing quite so satisfying as joining the opposition and thus giving the shaft to the Boyington household's grand master of arrogance.

"You guys got any special field?"

"Corporate and tax law." Brock Herron understated, relishing the irony.

"Came to the right store, huh? Well, we can put you to work at our going wage, free Coke and coffee." Kuzyk raked them with another appraising glance. "But there's an if. If you come aboard, I'm not going to keep it a secret. You're good publicity copy and Eddie can use all of that he can get."

"No problem." Cal Boyington's game plan: keep one step ahead of everybody at all times. "We talked that over before we left New Haven."

"Interviewers? The works?"

"Sure, but of course, we're also here to do a job." Cal's eyes, gun slits in the fortress of hair, were ready to mow down the enemies of humanity and brotherhood.

"Okay, you can go to work tomorrow, eight sharp," said Joe, "but right now, we'll start cashing in on the publicity."

The RBC camera crew was moving in like an army of occupation. Lights, backpacks, antenna, research girls, producer, commentator, shields, rods and boxes clumped and wheeled into the room and set up camp in the area where Teegee directed the sorting and counting of contributions. A man in a lemon shirt and striped bell-bottom trousers, his blond hair sprayed in place to the rearmost ringlet, sang out orders that relocated people, objects and intentions, thus beginning the subtle process by which reality is elevated to the magic box. Teegee was permitted to read portions of the letter from Widow Hudson, but certain angles and trapped fragments of conversation managed to communicate an aura of doubt as to the letter's authenticity.

When the crew completed its shots of the counting, Joe Kuzyk offered his newest recruits to the director in the lemon shirt. When Joe explained their bloodlines, the director demanded identification, studied the offered cards and instructed a research girl to phone the Herron and Boyington residences.

"Okay, we'll do a two-minute spot," he said, "subject to the check-out."

Lights focused, a camera aimed and an interviewer, faultlessly suited and cravatted, stepped forward with a hand mike. Joe and Teegee listened closely, noted all questions and answers and agreed that the interview was a fair one. But later, in Joe's office long after the workers left for the day, Teegee and Joe were far less satisfied when they watched the RBC news on a television set. In the interview, cut to one minute, Brock and Cal came through as callow dissidents, less fired by Eddie Quinn's visions than by a desire to elude the clutches of parents and affluence. As for the shots of the counting, they had a vaguely counterfeit quality, hinting that perhaps the Quinn staff had swelled the loot by dumping some of its own money on the drop cloth.

The news show concluded with three-minute shots of both candidates in Missouri, Pinholster in St. Louis, dwelling on the foreign perils lurking for the next President on various unruly continents, and Eddie speaking to the conservationists in Springfield. Eddie's great shoulders filled the screen with formidable bulk.

"He's got power, that fellow," said Joe, the admiring fellow politician.

"Yeah," breathed Teegee. "Kind of animal."

The camera caught Quinn's finale.

"And so, if I ever become President," said Eddie, "I'm going to freeze all the undeveloped waterfront land in this nation for the people. We'll use the right of eminent domain and we'll buy the property at fair prices, and we'll put that beautiful land in trust for all of us to enjoy."

They could see Eddie thrusting forward at the lectern, strong, intent, yet with the jaunty smile of a man who relishes his work. "Do you know that a rich man recently paid $240,000 for one acre of shorefront at Sea Island, Georgia? That's true. Think of it! He paid more for one small piece of ground than some people earn in a lifetime. In California, one man owns a whole headland jutting into the Pacific Ocean, acres and acres of it, just so he can enjoy the view all by himself. It's worth a couple of million. Believe it? It's true. From Palm Beach to Bar Harbor on the Atlantic and from San Diego to Puget Sound on the Pacific, it's the rich who hold the finest land. And they even try to keep us off the beaches with fences and dogs and guards and searchlights.

"Well, my friends, that's gonna change. The shorelands and the river fronts and the lake fronts belong to all the people. We too have a right to see the beautiful sunrise off Palm Beach, hear the waves rolling into Santa Barbara and see the fish jumping in those private lakes. And if you'll elect me, we'll reclaim most of the waterfronts in American for our children and our children's children."

Eddie threw his right arm upward and outward in the gesture that had now become his campaign trade mark.

Joe switched off the set. "Eddie," he said to the collapsing image, "you're something else." He turned to Teegee. "You know how that started?"

She shook her head.

"My bright boys came up with an idea for Eddie's speech tonight. They proposed that the federal government set standards for future building on undeveloped shorelands, mostly to preserve wildlife and the natural state. They had a lot of for-instances. So I phoned Fenelli after the RBC filming. Now look what Eddie does with it! He bawls out the wealthy and says he's going to buy up hundreds of miles of shorefront, river lands, lakeside, seaside."

"I don't think that's so crazy."

"No, neither do I. It's just that I never know what he'll do with an idea. He's a pistol." Joe rubbed his tired eyes. "I only wish he had a chance."

"You don't think he does?" The flurry of the day had left Teegee exhausted, yet dreaming of an office in the White House. "He's up in the polls, and all those volunteers and that money pouring in."

"No way." Joe reached for his coat spread over a chair. "He's got a long way to go in the polls and only ten days left. Any campaign draws volunteers. As for the money, you got a little better than 40,000 contributions. Am I right? That's damn good for one day, but just remember there are more than 200,000,000 people in this country."

Teegee looked glum as she slung her macramé bag over her shoulder.

"Perk up, kid," said Joe. "We're in this to wise up the people, and Eddie's doing a great job of it. He'll change the climate and someday, eight, twelve years from now, we'll elect somebody like Eddie Quinn, by God."

But eight years seemed like an eternity to Teegee as they walked past the vacant desks, the littered aisles, the hooded typewriters, the empty coat hangers and the locked safe. She wondered how Joe could take it so philosophically. Maybe Bill and that family tribe that pursued Eddie in Indiana were right.

She turned out the lights at the door. Maybe, she thought, the system corrupts or debilitates everybody. Teegee fumbled in her bag for her last joint.

Ted Witherspoon called Charlie Herron from his long, low home nestled on a waterfront of Highland Park, the exclusive Dallas enclave. It was 1 A.M.

"Charlie, I saw your boy on television." Ted still fumed over Kate's presence in the Quinn campaign entourage. Misery, if it did not love company, certainly welcomed news of those similarly afflicted. "What gives with the kid?"

"Same old story," said Herron. "I spend fifty thousand dollars on his education from prep school to law school, give him a car, a boat and a trust fund, so then he turns around and says, 'Up yours.' What can you do? I don't know. Hell, I think the country's had it."

The score now tied on family defections, Witherspoon shifted aim to the chief target. "Charlie, we're getting closer on that sex film. Somebody paid a thousand dollars for a strip of the negative."

"Who?"

"Not sure yet. Steve ought to have it by tomorrow. Listen, what about Steve's stuff on Mabel Quinn? She's ready to talk. Why don't we have Rich put some newspapermen on to her?"

"I thought of that, but I'm not so sure. She'd come off as the typical spurned, embittered wife. It might create sympathy for Quinn."

"But she told the investigator that she threw Eddie out of the house because he was screwing everything loose around town except the keyholes."

"Yeah, but all that's years ago now," said Herron. "Let's leave it up to Rich. He ought to be able to judge public reaction—if he can judge anything. . . . Say, did you get a call from Seymour Wick, Pinholster's finance chairman?"

"Yeah, Charlie. I sent my Washington man over to Wick this afternoon with twenty-five bills. Cash."

In many circles, a bill means one hundred dollars. On the playing fields of Witherspoon, Herron and Cuthbert and their friends, a bill was one thousand dollars.

"I'm taking thirty to Washington Monday," said Herron. "It's a sad damn election when I'm reduced to giving money to a character out in left field like Pinholster."

"What can we do? Anyway, it's a good investment, Charlie. The more of our kind of money he accepts, the more friendly Pinholster will have to be after January 20."

"I know. Still . . ."

"Cheer up. I'll call you tomorrow after the next batch from Kipke."

"If Kipke doesn't come up with something we can put our teeth into by tomorrow, I say let's end it. What the hell, Ted, Quinn's beating himself anyway. The man gets wilder by the day. The people aren't buying him."

"Is that what they're saying around the Chicago Club?"

"Is that a crack?"

"Well, that's what they say here at the Petroleum Club. But you talk to the guy at the gas station and you get a different story."

"Not me. I hear the same thing all over. Well, have a good sleep."

But Ted Witherspoon slept poorly. And in one of his spells of ragged wakefulness, he recalled that the first time his friends of the Chicago Club and the Dallas Petroleum Club agreed on a sure winner, the year was 1948. The sure winner was Thomas E. Dewey.

14

A breeze puffed the curtains as warm afternoon sunlight spilled through the open windows of the Skirvin Hotel suite in Oklahoma City. The air had a lazy touch, unusual for late October, and Eddie slouched back, a leg draped over the arm of the chintz-covered easy chair. On an end table beside him rested a miniature yellow racing car that a young admirer had pressed on him earlier in the day. The debris of several Sunday newspapers lay at his feet. It should have been an hour for drowsing.

Instead Eddie was buffeted by voices. Margot Hicks, Hunk Janiszewski and Phil Liccardo all talked at once. The Quinn S&T board pursued its first hot quarrel of the campaign. A simple issue, whether Eddie should descend to the lobby to greet Governor Pinholster, had grown to mountainous, symbolic proportions. Hugh Pinholster was due at the Skirvin within an hour for his joint CIA briefing with Quinn, yet Eddie's staff still bickered over protocol. Not since the Kennedy-Nixon campaign debates of 1960 had so many words been expended on the tactical implications of who first greeted whom where.

"There'll be reporters and TV men swarmin' all over the lobby when ol' Pinpooper comes in," said Hunk. "Why shouldn't Eddie get some of the publicity instead of letting the other guy hog it all?"

Pete Stackpole and Phil Liccardo supported Hunk, but Margot and R Dan Fenelli thought Eddie would be uncool to muscle in on Pinholster's entry.

Jeff Smithers, Pinholster's manager, had called Stackpole that morning and suggested that the two candidates meet at 4 P.M. in the suite reserved for Ward Delafield, the director of the Central Intelligence Agency, then pose briefly for pictures and get down to business. Delafield's fifth-floor suite served as the demilitarized zone between Eddie's sixth-floor campaign rooms and the quarters Pinholster had reserved for the evening on the fourth floor. Pinholster would arrive at the hotel at 3:45 and go to his room to freshen up after the flight from St. Louis. Stackpole had finessed his answer, merely said that Eddie would be waiting at the hotel.

"I don't think it's earth-shaking one way or the other," said Kate Witherspoon. She had not taken part in the debate. "Eddie ought to do whatever's most comfortable."

Phil Liccardo started to speak, but Eddie cut in. "Okay, let's end it. Kate's right. This is no big deal. Pinholster suggested all this, why I don't know. It's his show. Now, if this was my own turf, well, I'd greet him at the door. But it's a hotel and the lobby isn't my property. So, I'll just meet him in Delafield's room and we'll play it by ear from there. . . . But right now, I'm going to do a little work on tomorrow's speech."

Eddie disappeared into the adjoining bedroom and the staff slowly dispersed. Stackpole shrugged. "It's Eddie's ball game."

Forty minutes later Hugh Pinholster swept into the Skirvin lobby like the commander of a conquering legion. His troops, three times the size of Eddie's entourage, required a full five minutes to pass through the hotel entrance. In marched a staff of thirty, a large delegation of Oklahoma politicians who had met Pinholster at the Will Rogers Airport, a press corps 150 strong and the usual oddball camp followers who flock to a winning candidate.

The governor, dressed in a casual blue blazer and blue-and-white striped shirt swung along with a zestful, confident stride, befitting the leading aspirant for an office still acclaimed as the world's most powerful. If America's golden seas of wheat and corn, its tens of thousands of automated factories, its host of quietly clicking computers, its lethal submarines, carriers and cataclysmic missiles no longer assured automatic domination of the planet, they still added up to a mighty force that other nations held in awe. The giant of western civilization might shudder with inner tension, flagellate itself with thongs of self-doubt and brood over its destiny. Yet its sheer industrial and military size made it a global presence without peer. If the giant flicked a finger or moved a foot, shock waves could inundate a tea plantation in Ceylon or topple another government in the chill, gaunt mountains of Bolivia.

The gaudy trappings and carnival excesses of presidential campaigns often obscured the face of the giant, but his shadow was always there. Today it might be seen silhouetting Governor Pinholster's trim figure as he moved through the lobby of yet another hotel in yet another city. Behind the pliant smile, a certain aura of dormant power marked him. People deferred to him as to a conqueror on the eve of fated victory. And this Sunday encouraging battle bulletins continued to flow from all parts of the nation. In New York *The Kingdom and the Power* endorsed Pinholster in a lead editorial. The Gallup and Harris polls showed him handsomely ahead. Bolting members of Quinn's party made news everywhere. Rumor had it that the President himself might desert his party's candidate and throw his prestige, waning but still alive, to Pinholster. Moreover, the warm Oklahoma sun blessed his arrival and the customary winds, sweeping off the plains, abated as though in obeisance.

Traveling newsmen covering both campaigns bunched around Pinholster and his Secret Service escort in the lobby. He halted only briefly. "Nothing now, men," he said. "We may have a joint statement afterward. . . . Hi, Jake. . . . What do you say, Gus?" He greeted old friends among the reporters traveling with Quinn as his agents carved a pathway to the elevators.

He ascended as might a prince to the robing rooms of coronation. Pursued by jostling, sweating photographers, he made his way to his fourth-floor rooms, stayed inside a few minutes, then walked up to the fifth floor and down the hallway to the open door of Ward Delafield's suite.

The CIA director, portly, self-assured yet deferential, greeted him with outstretched hand. The civilities went smoothly, for they were members of the same establishment, accustomed to influencing, leading and controlling lesser citizens of the republic. At the moment one held a powerful bureaucracy while the other commanded legions of dissent and reform, but they understood each other. They belonged to the same clubs, spoke with kindred intonations, shared a common imprint of prep school, college and social status. In another era, it might have been the crown prince come to the cardinal for holy benediction.

Eddie Quinn arrived a minute later and at once the easy atmosphere fractured. Pinholster beamed a greeting, but his grip was wary and the other hand on Eddie's shoulder just a trifle patronizing. Ward Delafield shook hands as he might with a plumber, a real estate broker or perhaps the Reverend Billy Graham. The barbarian was here.

Pinholster took charge of the photographers. "Okay, one minute will do it. . . . Right, Commissioner?" The cameramen wanted two snaps, the intelligence director between the two candidates, then just Pinholster and Quinn together. They shouted, commanded and stage-directed their subjects. "Okay," said Pinholster, "that's it." The UPI photographer, who had covered every campaign since that of Truman and Dewey, shot a withering glance at Pinholster from the same steely eyes that stabbed Mafia captains and Miss Americas with equal contempt. "I need one more," he said. Then the troops evacuated in a body, leaving the terrain, a newly shampooed plum-colored carpet, strewn with the debris of skirmishing, empty film boxes, plastic wrappings, matchbook covers, shards of a flashbulb and three trampled cigarette butts, one of which still smoldered. Delafield picked it up and dropped it in a wastebasket.

"Drink?" He nodded toward the portable bar, but his guests declined. Pinholster took charge again.

"Look, Ward, Commissioner Quinn has the memo covering your briefing of Senator Hudson. Since you and I covered the same ground in September, why don't we skip the summaries of the old material and move right into the current picture." He glanced at Eddie. "That suit you, Commissioner?"

"Call me Eddie." Quinn was measuring both men, trying to get the feel of character.

"Good. I'm Hugh. Let's make it first names all around. Okay, Ward?"

"Fine." Hearty WASP agreement from the CIA director, but Eddie caught the fine shade of reluctance.

They settled into three easy chairs, placed equidistant to a tolerance of inches, and became at once a precise triangle of purpose and a floating mass of desires, aversions and hang-ups. Delafield, a man whose thrice-weekly tennis failed to sweat off excess poundage, reached into a side pocket and fished out a small notebook. Eddie was disappointed. He had expected a welter of papers, all stamped or embossed with vivid classification markings, to emerge from a locked brief case or perhaps from a portable safe requiring multiple twirls of the dial before it opened. The CIA director adjusted rimless reading glasses, studied the notes, gargled discreetly.

"Let's begin with the Soviets," he said. "First, the Berlin Wall negotiations. Ryabchikov broke off the talks indefinitely on Thursday. No formal explanation, the usual Kremlin tactic, but Ambassador Howell was privately informed that the remark of the Commissioner, er, Eddie, about confining military service to men over fifty was a direct insult to Ryabchikov because it fell on his fiftieth birthday. Ordinarily we would dismiss this as an obviously overhandy excuse and assume that the Soviets merely wanted to await the results of the U.S. election. However, our excellent Kremlin source assures us that Ryabchikov was furious. The source talked to several Secretariat people who personally witnessed the Premier's rage." Delafield glanced at Eddie. "Outside the intelligence community, people are often misled into thinking of the Russian leaders as machinelike power technicians. We have evidence to the contrary. Like everyone else, they can be flattered, insulted, curried and offended." He paused as though to give Eddie time to absorb a reasonable amount of guilt.

"Isn't the result the same?" Eddie asked. "They knock off the talks until they see who'll call the shots over here."

"Ah, but they had other options." Delafield ticked them off on his fingers. "They could have asked for a recess. They could have fiddled with a minor point, stringing it out day after day until we voted over here. The head negotiator in Geneva could have contracted a sudden, mysterious disease. Any number of things. Inventive, the Russians, when it comes to delay."

Eddie had another thought. "How do you know this source isn't a double agent?"

Delafield's quick smile was only slightly condescending. He answered Eddie as he might an earnest college boy. "OB Three is our most reliable informant inside the Soviet Union. We've checked him out many ways, some of them of immense sophistication that he would have no possible way of suspecting. He's clean."

Eddie tried again. "But aren't the talks in Russia's interest right now? And if that's true, won't they be back soon to Geneva?"

"Long-range, yes. But in the meantime they can use the break-off for pressure in other areas." Delafield embraced Pinholster with a knowing look as if the governor were the kind of worldly leader who appreciated these nuances of diplomacy. It was at this point that Eddie made up his mind. He did not like Ward Delafield. A Porsche. Okay for flashy bursts on smooth highways, but no good on dusty, rock-strewn roads through the boondocks.

"More on Russia," said Delafield. "General Petrovsky has replaced Dinop in command of the first Siberian ICBM battalion. This has gone unreported in the press or in Soviet military journals. The transfer means much higher morale at this isolated missile command, for Petrovsky is a splendid officer. A tough disciplinarian, yes, but the type of general who will battle the highest authority to obtain the best for his men." Delafield ran on for several minutes about the sterling qualities of Petrovsky until Eddie, bored, began to yawn. He could think of no reason why he and Pinholster needed to know the Soviet officer like a blood brother, and he decided that Delafield enjoyed parading arcane details for the uninitiated. Even Pinholster glanced at his wrist watch and suggested that perhaps they better move on. The governor shucked his blazer and draped it over the back of a chair. Eddie did likewise, but Delafield remained properly jacketed.

Other points of interest loomed on the guided tour of potential villains and muggers in the alleyways of Russian politics. There was a new missile launcher aboard Soviet destroyers in the Indian Ocean and five unheralded literary dissidents in jail in Minsk. Or was it Pinsk? Delafield consulted his notebook preparatory to leaping across the Great Wall of China to lance the secrets of 850,000,000 oriental Communists.

"I have a question before we get to China," said Eddie. "How much does the CIA cost a year?"

Delafield assumed that slightly elongated look, jaw sagging and eyebrows lifted, of a clerk in Tiffany's whose customer inquires about price before fully examining all facets of the diamond clasp. "I beg your pardon," he said. Eddie repeated the question.

"I'm sorry, Commissioner." Delafield could not bring himself to say Eddie at such a juncture. "In giving me the guidelines for this briefing, the President told me to limit it to the intelligence picture. I'm not authorized to go into budgeting and interior policy of the Agency."

Eddie waved his hand. "Just wondered. I heard it was around a billion a year. Go ahead."

For the next ninety minutes the CIA director conducted a colorful peek-a-boo tour through the chancellories of the world. He disclosed which African dictator had made a secret deal with the Chinese, what Latin American officer would unhorse a junta with a colonels' revolution next month, the range of demolition the Arabs had in store for the Israelis and vice versa.

Once Delafield paused to remind Eddie that they were handling matters of overwhelming sensitivity. Parties, cabinets and regional alignments might totter at the least indiscreet whisper that U.S. intelligence agents were in their midst. Between his carefully chosen words, Delafield seemed to be warning Eddie that he was no longer a feckless, boyish candidate, scooting along the highways and scattering bright promises to the voters, but a man of high politics who must bear the full and terrifying burden of world statecraft. He had been admitted to the secret society of global security analysts and he must conduct himself accordingly, speaking warily of certain confidential arrangements, stepping with muffled tread along the hallways of intercontinental intrigue. Eddie noted that these veiled admonitions appeared to be directed solely at him as though Pinholster were already a seasoned clubman who knew the rules and customs— when visitors could be admitted to the trophy room or which aged employer held the key to the locker where the billiard cues were racked.

The names of obscure ministers, legislators and military officers fell like raindrops in a summer shower, all subverted to the cause of democracy by the busy, cash-laden apostles of the CIA. If Tanzania was about to spring a border raid and seize a few miserable Uganda guards, Delafield's men knew of the plan in advance through Col. Ubuto, subchief of the Tanzanian frontier forces. If Indonesia decided to reopen trade talks with Peking, the CIA was forewarned by an economics functionary who supplemented his meager income with CIA gratuities. As Delafield hustled over the continents, lifting a boudoir drape here or a manhole cover there, Eddie began to picture the world as a vast CIA-owned plantation in which diplomats, warriors and merchants labored week-long in the fields of nationalism, then queued up Friday evenings to deposit their work sheets in return for American dollars. One thing bugged Eddie. If the CIA knew so much, paid so high and manipulated so many, how come the United States was forever in trouble abroad?

Delafield concluded with a summary of the hot spots: Haiti, revolution due next month; France, determined to detonate one more H-bomb on the altar of amity; Russia, all relations with the U.S. retracted like a turtle's neck because of Eddie Quinn; Greece, Operation Socrates, the preventive detention of one hundred more intellectuals and student democrats to begin at 7 A.M. Athens time. Delafield, who liked to end his briefing tours on a catchy note, said the wife of one of Peru's military rulers had fled to the island of Santa Maria in the Azores with a demographer from the Nigerian embassy in Lima. And that, he said with a touch of Eric Sevareid world-weariness, was the way things were around the globe this October Sunday.

Eddie and Pinholster rose as one man, glad that the main event was over and that Delafield had not threatened them with the special, deluxe tour through the catacombs of Iraqi intelligence. The telephone rang. The CIA director, answering, shielded the instrument with his body as if the two politicians might ambush it from the rear.

"Delafield." He listened for a while. "That's from T Four, I take it? All right. Thanks."

He turned around, bright-eyed. "Operation Socrates has been moved up. The first police sweeps have already started." He sounded quite pleased. The craft of intelligence, like that of journalism, feeds on grief and catastrophe, and there is no reason, after all, why the couriers of evil tidings should go about with long faces and warty dispositions.

Pinholster thrust out his hand. "Good job, Ward. I think Eddie and I have a pretty fair idea of the sensitive areas. No problem about what to lay off of, as I see it. What about you, Eddie?"

Eddie hunched his shoulders as though to lighten his new burden. "I think I've got the picture." In fact, he thought, one more conniving, rentable foreign minister and he would have begged for an intermission.

"Eddie and I want to have a talk before we face the press," said Pinholster. "You mind if we just stay here, Ward? You're welcome to use my quarters if you want."

"Thanks, but I'm flying right back to Washington. One of the President's planes is waiting for me. Just make yourselves at home."

"Okay. Tell the newspapermen we'll see them later."

The good-bys were said, and Delafield was off, topcoat over his arm, a bounce to his step and a look on his face of mission accomplished.

"I think I could use a drink," said Pinholster. He walked to the portable bar and mixed a scotch and soda. Eddie declined his offer. "Oh, that's right," said Pinholster, "you don't use the stuff. Well, here's how." He lifted his glass.

They walked and stretched, chatting health, weather and other inconsequentials, before settling back into their chairs.

"You gonna keep that guy on at the CIA?" asked Eddie.

Pinholster's brows flicked upward. "Well, I hadn't thought of it. How does he strike you?"

"I don't trust him. Don't ask me why. I just don't."

"I could see that. I've known Ward a long time. Not a bad sort. He's got his pluses and minuses."

"I don't like that garbage about buying up generals and cabinet officers all over the world. We're supposed to be this great, open democracy, but we've got a secret international payroll with thugs, policemen and double-dealing politicians on the take. Any guy who'd betray his own country for CIA money, hell, I wouldn't trust him with my pocket comb."

Pinholster shook the ice in his glass. "In theory, I agree, but in practice to get information in this world, we have to pay for it. Of course, if you're saying the intelligence outfits need a good overhaul, I'd go along."

Now that Delafield had left, Eddie was studying his rival. His first impression had been uncertain and he still wasn't sure. On the one hand, Pinholster had an easy manner, no sandpaper, haughtiness or put-down acts. On the other, he had a glossy surface that hid the real man underneath. Quick talker, way of sliding off the hook, less than frank. In a phrase, thought Eddie, the jury's still out on this guy.

Pinholster stretched his legs, sipped at his drink. "Eddie, I want to thank you for running a decent campaign. No mud-slinging."

"I've no complaints with you either, Hugh. As for me, I've just been banging around the interstates, saying what comes naturally. My target is the big-money boys. I have nothing against you personally."

"I hope we can wind it up on the same level. . . . I guess you've been wondering why I wanted to talk to you. There are two things, neither of which I felt free to go into on the phone. The first is personal. This is sticky for me, Eddie, and I just don't know quite how . . ." He paused for another swallow of scotch and soda. "I might just as well tell the story. About a week ago a man from Chicago showed up at our Jackson Place headquarters and insisted on seeing Jeff Smithers alone. Said he had something that would sew up the election for me. Jeff's people stalled him, but he wouldn't leave and finally Jeff agreed to see him. He was a young fellow, a pale, sneaky type named Elroy Kimble. He had a small roll of film negative he wanted to sell Jeff for a thousand dollars. After seeing it, Smithers paid the asking price."

Pinholster walked over to the chair that held his jacket and withdrew a package from a side pocket. It was small, square, wrapped in paper and bound with tape. The governor handed it to Eddie.

"I haven't seen it, but Smithers says it contains film of your son Alfred and his wife indulging in various, well, group sex activities with other men and women. . . . It's yours. You can do what you want with it. I'm glad to be rid of it. I don't play that kind of game."

Eddie stared at the package, then at Pinholster, his thoughts swirling. That Al's sexual life involved swinging, he'd suspected from several hints Al had dropped, but that Irene was involved had never entered his mind. His first flash reaction was one of astonishment, the second a dull, aching sadness. He and the boys had never been close and Al, especially, treated him as though he were a harmless clown who survived less by ability than by luck. What distressed Eddie now was not so much the sexual experimenting—God knows he'd done his share of philandering—but that he and Al were as remote as strangers. Then his thoughts ricocheted to his rival. Why had Pinholster confronted him with the story and package instead of just destroying the evidence in silence? The mere posing of the problem angered him.

"Why the hell tell me?" Eddie flipped the thin package to the coffee table and it slid across the top. "If that's your idea of doing me a favor . . ."

"Hold it, Eddie. I haven't finished. I would have burned the damn thing and kept quiet about it, but a few days ago Kimble called Jeff and tried to buy back the film for fifteen hundred dollars. Said it had become hot political merchandise. If other people knew, then sooner or later you would, and I didn't want you to think that I was involved in some dirty deal to smear you through your son."

"I see." But Eddie didn't understand. The reasoning appeared flimsy to him and he prepared to bracket Pinholster in a class he disliked: those who made sure that the generous size of their contribution to good works was known to all. And if Pinholster were sincere, why hadn't he ordered the film destroyed the day Smithers bought it?

"But there's a more important reason, Eddie, why I wanted to clear the air with you and get on a basis where we could level."

Pinholster leaned forward and propped his elbows on his knees. Eddie waited vigilantly. The jury was still out on this man.

"I don't know about you, Eddie, but I think this country is in big, deep trouble. I don't ring the alarm bells in my speeches, but I feel the danger in my bones. We're fracturing, flying apart, rushing away from one another. Look at all the signs of coming breakdown. Millions of people, adults as well as kids, strung out on drugs. More have armed themselves. Hundreds of miles of city streets are no longer safe. Crime rises month by month. Murder of policemen has become commonplace. Authority has a hard time everywhere. The prisons breed more criminals and violent revolutionaries. Public buildings aren't safe from senseless bombing. Discipline in the armed forces is shattered. People are frightened into immobility. We withdraw into smaller and smaller subcultures. Meanwhile, as you've been saying, the rich get richer and the poor get poorer." He paused. "Do you buy that diagnosis?"

"Some, but not all," said Eddie. "We've still got a lot going for us. If we can even things up, give working people a better shake, I think we can make it all right."

"I wish I could agree. I go along with a lot of your objectives, Eddie, even if I don't buy some of your approaches. But I'm more pessimistic. A hell of a lot more."

Pinholster leaned back in his chair. The effortless smile and easy air had vanished. Eddie sensed intuitively that Pinholster, whether right or wrong, believed what he was saying. He was a troubled man.

"Whatever we think about the shape of the country," said Pinholster, "I think we can agree on one thing. Whoever's elected next week is going to face a job that only God or a political genius could handle right. I'm neither, and with all due respect, I don't think you qualify as the first either."

"Drop me on both counts. A genius, I'm not. I'm just a pinch-hitter trying to do his best with two outs in the ninth."

"I think the whole country's in the ninth inning. . . . Anyway, what I'm leading up to is this. Given the situation, the winner a week from Tuesday is going to need all the help he can get, including first and foremost, the ungrudging support of the man who loses."

Eddie felt the pressure ebb. So that's where Pinholster had been heading. He grinned. "Relax, Hugh. The minute the last votes are in, the political war is over. You're the President-elect then and you'll get whatever backing I can give you. . . . Funny thing, you and I are closer in what we say in the campaign than I am to the guys who nominated me—or to Hudson's line, for that matter."

"Thanks, friend. I know you mean it. The same goes in reverse. If you're elected, I'll do everything in my power to see you off to a good start. A deal. Can we shake on that?"

They did, gripping firmly. Then Eddie laughed as he settled back.

"That's like the winner of the Indianapolis 500 shaking hands with a stock-car driver from the sticks," he said. "Me, I'm lucky if I can win the nomination for governor back home."

"You don't think you have a chance next week?" Pinholster eyed him closely.

"You kidding? Of course not."

"What's your guess on the results?"

"Oh, I might take a few states," said Eddie. "Pete Stackpole and I went over the figures last night. I'll give you a fair run here and there, but hell, man, you've got a landslide."

Pinholster stood up. "I think I'll freshen my drink. . . . A ginger ale?" Eddie nodded and the governor made a business of fussing at the bar. He handed the soft drink to Eddie, then stood for a moment looking out the window at the Oklahoma City skyline, fading now into the shapes of twilight.

"You ever hear of the Swensson poll?"

"Sure. I hear he's hired out to you. Some newspaper mentioned it."

"That's right. We're paying the guy a small fortune, but he's worth it." Pinholster dwelled for several minutes on Arnold Swensson's statistical wizardry, then took a slip of paper from his pants pocket and handed it to Eddie.

"Those are today's numbers as of seven A.M."

Eddie looked at the slip. "A—1030. B—816. C—154. D—51.5. E—40.8. F—7.7. G—+1. Pinholster stood behind Eddie and interpreted. "That's a poll of two thousand people across the country yesterday," he said. "I'm A and you're B. I'm D and you're E in percentages.

F is the per cent of undecided. G is your percentage gain or loss in the last twenty-four hours. As you can see, you're up one per cent."

Pinholster went back to his chair and Eddie offered him the paper. "No," said Pinholster. "Keep it."

"Interesting," said Eddie. "About what I thought. I've gained some, but you're way ahead."

"Today, yes. But the country isn't voting today." Pinholster eyed his drink, took a sudden, long pull at it. "What pollers look for, as you know, is a trend. And it seems that we have a trend running this time that's not good for the Pinholster team. You see that number, plus one after G?"

Eddie glanced at the paper again.

"That number is beginning to haunt me. Ever since the night you were nominated, Eddie, you've been gaining an average 1.1 per cent every twenty-four hours. Some days it's one, some days one point two, but steady on, day after day. Nothing either of us says seems to make any difference. Each day you chisel a little off me and a little into the undecided vote. Goddamnedest thing, it even works in four-hour segements. Those figures are as of seven A.M. today, but in the polling from ten to two o'clock today—I got Swensson's call on it out at the airport—you increased another 0.3 per cent. It's uncanny, as if some big computer had programmed a steady shift from me to you."

Eddie felt a tightening sensation and was suddenly aware of his stomach. He worried the glass of ginger ale.

"You don't have to be a Ph.D. in math," Pinholster continued, "to figure what's going to happen if the trend continues until election day. Nine days to go, and you add 9.9 to your 40.8 as of today. That gives you 50.7 per cent of the popular vote and—assuming the electoral votes break right, and this poll is weighted for the electoral count—Eddie Quinn is President-elect of the United States."

Eddie gripped his glass and stared at Pinholster. He felt a rush of anxiety. He heard a low buzz of conversation from the corridor where Flannery and Baker were talking to Pinholster's Secret Service guards. Through the window he saw a jet paint a smoky trail across the dome of the darkening sky.

"But you know that doesn't figure, pal," he said after a bit. "A nobody like me goes up for a while, sure, but then he levels off and finishes with a nice round of applause for the also-ran."

Pinholster shook his head slowly. "That's what I tried to tell myself, but Swensson points out that this trend started the first day and never varied. It's been under way ten days now. Of course, Swensson talks about what he calls the variables. The poll can be off a point or so. Local pols rig voting machines in some cities. A big scandal could break, or the Arabs start bombing Israel. But that's all ifs, buts and maybes. On the straight numbers, Eddie, this is going to be one hell of a tight election, and you stand just as much chance of winning it as I do."

Eddie sat very still. He could feel himself breathing and the pulse of his blood. "Why are you spilling this?"

Pinholster studied his glass, tracing his fingers around the edge. "Why? . . . Well, I don't want to sound pretentious, but when I said I was worried about the country, I meant every word of it. Look, Eddie, I started out to win the big job three years ago. At first, I was all ambition. My game is politics and I took it for granted that winning the presidency was the name of the game.

"Then, a month ago, when I took a big lead over Hudson, I knew I had the election in the bag. At that point, something happened to me. I began to think about the immensity of the job, the endless dilemmas, the possibility that the system might collapse under me. Suddenly, the fate of the country seemed more important than Hugh Pinholster's."

He paused, looked directly at Eddie without a trace of a smile. "A couple of nights I actually couldn't sleep. I'm not exaggerating. And once, Eddie, just before a speech in New York, I had this sudden feeling of panic. I felt I could never cut it, that I'd made a terrible mistake, that the people needed a man much wiser and more confident than I was. The feeling didn't last long. I got a grip on myself, made myself realize that if I wasn't omniscient, neither was anybody else—especially Hudson. I was all right after that, but the experience sobered me."

Pinholster smiled faintly and shrugged in a self-deprecatory fashion. "I know I sound quite the opposite in public. Nice, smooth patter, lots of solutions, the once-over-lightly gig as one writer called it. Well, that's my style and I can't change. But inside, Eddie, I'm hurting, not constantly, but enough. It'll probably sound corny to you, but what I hurt for isn't me, but our country. . . . Eddie, every move you make is that of a man who doesn't think he has the chance of a snowball in hell. I wish, for your sake, that were true. But it isn't. You have a fifty-fifty chance of becoming the next President of the United States and, by God, Eddie, you have a right to know it, so you can prepare yourself."

A picture flashed from old memories. Eddie could see himself standing behind the tailgate of a dump truck loaded with two tons of gravel. The truck body was raised and suddenly the automatic gate opened. Eddie leaped to one side, a fraction of a second before the avalanche of egg-sized rocks would have crushed his legs. But now, he couldn't move. Nor would his brain comprehend. He merely sat rooted in the chair, a scrap of matter frozen in time.

"I suppose I have another motive," said Pinholster quietly. "I couldn't tell Jeff Smithers or Hutch Boyington about that panic feeling. I couldn't even tell my wife. Funny, the only person I've wanted to tell is you. Maybe what I'm trying to say, Eddie, is that we're both in this thing together—just the two of us—and God help the man who wins."

Eddie rose and walked to the window. The sun had sunk behind the tall office buildings, silhouetting the city like a graveyard of giants. Far to the west, fading rays streaked a lavender cloud, and the sky's dome flattened into dusk. Eddie struggled with a doubt, testing it as a barrier.

"Are you telling the truth about that poll, Hugh?" he felt weightless, suspended.

"Yes." The word came as from a distance. "I have yesterday's print-out in my room. You're welcome to look at it."

Eddie turned, walked the few steps slowly and stood before Pinholster. He appraised him anew as though he were a stranger. The room had darkened and Pinholster's face was obscured by shadow.

"No," said Eddie. "I'll take your word for it." The jury's verdict was in. Pinholster might not be his kind, but he did trust him. And with the realization, Eddie came back to solid ground, heavily.

"I guess I didn't do you any favor." Pinholster smiled. "But for that matter, neither did Herron and Cuthbert and your other friends in Houston."

"Yeah." The desire to talk had evaporated. Eddie became aware of a weight on his shoulders. Strange. He felt older. "Well, I guess there's nothing more to say."

Pinholster arose and reached for his jacket. Eddie remembered his own coat, then saw the package on the coffee table. He stuffed it into a side pocket. Pinholster noted the movement, but said nothing. They readied themselves in silence, using a wall mirror to adjust their ties.

"We've got to face the mob," said Pinholster.

"Let's just say we discussed the briefing and the conduct of the final weeks of the campaign. Keep it short. You do the talking, Hugh."

"Oh no, Eddie." Pinholster grinned. "We both talk, fifty-fifty."

They moved to the door and shook hands once more, awkwardly this time.

"Good luck," said Pinholster. "And I almost mean that."

"Happy landings, Hugh. And I'm damn sure I mean it."

In the corridor, Secret Service agents boxed and separated them. They rounded a corner, prisoners both, and headed for a swarm of newsmen who filled the hallway from wall to elevators. Again they posed for photographs as they answered questions. Pinholster said they had a good briefing, followed by a man-to-man discussion of the campaign. Eddie said he and Pinholster took a look at the general picture after their briefing. Then they parted, Eddie riding an elevator to the sixth floor with Flannery and Baker.

Back in his own suite, Eddie instructed Flannery that nobody, but nobody, and that included Pete and Kate, was to disturb him before 9 o'clock. Inside, he locked the door, then called Pete Stackpole's room.

"Pete, I'm holing up here alone for a while. I'll see you at nine to go over the Teamster speech. Just you, R Danny and Kate. Okay?"

"Sure, Eddie. . . . Something wrong?"

"No, nothing—or maybe everything. I'm okay. See you later."

Eddie shucked off his clothes down to his shorts, pulled the big easy chair around to face the night skyline and lowered the window to a crack. It was growing chill now. He sank into the chair and propped his feet on an upholstered footstool.

He'd had flashes of premonition yesterday, the growing crowds across Missouri and then Joe Kuzyk's phone call from Washington about those mail sacks full of ones and fives. Last night in Springfield, that quick, streaking thought—what if he won? It had flipped away, but now it was back, a big, dark question mark, demanding to be faced.

Pinholster hadn't lied about the poll, of that he felt sure. But how about the film of Al and Irene? Why hadn't Pinholster just burned the thing? There was a showy side to Pinholster. A guy who wanted full marks for good works.

On impulse Eddie left his chair, found the package in his coat pocket and ripped off the wrapping. Slowly, methodically, he tore the tough film to shreds, even as memories of Al as a boy unrolled in his mind. He scrambled the pieces of film, then stuffed them back into the box and retaped the package. R Danny could dispose of it later.

Al's life was his own, Eddie thought as he resettled himself in the chair, and Eddie was not one to moralize. They were all alone now, Al and Eddie and Eddie, Jr., and Mabel. He had done it all wrong in those early days, and so had Mabel, and now there was no way to reknit the past. Jesus, how he'd messed up a family. A great wave of pain washed over him, carrying memories like debris swept up from a littered beach. A scattering of scenes, some poignant, all lonely, all gray, all gone. Big Eddie, the hale fellow, the quick comrade, the sure-fire stud who went from woman to woman. His own man, he had told himself, possessed by no one and possessing none. And now so alone, he ached. Could he love Kate, with all this crud from other years weighing him down like lead?

An hour went by before Eddie left the swamp of the past and returned again to the dark question mark. Eddie Quinn, the President? It was incredible. Why hadn't they left him alone in the Apollo Motel? What crazy impulse seized Pete Stackpole and why hadn't the kingmakers laughed him out of the Astroworld? My God, he was way, way over his head. It was all a game, he had said at the start.

Eddie Quinn, playing it for laughs. Some game, a black cave of reality.

That poll. Even if it was off a few points, it meant that right now, right at this moment, millions of people were staking their future on him. They were trusting him to make the "fair shake" come true, so they and their kids could live a better life, so the system would work, so they could escape another of those bloody wars that convulsed the world every few decades. They counted on Eddie to stave off revolution, preserve their homes and their jobs and let them live in peace. Even if they weren't aware of it, Eddie knew they hungered for him to be the man with an answer. Him! The thought was overpowering. Why, a month ago he had even wondered if he could cut the job of running the state of New Jersey.

Abruptly he felt tired. Weariness consumed him and he dropped into a deep well of fatigue. When the knock came at the door at 9 o'clock, Eddie was in a fitful sleep.

15

R Dan Fenelli leaned against a table, his arms folded, his glasses shoved atop his thatch of black hair and his brows arching in dismay.

"That's pap, Eddie. Cream and sugar on the top. Underneath nothing but pap."

"It'll make a good speech," said Eddie defensively. "It's what I ought to be saying right now." He was slumped in the big easy chair of the Skirvin Hotel suite.

"That wouldn't even have made a decent speech for old man Hudson," said Fenelli with disgust. "Kate . . . Pete . . . what are we going to do with this character?" He looked at his fellow advisers, seeking help.

"Maybe we ought to call it quits for tonight and go at it again in the morning on the plane," said Stackpole. He was sitting on the floor, coatless, collar open at the neck.

Kate Witherspoon nodded agreement. "Yes, I've about had it. We're not operating on the same wave length tonight with our leader."

If Eddie caught the sarcasm in Kate's tone, he gave no evidence of it. "No, let's wind this up now," he said. He was stubborn and uncharacteristically remote.

It was 11 o'clock and they had been laboring for an hour over Eddie's scheduled speech to a Teamsters' regional convention in Los Angeles the next afternoon. They had gathered after awakening Eddie at 9 and had eaten a light supper in the sitting room.

During dinner Eddie spoke only guardedly of his CIA briefing and said nothing at all about his afternoon talk with Pinholster. From the start it was obvious to his friends that Eddie had undergone an inexplicable change. That morning he had agreed enthusiastically when Fenelli suggested a speech, entitled "Whose Money Talks?" charging that all too many members of Congress voted the interests of large campaign contributors. The theme was to be nailed down with specifics. One of Joe Kuzyk's teams of young lawyers had supplied case histories of six prominent senators, three from each party, who unfailingly followed the wishes of big corporate donors on major issues. Eddie was to list dates, names, gifts and votes. The machinery of government, Eddie was to contend, had been geared to produce benefits for the favored few to the detriment of the neglected many. That morning Eddie blessed the outline with a quick okay, said they would meet in the evening to flesh out the form. Eddie envisioned it as his No. 1 address of the campaign.

Now, for a haggling, abrasive, incomprehensible hour, in Fenelli's view, Eddie had first backed away from the theme and finally staged a full retreat. Instead of a bold, slashing attack on government by and for the few, Eddie came up with bland fare: shoulders-to-the-wheel, stars and stripes waving, vague promises of remaking Washington for the people and the inevitable "fair shake" for everyone.

"It's a copout," said Fenelli. "That's not Eddie Quinn. That's crap that any high school orator would be ashamed of."

"After listening to that," said Kate, "I can just see Marsha Hudson puking." She was sitting opposite Eddie, eying him through a haze of cigarette smoke.

Eddie's distant, shell-like posture, so different from his usual open, playful warmth, exasperated her. She did not understand it and she couldn't imagine being swept into mutual passion with this man before her. Could this be the real Eddie and the one of the Apollo Motel and the Potomac shack but a figment?

"How does Marsha Hudson get into the act?" asked Eddie. He sounded badgered, querulous.

"As I recall her letter," said Kate dryly, "she gave you three thousand dollars to keep on saying what you'd been saying regardless of who tried to stop you. It didn't enter her mind that you might censor yourself."

"I'll say the same thing in this speech as I've said all along." Eddie was testy.

"With about as many teeth as a day-old baby," said Stackpole.

"God damn it." Eddie flared. "I've been on the attack long enough. It's time I begin to sound responsible."

"Oh ho. Responsible, huh?" said Fenelli. "Well, how responsible is it to let down those thousands of people who're sending you one- and five-dollar bills? How about your responsibility to Kate who's canceled her schedule back home, risking her district, to help you get the message across? And Pete? Hell, he's lost a career on account of you. And what about all those volunteers back in Washington? We all believed in you because you were willing to wade in, no holds barred, and tell this country what's wrong with it. But now, Jesus." Fenelli shrugged, a gesture of helplessness. "Tomorrow you're going to come off sounding like Norman Vincent Peale at his worst."

Stackpole hoisted himself from the floor, brushed at his trousers. "Let's try it from another angle. What's your specific beef, Eddie, about naming the six senators?"

"Yeah," said Fenelli. "They're a classic example of everything you've been pounding away at—that big money buys big privilege in Washington and big privilege runs the country for its own benefit. Now Joe Kuzyk's boys provide you with real live ammo for your guns, but you won't use it. Why?"

"I've got to look ahead."

"Just what does that mean?" asked Fenelli.

Eddie looked from one adviser to the other. "The reason may not be plain to you, R Danny, but it should be to an old pro like you, Pete."

Stackpole cocked his head and looked at Eddie with a puzzled frown. "What's supposed to be so obvious to me? I don't get it."

"I may have to deal with those men in the Senate," said Eddie, "and they've got long memories."

Stackpole still looked perplexed. "So now you've decided to run for the Senate?"

Eddie shook his head. "No. I mean if I'm elected President."

They all stared at him. Kate asked: "You said . . . President, Eddie?"

"Yeah, I think that's the office I'm theoretically running for." His sally into sarcasm fell flat.

Kate eyed him intently over a stream of cigarette smoke. "Eddie, when did you discover you were going to be elected President?"

"I said 'if.' "

"All right then," she insisted gently. "When did you decide you might be elected?"

"I didn't decide. I was told."

"Who told you?" Stackpole shot the question.

"Pinholster."

After a gap of silence, Fenelli said: "Come on, Eddie. Cut the mystery. What's this all about?"

"There's no mystery. Hugh showed me the latest figures from Swensson's poll in confidence. There's a steady trend my way. Swensson's projection gives me a fifty-fifty chance, even a fraction better, of making it on election day."

"Oh, Swensson," said Kate. "Good reputation."

Eddie took the slip of paper from his pocket and handed it to Kate. He explained the meaning of the numbers and letters and told, as the slip was passed, of his consistent rise each day and the latest four-hour results phoned to Pinholster.

"Did it occur to you that Pinholster might be conning you—for his own reasons?" asked Pete.

"Yes, at first. But I believe he's telling the truth." Eddie related the gist of what Pinholster had said, withholding only the incident of his rival's brief attack of panic. A confidence of such a personal nature was not to be violated, he felt.

"All very noble and generous," said Stackpole. "Only thing is, I don't trust that guy."

"I got a feeling he was leveling on this. You don't believe the poll, Pete?"

"The poll could be right," said Pete. "We all know you're gaining. We can feel it. The projection is something else. You can't win an election in this country without a lot of television—especially in this short time. About all the TV exposure we're getting is the news shows. To win, we'd need the kind of dough Pinholster has to spread around on a lot of paid spots and shows. So, no, I don't buy the projection. . . . But that's not the point. The point is Pinholster's motive. If he could hear you right now, he'd be one happy candidate. Why? Because you're getting ready to do exactly what needs to be done to lock up a Pinholster victory."

"How so?"

"You don't understand that, Eddie?" asked Kate.

"No. Frankly, I don't."

Kate leaned toward him. "Eddie, I haven't been in politics very long, but long enough to know that you can't suddenly change your image with the voters." She gestured with her cigarette. "You can't throw the voters strong meat day after day, then poof, like that, at the last minute, start serving pap, as R Danny calls it. Your enemies aren't paying attention anyway, and you confuse and put off your supporters."

"But I'm not changing my pitch," said Eddie doggedly. "I'm just toning it down."

"Crap," said Fenelli. "You've been punching hard, Eddie. Sure, you shock people, but then they start thinking about what you've said, and they say, 'Thank God, at long last here's a politician who believes what he says and who says what needs saying and the hell with the consequences.' The ordinary guy's no dummy. He thinks about what you say, decides he trusts you and he believes that you'll really start moving things his way." Fenelli rose from his perch on the table and began bobbing excitedly about the room, gesturing, jingling coins in his pocket. "Pinholster's right about what he told you. The country's not far from a nervous breakdown. If we don't change fast, radically—and that's been your message—we could split apart. I mean it. I know. I've been around."

Fenelli walked over and stood in front of his old roommate. "Listen, Eddie, you know my hunches are pretty good sometimes, and I've got one now. . . . I believe Pinholster as you do, but I think he had another motive for telling you all that. I think he senses that you may be a better man for this day and this hour of history than he is. He must realize that people don't trust him, and he knows that a hell of a lot of them do believe in you." He paused. "And you better make damn sure, buddy, that you don't forfeit that trust."

Eddie's internal struggle was evident in his face. "The President accused me of talking like a boy running for president of the sophomore class. Okay, he was sore, but I know what he means. It just never entered my head, seriously, that I might be elected—until today."

Kate took over. "Eddie, remember what you said at our first idea session in Washington." She stubbed out her cigarette and tilted her head. "I'm not sure of your exact words, but when Phil gave the Gallup Poll figures, you said that if we started thinking we had a chance to win, then you'd begin to trim and straddle and play it safe. You said to hell with that. You weren't going to butter up any organization or bloc, but were going to lay it on the line. Don't you believe that any more?"

"Sure, I do. It's just a matter of style and a way of saying things," said Eddie. "How could I ever get any legislation through the Senate if those six boys were just laying for me, waiting to get even?"

The phone rang. Stackpole answered, listened awhile as he nervously stroked his thinning hair. "What are those other names?" he asked. He listened silently for a full minute, then said: "Nice work, Teegee. Thanks, honey."

"Very interesting," said Pete as he hung up. "Teegee's been keeping in touch with a friend at Pinholster headquarters. Ted Witherspoon's Washington man, Ed Dunleavy, delivered twenty-five grand in cash yesterday to Seymour Wicks at the Jackson Place offices."

"Bastard," said Kate without particular emotion.

"Another of our kingmakers, Senator Framingham," said Stackpole, "gave the Pinholster people a secret cash gift of three thousand dollars. A few other names you may recognize have forked over heavy cash—Field, Heffernan, Rue, Waldron." They were all party leaders, two of them national committeemen, prominent in the Hudson campaign. "Looks as if our fat cats don't want their own candidate to win."

"Damn it, Eddie," said Fenelli, "while you sit around figuring out how to be a nice, mealy-mouthed statesmen, these guys are cutting your balls off."

"Do you still think it's all just a game, Eddie?" asked Kate in a tone of mock sweetness.

"They play rough," said Pete. "I know those bastards from way back."

The wrangling dragged on until midnight when it became apparent that Eddie wasn't listening any more. He seemed caged in a world of his own, visible and mechanically responsive to those outside, but dwelling apart, sunk in himself. Several times Eddie asked Fenelli to repeat what Fenelli had just said to him with great force. Once Eddie abruptly left the group and stood for several minutes, gazing out the window into the reaches of the night sky. His face, which usually mirrored quick rushes of emotion, was now expressionless.

"This is a waste of time," said Pete Stackpole at last. He went to the closet and reclaimed his jacket, rattling the coat hangers irritably as he did so. "We'll see you in the morning, Eddie. We leave the hotel at nine."

"Okay, I'll sleep on it." Eddie stood up. "I didn't realize I was so tired. A nap this evening and I'm still beat."

Eddie moved toward the door with Fenelli and Stackpole, then realized that Kate was not with them. He turned, saw her still sitting in her chair and looked at her quizzically.

"I'll stay on for a few minutes, if I may." She offered no further explanation.

"Yeah, well . . ." Eddie was noncommittal. Perplexed, he said his good nights to the two men and ushered them out the door.

When he returned, he found her staring at him. "Fix you a drink?" he offered.

Kate shook her head. She said nothing and after a hesitant moment, Eddie lowered himself into the same chair he had occupied through the futile session. They faced each other unsmilingly. Eddie began to feel uncomfortable.

"Sorry, Kate. I know I'm not myself. I just can't get used to this new idea. . . . Can you understand that?"

"I think so." She slowly drew another cigarette from her pack and lit it with her gold lighter. She studied him through the blur of smoke. "But right now let's not talk about that. Let's talk about us."

"Okay." Eddie was relieved.

"Where are we, Eddie?"

"In our"—his smile, a thin one, was his first in an hour—"our big thing, as Teegee would call it?"

"Yes. You. Me. Us. How we feel about it."

"Sounds like you're quizzing me, and I don't like tests. Whatever it is, it just happens. Talking about it is for the birds."

"That's true—usually. But once in a while it helps to talk it out. Eddie, you don't know much more about me than you did the first night. Good old Kate. Not a bad lay. Nice dame to have around. Has pretty good ideas—for a woman."

"Come on, baby. It's more than that."

"Eddie. I stopped playing games many months ago. I went to bed with you that first night because I felt something special about you. I had a hunch it might be good and it was. Same feeling the night in Flannery's shack. And in—where was it?—Cleveland, then Cincinnati and last night. Very strong, Eddie, each time . . . Now I'm curious. Not curious yellow, just wondering. What's with us right here and now?" She glanced at her small, jeweled wrist watch. "Twelve-seventeen Central Time, Oklahoma City."

Eddie shifted uneasily in his chair. "Am I supposed to say whether I love you? Is that the pitch?"

"You're not *supposed* to say anything." She could sense his tension. "No, love's a baggy word. You can throw anything into it. I'm asking something much simpler, like what you feel about me right at this moment?"

"Not much." He surprised himself. "I mean, I'm not thinking about us. Christ, Kate, you know what's bugging me."

She was pleased to see a spark of fire at last. Eddie had been withdrawn into himself for hours. Kate inhaled, blew a thin spike of smoke, then asked: "Eddie, how long has it been since you really cared for anyone?"

"What a question!" He glared at her, then hunched his shoulders as though such an inquiry deserved no answer.

"Well, how long?" she insisted quietly.

"I'm not on any witness stand and we're going to end this school-kid examination right now."

"You would have answered me last night."

"Last night was different."

"Why?"

"Why?" he repeated grimly. "Where have you been for the last three hours? Last night I had no idea I might be elected."

"My, my." She put on her most serene smile. "Such a big worry."

"Don't give me that great-lady act," he said. "How the hell would you feel if you suddenly learned you might be elected President?"

"I'd love it."

"Bullshit."

She let his anger simmer for a time. "You don't know me at all, Eddie. You haven't bothered. . . . But let me give you a clue to part of me. Okay, I know you're beat, but listen just a minute. If I learned I had a chance to be President, I'd give it everything I had. I'd rip through the campaign with all stops out. I'd give 'em hell. Oh, nobody would get in my way. And whatever I did, I'll tell you one thing I wouldn't do. I wouldn't sulk around a hotel room half the night in a funk like some dumb, scared truck driver."

"Say that again." Eddie sat stunned.

"A dumb, scared truck driver," she repeated with elaborate care.

"Is that what you really think of me?" Now he struggled to contain his anger.

"Until tonight, no." She delayed again, smoking. "Until tonight, I thought you were a man, a big man who knew who he was, who said what he believed and to hell with his critics. I thought you had guts, Eddie. But now, you're running scared. That man, I don't see."

Eddie clutched the arms of his chair, then stood up and walked to her. He snatched the cigarette away and mashed it in the tray. He pulled her roughly to her feet.

"I'm not a man?"

His eyes drilled hers. His fingers gripped her shoulders.

"Answer me." He shook her.

"Not till you take your hands off me." She looked back at him steadily.

"You're a bitch, Kate."

She could feel his fingers tighten.

"Is this your usual big scene, Eddie?" Her voice turned saccharine. "You rip off the dress, try to prove your manhood by raping the girl?"

He grasped the neckline of her knit dress.

"You'd like that, wouldn't you?"

"No."

He bunched a piece of the dress in his fist.

She cracked a smile. "Know why?"

He shook his head slightly, still glaring at her.

"Because then we'd have to ask Flannery to fetch me a new dress from my room, wouldn't we?"

He stared at her bewildered. His hands fell away.

Kate stepped quickly to a floor lamp, held it with one hand, put the other hand behind her head and arched her hips forward.

"Oh, Mr. Flannery." Her voice fluttered girlishly. "Would you please bring me the black chiffon from my room? My dress has just been ripped off by a man who's running for President."

Kate swung her pelvis in a mock-burlesque grind and bump.

"And Mr. Flannery, please bring me one of my new instant pills from the little red box in the medicine cabinet."

Eddie grinned. Kate did the grinds once more.

"Quick, Mr. Flannery. The candidate's in a better mood. . . . Hurry, hurry, let's have fun. Who says there ain't no easy run?"

Eddie laughed out loud now and Kate, playing it slinky, walked toward him, swinging her hips in feigned provocation. He pulled her to him and they capped the embrace with a long, rough kiss.

"I take it back," said Eddie. "You're no bitch—bitch."

"Sometimes. And sometimes I'm still the frustrated Wellesley junior who yearned to be an actress."

"As a bitch, you make a good psychologist."

She threw a quick, surprised look at him, then stepped to the table where her cigarettes lay. "A psychologist, Eddie?"

"Sure. I may be an old truck driver." The tensions had ebbed away. "But stupid, no. I know what you were up to."

She lit a cigarette. "What was I doing?"

"Psyching me up. First you get me mad, then you switch and play it for laughs—let's bring this big rigger down to earth."

"Did it work?"

"No comment. Anyway, I feel better—or easier."

They settled back in their chairs.

"There's something serious I want to say, Eddie." She could sense him listening closely now and she knew the intimacy was edging back. "When I joined up with you, there was the sex pull, sure. Also I wanted to sell you on population control, among other things, but there was something more. In your acceptance speech and then the press conference, I felt I was seeing a new kind of politician. With the right breaks, you could go all the way, maybe not this year, but someday. To be part of that was exciting." She paused. He was following, no longer tuned out. "But lately, something else has happened. You've made me think, just as you've made other people think. I'm going to be a different kind of congresswoman next term. The country does need your 'fair shake' overhaul, or something very like it. And damn it, I think it needs you too, Eddie. So don't change, please. Period. End of sermon."

"Things came at me awful fast this afternoon. And then Pete and R Danny rode me too hard. I didn't like it."

Kate nodded. "But you're not the only one under pressure. Pete and R Dan and I had a long talk this afternoon while you and Pinholster were together, and I learned something they haven't told you." She watched him for a moment as smoke coiled from her cigarette. "Pete's in debt. He has a large personal loan from a bank in Newark. Yesterday one of the officers phoned him and said they were calling the loan. All very businesslike, but Pete can sense these things and he knows the heat is on. If Pete quit you cold, the bank just might say, oh, well, the loan's okay then. Pete's sure of that. He suspects Charlie Herron's hand somewhere. Pete has no way to raise seventy-five thousand dollars right now. But he's sticking with you, even if it means bankruptcy. Why? Because you've made a believer out of him. And for a hard-nosed operator like Pete, that's a conversion right out of the old revival tent."

"I didn't know. I wish he'd told me."

"R Danny had his lumps too," said Kate. "A big contributor to the Center called him and said it was about time he 'muzzled the wild man.' And that from a so-called liberal. The whole establishment's afraid of you, Eddie. You're more of a threat than the revolutionaries. The people are listening to you."

"I guess that's what's bugging me. It's one thing to rattle along the expressways, throwing out ideas. It's something else to sit there in the White House and deliver."

"But that's the way it is, Eddie. To coin a phrase, this thing may be bigger than all of us."

They sat for a while without speaking, then Kate asked: "How do you feel now, Eddie?"

"Okay, I guess."

"No. Tell me, please. Honestly. How do you feel?'

"I feel lonely, Kate."

"Lonely?"

"Lonely as hell."

There was pain and a bleakness in Eddie's expression that Kate had not seen before. She walked over to him, sat on the arm of the chair and kissed him. They embraced, holding each other tenderly for long minutes. Then, suddenly, Eddie began to talk. He told about the film, about Pinholster's hour of panic, about his own feeling of inadequacy. Kate moved quietly back to her own chair as Eddie talked on like unpent waters coursing along a once familiar riverbed. He talked of his sons, of his boyhood, of his mother withdrawn within her shell, his trucking days, the separation from Mabel, first politics, the run for Congress, the Turnpike job. As he talked, the old confidence seeped back and several times he made her laugh with anecdotes about his days as mayor.

"Doesn't sound much like the making of a President, does it?" he asked at last. But his tone was lighter now, consciously self-deprecatory without apology.

"Oh, but it does," said Kate, "if—if you can just flip the whole scene and see it from a new angle."

"How's that?"

"You like to simplify. Well, do it now. Remember what Pinholster told you, that he finally realized that he was better fitted than Hudson? That's what it all boils down to. It isn't whether there are a thousand people better qualified to be President than you. The question is, who's the best, you or Pinholster? You know yourself. You have a feeling about Pinholster. So, who'll you vote for a week from Tuesday?"

"Me."

"Just once?"

He grinned. "They're very strict in my precinct. . . . How about you, Kate?"

"I intend to vote for me—and for you. Tonight for a spell I thought maybe I'd picked the wrong man. I'm a practical politician. I don't like to go with losers, and I positively hate going with losers who beat themselves."

"How'd you like a winner?"

"I'd love it. I'd sashay into that White House oval office, tell Flannery, 'Out of my way, Jim,' give a couple of secretaries the back of my hand, plump my fanny down on your desk and say, 'Mr. President, I've come to collect.'"

"And what's the pay-off?"

"The baby tax, my dispensaries, a dozen edicts I haven't thought of yet, maybe a *Time* cover story on America's most powerful woman and two hours with you in the Lincoln bed."

"How about starting with the last, in a Skirvin bed, and working our way back?"

"Winners only?"

"Hell, yes. In this outfit, vertical or horizontal, no losers allowed."

"Well, then, what are we waiting for?"

Kate gathered up her cigarettes and lighter and walked to the bedroom. She halted in the doorway, reached over her shoulder and tapped her back. "Help, Eddie. The zipper snags."

It was almost 3 o'clock when Eddie felt Kate stir at his side. She had dozed off, her head on his shoulder, her hair flung across his chest, her body warm and moist along the length of his.

"Awake?" she asked softly.

"Yeah. You fell asleep."

"I know. It was so good. Suppose it's love?"

"Could be. Whatever it is, I want it."

"Mmm . . . What have you been thinking?"

"About you, us—some."

"And?"

"The speech. Fenelli's right. Those six senators show just how the people get taken. I hope I can put it across. I'm sure as hell going to try."

"You will, Eddie. We're winners, you and I."

At that moment, 2:58 A.M. in Oklahoma City, 3:58 in the East, a loser died. Five hours earlier he had fallen against a car fender, a bullet through his neck, on a street of broken storefronts and wasted hopes 1400 miles from the Skirvin Hotel. He was a black man named George Dawson. A white policeman shot him.

16

The phone drilled Eddie's deep sleep at 8 o'clock. He came awake on the second ring and knocked over a glass of water while reaching across the bedside table. Kate murmured in protest as she rolled on her side.

"'Morning, Eddie." It was Pete Stackpole. "It's that time."

"Okay, okay." Eddie slowly shed the hood of sleep.

"How do you feel?"

Eddie yawned and stretched. "Pretty good." He glanced at Kate, then around the room. Sunlight filtered through the drawn curtains. His mind gradually narrowed into focus. "Pete, you guys were right about the speech. . . . Lemme see. How about fifteen minutes from now? I'll get Kate and R Danny in and we'll start work over coffee."

"Sure. You sound more like your old self."

"Yeah. I'm ready to get in and slug."

"That's the boy. . . . Eddie, I hate to hit you with this, but I've got bad news. Your friend, George Dawson. He, well, he was killed last night."

"George! . . . How?"

"Shot by a white cop in Merton about eleven o'clock their time. Now there's a riot under way. All hell to pay. Two blacks and one white dead so far. The state police are in and they may have to bring in the Guard. Looks bad."

"What about George?" Eddie struggled to accommodate the thought of death. "How did it happen?"

"We're not sure. First reports sound like he was shot by mistake.

Something about a party and a robbery. George was on his way to his car, I think."

"That must be mine. I let him borrow my old Impala while I was away."

"I'll know more in a few minutes. I've got a call in to the mayor and Phil's trying to reach somebody in Governor McCabe's office. See you in fifteen minutes. Sorry, Eddie."

Eddie looked around for Kate, but she was already in the shower. Later, as they dressed hurriedly, Eddie relayed Stackpole's news.

"George is a guy who ducks trouble," he said. "I don't think he ever carried a gun in his life. . . . The poor bastard. . . . Remember, you met him in Detroit last week when he flew over for my walk in black town."

"Of course," said Kate. "I liked him. He had a funny way of shooting up his eyebrows as if everything surprised him, when actually, I suppose, nothing did."

"Not much. George knew the score."

A waiter wheeled in a table and set out orange juice, cups and two large pots of coffee. Kate went to her own room to change into another outfit, returning as the rest of the staff arrived. Phil Liccardo handed Eddie a sheet of yellow paper.

"Vince Anderson gave it to me," he said. "It's off the AP wire."

Merton (AP)—This New Jersey city of 100,000 inhabitants exploded in racial violence last night after a black man, friend of Presidential Candidate Edward N. Quinn, was shot and mortally wounded by a white policeman.

Gunfire rattled in the city, store windows were smashed and cars overturned. At 7 A.M. at least three persons were known to be dead and more than a score injured seriously.

Rioting continued despite a declaration of emergency, ordering civilians off the streets, by Mayor Anthony Bianco. State police responded to a call for help from the Merton police department in the early hours.

The victim of the shooting which apparently triggered the riot was George Dawson, 49, friend and motel neighbor of Candidate Quinn who was in Oklahoma City on a western leg of his campaign.

Dawson, shot in the back of the neck shortly before 11 P.M.

(EDT), slumped against a fender of a car owned by Quinn and died five hours later in a hospital.

Sgt. Frank Kocsak, the officer who shot Dawson, said Dawson failed to halt when ordered to do so near the scene of a robbery of a liquor store. Police said Dawson reportedly attended a drinking party in the neighborhood.

The victim's mother, Mrs. Sarah Dawson, 71, angrily disputed the police version. She said her son spent the evening at her house and was on his way home to his motel room near New Brunswick. She said Candidate Quinn had lent his now famous 1968 Impala model Chevrolet sedan to Dawson for the duration of the campaign.

Quinn mentioned Dawson at his first press conference and subsequently Dawson was interviewed by press and television and accompanied Quinn last week on a night walk through Detroit's ghetto.

Merton, scene of past racial skirmishes between blacks and the large Italian and Polish communities, resembled a battlefield this morning as. . . .

Eddie laid the teletype copy on the breakfast table. "What a hardluck guy. No sooner did George get a leg up, than wham, something shoved him back down again. This time for keeps."

"The mayor's office tells me there're two more dead," said Stackpole. "They've closed off about twenty blocks in the black section. Bianco's asking for the Guard."

"The Guard's alerted," said Liccardo, "but the governor's holding off to see if the local and state police can contain it."

They stood around the table, nervously drinking coffee, talking swiftly, trying to assess the meaning of an event unrolling half a continent away. For all its bravado, flashy tone and confident victory claims, an American presidential campaign is a fragile, vulnerable thing. A candidate can be damaged by heedless remarks of friends, scarred by the acts of strangers, ambushed by a deceptively docile issue or destroyed by a far-off happening that taps buried passions in millions of voters. Any untoward development is suspect, for it may portend sudden change that rends supposedly foolproof strategy.

"If there had to be a riot," said Stackpole, "why not in Connecticut where it's Pinholster's baby?"

"Are you saying Eddie ought to do something about this because it's in New Jersey?" asked Kate.

"Not necessarily. But it taints him. A lot of idiots will blame Eddie, guilt by association."

"We should put out a statement of condolence for Dawson's family," said Liccardo.

Eddie was already writing it on a scrap of notepaper. "I wish I was back there right now," he said.

"In Merton?" Hunk Janiszewski was incredulous. "You're nuts, Eddie. What would you do? You're not the boss there."

"I'm running for President. That gives me some muscle. I sure don't feel right flying to California. That's the wrong way this morning."

"We better start moving," said Stackpole. "We have to leave the hotel at nine if we're going to make the L.A. speech in time."

"Let's get the bags down in the lobby," said Eddie, "then just hold there for a while."

The next ten minutes passed in small, hurried preparations for departure. Eddie was stowing his toilet kit in his bag when the phone rang. Stackpole answered.

"McCabe for you," he said. Clark McCabe, governor of New Jersey and a party leader, had named Eddie to the Turnpike Commission but had not endorsed him for President.

"Have you heard about our problem on Beckdale Street?" asked McCabe after the hellos.

"No, what happened?"

"Fourteen armed black men seized a three-story apartment house, the Beckdale Arms, in the Polish section." McCabe's speech was rapid, concise. "That was about dawn. They're holding seven white tenants as hostages. The blacks are members of a revolutionary outfit called Brothers of the Night. They threaten to shoot anyone, white or black, who approaches the building without their permission. If we move in or use tear gas, they say they'll kill the hostages.

"They've put out a list of five demands, including amnesty, of course. They'll free the hostages and leave the building if we accept the demands, which they label non-negotiable. When I asked to come into the Beckdale Arms to talk, they replied they would shoot.

The reason I'm calling you is this: They say the only person in—uh —authority they'll talk to is you—because, they say, you were a friend of George Dawson. What I'm doing is relaying their message to you."

Eddie knew the governor, but had spoken to him only infrequently on Turnpike and party business. He regarded McCabe as a capable politician, but inclined to be officious and legalistic. He was the kind of man who petted dogs, but seldom stroked wounded human egos.

"Are you asking me to come there, Governor?"

"I'm giving you the facts. I'm not making an official request."

"Well, do you want me to come?"

"It might buy time. The danger's obvious. It's entirely up to you."

"If I wasn't in this, what would you do?"

"Our first job is to stop the fighting in Merton and secure the city. After that I'll face what to do about the apartment. I might consider amnesty, but the other demands are unacceptable on their face. We might be able to negotiate something, but they refuse to talk to me."

Eddie considered. He had no idea what he could accomplish, but he sensed that at this hour, flying in the opposite direction from Merton was unthinkable.

"Okay, I'll come," he said. "We'll leave right away for the airport. That ought to put our charter jet down in Newark about three hours or so from now."

"All right. I'll have a state police car there for you. Jerry Babson, my black minorities man, will come along and brief you on the ride down."

Eddie turned to his staff and filled in the gaps in conversation from the governor's end.

"Bad news," said Liccardo. "That's like trying to get the Panthers and the Mafia together at a prayer breakfast."

"Maybe you have to go, but it's mission impossible," said Stackpole. "Now, whatever happens in Merton, you're the goat. It's tails you lose, heads Pinholster wins."

The staff scattered into a scramble of last-minute errands. Doors banged, handbags were stuffed, coats found, toilets visited, orders shouted. Jim Flannery, adapting like a chameleon to the new campaign coloration, assigned a Secret Service agent to remain behind and make telephoned security arrangements for a candidate arriving in Newark instead of Los Angeles. Phil Liccardo, scurrying off to alert the press, had visions of another epic luggage debacle, with Sybil Jamieson's lost bag finally reaching her three days after the election. Marching to the elevator, Eddie and staff revamped campaign plans. R Dan Fenelli would deliver Eddie's speech to the Teamsters, flying commercial if possible, otherwise chartering on a fly-now-pay-later-maybe scheme. Pete Stackpole would cancel Eddie's California dates, fly the staff from Newark to Washington. Only Margot Hicks and Phil Liccardo would accompany Eddie to Merton. Odds and ends: Order press buses in Newark. Cancel hotel reservations in Los Angeles. Call county leaders in California. Call off the advance men. And suddenly Eddie remembered. That damn film. The shredded negative was still in the box in his jacket pocket.

Eddie plowed through milling reporters in the Skirvin lobby, climbed into the Electra 225 and led the caravan under police escort on a breakneck ride to Will Rogers Airport. On arrival he buttonholed Fenelli as he emerged from a staff car.

"Burn this somewhere for me," he said, handing the box to Fenelli. "I don't care how, just make sure you burn it. I'll tell you sometime. . . . And R Danny, name all six senators in that speech. Lay it all on the line like we first talked about. You know, the works. I'll stand behind it."

"Will do, Eddie. What changed your mind?"

"I guess it boils down to something Kate said. It isn't whether I'm good enough to be President. It's just whether I'd be better than Pinholster. Looked at that way, it's like this Merton thing. There's no choice."

Three hours later Eddie raced south on the New Jersey Turnpike in the second of three state police cars. State troopers and Secret Service agents rode in the first and third cars. The newsmen, shepherded by Liccardo, lagged far behind in a press bus delayed by the stowing of baggage. With Eddie were Jim Flannery and Oscar Baker, Margot Hicks and Jerry Babson, the governor's black adviser on negritude, welfare and rebellion. A fastidious man with a mincing accent, Babson proved to be even less black in attitude than he was in skin color, a pale tan. He reported factually enough on the racial battle, but he knew little more about the Merton ghetto than Eddie did. Margot soon began to fence with Babson as she might with a white man.

As he sped along the Turnpike, where every overpass, grade and interchange was as familiar to Eddie as the contours of his own body, he tuned one ear to Babson and fixed his mind on Merton, the state's fourth-largest city.

Urbanologists studied Merton, clergymen prayed for it, business-men fled it and inhabitants endured it. Within its twenty square miles, Merton nurtured every virus and bacillus of the eastern sea-board's common variety of urban plague and boasted a few unique strains of its own. Its history paralleled that of many cities. A village in Revolutionary War days—Washington fought, tarried and was memorialized in granite there—Merton prospered and slowly grew as a city of British stock. Then, more than a century ago, began the successive waves of immigration from other countries of Europe. German, Irish, Polish, Russian, Hungarian, Slav and Italian workers poured in to man the machine shops, factories and mills. As Merton became a grimy, low-wage industrial center, where employees were herded into biennial Republican torchlight parades under penalty of job blacklisting for those who declined, the class structure jelled. The old WASP families controlled the banks and mills and dwelled in the big Victorian homes, the Irish ran the politics and police force and the Poles, Slavs and Italians did the manual labor.

Then, after the depression and World War II, came the great tide of blacks from southern farms and hamlets. As the impoverished blacks moved in, affluent whites moved out. Merton, for the first time in its history, lost population in 1950, again in 1960 and 1970. Industry decamped to the west and south. Department stores, services and entertainment facilities deserted the city in pursuit of the fleeing money—to the new shopping centers in the leafy suburbs which now ringed Merton like a white noose. Merton's class structure shifted. WASPs, now largely absentee, still controlled the financing and shrunken industry, but Italians ran the city government while blacks and Puerto Ricans, now half the population, fought to wrest some of the dwindling jobs from the resident Poles and Italians. Taxes climbed while the tax base shrank.

Now the city's face mirrored its neglect. In the downtown section blank marquees jutted from abandoned movie theaters, boarded storefronts gaped like toothless crones, sooty show windows wore the finger-tracings of graffiti and loudspeakers blared from sleazy discount stores. An expressway, carrying cars shuttling from one suburban outpost to another, cut through one part of the city while a great scar defaced another. This was the scar of urban renewal. Like the ravages of strip mining, its devastation was as real as the renewal was conjectural. On residential streets only a few of the frame bungalows and brick row houses evinced intentions of permanency by new paint and mortar. Some blocks looked as though the dwellings had been strafed by attack planes in some forgotten war and never repaired.

The people of Merton had lost hope for the city. Unemployment stood high. Drug addicts robbed and mugged. A third of the population subsisted on welfare checks. Every month another business moved out of town. White, black and Puerto Rican children battled one another in the decaying schools where defeated teachers spoke of Walt Whitman and Mark Twain but yearned for survival kits. Everyone knew that Merton was dying. Some believed that a remedy for the fatal affliction must exist somewhere. A few thought they knew what it was. No one knew where to find it.

Eddie, himself an outer-city man more at home in the highway strips and townless sprawls of the resettled white world than on a city block, had no answer for Merton or the hundred Mertons of America. The thought depressed him as the patrol cars left the Turnpike and raced toward the bleeding city on a four-lane divided highway. Motels, gas stations, shopping centers, diners, nursing homes, industrial parks, bowling alleys, restaurants and skating rinks —the landmarks of Nowhere, U.S.A.—fled past. The signs and shapes were all familiar. Eddie had traveled the road scores of times. But today the familiar provided scant comfort.

He met Governor Clark McCabe by appointment at a state motor vehicle inspection station outside the city limits. The governor had only the police version of George Dawson's death. Sergeant Kocsak and another officer, patrolling in a squad car, were dispatched to a liquor store where a burglar alarm sounded. They saw a black man running from a side door, carrying several objects. One officer cornered the suspect while Kocsak ran to the front. He saw a man walking rapidly away with a bundle under his arm. Kocsak ordered the man to halt. Instead this suspect hurried toward a parked car. Kocsak fired, hitting his target in the back of the neck. George Dawson fell against the fender of Eddie's car. His package contained his own shirts, shorts and socks, newly laundered by his mother. The mother lived next door to the liquor store. A drinking party was in progress on the other side of Mrs. Sarah Dawson's cottage. Eddie's car was parked about a hundred feet farther along the block. Police said Dawson had been at the party. Mrs. Dawson said George had been there only briefly, had spent most of the evening at her house. Whatever the facts, said McCabe, inebriated blacks poured out of the party house at the sound of the single shot. Ten minutes later the riot, touched off by the drinkers, was in full swing. George died five hours later in a hospital.

"Shot for carrying a package." Eddie shook his head in disbelief. "George was a tall man. His neck is a helluva long way from his legs where I thought cops were supposed to aim."

"I know how you feel," said McCabe. "Kocsak apparently didn't do anything right. . . . But that will have to wait. Right now I've got a small war on my hands."

The governor dealt out the latest riot report in uncluttered, efficient prose while Eddie drank coffee from a paper cup. They talked briefly by phone with Mayor Bianco in his downtown city hall office. Riot status: Death toll, 6. Injuries, 100 plus. Arrests, 172. Police had cleared all major streets, forced evacuation of a park where blacks and Italians had exchanged rocks, bottles and some shots. City under partial curfew. National Guard units bivouacked just outside city limits. Most people now indoors with streets deserted. Pedestrians or motorists found within a twenty-block inner-city area subject to automatic arrest. Brothers of the Night appearing at open windows of the Beckdale Arms with rifles and shotguns. Hostages believed unharmed. Telephone communication possible. Brothers waiting for Eddie.

Demands of Brothers of the Night: (1) Mayor Bianco must agree to bring first-degree murder charges against Officer Kocsak. (2) Withdrawal of all police, local and state, from black neighborhoods. (3) All blacks under arrest must be turned over to an all-black "council of justice" to be named by the Brothers of the Night. (4) McCabe must agree to allot $5,000,000 in emergency aid to Merton, the money to be spent by a black committee named by the Brothers. (5) Blanket amnesty for Brothers of the Night.

Agreement of Governor and Commissioner: Eddie empowered to negotiate these demands, but McCabe must approve. Governor willing to grant amnesty for seizure of hostages and building, but not for past crimes, if any.

"The Beckdale Arms is the key now," said McCabe as they parted. "If we can clear the building, the riot's over. But fighting will continue as long as those white hostages are held by armed blacks."

Four patrol cars, flanked now by a motorcycle escort, entered the city with the governor and Jerry Babson in the lead automobile. The press bus had caught up and now kept pace in the rear. As Eddie and Margot rode through the deserted streets, they could see people peering from closed windows. A few stood on porches and an occasional venturesome boy could be spotted on a roof. It was a chill, dank, shadowless afternoon, the sky an unbroken sheet of gray with no glow to mark the location of the sun.

"You'll get a lot of rap from the Brothers," said Margot. "Wait it out, Eddie, even if they talk you back to slavery. My guess is they'll give some in the end—provided McCabe does too. Both sides gotta give. No other way."

"What do you suppose they really want, Margot?"

She looked at him with dismay. "For a man supposed to be a quick study, you sure take your time digging the black scene." She spoke as one weary of explanations. "They want the same as every other nigger in this country—a piece of the action. How many years we got to keep sayin' that to you people?"

Flannery turned toward them. "I talked to the chief in Washington. He ordered me to repeat what I told you on the plane. The Service turns thumbs down on you entering that building and we can't accept responsibility for your safety if you go in."

"The party line of you bureaucrats," Eddie chided. "Any more bright ideas, pal?"

"Well, I intend to go in with you. Not that it'll make any difference."

"So do I," said Margot, "and I might make a difference."

"Well, we'll have a picnic," said Eddie. "Who's bringing the franks and beer?"

Leafless maples bordered Beckdale, a street of modest frame houses, small browning lawns and dejected shrubs. Trash cans and refuse heaps stood along the curb, awaiting collection. The cars halted in front of a grocery store, commandeered as the governor's riot headquarters. Eddie jotted down the store's phone number and shook hands with McCabe.

In step with Flannery and Baker, Eddie and Margot Hicks walked down the block to the barricaded intersection as the political writers, spilling out of the press bus, joined local newsmen to become riot reporters. Phil Liccardo bustled about. A dozen Merton policemen and New Jersey state troopers in light blue uniforms paced the street behind a row of wooden traffic barriers. An officer pointed out the Beckdale Arms, a dingy red-brick structure midway in the surrounded block. Flannery and Baker removed their shoulder holsters and gave the weapons to a state trooper for safekeeping.

A Merton lieutenant aimed a bullhorn toward the apartment house. "Commissioner Quinn and party, all unarmed, are now coming to the Beckdale Arms." The words rumbled down the empty street.

The four emissaries stepped through the barricade and walked slowly abreast down the center of the pavement. The small, white frame houses stood in silence, blinds drawn at most windows. Here and there people watched from doorways. Far down the block a dog, as smudged and gray as the overcast, trotted along the sidewalk. In the distance a police siren wailed as though in pain.

"Hold it!" The shout came from the apartment house about 100 feet away. A black man under a halo of hair leaned out of a window.

The muzzle of a shotgun protruded from the sill. "Which one is Eddie Quinn?"

"I am." Eddie raised a hand.

"Who those dudes with you?"

"Secret Service."

"No way. Send 'em back. And the black chick?"

"Margot Hicks. She's on my staff."

"Same answer. You alone or no talk."

Eddie shrugged. "Well, I guess that's it."

Flannery gripped Eddie's elbow. "I know your mind's made up. Take it easy, Eddie."

"I wish you'd do something for me, Margot," said Eddie. "Get the facts on George's death. When you talk to Mrs. Dawson, tell her I'll come by as soon as this is over. If the police try to shove you around, tell the press about it."

"Same old story, Eddie." Margot flicked a cynical glance at him. "Black girl sure to be hassled by the cops, huh?"

"It's not my town, honey, but I know it from way back."

Margot, Flannery and Baker turned and began walking toward the barriers. It took Eddie only a few seconds to reach the apartment house door. It was opened by a young black man wearing a zippered jacket and a dark blue beret. Eddie found himself in a small, white-tiled hallway with a row of mailboxes on the wall. The man frisked him quickly, then said: "Follow me." He carried a hand gun.

They mounted the stairs. At the first floor, two men carrying weapons paced along a dark corridor. The escort climbed another flight, led Eddie down another dim hallway, rapped once on a door, then opened it.

Four black men sat in a semicircle, facing the door. The room, apparently the parlor of an apartment, reeked of stale food as though fumes from a thousand sauerkraut dinners had settled into the wall-paper amid the pattern of nymphs and roses. Heavy furniture be-spoke a faded, turn-of-the-century middle-class propriety. A cabinet with glass doors held shelves crowded with enameled figurines. On the wall hung a framed print of the Virgin in dimming colors. Eddie could imagine the tenants, a pair of elderly ladies who wor-shiped at early Mass at Our Lady of Mount Carmel.

Then his eyes found the arsenal. Two pistols, a shotgun and two rifles rested on a cedar chest near the window. Beside them lay a few gas masks.

"Have a seat." The speaker's voice had a mocking lilt. He was very black, his wiry hair short-cropped. He wore a blue turtle-neck sweater beneath a frayed gray cardigan. He pointed toward a wicker chair with a high, fanlike back.

Eddie eased into the chair, which faced the four men.

"I'm Brother Ned." The ebony face radiated as though Eddie's arrival brought him untold happiness. "This here's Brother Saint . . . Brother Julian . . . and Brother Mwimba."

Brother Saint, short and pudgy, had a pitted face that alternately glowered and pouted. He wore sneakers, old denim pants and a heavy woolen shirt.

Brother Julian, who peered through granny glasses, had sharp, narrow features, an almond complexion. He wore, surprisingly, a business suit, button-down shirt and tie.

Brother Mwimba wore a brilliant dashiki of golds and scarlets. His features and eyes were soft and his Afro formed an immense halo. Eddie recognized him as the man who had challenged him from the window.

"Glad to know you. I'm Eddie Quinn."

"What can we do for you?" asked Ned. A benevolent smile flooded his face.

"I'd like to see the hostages first. Then, I guess, we'd better settle on the ground rules here."

"You *demand* to see the prisoners?" Mwimba's tone was low, rich and slightly menacing.

"I'm not demanding anything," said Eddie evenly. "Still, if any of the people you're holding has been hurt, we've got a different ball game, haven't we?"

"Man, you call this a ball game?" asked Brother Julian. His enunciation was unslurred, precise and cold.

"You know what I mean. It's just my way of saying it."

"Eddie don't trust us." Ned's eyes shone above a great wreath of a smile. Eddie wondered if he wore joy as a mask.

"No, I don't. Just reverse the deal. Would you?"

Mwimba answered softly. "Don't have to turn it around. I don't trust the man, no way, no time, no place."

"I'm not the man. I'm Eddie Quinn."

Brother Saint, who had been slumped in his chair, hands folded on his stomach as though dozing, sprang up and flung out his arms. "He not the man, he not the man," he said in a high singsong chant. He began to pace back and forth in a rolling gait, arms flailing the air. Eddie watched in astonishment.

"He's not the man. Oh Lord, nobody ever the man," sang the Saint in the reedy voice of a country preacher. "Who hold us in slavery for three hundred years? The man? No. Ain't no man. . . . Who hang Nat Turner down in Virginia? The man? No, ain't no man. . . . What mother never told us that Crispus Attucks died when them British redcoats up in Boss-town shot him? The man? Who-ee, no. Ain't no man." The Saint sang his high-pitched way through major Negro names in American history, Benjamin Banneker, Frederic Douglass, Lewis Latimer, Richard Wright, Dorie Miller, rolling and swaying around the room and occasionally halting in front of Eddie for a private rendition.

"So the Saint was born in B-more in the man-made depression and the man wouldn't give his daddy no job 'cause he have this rule for his unfreed slaves, first fired, last hired. Only there ain't no man, so maybe Brother Saint was only dreaming it." He was shouting in cadence now. "And then we come to Mirth-town, ha, ha, where the man has this statue of George Washington pointing south, which means, 'Nigger, go back where you come from.' And the man keeps us on his tight-ass welfare so's we won't take no jobs away from the man's white friends. An' Mayor Bianco, who shovels the man's shit, he says he ain't gonna have no law of the jungle, but the man's law of his own order.

"Then the chief of the pigs, who hassled niggers on his way up the force, says he believes in equal hiring which must mean one nigger is worth three honkies because that's how they put on new cops in Mirthtown. And they pick up black kids and send them off to Livingston College so they'll feel worse when they get out with them degrees that qualify them to rake the man's yard and deliver him another living-color TV set."

The Saint swayed back and forth, chanting his litany of white infamy and oppression in Merton. Brother Ned beamed on the performance as he might at the opening night of a black musical, but when Brother Mwimba began to click his fingers in rhythm, Eddie suspected that the Saint's act was not a new one. Julian watched with a tight smile. At first bewildered, Eddie became caught up in the imagery and found himself relishing apt allusions to several white politicians in Merton. The Saint's hate came through unvarnished, yet he obviously enjoyed his starring role.

"Oh, there ain't no man in Mirthtown, ain't no man in the Whitey House, ain't no man nowhere," he chanted in conclusion. "So couldn't have been the man who shot George Dawson in the back for the crime of fixin' to drive home with his clean rags."

The Saint sank back in his chair, breathing heavily and glaring at Eddie. The finale chilled the echoing memory of Brother Saint's mordant banter. There was a long silence.

"Do you think George would be dead now if he'd been white?" asked Julian.

"No, I don't," said Eddie.

"Any cop ever shoot you when you carrying your clothes and minding your business?" It was Julian again.

"No."

"You care about George?" asked Mwimba.

"I liked him. We weren't old friends, but we were friends. It's hard to realize he's gone."

All four men eyed him intently during these quick exchanges. There was more silence.

"How about if we let him see the prisoners?" asked Ned brightly. Julian nodded, followed in turn by Mwimba and the Saint. Eddie thought he was witnessing the junta's pecking order and he filed the scene away for future reference.

"Come with me," said Ned. He picked up a revolver from the chest, jammed it in his belt and, with a flashing smile, led Eddie to the door. Eddie found Brother Ned's effulgence strangely unsettling.

They walked along the gray hallway to a door near the rear of the building. Ned rapped once and said, "Open up, Jesse. It's Ned."

A tall, somber young black man cracked the door, looked out, then opened. He held a pistol.

Eddie entered another living room, this one filled with plastic-covered furniture. Seven white people looked at him as though he were an explorer newly arrived at the wilderness base camp. Four women, three of them elderly and one a young blond with her hair in curlers, sat at a card table in the midst of a game. Three somewhat seedy middle-aged men lounged about, one of them on a sofa with a magazine in his lap.

"Ask 'em whatever you want," said Ned.

"My name's Eddie Quinn. I'm here to find out how you're being treated."

A birdlike woman lowered her spectacles and eyed Eddie over the rims. "Aren't you that Eddie Quinn that's running for President?" Eddie nodded. "Well, for the love of God," she said. "How do you like that?"

"Yeah, I saw you on TV," said the blond in curlers. She swept Eddie with a glance tailored to fit tigers, Zsa Zsa Gabor, pygmies, golf champions, Mayor Lindsay, Bill Buckley and other celebrities of the tube.

"Has anyone been hurt?"

Six people shook their heads. The frail little woman with the glasses said: "Jesse twisted my wrist some, but I don't know as he meant to."

"How are you being treated?"

"Okay. They let us fix lunch," said the blond. "We're going to run out of cigarettes soon is all."

Eddie explained his mission. They were avid for news, anxious to know when they would be released, the state of the riot, whether the curfew was still on, what the mayor and governor were doing and why they were not permitted to have a radio. Eddie realized they were unaware of the announced threat to kill them should the building be attacked. Unconscious of the full danger and with the original terror of the seizure hours behind them, they were verging on boredom. Careful not to alarm the hostage tenants, Eddie merely said that he was here to talk to the Brothers and would return later. He wrote down their names and identification on a piece of paper.

"We could use some ciggies and Seven Crown," said the blond as Eddie left.

In the hallway Brother Ned wrapped Eddie in a sunburst of good will. "See, not a scratch on 'em." This time the radiance struck Eddie as more menacing than peculiar. He wondered if Ned could slice him with a knife without losing his smile. Returning to the front apartment, Eddie tried to grasp the essence of the Brothers. Were they disciplined revolutionaries, men resolved to establish some black clout in the system or perhaps angry warriors with no clear goal? Eddie had only a few clues thus far and he needed more before he could chart a course.

In the parlor where sauerkraut reigned in memory the four Brothers faced Eddie like a tribunal as he settled into the wicker chair again.

"Why are you here?" asked Julian. In his suit and tie, he looked oddly out of place, like a broker in a longshoremen's hiring hall.

The question puzzled Eddie. "Because you asked me to come."

"Oh no," said Mwimba. "McCabe wanted to come in. We said no. Only white dude we'd allow up is you because you claim Dawson for a friend."

"We willing to talk to you, but we didn't ask you to come." Ned blessed him with another smile. "We got nothin' to say. We made our demands. When McCabe accepts, we hand him the building and the people. Until then, well, we in no hurry."

"What if he doesn't accept?"

"He has to," said Julian. "No white governor wants the blood of seven white people on his hands." He was cool, precise. "Nigger blood of fourteen Brothers, sure. Whites, no."

Eddie decided to test. "How would you kill them?"

"Killin's not hard," said Mwimba quietly.

"No?" Eddie looked him in the eye. "Would you tell me just how you'd go about killing that little old lady with the glasses in the back room? Would you put a gun to her ear and pull the trigger? Press a knife to her throat and slash the jugular?"

"If my life or hers, the how wouldn't matter," said Mwimba.

"How about you, Brother Ned? Would you shove the muzzle down her throat and fire?"

"That's not . . ."

But the Saint shouted: "Ax me!" He heaved from his chair, seized a pistol from the chest and waved it at Eddie. "You do it just like ol' pig-fart Kocsak done it to George Dawson. You aim for the back of the brain and let fly." The Saint pranced to stage center, brandishing his gun. "Quinn, you like all the white mothers in Mirthtown, the U.S. and A. and the whole goddamn white world. White pig kill your friend, George, and you don't give it no never-mind, but if one little old woman in a white skin get hurt, oh, that's wicked, man. That's deary me, oh, my, my. George your friend? Shee-it! You cry one little tear? You demand justice from Bianco, the greaseball? Or from Governor Mac Rape? Oh no. George lyin' there on the slab with a bullet through his neck, and you worrying about some old white broad you only seen but once."

The Saint rolled and swayed about the room, shouting and cursing. The cadence was gone now and wild diatribe replaced the biting humor. He soon dropped Eddie and George as topics and began to catalogue the sins of Merton's white officials, police and business-men. Watching the other blacks, trying to read their thoughts, Eddie saw a look of amused tolerance on Ned's face. Julian looked bored, almost as if he might yawn any second. Suddenly Eddie understood the Saint's role. The tubby man, with his pouting and glowering face pitted from an old bout with smallpox, was the Brothers' fili-busterer. When they wanted to play for time, the Saint sprang into action, strutted the boards while they pondered their next move. As the Saint reached his climax, Eddie noted that Ned, Julian and Mwimba were studying him, Eddie, for his reactions. At last the Saint dropped the revolver on the chest and sank back into his chair, panting and fixing Eddie with a stare of malevolent challenge.

Eddie waited a minute, then asked: "Ned, how would you kill that little lady with the glasses?"

Ned bathed Eddie in sunbeams. "Now, Eddie, you know we ain't ever going to face wastin' the old woman. Never come to that. They not going to attack us as long as we holding them whites. So we all just lay back and take it easy and two, three days from now, ol' McCabe'll get tired of waitin' on us and he'll give us what we ask.

We got plenty of chow around and if we run out, I guess nobody outside'll let them white people starve."

Eddie made up his mind. The hostages were not in immediate danger. These men might kill, but they were not killers. "Can we talk about your demands?" he asked.

"Go ahead," said Julian. "It's a free country—for whites. If you want to talk, nobody here gonna stop you."

"Are the demands written down someplace?"

"Yeah." Ned motioned with his head. "Brother Saint, give Eddie that paper from off the table." The Saint obediently did as told, but glared at Eddie as he handed him a sheet of lined yellow tablet paper. Now Eddie was sure of two links in the brotherly chain, Ned first, the Saint last. There were five numbered, hand-written paragraphs on the paper.

"Number One," Eddie read aloud. "'Mayor Bianco must agree bring first-degree murder charges against Officer Kocsak.' I want justice done here as much as you do. Despite what Brother Saint says, George dyin' was tough for me to take. He was my friend. He taught me a lot. Why, he made me read three books that gave me some ideas for this campaign I'm in." Eddie talked for five minutes about his friendship with Dawson. No one interrupted him. "But now you say 'first-degree murder.' That means premeditated, that Kocsak planned to kill George and set out to do it. We don't know the facts yet, but we're pretty sure that's not true. Kocsak wasn't hunting for George. He shot him near the scene of a burglary. It was a helluva terrible thing to do and I want to see Kocsak tried for it, but first-degree murder won't stick."

"He planned to shoot Dawson when he aimed the gun," said Mwimba.

"That's true, but probably not before he saw Dawson on the street. And it was dark, so he couldn't have known it was Dawson."

"Any old nigger would do," said Julian.

"Maybe." Eddie thought for a while. "Look, I think you Brothers are missing something. We all want justice done. What I'd like to see is immediate suspension of Kocsak from duty pending an investigation."

"Investigation!" Julian scoffed. "The man asks Kocsak a couple of questions and lets him go."

"Not this time. Suppose you demand an investigation by attorneys, most of them black, appointed by the governor? If you did that, I'd join you in the demand. Then if the committee recommends a murder charge and the county prosecutor refuses to go ahead, I promise I'll come back to Merton and raise hell until he does."

"Same old shit," the Saint growled.

"No. Suppose it was a black cop who shot? Wouldn't you want an investigation?"

"Tom shoot a Brother," said Mwimba, "and he ought to be locked up and put to trial."

"Wanton murder of black people on the streets by police has got to stop," said Julian. "Kocsak saw a black face, so bang, he shoots. On a white block, he'd go up to that car, very polite, and say, 'Excuse me, friend. What have you got in that bundle, please, sir?'"

"You're right, Brother Julian," said Eddie. "And a big investigation might make people realize just that."

"Did I hear right?" asked Ned. "You say you'd join us if we ask for an investigation?"

"That's what I said."

"How would you write that up?"

My God, thought Eddie, we're negotiating. "Well, let's try it together." He turned the sheet on the back. Julian handed him a pencil. Eddie pulled his chair close to the others. "Number One. Immediate suspension . . ." Julian suggested a phrase, Eddie another. Mwimba added some words as did Ned. Only the Saint contributed nothing. Twenty minutes later, Eddie read aloud:

We, the Brothers of the Night, will evacuate the Beckdale Arms and release all persons held by us upon agreement by the proper authorities to do the following:

1. Mayor Bianco to suspend immediately Sergeant Frank Kocsak from the Merton police force. Governor McCabe within three days to appoint a committee of attorneys, a majority of

whom shall be black, to investigate the killing of George Dawson by Sergeant Kocsak. The governor to present the committee's report to the county prosecutor with a recommendation for appropriate action. (Edward N. Quinn urges the same action as that demanded by the Brothers of the Night.)

Mwimba looked pleased and Brother Ned showered his smiles about. Eddie found Ned's radiance less threatening now. Actually he did not know what to make of Ned. Eddie turned to the second demand.

"You ask withdrawal of all police, state and local, from black neighborhoods," he said. "Are you sure all black people want that? I'll bet a lot of them want police protection."

"They don't want no white pigs around," said the Saint, scowling.

"Wait a minute," said Julian to Eddie. "What are you trying to do? Are you fixing to water down all our demands?"

"I'm trying to end the shooting in Merton. You guys are playing a big hand. Hell, you're holding seven people under threat of death. But you've also got some legitimate beefs. What I want to do is go back to McCabe with reasonable demands—only I'd call them requests—that I could support myself."

"You also politicking to get y'self a big job," said Mwimba with suspicion.

"Sure I am. But I can't make any votes whatever I do in this building. Believe me."

"Yeah, the election." Julian digressed. "What are you going to do about the cities if you're elected? The more they go black, the faster the jobs melt away."

"I honestly don't know. It's a helluva mess. But I'm sure of one thing. If I make it, I'm going to have black men and white men try to figure it out together. Women too. When I say, 'fair shake,' I mean it."

"Easy to make big promises," said the Saint. "The man born to lie. And you the man, just like Mac Rape."

"I don't think I lie. The fat boys have been taking us all for years, playing the races against each other, while they get more and we get less. That's what Charles Evers down in Mississippi says—and that black man's right on. When are we going to wise up and work together for that 'fair shake' we've got coming?"

Eddie plodded on, using many of the arguments from his standard campaign pitch. Soon Ned and Mwimba joined in, then Julian and finally the Saint. They talked politics until the gray afternoon slid into muddy twilight. Eddie sensed that with each passing minute he was accumulating a kind of trust, wary and grudging, yet visible. He made no effort to push the Brothers, pursuing with them every detour and meandering digression.

Dusk melted into night. Ned switched on a floor lamp. "Saint, go wake them sleepin' Brothers and change the guard. We got to watch sharp now it's dark." After the Saint left, carrying a rifle, Brother Ned spoke to Eddie.

"Let's go back to Point Two. You was sayin'?"

"You want all police out of black neighborhoods. Why don't you make that 'white police'? How many black cops on the Merton force?"

"Nineteen per cent black," said Julian quickly. "Should be fifty."

"Well, that's enough to give protection in black sections. With black cops patrolling, you get what you want, the white ones off your back. And that would be hard for McCabe to say no to. But if you say all police, you're asking a governor to deny protection to a lot of citizens."

Ned looked questioningly at Julian and Mwimba. They both nodded. "Okay, let's write it up," said Ned. Again they labored with paper and pencil and produced:

2. Withdraw all white police, local and state, from black neighborhoods, substituting all-black city patrols until the emergency is over.

A single loud rap shook the door. "Kapanga," said a voice. "Come in, Brother Kap," said Ned. A slight black boy, not more than fifteen years old, appeared in the doorway. He proudly carried a hand gun.

"Governor on the phone," he said. "He want him." He pointed to Eddie.

"You take him," ordered Ned.

Eddie followed the boy across the hallway into the dimly lit living room of another apartment. The cradle phone rested on a table.

"You all right?" asked McCabe after Eddie identified himself.

"Okay."

"Where do we stand?"

"We're talking. Some progress. What's it like outside?"

"Tense, but holding. Some sniper fire and another store looted. I'm going to try to get through the night without bringing the Guard in. An incident with your Miss Hicks and a patrolman outside Dawson's mother's house, but we straightened that out. She's in with the mother now. . . . How about the hostages?"

"In good shape when I saw them a couple of hours ago."

"Any chance of something from you tonight?"

"Maybe, maybe not. Like I say, we're talking."

"They brought me a cot. I'll be here all night. If there's a break, you get me up, Eddie."

"Will do."

They said quick good-bys and the boy escorted Eddie back to the parlor as though he were a spy caught behind enemy lines. While Kapanga stood in the doorway, Eddie repeated the conversation as accurately as he could.

"That what he said, as far as you heard?" Ned asked the boy. Kapanga confirmed Eddie's account, then closed the door.

Demand Number Three, that all blacks under arrest be tried by an all-black "council of justice," named by the Brothers of the Night, was discussed next. Eddie argued that no governor anywhere could agree to turn over the law's machinery to a rump court, whether white, black or yellow. The Brothers contended that "the man's" justice was a mockery for blacks. Julian gave a long, learned lecture on operation of the people's courts in Havana. Mwimba told of once being held for three months on a breaking and entering charge, only to have the prosecutor concede at last that the police had arrested the wrong man. The Saint staged another furious ballet depicting Mayor Bianco's triple standard of punishment for alleged offenders, light for fellow Italians, moderate for other whites, vindictive for blacks. The talk ran on and on. Kapanga came in silently with hot servings of pork and beans and coffee. The Saint disappeared somewhere for an hour. Once Mwimba took a revolver from the chest, emptied the chamber and slowly and methodically cleaned the gun, then reloaded it. Eleven o'clock passed with no movement.

"Tell you what," said Eddie finally. "Why don't we pass over Number Three and see if we can agree on the last two points? Then we come back to Three?"

This fetched assent. Eddie, taking heart, read from the yellow sheet: "Four. Governor McCabe agrees to allot $5,000,000 in emergency aid to Merton, the money to be spent by a black committee named by the Brothers of the Night."

"Now I don't know for sure," said Eddie, "but my guess is that McCabe might buy that if we just changed a few words. In the first place, McCabe probably would have to ask the legislature for the money. Also, you don't need all-black committees to achieve your purpose. A majority of Merton is non-white now, so why not say an advisory committee that follows the city's racial lines?"

"If Bianco names the committee," said Julian, "city hall will graft half the money and his friends will get contracts for the rest."

"Okay. Let's have a state agency control the money," said Eddie. "What we want to do is present McCabe with something reasonable he'll find it hard to refuse."

Julian offered an, idea and Ned another. As they talked, Eddie slowly completed his estimate of the Brothers. They did not, he decided, want to go down with guns blazing. They would prefer not to fight at all. What they wanted, as Margot had surmised, was a big piece of the action in Merton. In a phrase, black power. This, Eddie realized, was an old-fashioned political negotiation and—if he could just forget those guns on the chest—he could operate by familiar rules. The thought gave him confidence and he pressed on although he could feel fatigue lapping at his body.

Shortly after midnight, Eddie read off the proposed demand:

4. Governor McCabe to request the legislature and/or federal government for an emergency fund of $5,000,000 to improve economic conditions for blacks and Puerto Ricans in the city of

Merton. The governor pledges to use the power and influence of his office to obtain the funds. The governor to create a state agency to administer the fund, the agency to be headed by a person of the black race and advised by a committee, appointed by the governor, whose members accurately reflect the racial composition of Merton.

"All them words," scoffed the Saint, "and nothin' in there about the Brothers."

"Don't worry," said Eddie. "If McCabe agrees to this, the Brothers will have plenty of clout in this town."

"Julian?" Ned looked inquiringly at the dapper Brother with the granny glasses.

"It's okay," said Julian.

Mwimba nodded. The Saint cursed but said he'd go along if the other three agreed.

"All right then," said Ned. He beamed his locomotive headlight smile at Eddie. "The next is amnesty and there ain't no rapping to do. Amnesty. That means we go free and the man won't touch us."

"Right," said Eddie, "but let's be sure we all mean the same thing. I don't want any of you claiming later that I double-crossed you. Amnesty for holding this building and the hostages, that's one thing. But amnesty for what some Brother did yesterday or last year, that's something else."

"Amnesty or nothin'," said Mwimba. He folded his arms over his brilliant dashiki like a tribal judge.

"No Brother goin' out of here without it," said the Saint.

"Look at it from my side," said Eddie, realizing with a start that he would never have dared such an appeal three hours ago. "If I make an amnesty pitch to McCabe, look at all the laws I'm asking him to ignore. Violation of the state gun laws. Assault with a dangerous weapon. Unlawful assembly. Seizure of property. Kidnaping, God knows what else."

"How many laws the man break every day when he after a nigger?" asked Mwimba. "He got two laws, one for him, one for us."

"I won't argue that. I'm just trying to explain my position. Hell, do you realize that if the President wanted to, he probably could come after you with the FBI under the kidnap law? And that carries up to the death penalty."

"If they try that," said Julian calmly, "there'll be enough death to go around."

"I know what's involved. I'm just saying that blanket amnesty is a big deal. Let's try it another way. Is any brother in this building a fugitive from any criminal charge?"

The four men eyed one another, questioning. "How about Sonny?" asked Ned. "Naw," said Mwimba, "they give Sonny a no bill last week." They pondered for a time.

"No, none's we know of," said Ned.

"I'm out on parole," said Julian. He gazed placidly at Eddie. "Murder." He said it as if he had broken a school window by mistake.

Ned beamed with pride. "Brother Julian done eight years in Trenton State for the man."

Eddie kept his face expressionless. "Amnesty would cover anyone on parole," he said. "Well, if nobody's got an old rap against him, we've got no problem. Something else. In taking the apartments, did you shoot at or harm anyone? Or since you took over?"

Julian shook his head. "Not a gun fired. And nobody hurt."

"Then it's pretty simple." Eddie thought as he studied the yellow sheet. "How about something like this? Number Five. 'Grant full amnesty to all Brothers of the Night inside the Beckdale Arms for all events connected with the seizure and occupation of the Beckdale Arms and pledge no reprisals or harassment of the Brothers.'"

"We been gathering the guns some time," said Ned. "They could get us for that. . . . But every white man got him a gun, so it ain't one-sided."

"We can cover that," said Eddie, "by making it 'all events connected with or leading up to the seizure . . .' That would do it."

"Write it down so's we can study it," said Ned.

Five minutes later the Brothers agreed on the wording.

"Now back to Number Three," said Ned. "Brother Saint, go ask Brother Kap to bring us some more coffee."

Eddie would remember the next three hours as some of the most grueling of his life. He was groggy in mind and body, having slept less than four hours the night before. Oklahoma City seemed a decade in the past. Once, while the Saint erupted in another mocking charade, Eddie suddenly realized that this was Tuesday morning. Just seven days from now, the polls would open and unknown millions would pull levers in voting machines that bore his name and Hugh Pinholster's. The campaign itself seemed like a distant drama played out by unreal characters. His life was here in this dusty parlor beneath a faded print of the Virgin and surrounded by four black men whose every gesture, intonation and foible was becoming as commonplace to him as his own. Now and then he thought of Kate. He wanted her near. After the election, a week somewhere with Kate. Newsmen quickly abandon defeated candidates. Seen from this perspective, where a dim light shone on browning wallpaper of nymphs and roses, Swensson's projected fifty-fifty election was a mirage. Pinholster would win going away.

At times Eddie feared the Brothers would banish talk and order him from the Beckdale Arms. While Ned and Julian edged cautiously toward compromise, Mwimba and the Saint were adamant that all blacks arrested during the riot be handed over to the Brothers of the Night. Eddie surmised that McCabe would never consent, might even risk some desperate measure, such as a surprise helicopter assault with tear gas, rather than yield. Eddie tried every persuasive technique he knew, but the Brothers would bend only so far.

Then, suddenly, a break came. Eddie mentioned, in casual passing, the possibility of a special grand jury. At once the Brothers showed interest, and it developed that Julian, Mwimba and the Saint all had been bound over to the grand jury in years past. Yeah, said Mwimba, suppose McCabe agreed that a special grand jury, with mostly black members, should pass on the riot cases. Soon Ned had taken over and made the idea his own. They discussed wording for half an hour and then Ned, with an air of triumph, ordered Eddie to "write it up." They all huddled over the yellow sheet, advising and changing, while Eddie wrote:

3. Governor McCabe to urge the courts to impanel a special grand jury, not less than twelve of whose twenty-three members

shall be black, to hear all cases of persons bound over to the grand jury as a result of arrests in the city of Merton, Oct. 25–26. All persons currently being held shall be arraigned promptly and those bound over shall be released without bail except for those accused of capital offenses. The governor to urge swift judicial action and speedy trial of those indicted.

Ned handed the yellow sheet, now covered with writing on both sides, to Julian and ordered him to read all five points aloud. "Listen careful," he said, "because we gonna hold the man to everything."

The reading was completed with only several minor alterations. Julian drew two lines at the bottom of the reverse side. Underneath one he wrote "for the Brothers of the Night" and beneath the other, "Governor." To one side, under a third line, Julian wrote: "Witness: Hon. Eddie Quinn."

The Brothers all signed in turn, Ned Gatewood, Julian Fenton, Mwimba Odote and Saint Draper. Eddie scrawled his name above the witness line.

Eddie asked permission to call the governor. Escorted across the hall by Kapanga, Eddie noted the time, 4:16. He dialed the grocery store number and after several rings a man's voice answered.

"This is Eddie Quinn at the Beckdale. Please wake up the governor and tell him I'm coming out. And notify the police at the barricade. I don't want my ass shot off."

Back in the parlor Eddie spoke to Ned. "I can't guarantee anything, but if I can get the governor's signature, I'm going to tell him you'll come out unarmed, leaving your weapons here for the police. The hostages can either come out or stay here if they wish. Is that okay?"

"Yeah, but you got to bring that paper back first, so we can see McCabe signed."

"All right. If he refuses to sign, I promise to bring it back anyway. Will you take my word for that?"

"Yeah."

"One other thing. I have to check on the condition of the hostages before I leave."

"They okay. You willin' to take my word?" Ned flashed a dazzling grin.

Eddie hesitated only a moment. "All right." He extended his hand.

Ned slapped the palm smartly. "You tell the governor ain't a hair on them white heads been touched."

"Don't mean they won't be if Mac Rape crosses us up," said the Saint, aiming a last satanic glare at Eddie.

This time Ned walked Eddie down the two flights to the entrance. "You ain't so bad," he said as they parted. "Your skin black, Eddie, and you be doin' the same thing. Wasn't a black man shot George Dawson."

Eddie left through the door he had entered almost thirteen hours before. He took a deep breath. The air had freshened and the overcast was crumbling to the north, exposing a splash of stars. He walked rapidly down the middle of the street. Beckdale had no street lamps, but lights flickered in several houses, casting shadows on the small, patchy lawns. George Dawson gone, felled by a single bullet. Six people dead. The Brothers of the Night, torn by hate, fear and hope, struggling for they knew not what. Christ, what a mess, and this was the country he was asking to run for four years. Better he have his head examined. Eddie could hear the tread of his feet, a forlorn beat in the soundless night. Seldom had he felt so tired.

"Is that you, Commissioner?" a voice asked.

"Right."

Once more he was back with his fellow whites at the barricades.

17

Moving figures loomed in the darkness as a state trooper pulled a traffic barrier aside, permitting Eddie to walk through. Jim Flannery appeared at his side.

"Hi, Jim. You been up all night?"

"No. Baker and I've been spelling each other. You okay?

"Fine. Except I could sleep for a week."

"The governor's up and waiting." Flannery edged Eddie across the street. A dozen media men, sentinels for a sleeping press corps, crowded about them. At the curb Eddie could see the bulk of a mobile television unit.

"How are the hostages? . . . Have you got an agreement? . . . How many guns in there?" The questions shot out of the night.

Eddie halted. "The hostages are in good shape," he said. "No one has been mistreated, including me. I have talked to the Brothers of the Night and now I'm going to see the governor. That's all for now."

Eddie and Flannery moved forward, but a persistent man with a microphone barred their way in the name of electronic journalism. "Are you bringing an offer to the governor?"

"Sorry, nothing more now." Eddie edged forward. The television reporter blocked his path. Flannery slid neatly between them, shoving the questioner aside. He convoyed Eddie to the brightly lighted grocery store.

Three state policemen guarded the entrance to the small frame building. Show window posters boasted of bargains in pork chops, sweet potatoes and pumpkins. Eddie and Flannery passed the cash register and threaded an aisle between breakfast cereals and canned goods. The governor stood in the doorway of the back room, vigorously rubbing his face with a towel.

They shook hands and the governor closed the door as Flannery took up a guard position. Eddie found himself in a stockroom crammed with crates, cartons, boxes and some exposed merchandise, including a bundle of new brooms and a row of pumpkins awaiting the Halloween trade. The governor's cot with rumpled blankets and sheets stood against one wall. A fluorescent tube overhead threw harsh light around the room and Eddie realized his eyes ached. A door opened on a small washroom.

"I could use a clean-up myself," said Eddie. At the basin, he lathered with a dirty bar of soap, doused his face with handfuls of cold water. As he dried on the paper towel, Eddie saw his face in the smudged mirror. He looked puffy. Brown and white stubble bristled along his jaw.

The two men sat down on straight-backed wooden chairs. Clark McCabe showed few signs of ordeal. He was a hard-muscled man, noted for his setting-up exercises and self-discipline. Handsome, patrician features sloped into sad, pale eyes that hinted of some long-ago compromise that flawed him. He was competent, correct and humorless, a man of law in a world of disorder.

"Well, Eddie, where do we stand?"

Eddie sketched the current scene at the Beckdale Arms, then drew the yellow sheet from his jacket pocket. His shirt, soiled by patches of dried sweat, felt stiff against his skin. His tie hung loose from his open collar, unbuttoned thirteen hours before in the parlor of the ancient nymphs and roses. McCabe put on his reading glasses and read slowly through the demands.

"What did you say about this to the newsmen outside?" asked McCabe when he finished reading. He betrayed no reaction.

"Nothing. They don't even know I have a paper."

"I see you endorse the first point yourself."

"Yes. Something's dead wrong with a police force that shoots a guy who's merely walking toward a car. As George's friend, I want to know exactly what happened and why."

"What do you recommend I do about these five demands?" McCabe put the question in a flat, resigned voice as though he were a magistrate in a night court.

"I think you ought to accept them."

"Straight out? No change of a word or comma? Just buy it as is?"

"Well if you have serious objections, I'll go back to the Arms with them. But given what you're up against, I think those are terms you can live with."

McCabe stood up, slowly rolled the paper into a tube and tossed it on a nearby crate.

"No. That list is out."

Eddie gaped. Of all the reactions, flat rejection was one he had not reckoned with. They eyed each other. Eddie could hear the drip of a faucet in the washroom.

"Why?"

"Those are orders to a governor of a state," said McCabe. "I won't take orders from men who hold a gun at my head."

"*Your* head? What about these seven people inside the Arms?"

"I'm speaking symbolically. You know that."

"There's no symbolic crap up the street. There are fourteen black guys with weapons. They hold seven unarmed whites. They'll shoot at any uniform that walks up the block."

McCabe retrieved the roll of paper and toyed with it as he resettled on the chair. "Lawbreakers are trying to blackmail the elected authority of this state. I can't tolerate that."

"God damn it, let's review this deal." Eddie's voice grew taut with anger. "You've got a riot on your hands, touched off by a trigger-happy cop who shot a friend of mine from the back. I'm asked to fly fourteen hundred miles to talk to the Brothers. You give me the go-ahead to negotiate for you. I spend all night with those guys. I get 'em to tone down every one of their demands. I come out with a reasonable compromise. You turn it down flat without even discussing the points with me. Instead you start talking about your symbols and authority. Just what the hell gives with you, McCabe?"

"This isn't negotiation. It's surrender. If I sign that paper, I set a precedent that will haunt half the mayors and governors in the country."

"And if you don't come to terms, you may have a pile of dead bodies on Beckdale Street . . . and maybe soon a race war in Merton that could make this outbreak look like playground stuff."

"We can take the Beckdale Arms without any loss of life."

"Oh?" Eddie looked puzzled. "Like how?"

"A gas attack. The FBI tells me they can provide us with their non-lethal gas that immobilizes instantly. Either we can lob it in with rocket canisters or via some of those new, fast robot gadgets that scuttle into a building."

"Then wham, the Brothers, wearing gas masks, start shooting up the block."

"They have gas masks?"

"I saw a few. How many they have, I don't know."

The governor unrolled the paper, skimmed through the contents again. "I have other things to consider," he said. He ticked off some of them. Five governors had wired him, urging that he take a firm stand. Russell Bishop called from the White House, relaying word that the President feared unwise concessions might undermine his law-and-order posture and encourage lawbreakers and revolutionaries everywhere. Mayor Bianco and the Merton police chief believed only stern measures now could prevent outbreaks in the future.

"And another development," said McCabe. "The police radio picked up a report that busloads of armed blacks are heading this way from New York and Philadelphia."

"Do you believe that?"

"It's possible. The report came in an hour ago, I'm told."

"Look, Clark. I'm no police expert and I know you've lived through a couple of riots as governor." Eddie lowered his voice and spoke with quiet emphasis. "But I suspect that report's a phony. You hear that kind of rumor during every racial fight. Armed blacks in buses? Man, that takes big organization. You mean police in New York and Philly just stand around watching guys with rifles climb into chartered buses? Hell, that doesn't make sense. . . . Have you heard any details?"

"No, I was told when I woke up. I asked Jerry Babson to check back on the report and see where it came from."

"I'll lay you ten to one there's nothing to it. . . . Clark, I look at this race hassle this way. We've only got two ways to go—shooting or talking. Lately we've used more guns than mouth. And the guns haven't worked. The blacks keep pushing, and they'll keep on shoving until we cut them into the action." Eddie paused. "I know those Brothers of the Night now. They're not out to kill anybody. What they want is some say in how this town is run. In a showdown like this, both sides gotta give."

McCabe's pale eyes showed no reaction. "I wind up this job next year. I know you're planning to make a run for it. If you're in the hot seat, you'll see things differently."

"I haven't thought about politics for hours. But since you bring up the subject, let me tell you something, Governor. If you refuse to meet these guys part way, I'm going to walk out to those newspapermen and tell them the whole story. I'll say that between talking compromise and possible death, the governor of this state refused to bargain."

"That's a wild exaggeration," said McCabe with sudden heat. "The issue here is whether I'll give in to blackmail by armed lawbreakers."

"And what law was broken when a cop put a bullet in George Dawson's neck? From what we know, George's only crime was walking to a car with a bundle of clean shirts."

The two men sat eying each other in the garish light from the fluorescent tube. There was a knock on the door and Jerry Babson looked in.

"That bus report didn't check out, Governor," he said. "Apparently it originated with some ham radio operator. There's no unusual traffic toward Merton."

"Thanks, Jerry," said McCabe. Babson withdrew his head and closed the door.

"Well, thank God for that," said McCabe.

Eddie let the point pass without comment. "I can appreciate the heat you're getting, but do me a favor, will you? Let's go through the agreement item by item and see which ones you can't buy.

I honestly don't think there's much that you might not have thought up on your own."

McCabe read slowly through the document again. "Point Two is irrelevant now," he said. "We've already withdrawn all white police from the black areas and substituted black patrols." Soon they were discussing the demand for amnesty, then other points. McCabe said he doubted he could persuade the legislature to vote $5,000,000 for Merton, but he acknowledged the money was needed and thought he could make the effort in good faith. Twenty minutes later, McCabe had conceded that the demands were not beyond reason.

"So why not sign?" asked Eddie. "And get Merton out of curfew and back to work?"

"No. I can't do that." McCabe pondered as he eyed the paper. "There's another way, though." He stood up. "Let's see if I can get Bianco out of bed."

Eddie waited while the governor used the wall pay phone in the front of the grocery store. Eddie stared at a carton of detergent, trying to fight off sleep. His neck ached and his feet felt as if stitched to his shoes. Ten minutes passed before McCabe returned, carrying a brown paper bag.

"Bianco's tough. You have to use the meat-ax on him," he said. "He's agreed to suspend Kocsak first thing in the morning, pending investigation. . . . Now, Eddie, I can't sign an ultimatum while those men hold the Beckdale Arms with guns. But I've decided that I can make an offer myself. I can write and sign a pledge of action dependent on their surrendering the building. Unless they're on a suicide trip, this ought to do it. This bag is the best thing I could find to write on."

Using the carton of detergent as a desk, McCabe wrote on a paper bag with a ball-point pen while Eddie looked over his shoulder.

5:45 A.M., Oct. 26

Following negotiations conducted by Edward N. Quinn and upon agreement by the Brothers of the Night to release all hostages and leave the Beckdale Arms without weapons of any kind, I will pledge to do the following:

1. Appoint a committee of attorneys, a majority of whom

shall be black, to investigate the shooting of George Dawson by Sergeant Frank Kocsak, who is being suspended from duty this morning by Mayor Bianco pending outcome of the inquiry. I will forward the committee's report to the county prosecutor with request for appropriate action.

2. Urge the impaneling of a special grand jury, including a majority of black members, to hear all cases of persons bound over as a result of arrests in the city of Merton, Oct. 25–26; urge prompt release on their own recognizance of such persons except those accused of capital offenses; urge swift action by the grand jury and the courts on all riot-connected cases.

3. Request the legislature and/or the federal government to provide $5,000,000 for the improvement of black and Puerto Rican living conditions in Merton, using the power and influence of my office to obtain such funds; create a special state agency, headed by a member of the black race, to administer such funds under advice of an appointed committee that will reflect the racial composition of Merton.

4. Grant amnesty to those Brothers of the Night inside the Beckdale Arms for all events connected with and leading up to the seizure of the apartment; pledge no reprisals or harassment of the Brothers.

(Note: Black residential and commercial areas of Merton are now being patrolled exclusively by black officers.)

McCabe affixed his signature with a flourish. Eddie folded the bag into his jacket pocket.

"You went as far as anyone could expect," said Eddie. "I hope this ends it."

"In this kind of dilemma, you're damned if you do and damned if you don't," said McCabe unhappily. "But I don't want it to stand on the record that I didn't try."

Eddie walked to the door, picked up Flannery as his escort and made his way once more to the blocked intersection. The media population, alerted to a possible break, had swelled, now numbered several dozen men and women. Eddie did not stop. "Nothing yet," he said, fending off several microphones as he slipped past the barriers. Gray light in the east forecast the dawn and a lone house sparrow hopped along the curb.

Kapanga, looking self-consciously forbidding, admitted Eddie to the apartment house lobby and led him up to the second-floor sitting room. The four Brothers awaited Eddie, ringed like judges in the same semicircle under the print of the sorrowing Virgin. Eddie gave the governor's statement to Ned.

"He wanted to do it his way," said Eddie, "but the result's the same. He accepts, as you can see."

Ned held the brown paper bag while the Brothers clustered about him. They read it through with great care.

"Shee-it!" The Saint fixed Eddie with a look of scorn. "Mac Rape actin' like he givin' us something. Man, we tellin' *him*."

"Where's our paper?" asked Julian. Eddie handed him the yellow sheet. Julian laid the two documents on the floor and studied them line by line.

"He change much?" asked Ned.

Julian shook his head. "Some words, but what we want is all down there." The Brothers eyed one another.

"Put yourself in McCabe's place," said Eddie. "If he signs your paper, he thinks he's surrendering the authority of the state. But if he makes the promise, it's an offer. Face-saving, but what the hell, either way, you get what you want."

"You guarantee this, Eddie?" asked Ned.

"If McCabe doesn't make good, I'll be the first to call him a double-crosser. But he will. He'll be committed in public."

"Bastard ought to surrender," growled the Saint.

But Ned bathed Eddie with a radiant smile. "Okay, I vote to leave." Julian and Mwimba nodded assent. The Saint shrugged, a defeated victor.

Ned promptly changed into the commander. "Saint, round up all the Brothers. . . . Stack the guns in this room. . . . Brother Mwimba, wake up the prisoners. . . . You take the governor's bag, Eddie. We keep the yellow sheet. . . . Julian, call the store and tell 'em we comin' out. . . . Let's go. I wanta get home to the old lady."

It was an odd parade that marched down the center of Beckdale Street toward the barricades ten minutes later. Eddie and Ned walked side by side in the lead, Eddie in his rumpled suit, tie sagging, and Ned, smiling triumphantly, in his blue turtle-neck and ragged gray cardigan. Behind them like twittering birds came the three elderly women and their stout blond friend, her hair still in curlers. The three white men marched in step, thin shoulders back, trying valiantly to achieve the cut of heroes. Behind them, striding two abreast in cadence, came the Brothers of the Night. In the rear, a solitary figure, Mwimba, swung along in his splendid dashiki. A pink glow suffused the eastern sky, lights winked in the white bungalows, autumn birds bickered for the dawn in the maple trees and, behind the barricades, a clatter of voices and machines smothered the approaching tread of Eddie's rakish band.

State troopers pulled the center barrier aside. Eddie and Ned led the way into a noisy throng of some five hundred people, police, newsmen, officials, photographers, TV crews, white and black onlookers. Floodlights suddenly etched the crowd in eerie brilliance so that everyone seemed a figure in a wax museum. Flannery materialized at Eddie's elbow and Margot Hicks and Phil Liccardo pushed toward him. Under instructions of television directors, chaos quickly shaped into that manageable kid of disorder peculiar to the electronic age. Bathed by thousands of kilowatts, Governor McCabe shook hands with Eddie and bowed stiffly to Ned who beamed happily into the cameras as though he were the groom at a wedding party. The governor said a few formal words of solemn rejoicing, then took the paper bag from Eddie and read his statement into the nest of microphones.

Phil Liccardo squeezed next to Eddie. "When it's your turn, keep it short and make it good. Talk stopped the shooting. Right? . . . You'll never have another platform like this before election day." Eddie remembered that the voting was only seven days off. He braced himself, summoned reserve strength despite his slough of fatigue.

Then four microphones were thrusting at him, the lights beat on his stubbled face and a voice said: "And here's Edward Quinn, the candidate for President, who negotiated release of the hostages after an emergency flight from Oklahoma. Mr. Quinn."

"We should all be thankful," said Eddie, turning to the cameras, "that this potentially tragic episode ended without bloodshed and without harm to anyone. Both Governor McCabe and the Brothers of the Night acted reasonably. It's always easy, on both sides, to threaten violence. It's much tougher to talk our way to a compromise on the bitter differences that divide us. I hope this is a lesson for Americans. Both sides gave a bit because they realized in their hearts that we all must live together—or tear ourselves apart in civil war. I'm glad I could help."

He turned away, and as the microphones were switched to Brother Ned, Eddie could feel his last reserve of energy draining away. He leaned against Flannery. "Nice going," said Liccardo. Margot smiled at him. "That was good, Eddie," she said. "I don't know about votes, but you did right."

Eddie lived through the next hour in a daze from which his memory later could isolate only a few blurred scenes . . . listening to Ned praise him on television . . . briefing Liccardo on highlights of the long night . . . talking to Vince Anderson as they drove to the home of Sarah Dawson, George's mother . . . the feel of Mrs. Dawson sobbing on his shoulder . . . the sight of an enraged white man, standing on a corner as Eddie's car passed, loosing a stream of profanity and yelling, "Nigger lover." . . . talking to Pete Stackpole in Washington from a gas-station phone booth and telling him no campaigning until tomorrow, that he would sleep all day in his room at the Buccaneer Motor Lodge near New Brunswick . . . the last sight of Merton through the rear window and the morning sun shouldering away a cloud bank and reaching for the wounded city.

The Secret Service had driven the Continental Mark IV up from Washington and Eddie yielded to its luxury as they rolled along the familiar New Jersey Turnpike toward his motel.

"You know I was born right along here," said Eddie as they halted at the Exit Nine tollgate.

"Before they built the Turnpike, wasn't it?" asked Flannery from the front seat.

"Yeah . . . Hey, Jim, you've seen a lot of politics. What do you think? Will last night help me or hurt me?"

"You ought to pick up black votes. The whites, I don't know."

"Well, we'll have the answer in seven days."

Fifteen minutes later Eddie was asleep in his motel king-sized bed. The room next door, George Dawson's for six months, already was occupied by new tenants.

Eleven hours later, while Eddie stirred into wakefulness in the Buccaneer, Arnold Swensson put through his 7:15 P.M. call to Governor Hugh Pinholster at the Brown Palace Hotel in Denver.

"This covers the thousand people polled since we talked this morning, Governor," said Swensson. "A—498. B—452. C—50. D—49.8. E—45.2. F—5.0. And G—plus 2.2."

"God." Pinholster took a second to absorb the blow. "Quinn up two point two per cent in twelve hours. That's four times his usual increase. Well, I guess that answers our question of this morning."

"Yes. I think this gives a fair picture of the initial reaction to Quinn's all-night scenario. Of course, we don't know about the second thoughts. We'll get that tomorrow."

Swensson felt no pride in his numbers tonight. Quinn had put an unseemly bulge in the trend line by his highly unorthodox behavior in some minor outpost in the trackless globopolis of New Jersey, a corridor of swampy weather and toadstool habitations that called itself a state.

"Where do those new Quinn votes come from?" asked Pinholster.

"Just let me eyeball some numbers from the depths." Swensson bent to his task. "Yes. Mostly black voters switching from you. The white vote holds steady, only a fractional rise for Quinn that isn't significant."

"Well, we're in a horse race for sure, then." Pinholster tried to draw a note of competitive cheer from the shadows of his spiritual cellar.

"Yes . . . I'll call the usual time in the morning. Let's see if that jump in the trend flattens out overnight."

Swensson hung up in a mood of resentment. He was annoyed with Eddie for causing a sudden hump in the otherwise beautifully escalating blue line on the graph. An ill-mannered man, the sort who'd try to rush things. And so enmeshed in the aesthetics of his numbers was Swensson that it was a half hour before he realized that Quinn's disfiguring hump might be worth $19,000 in gambling winnings to him.

18

Some four thousand people filled a Philadelphia street intersection and spilled across a corner parking lot three nights later to see and cheer the man who had made the two-martini, expense-account lunch as un-American as the Communist Party. They boomed approval as Eddie Quinn vowed to "run the big bankers, the brokers and the bond-clippers out of the lobbies of Washington" and repopulate the nation's capital with new legions of the white- and blue-collar masses. His voice hoarse from constant use, ruddy face moist with sweat, the broad shoulders heaving, Eddie waged political war with every muscle and pore.

Time and again he flung his right arm upward and outward in the gesture now known to millions. With its thrust from the shoulder, palm out, fingers spread, the movement bespoke command, mission, appeal, challenge. "When he shoots out that arm," wrote a Philadelphia *Bulletin* columnist that day, "Eddie is at once the U.S. cavalry commander ordering a charge on the western plains, the bearer of the Olympic torch and the college student flashing his peace sign. Some of Quinn's Negro followers may even note the similarity to the black power salute, for were Eddie but to close his fingers, he would indeed be raising the black fist of defiance. Where Harry Truman chopped and Jack Kennedy pointed a hooked index finger, Eddie Quinn slams his whole arm toward the sky."

Eddie's juices flowed and his blood heated as he carried his assault to the towers of privilege in this last of ten speeches that day in the slums, ethnic neighborhoods and shopping centers of Philadelphia. His stance was that of Al Smith's happy warrior of long ago. Warrior? This was Friday, October 29, only four days before the election, and Eddie, all self-doubts buried in a hotel room in Oklahoma City, swore that he would fight until the final hour. Happy? Ever since he emerged at dawn from the Beckdale Arms in Merton, the good news had come in, at first in trickles, then in a swiftly coursing current and now, at last, like a great, broad river in flood.

Pete Stackpole stood anonymously in the crowd about 100 feet from his candidate, gauging the temper of the people. Pete knew the signs and tokens of political upset. It was easy to spot the tangible evidence, rising money, polls and crowds, but for an old pro the auguries that fascinated and grabbed him were the intangibles—overheard snatches of conversation, the jokes, the silent shift of the big gamblers' money, the fervor of volunteers, a certain electric quality crackling along the campaign route. And when the intangibles began to cluster about the ridiculed underdog, high drama was in the making. It had happened to Harry Truman in 1948—and he won by a hair. It had happened to Hubert Humphrey in 1968—and he lost by a whisker. Now it was happening to Eddie Quinn.

Most voting shifts, Pete knew, were not large ones despite all the lurid headlines about landslides, avalanches, power sweeps and towering majorities. Stackpole often explained it to his amateur friends this way: Picture one hundred people standing in two rows, fifty to a row, comely secretaries, farmers, paunchy businessmen, long-haired students, hard-hat construction workers and fussy little grandmothers. Fifty-fifty, a dead heat. Now move one person from the second row to the front row. Presto. A close but clear-cut victory, fifty-one to forty-nine. Now move four more citizens from the second to the front row. Wham! A landslide, fifty-five to forty-five. Persuade just five people in every hundred to switch from Aaron to Zilch, Pete would argue, and the photo finish becomes Zilch's runaway race by ten lengths.

But this fall the shift had been heavier. When Eddie started, the numbers read Pinholster 56, Eddie 32 and Mr. Don't Know 12. Today, only two weeks later, Gallup made it Pinholster 49, Quinn 46, undecided 5. Harris said Pinholster 49, Quinn 46.5, undecided 4.5. As published today, Pete knew, these figures were at least twenty-four hours old and included some people polled as much as two days ago. In his pocket Pete Stackpole carried a slip of paper with very, very fresh numbers, smuggled out of Arnold Swensson's bucket shop of polling by a pro-Quinn employee. Pete had shown the slip to Eddie just before he launched his street-corner speech. The numbers, disgorged by computer at 3 P.M., read: Pinholster 48.4, Quinn 47.7, undecided 3.9. The trend was climbing ever upward and now Pete sensed that, with all the TV and radio saturation scheduled for the weekend, the trend pointed at the least to a hairline finish with ultimate decision dependent on the fall of the electoral count or at the most a clear victory for Eddie.

As he stood in the warm October night and listened to Eddie castigate the privileged establishment from Southampton to La Jolla, Pete reviewed the four days and three nights of escalating campaign hopes since Eddie led white hostages and black Brothers through the barricades of Beckdale Street.

On Tuesday, while Eddie slumbered, the nation reacted to the compromise of Merton, at first slowly, then with a flowering of comment via TV interviews, news and panel shows. A large percentage of blacks hailed it as a victory, giving Quinn grudging-to-high marks for his negotiation. Some embittered whites denounced it as a sellout, but the majority either accepted it as the best of a bad bargain or backed Eddie for avoiding bloodshed. As it became common knowledge that George Dawson was an innocent man slain on his way to the car of his friend, Eddie Quinn, white sympathy for Eddie's feelings rose. In the end it appeared that Eddie, whether consciously or unknowingly, struck a note the country wanted, a bending by both the authorities and the black militants and, above all, an end to killing. If the people were emotionally exhausted by the constant threat of black revolution, they were also sick of racial slaughter. Optimists said Eddie Quinn pointed the way toward peace. Pessimists said he merely bought a little time. Either way, Eddie filled the bill and his dawn performance before the cameras on Beckdale Street, where Eddie stood frayed and haggard but solidly in command, was seen by millions of TV viewers watching later news shows. Eddie's deed blotted Pinholster from the public eye that day.

Pete Stackpole did that Tuesday what he had ached to do since the day Charlie Herron wrathfully cut off Eddie's funds. He hired a media director and production crew with orders to slap together a crash program that would fill the weekend air waves with Eddie Quinn. Also hired was a TV and radio time buyer. Pete took a chance. Although contributions were flowing in to Teegee Churchill at headquarters at the rate of $100,000 a day, he knew he had insufficient money for the expensive network spots. But Pete speculated that the big fair-weather donors, those who liked to be with the winner, would soon begin to hedge their bets with late gifts to the Quinn campaign.

Routed from his Buccaneer Motor Lodge bed early Tuesday evening, Eddie was driven to New York City where he worked until 2 A.M. in a West Side studio making 30-second television and radio spots. Eddie protested. He longed to light out for the outer-city highway strips to meet and harangue the folks, but Pete and Phil Liccardo dissuaded him. A network TV spot, they argued, could reach more voters in one minute than Eddie could meet in person if he traveled the campaign route for a year. The television experts schooled him in a folksy, conversational approach, pure Eddie Quinn, that pointed a sharp contrast with Pinholster, who was flooding the channels but tending to lecture and preach at his audience. Ever the quick learner, Eddie soon shaped a style that would bring him into the living room as that friendly guy up the block who has some sensible ideas on how to rout the Hell's Angels marauders of war, poverty, pollution, inflation, holocaust, unemployment, cancer, heroin, trade deficits, famine, racial venom, bad breath and quarter parking meters.

Eddie, the valedictorian of the motor era, climaxed his 30-second spot appeals by vowing to "run the chauffeur-driven executive limos off the exit ramps so we ordinary Americans can have a clear shot on the thruway of pride, liberty and prosperity."

Wednesday morning, motorcading through Boston suburbs, Eddie called for national recruitment of a "Community Medical Corps" of 700,000 men and women who would serve as mini-doctors capable of treating 90 per cent of humanity's ills. These paramedics, said Eddie, would receive six months' training, staff free neighborhood clinics and minister to common colds, flu, sore feet, lacerations, bee stings and shriveled egos. If a patient needed more sophisticated care, he would be referred to one of the nation's 350,000 licensed physicians. Eddie said the Community Medical Corps would erase America's "greatest shame, our care of the human body" and would smash the health monopoly of the American Medical Association.

Jumping from health to wealth, Eddie proposed a new share-the-dough equalizer to a noonday throng of 20,000 people on the Boston Commons. He pledged, if elected, to demand of Congress a fortune-smashing lottery. When a multimillionaire died, he would be permitted to will $10,000,000 to his family, "enough to send his grandkids to Groton and Harvard and over to the Alps for skiing." Anything above this "ten kilo-grand," said Eddie, would be split 30 per cent to the government and 70 per cent to the taxpayers. All Social Security and taxpayer numbers would be fed into a computer which would cough up as many random individual $100,000 prizes as the fortune permitted. The crowd roared hungrily.

Joe Kuzyk phoned from Washington, confirmed Pete's hunch about big money givers. A dozen checks, ranging up to $25,000, reached headquarters that morning. Eddie ordered Pete to refuse any contribution above $3000, saying he would not be under obligation "to the oligarchs." Eddie nailed this into official policy in an afternoon speech in Providence, Rhode Island, where he said anybody donating more than $3000 to a candidate "is either in love with the guy or is trying to bribe him." Belatedly Eddie realized that Kate gave his campaign $10,000, but decided the definition still fit.

That Wednesday saw a series of fast political developments. Pete Stackpole got private evidence that the big money crowd feared that Eddie might win. He received word from his bank in Newark that his $75,000 unsecured loan would not be called after all. The New York Stock Exchange average dropped ten points as a rumor swept Wall Street that secret polls showed Eddie had a good chance to win. Oddsmakers, led by Jimmy the Greek, dropped the odds against Eddie to a scant three to two. Kate Witherspoon, campaigning for a few days for her own seat in Dallas, phoned to report that Eddie had a fighting chance to take Texas on combined worker, Chicano and black votes. The President, at a Washington press conference, refused to say how he would vote, urged every citizen to "consult his own conscience." Four well-heeled WASP cabinet officers promptly consulted their liberated consciences and announced they were bolting the party to vote for Pinholster. Quinn headquarters released a list of 1057 local ethnic clubs, Italian, Polish, Hungarian, Czech, Armenian, Greek, Cuban, Puerto Rican, Mexican and a few Irish, that had endorsed Eddie.

Speaking in New Haven Wednesday night on the campus of Yale University, Eddie said the last time he visited Yale he struck out with the bases loaded as short stop of the Seton Hall team. He vowed that would not happen this time at bat. He again impaled the six senators named by R Dan Fenelli in the Teamsters speech. Eddie claimed these senators "sold out your interests and mine to great plundering corporations for a few loaves of campaign bread." Answering a question on distribution of income, Eddie said "there's something wrong with a system where a stockbroker makes more with a few phone calls than a trash collector does in a year of wrestling with stinking garbage cans." The Yalies cheered, whether for the trash men or the lucky brokers, nobody knew. Stackpole moaned inwardly, then quickly calculated there were at least four sanitation toilers for every stockbroker in the country.

On Thursday Eddie, motorcading southward through Connecticut, New York and New Jersey, told largely female audiences in the shopping centers that he would carry "the lesson of the Beckdale Arms" into foreign affairs, would travel to Moscow and Peking for "talk-don't shoot" conferences with Communist bigwigs. He said he would keep talking until the world defused nuclear bombs and dismantled the lethal ocean-hopping missiles. Eddie got a cool reception in the upper-crust suburbs, but was mobbed twice by eager women outside discount stores. Once he was forced to change shirts in the Continental Mark IV because of lipstick prints on the collar.

Eddie broke his tour that afternoon to fly to Merton in a small charter plane to attend George Dawson's funeral. He stood by the grave with George's mother, then signed over the deed to his old Impala to Mrs. Dawson's pastor with an understanding the Impala would be raffled off, proceeds going to Mrs. Dawson. Merton was quiet. Black high school seniors contributed $17.75 to Eddie's campaign as a memorial to Dawson.

Thursday night in Camden, New Jersey, Eddie pledged that a "rebirth of the cities" would be his top priority in the White House. Candidly he said he was not sure what to do yet, but for starters he would consider a ten-year moratorium on federal corporate taxes for any company that would move into a city and provide employment for ten or more persons. Also, he said, he was weighing a possible tax penalty on companies that moved out. Eddie also said he favored repealing the child labor laws and letting able-bodied kids go to work.

Friday morning the candidate was joined by his son, Eddie, Jr., the appliance salesman, as he campaigned the streets of Philadelphia. Eddie, Jr., a stolid, withdrawn young man, had always treated his father as a kind of tired joke, but as he listened to Eddie, now a political celebrity, flay the rich and the mighty, a new respect took root.

At one street-corner stop, Eddie, Jr., was scrambling into the back of the flat-bed truck when a policeman grabbed his arm and pulled him to the pavement.

"What's the idea?" Eddie, Jr., was indignant. "That's my old man up there." The patrolman's glance was one of utter disbelief.

Eddie leaned from the truck. "Let him up, officer. He's my son. He's worth more votes today than I am."

Reunited on the truck, father and son got a stout hand from the crowd for this victory over authority. By late afternoon, Eddie, Jr., having shed his shell, was basking in the reflected acclaim for the candidate. And Eddie added a local twist to his remarks: "As your fellow Philadelphian, my son, Eddie, Jr., was telling me just now . . ."

While Eddie toured the city of brotherly love, politics dominated the country in the shadow of the election. The stock market plunged on the heels of more bullish Quinn news. The first wave of Quinn's 30-second spots hit the daily TV soap operas. Checkers reported that women devotees preferred Eddie's commercials to deodorants, hand lotions or the little acid men who scampered about hammering on the inner walls of the stomach. The Gallup and Harris polls re-

flected the Quinn surge. Archibald D. Prudhon, a horticulturalist
who had accurately forecast every presidential winner since F.D.R.
in 1932, said it was Quinn in a squeaker. The presidents of
twelve major unions, breaking with the AFL-CIO neutrality stand,
came out for Eddie. The manufacturer of campaign buttons and
bumper stickers said Quinn was outselling Pinholster five to three. A
survey of professional football players showed that high-salaried
quarterbacks, running backs and wide receivers favored Pinholster,
while centers, guards, tackles and linebackers liked Quinn. In Las
Vegas, Jimmy the Greek dropped the election odds to even money.
A poll showed doctors were nine to one for Pinholster, nurses eight
to one for Quinn. In Washington, Joe Kuzyk revealed that the total
of all Quinn gifts from a nickel to $3000 totaled $1,050,000.

Now this Friday night, standing in the street-corner crowd under
a mellow moon and a star-studded sky, Pete Stackpole watched with
wonder and pride as his candidate drummed toward his climax. Eddie
was a confident orator now, mixing colloquialisms and earthy anecdotes with facts and figures and an occasional lofty quotation supplied by Fenelli or a lyrical flight of his own.

"And so," concluded Eddie, "go out and vote for me next Tuesday, twice if you can get by with it, and we'll take this great
country of ours away from the executive-suite crowd, the patty-de-
foy-grass expense-account lunch boys, the deductible beach- and
yacht-club gang and the big selfish conglomerate presidents who
raise prices, pollute the air and duck through the biggest tax loopholes in the whole Western world. Vote for me and next Tuesday
we'll hand the government of the United States of America back to
the people it belongs to, the ordinary people like you and me and
my Uncle Hunk and everybody else who puts in an honest day's
work and deserves a fair shake. A fair shake! That's all we want.
And with your help on Tuesday, by God we're going to get it.
Thanks and good night."

Eddie jumped down from the flat-bed truck into a pack of auto-
graph hunters while Flannery and Baker tensed at his side like a
pair of purebred pointers. Eddie bid good-by to his son, promising
to call election night. Margot Hicks, Hunk Janiszewski, Fenelli and
Phil Liccardo made their way to the staff cars, parked down the

block, while the Secret Service men convoyed their charge to the glossy Continental a few minutes later.

"Off to the big apple," said Eddie.

"Plenty of time," said Pete. "We're reserved on a ten-thirty flight to New York. Nice easy ride to the airport. Then we're going to tuck you into bed early at the Waldorf. That schedule in Brooklyn and Queens tomorrow is a bitch."

"Hell with the plane, Pete. Let's drive. Nice straight haul up the Turnpike out of Camden."

"More wear and tear, Eddie. Your throat sounds like a rusty gate already."

"No. Riding relaxes me. Especially the Turnpike."

Pete acquiesced. "Okay. I'll let the staff fly up. You and I can talk in the car."

The Quinn disciples parted, Fenelli and the other staffers heading for the airport in two cars while the press bus trailed behind. Eddie, Pete, Flannery and Baker boarded the Lincoln Continental. Agent Baker took the wheel, maneuvering the limousine through city streets toward the Delaware River and the span leading to Camden, New Jersey.

"Four more days to go," said Pete. "Actually, only three for campaigning. Voters don't like a candidate to push it on election day. Besides, we'll have the spots working for us all day Tuesday."

"Feel great," said Eddie, "except for this lousy throat. I'm good for another month. What have we got left?"

"Eleven stops tomorrow in Manhattan, Queens and Brooklyn. Tomorrow night the big speech in the Garden. Then the night flight to L.A. I hate that, but we have to show on the West Coast. Hollywood Bowl Sunday night. Chicago all day and night Monday. Back to vote in New Brunswick Tuesday morning. Then Washington, where we chew our nails and climb the wall until maybe three in the morning."

Eddie glanced at his watch. "Kate ought to be landing at Kennedy right now." The congresswoman was flying from Dallas to New York to speak on Eddie's behalf to a women's liberation coalition meeting. "She ought to get back to the hotel about twelve-thirty, give or take a few minutes."

Pete laughed. "Oh, so that's it: You can't see Kate until late, so we'll use the time floating up the Turnpike."

They traded news, tactics and hunches until they reached the tollgate entrance to the New Jersey Turnpike.

"Let me take over, Jim," said Eddie. "I haven't handled this boat since that day in Washington."

"No, better not, Eddie," said Flannery. "We haven't got a lead car and you're tired. You sit back and relax and Baker will give us an air-cushion ride."

Eddie insisted. "I feel fine. Driving does more for me than a sauna bath does for old Rich Cuthbert. Besides, I know the Turnpike like the palm of my hand. Move over, Bake."

The candidate had his way and the long, sleek car soon was purring north with Eddie at the wheel, Flannery at his side and Stackpole and Baker in the rear seat.

"You may be a gas as a candidate, but your arithmetic stinks," said Stackpole.

"How so?"

"Kate speaks at eight-thirty. Even with questions, she ought to be back at the Waldorf before eleven."

"Now you tell me. I thought her talk was at ten." Eddie pressed the accelerator and the car gained speed.

"Easy, Eddie," said Flannery. "This is a sixty-mile limit. You've got it over seventy."

"No problem, Jim. I've hit ninety along here with no sweat." Eddie began to whistle.

Pete told his best street-corner story of the day. Eddie topped him with his tale of the fat woman with the garlic breath who threw her arms around his neck after the Walnut Street rally and whispered: "You're a goddamn Communist, Eddie, but I love you." Soon they were regaling each other and the Secret Service agents with campaign lore from Houston to Batesville. "Or was it Batesburg?" asked Pete.

They laughed once more. Eddie could feel his spirits soaring. The news was excellent, the companionship as good. Stars sprinkled the sky, he was on his way to see Kate and the Mark IV hummed along in the center lane while the mileposts flashed by.

"Hey, Pete. Who says there ain't no easy run?"

"Hold down on that ego trip, pal," said Pete. "You haven't got it made yet, and even if you do win, remember, you'll only be the thirty-seventh-and-a-half President."

"Half or full, they still pay two hundred grand a year."

Not only that, thought Eddie. With the glow of the dashboard before him, the wheel smooth to his touch and the sense of elegance all about him, he was going first class all the way.

Ahead on the right, parallel to the flow of traffic, a single car moved swiftly along an entrance ramp.

19

To Pete Stackpole in the rear seat, it was a great explosion. To Agent Oscar Baker beside him on the left, it came clearly as a scream of tires amid a grotesque clashing of metal. Jim Flannery, unaware of sound, felt as though someone had shoved him rudely and violently against Eddie's shoulder. Eddie heard and felt nothing at all.

In a sense Eddie never knew what happened. In another sense he knew everything that mattered in a vivid fraction of a second in which a dozen fragmentary scenes lashed the negative of his memory with such speed as to be called instantaneous. Then a giant hood fell.

Those who have survived the impact of two automobiles colliding at high speed know that events do not stamp the memory in sequential, linear order. Rather they drive inward as from the circumference of a circle, pelting the core of the mind with the fury and random impact of a hurricane. Recovering from the shock of yielding defenseless flesh to four tons of pulverizing steel, aluminum, wire, plastic and glass, the passenger recalls the immediate past as he might a dimly remembered nightmare. If asked to testify later in court, he is bewildered by lawyers who strive to stretch an inchoate happening into an orderly chain of cause and effect, time and place, sequence, beginning and end. At this point the law becomes a mad jester and memory's chaos the only sanity.

Eddie could remember clearly enough the scene just before the accident. The Continental rolled north in the center of three lanes on the New Jersey Turnpike about thirty-five miles from the Lincoln Tunnel into New York City. Vision was good, the moonlit night flawless so that the Milky Way glittered like a tiara. Traffic was moderate for a Friday night and Eddie kept the needle of the speedometer just above seventy. As they approached Exit Nine at New Brunswick, Eddie pointed left to a lighted building, the administrative offices of the Turnpike Authority where Eddie had spent his working days during the last three years. Exit Nine flashed by. Just beyond, a car moved along the entrance lane that bled into the expressway.

Eddie gave the vehicle only peripheral attention as it rolled into the outer lane and he prepared to pass it in his center strip. The overtaking should have been routine, one of thousands of similar passings on the Turnpike that day and akin to more thousands that Eddie had negotiated in his three decades of driving. Still, car buff that he was, he glimpsed the type, a Chevrolet. A Caprice, he thought.

Suddenly red tail lights veered directly in front of him. Instead of straightening out in the right-hand lane, the Chevrolet incomprehensibly was cutting across the jagged white line into the center strip. Thoughts and impressions imploded with computer speed. . . . His headlights on a rear window, the shape of the car's trunk, the glow of crimson lights, a mud-streaked bumper . . . the tug of the seat belt at his belly . . . an upward blurring movement of Jim Flannery's arm beside him . . . did Jim cry out? . . . lights of southbound cars like great orbs of hurrying insects . . . a corner of the mind saying the crazy bastard, drunk or what? . . . the sure knowledge that a crash was coming . . . a flash of Kate, her face, her hair . . . and, curiously, the shape of the old Impala when he came out of the motor lodge one morning and saw it sagging because of a rear flat. And during this wild dance of the mind his right foot hit the brake and his hands threw the wheel to the left. Then nothing.

The Continental smashed into the left side of the Chevrolet's rear bumper. For several seconds after this irrelevance of fate a hundred events erupted without design, but a sequential, and therefore perhaps false, reconstruction of what occurred might go like this:

Eddie was thrown with great force against the left side window, cracking the pane, gashing his scalp and knocking himself unconscious. The Mark IV shuddered, lurched, stayed upright and raced out of control down the highway and across the inner lane. Hurled against Eddie, Jim Flannery reacted with an automatic movement, less instinctive than one resulting from long, thorough preparation. He unsnapped his seat belt with a glancing swipe at his stomach and even as he was half sprawled across Eddie, he threw out his right foot and jammed the brake pedal. He also grabbed the wheel and tried to pull it to the right. He may have succeeded, for the long car struck the center guard rail at only a slight angle. It sideswiped the low steel fence with a sickening grind of fenders, doors and chrome, rebounded a few feet, teetered for a moment and came to an upright halt perhaps a hundred yards from the point of impact. Flannery reached out and switched off the ignition key, noting that his arm trembled convulsively. A mist of dust oddly enveloped the plush interior of the automobile.

Flannery squirmed, slapped himself in several places, saw that Eddie was inert, then turned around. Baker sat jammed in the left corner, hands clutching his arms, eyes wide with fright. Stackpole, thrown against Baker, was righting himself as clumsily as a drunk.

"Out!" Flannery's attempt at a shout emerged as a feral croak. "Could be fire."

Flannery and Stackpole threw themselves at the right-hand doors. Luckily both doors had sprung open. They scrambled out. "Other side," said Flannery. "Eddie's out cold." They ran around the car. Flannery found that the left front door, against which Eddie's body was jammed, could be opened. Stackpole reached in and lifted Eddie's shoulders while Flannery supported the legs. Quickly, but as gently as they could, they lifted the big man out. Blood flowed over Eddie's left ear. Headlights stroked the scene in crazy patterns and they could hear the screech of tires as oncoming cars braked and swerved.

Baker, finding the rear door on his side jammed, stumbled out through the same right-hand door used by Stackpole before him. He took several small, tentative steps, found that his limbs worked, then half ran and half staggered around the rear of the car.

"Help," said Flannery. "Move him back . . . fire."

Baker helped Stackpole carry Eddie's torso while Flannery supported the legs. They carried Eddie along the brown grass strip flanking the guard rail. The three men shuffled and scraped, moving crablike away from the automobile. "Here," said Flannery. They lowered Eddie to the ground. Baker, his arms trembling, struggled out of his jacket, wadded it and placed it under Eddie's head. Flannery also shed his jacket and spread it over Eddie's chest. They could see him breathing although his eyes were closed. "He's alive," said Jim. Headlights bathed the scene and the two coatless agents stood with their shoulder holsters exposed over white shirts.

Pete's legs felt watery, his left arm quivered uncontrollably, but his brain seemed to function with unusual precision and clarity. Like a flash, as he would recall later, he saw a hand pulling a lever to close the curtains of a voting booth.

"You were driving, Jim," said Pete. "Eddie was in the back seat with me."

Flannery and Baker gaped at Stackpole. Then Jim understood. He shook his head. "Won't work, Pete. No time to put it together."

"You were driving!" Pete's voice shook with a near-manic intensity. "Who knows, the other guy may be dead."

All three men glanced involuntarily to the east. Across the roadway, perhaps another fifty yards farther along, they could see an overturned car, wheels in the air. Traffic braked across the three lanes. Gas fumes swirled in the glare of headlights. A man was coming toward them along the guard rail. They heard shouts and in the distance the thin, wavering cry of a siren.

"You want Eddie to win?" Pete's question came out with a rough, growling sound. "Quick. Answer me!"

Flannery's mind flashed across a web of mutual commitments, first spun by the exchange of favors when he met Eddie at the Apollo Motel. "Yes."

"Okay then?" asked Stackpole. It was less of a question than a swift command. Pete was shivering now.

"Okay, but let's think it fast," said Flannery.

"Leave it to me. You guys say nothing except to police if asked." Pete spoke with frantic haste. "I do all the talking. . . . You were driving, Bake beside you. Eddie and I in the back, Eddie to the left. We pulled him out the right rear door. When in doubt, blame it on shock. We'll get it straight later. Right?"

"Blood on the front window?" asked Flannery. "And our top-coats?"

All four men had removed their topcoats in the car, preferring the comfort of the heater's warmth. The night was cool, perhaps fifty degrees.

Stackpole hurried back to the car. Wisps of smoke curled from the hood. He climbed in the front. Although his whole body shook, he leaned over the seat and snatched up his coat and Baker's from the rear, then gathered in those of Flannery and Quinn from the front seat. As he stepped out, he threw the coats to the ground. He glanced to the rear. The man approaching along the center guard rail was only a few yards away. The bulk of the car shadowed the open front door. Pete saw a smudge of blood on the cracked window. He whipped his handkerchief from a hip pocket, spit on the cloth and rubbed at the stain. Had Eddie's feet dragged on the ground? Gathering up the coats, Pete scuffed at the soil where patches of dried grass stood like islands in the brown dirt. He tramped about, kicking at the ground. He glanced at the left rear window. It had a single, jagged crack. Good. Enough to explain Eddie's head injury if he lived. Lived? What a thought. Pete walked back along the guard rail.

The stranger, a short, hairy man in a windbreaker, stood with Flannery and Baker looking down at the body on the ground. Eddie's eyes opened, stared straight up, then flicked from one face to another above him. He shivered beneath the jacket.

Eddie spoke faintly. "I'm cold."

Pete spread two of the topcoats over him, then threw himself flat on the ground at Eddie's right side. Pete whispered into his ear.

"Don't talk, Eddie. Don't move. You're okay. . . . Listen carefully. You were not driving, repeat, not. Jim was driving. Jim Flannery. You were in the back seat with me. Understand? . . . If you've got it, squeeze my hand."

Pete placed his hand in Eddie's. After a moment, he felt Eddie's hand tighten on his.

"Good. You say nothing, Eddie. Nothing. You're in shock. You won't be expected to talk. We'll handle it. Now relax, pal. They'll have you in a bed soon."

Pete patted Eddie's hand, then stood up and brushed himself off. "I told him he was okay," he explained for the benefit of the stranger in the windbreaker. Pete nudged Flannery to one side.

"It wasn't your fault, Jim," he said. "That crazy bastard cut across your lane. Tire marks ought to prove it. The guy may admit it himself if he's alive."

"Won't help me." Flannery shook his head. "At the least, I'll be busted off the detail."

Pete gripped both of Flannery's arms. "Listen, Jim, if Eddie comes out of this okay, he's going to be President." He motioned with his head toward Eddie. "What he says will go. You'll have no problems, believe me. It's a gamble we have to take."

"I told you okay. I want him to win as much as you do."

They turned around. Baker was upright but shaking badly. Flannery threw his arms around the other agent. Baker's hands fluttered on Flannery's shirt sleeves and a great wave of cold engulfed him. His teeth began to chatter and he found it impossible to control his jaw. "Jesus Christ," he muttered. "What's happening?"

Flannery eased him to a sitting position, grabbed up one of the spare topcoats and draped it over Baker's shoulders. Baker clutched at his knees to steady himself just as a state police patrol car, siren dying to a moan and roof lights stabbing the night, squealed to a stop behind a tangle of cars blocking the inner lanes. Traffic continued to crawl on the outside lane, accelerating when past the accident scene, then fleeing north as if pursued by ghosts. Only four minutes had passed since the Continental struck the Chevrolet.

Eddie could not have picked a more convenient spot on the Turnpike to suffer the first major accident of his thirty years of driving. At Exit Nine, the interchange for New Brunswick, the Turnpike administration building housed communications and control for the large state police unit assigned to patrol the expressway. Dispatchers stood duty in shifts around the clock in a third-story, glass-enclosed room affording a view of the highway in three directions.

Sergeant Arthur Gelentser, a night-shift dispatcher, had been standing by the window, watching the endless river of speeding cars when he saw one vehicle suddenly shoot off to the right and another to the left on the northbound segment of the divided highway. Both cars lurched drunkenly off the roadbed and one turned over completely. Gelentser stepped to the control console, picked up the microphone, flicked a switch and called Troop D's Patrol Car 19 assigned to cover northerly traffic in the area.

"D Nineteen. D Nineteen. Signal Twenty-eight."

"D Nineteen to New Brunswick. I'm at Mile Eighty north."

"Signal Eleven at Milepost Eighty-four northbound. Two cars. Traffic building."

"D Nineteen to New Brunswick. On my way."

Turning away from the mike, Gelentser pressed a button which activated flashing signs on overpasses south of Exit Nine: "Accident ahead." The press of another button lowered the speed limit to forty miles an hour from the normal sixty on northbound roadway signs in the same area.

Gelentser then made three swift phone calls. First he called an ambulance service, two miles from the Turnpike, and gave the location of the accident. Then he called the emergency ward of the Middlesex General Hospital in New Brunswick, notifying the duty nurse of the possible arrival of highway casualties within a few minutes. Finally he called the nearest all-night wrecker. Hanging up, Gelentser turned toward the window, but the phone rang before he could take a first step. It was a collector at the Exit Nine southbound tollgate, relaying word of the accident as given by an excited motorist who had witnessed it across the center guard rail. Gelentser did all this with no obvious emotion. The Turnpike, although one of the safest in the country, averaged five accidents every twenty-four hours. Fridays were worse. On a typical Friday, eight crashes occurred.

Gelentser's police broadcast was picked up by the open radio of Patrol Car 19 then cruising the northbound segment four miles below Exit Nine. Trooper Hub Young flipped on his siren and roof lights and accelerated to eighty miles an hour.

When Young braked to a halt just beyond Exit Nine, he found traffic strangled. Vehicles now blocked both inner lanes while continuing cars and trucks crept northward in the single outside strip. Young unloaded flares from the trunk of his patrol car and placed them on the inner lane. Then he ordered the halted cars, more than thirty of them, to move on. His first duty was to prevent more crashes and mayhem.

Trooper Young's trained eye took in the scene near the smashed Continental in one comprehending glance. One man prone, covered by coats, another sitting with a topcoat draped over his shoulders. The sight of a shirt-sleeved man wearing a shoulder holster with protruding revolver butt did not surprise him. Law officer, he judged at once. No hood would remove his coat to help anyone if it meant revealing a pistol. Still, Young's glance at the holster was a questioning one.

"Secret Service," Flannery explained. He flipped open a black leather holder and showed the identification card, then pointed to Eddie. "He's Eddie Quinn, the presidential candidate. Head wound and shock. I don't know what else." Flannery pointed across the roadway. "The other car turned over. Came flying out of the entrance and cut me off in the center lane."

Young stared at the man lying beneath the coats. "For God's sake! Eddie Quinn, the commissioner." He gave the identity card a cursory look. "Okay. The ambulance will be here in a minute. We'll catch up with you in emergency at the hospital. I'll have to check the other car."

Trooper Young trotted back to his patrol car and flicked on his transmitter. "This is Young in Nineteen. . . . Sergeant, we've got a VIP injured. He's Eddie Quinn, the Turnpike commissioner who's running for President. Head wound and shock. Got it?"

The Chevrolet Caprice lay on its roof like an overturned beetle. Only after the arrival of more state troopers and the passage of minutes could the lone occupant be hauled from the twisted wreckage. He was a young man and he was dead, his face smashed beyond recognition. Apparently not having fastened his seat belt, he probably had died instantly when his head rammed the windshield. Police found his driver's license in the pocket of a leather jacket that had been torn half off his shoulders. His name was William F. Deitz, aged thirty, and he lived in Albany, New York. Other identity cards listed him as a telephone repairman, married, the father of two children, an army veteran of the Vietnam war.

Near the Continental an ambulance driver and his assistant slid a stretcher under Eddie and lifted him into the red-and-white ambulance just eleven minutes after collision. Stackpole bent over and whispered to Eddie during the transfer. "Remember, Jim was driving. You don't know a thing." Pete rode to the hospital in a state police car with the two Secret Service agents. Twice a fit of shivering came over Baker, but by the time they reached the hospital, he was in reasonable command of himself, although weak and shaky.

The Middlesex General Hospital is an old red brick structure, surmounted by a towering new center section, located near downtown New Brunswick a few miles from the Turnpike's Exit Nine. A rear ramp, covered by a metal canopy, leads to the emergency ward.

The ambulance attendants placed Eddie's stretcher on a dolly, rolled him into a brightly lit room and shifted him carefully to the padded center table. Alerted by Sergeant Gelentser that Presidential Candidate Quinn was about to arrive with a head wound and perhaps other injuries, the hospital staff prepared for prompt examination. Ward Inglis, a leading neurologist who had attended hundreds of traffic casualties in his earlier days and who still responded to cases involving possible brain damage, had been summoned from his nearby home. A heavy-set, amiable, methodical man, Dr. Inglis hurried in just ahead of the victim and awaited him with a staff doctor, an interne and two nurses.

As he leaned over Quinn, whose clothes were rumpled and soiled, Inglis noted that his patient turned his head to watch. The specialist inspected the blood-clotted gash about two inches above Eddie's left ear while he asked his routine opening question when confronted with possible brain damage: "What's your name?" Eddie replied in a weak voice. A nurse measured the pulse in the right wrist as Inglis inspected the eyes, then peered once more into the eyes through an opthalmoscope for telltale signs of brain injury. Inglis inspected the ears for blood, found none.

"What do you do, Mr. Quinn?" It was Inglis's standard second question when testing for normal functioning of the brain.

Eddie smiled wanly. "Well, I was running for President. . . ."

"Oh, I think you're still in business, young fellow."

Inglis loosened his patient's belt and pulled up the shirt, exposing the stomach. Using a plastic tongue blade, the physician scratched the skin in four places, taking note of flesh reactions. Meanwhile a nurse was taking Eddie's blood pressure with a rubber belt tightened on his arm.

"What happened to you?" asked Inglis. He slowly fingered Eddie's collarbone, then felt the shoulders.

"We were driving the center lane of the Turnpike," said Eddie in a nearly normal voice. "An entering car cut in front of us. We hit the rear bumper, I guess, and I blacked out. When I came to, I was lying on the ground with some coats over me."

Inglis turned to Pete Stackpole, standing a few feet away. "About how long was Mr. Quinn unconscious?"

"I'd guess something over a minute," said Pete, speaking loudly enough for Eddie to hear. "I think he came to while we were pulling him from the back seat."

Inglis listened to Eddie's heart with a stethoscope. "Okay, now move that right arm and shoulder for me." The doctor felt the arm. "All right, now the left arm." He repeated with both legs, then pressed his hands on Eddie's stomach. Finally he tapped elbows, knees and ankles for reflex action. All joints responded normally.

"You seem to be in pretty good shape, Mr. Quinn. We'll just clean out that little cut on your scalp and sew it up." A nurse cleansed the wound with a saline solution, then the interne injected Novocain near the gash. "You won't feel a thing."

Inglis swiftly took five stitches in the scalp. A nurse affixed a bandage pad with adhesive tape.

"Okay. Now they're going to take some X rays," said Inglis. "I'll see you in a few minutes."

An attendant wheeled Eddie into the X-ray room where, for the first time, his clothes were removed and he was given a hospital gown. Eddie found he could move about quite easily under command of a technician who operated a wall switch, focused the machine, changed plates and helped Eddie turn into various positions. Minutes later, after scanning the wet plates, Dr. Inglis tentatively pronounced Eddie free of any obvious brain or bone damage.

"But we can't be sure about that head of yours for some time yet," he said. "We're going to put you to bed now and let you get a good rest and night's sleep."

"I've a lot of campaigning left, Doc," said Quinn. His wide smile was back now. "I'm running behind the other guy."

"We'll see about that in the morning. Right now you're going to bed. No sedatives and no food. Liquids only if you're thirsty. They'll wake you up once in the middle of the night to see how you respond. Okay?"

A few minutes later Eddie lay between fresh sheets in a bed in a third-floor private room. Before he fell asleep he learned from the special duty nurse that Stackpole, Flannery and Baker were all uninjured, but he was not told that William F. Deitz, the driver of the other car, was dead. Eddie slept soundly until 3 A.M. when a nurse awakened him, said a few words, then tucked him back between the sheets. Again he fell asleep gradually. A sphygmomanometer was attached to his arm and once an hour the nurse pumped up the band and measured the blood pressure. She also took his pulse at regular intervals.

Flannery phoned in a preliminary report to the Secret Service night-duty agent in Washington soon after arriving at the hospital. He named himself as the driver and sketched the crash in broad outline. Medical examinations of the three Continental passengers revealed no injuries beyond a superficial cut on Baker's left ear. But Baker showed signs of shock and was ordered to bed by a staff physician.

Trooper Hub Young interviewed Stackpole and Flannery immediately after their physical examinations. The questioning was polite, routine and relatively swift. Reviewing his notes afterward, Young noted that both stories dovetailed. Flannery, driving at the speed limit, give or take a mile or two, was cut off suddenly by a sedan that unaccountably swerved into the center lane. Young noticed only one minor discrepancy. Flannery said that he and Baker had pulled Eddie out of the back seat from the right-hand door after

Stackpole staggered out. Stackpole said that he and Flannery removed Eddie, that Baker was in shock. The trooper attributed the differing versions to normal post-accident confusion and decided to wait until morning to clear up the unimportant detail.

Stackpole and Flannery found Dr. Inglis in a hospital corridor as he was preparing to leave for home. Inglis explained in simple language. He had long ago passed the point where he sought to impress bewildered laymen by scattering multisyllabic medical terms about.

"It looks like a simple scalp wound suffered at the time of a mild concussion," he said. "All our tests for serious damage came up negative. But when a man bangs his head and blacks out, there's always the danger of cerebral bleeding we haven't detected. If that doesn't develop, we ought to have your man out of here sometime Sunday. We'll see. So far, so good."

Commandeering an office in the hospital's administrative section, Flannery phoned his second report to Washington while Stackpole called Phil Liccardo at the Waldorf in New York. Phil was not in his room, but a page raised the breathless publicity man several minutes later.

"I've been trying to reach you," said Phil. "We got the word from Vince Anderson a couple of minutes ago. How's Eddie?"

"Okay, we think. He's asleep right now." Pete rapidly filled in the highlights. "Down play this, Phil, for God's sake. We've got a good, sound candidate with a minor head wound that only took five stiches. No cause for alarm. Is Kate around?"

"She's already in the press bus with the rest of the staff. We're coming over with the media. See you soonest. Middlesex General, right?"

"Yeah. Listen. No speeding. One accident tonight is enough."

"How about the other car?"

"A man driving by himself. He's dead. That could mean big trouble. When you get here, talk to me first."

Pete noticed that his right hand quivered as he hung up. The damn shakes again. He had out-talked the staff doctor who wanted to put him to bed. Pete had decided that he would not fold tonight until the cover story was nailed down tight with press and police.

But he felt chilly, strung out, his nerve ends snapping like frightened dogs. Where the hell was some hot coffee?

The New Jersey Turnpike's 1683rd accident of the year occurred at 10:07 P.M. and by midnight Eastern Time, every American listening to radio or television knew that Edward N. Quinn, candidate for President, had been injured in the crash of a car driven by James A. Flannery, head of the protective Secret Service detail. First word of the accident to reach the communications media came from a Middlesex General nurse whose husband was a night-beat man on the New Brunswick *Home News*. After quick checks with the state police and the emergency ward, the reporter phoned the Associated Press bureau in Newark. The AP put its first bulletin on the wire at 10:58 P.M.

After his call to the Waldorf, Stackpole found a vending machine in a hospital corridor. He carried two paper cups of black coffee to the office Flannery was using. The agent sat by a desk phone, staring moodily at the wall. Stackpole closed the door and handed Jim one of the cups. They both sipped at the hot brew.

"This is the hardest damn thing I've ever done in my life," said Flannery. "The fibs, as Ma used to call them, a guy gets used to, but this one is big, Pete." He looked miserable.

"What did they say in Washington?"

"I got through to the Chief the second time. He chewed me out. Why didn't we fly as per schedule? Why no lead car? Why no police escort? Why didn't I give that entering Chevy some space until I was sure it was squared away in the outside lane? How come Baker wasn't driving? Said the Service would catch hell from the media. Oh yeah. Postscript. It's all my fault and I'll face administrative charges of negligence."

"Quit worrying. Eddie'll straighten it out tomorrow with a phone call to the Chief."

"That won't help much. I'm responsible for the candidate's safety, not Eddie. The Chief won't forgive me for this."

"Damn it, Jim, you know you'd be worse off if we said that Eddie was driving. That, you could never explain away."

"I know that. " Flannery's bleak expression reflected his torment.

"Listen, Jim. If Eddie makes it, you're the certain head of the

White House detail and a good bet for the job when the Chief retires. Eddie feels like a brother toward you."

"If . . ." Flannery shrugged. "What about the press?"

"Leave that to me. You find a room and hit the sack so you can't be found tonight."

"Okay. They're sending us relief out of New York. Four agents. They ought to be here soon."

"All right." Pete took a long swallow of coffee. The hot liquid felt good going down. "Now let's go through it together. Here's what I told the trooper."

They soon discovered the discrepancy as they swapped questions and answers from Young's interviews. Pete said he would change his story on the minor point the next day. Flannery and Baker had lifted Eddie to the ground, then Stackpole had joined them in taking Eddie away from the car. They agreed that Flannery would go over the story once more with Baker when he awakened in the morning.

"I don't like loading you with this," said Stackpole as they walked to the door. "I only know one thing. Eddie Quinn cannot be the driver of a car involved in a crash that kills a man."

"Knock it off, Pete. I told you I want Eddie to win and I mean it. . . . God, why did I ever let him take the wheel?"

"He was the boss. And if we can pull this one off, he may be the boss for a long time to come."

Pete Stackpole did not reach his hospital bed until 3 o'clock in the morning. By the time he and Flannery finished their talk, a dozen newspapermen were roaming the hospital in search of him. Pete told his story briefly to reporters in the main lobby, then repeated it all over again when the contingent of newsmen covering Eddie's campaign arrived from the Waldorf. This time Pete spoke to more than 100 reporters under the glare of television lights and before a thicket of microphones. Questioning went on for half an hour. Although no one doubted Stackpole's essential but unstressed detail—that the Continental was driven by Flannery—the inquiries soon confirmed the Secret Service director's fear. The press intended to raise the issue of Service negligence. No accident occurs without a cause. A driver swerving into the wrong lane was not enough. Why were flying reservations canceled for a Turnpike ride? Why no lead car, no escort? Didn't Baker usually drive? How fast was Flannery going? Why couldn't they question Flannery tonight?

Later, while reporters quizzed nurses, doctors, attendants, police and even an obliging Dr. Inglis in the yard of his home, Pete Stackpole huddled with the Quinn staff, Kate, R Danny, Phil, Hunk and Margot. He told the same story—by now he actually could visualize Jim Flannery at the wheel at the moment of collision—and he stressed that no one should be alarmed about Eddie's condition. They had a good, strong candidate, intact in body and brain, and while they would have to cancel all New York appearances, including the big speech in Madison Square Garden, they might be able to fly to California Sunday. If not, perhaps a TV appearance could be scheduled to exhibit Eddie, hopefully hale and hearty, to the nation.

"Let's everybody hang loose," said Pete as they broke up. "This is a tough break, but if we all do our jobs, be calm, act like everything's under control, we can put Eddie over Tuesday."

Pete had a private talk with Kate, assured her that she had the full truth on Eddie's condition and that she probably could visit him in the morning. The staff and press found late accommodations in motels scattered over a wide area. At long last, Pete undressed and went to bed in a room down the hall from Eddie.

As he lay in bed, he knew the feeling of total exhaustion. His skin itched, his head ached, his right leg twitched and sleep fenced with him like a taunting enemy. The nurse had provided a sleeping pill in a small paper container on the bedside table. Pete gulped it down with the help of a glass of water. Things were under control, he told himself. Tough on the Service, rough as hell on Flannery, but with luck Eddie Quinn might make it. Pete had done his best, quickly and instinctively, at the worst of times. And with that consoling thought, Pete Stackpole fell asleep.

But computers compiling daily statistics in America's unending automotive warfare did not sleep. Digging statistically into the mountain of mashed limbs and bleeding flesh, they would include William Deitz, dead at Exit Nine, as one of 163 persons killed in motor vehicle accidents in the United States that day, Eddie Quinn as one of 5750 people injured by automobiles in those twenty-four hours and the mangled Continental and Chevrolet as routine reminders of but one of an incredible 46,000 motor accidents on that single Friday, October 29. Computer observation on the day's traffic slaughter and devastation: Statistically normal.

America's carnage of the streets and highways, the most savage and prolonged civil conflict of all time, was nearing the point where the death toll would double the total military fatalities of all the wars, Revolutionary through Vietnam, in the nation's history.

Kate Witherspoon did not know these precise figures, but as she skirmished for sleep that night, she recalled her first conversation about automobiles with Eddie in the Apollo Motel in Houston sixteen nights ago. She had said she often felt depressed in that car world which pleased him so much. Now, with Eddie's head gashed in his brush with death, Kate knew that depression was not the word. What she felt this night, only seventy-six hours before the polls opened, was hatred.

20

A little puffball of a woman in a starched white uniform was shaking a thermometer. Beyond her a closed door formed a precise oblong on the wall. Eddie stirred, opened his eyes wider and blinked at the daylight. Then he remembered.

He moved his shoulders, twisted on the bed, wriggled his hands and feet. His head felt a bit stuffy, but otherwise, he decided, he felt as he usually did on awakening.

"Am I okay?"

"Are you ever!" She winked. Her face had a comic cast as though she might have ordered it from a theatrical costumer. "You had a very healthy erection a few minutes ago. That takes care of one vital department."

"Oh." Eddie was unsure whether the good news outweighed her intimate surveillance. "What's your name?"

"I'm Edna Walsh and you're Eddie Quinn and right now you're going to open your mouth so I can take your temperature."

Eddie closed his lips over the glass tube while Nurse Walsh held his wrist and checked his pulse. "How'm I doing?" he asked after she took the reading.

"That's for the doctor to answer." She paused with a grin. "But between us, you could walk out of here right now and make a speech. . . . It's nine-thirty and Dr. Inglis will be here in a couple of minutes. If you're interested, you've got the whole country upset, this place is swarming with nosy newspapermen and three people are trying to get in ahead of Dr. Inglis, something we won't allow even for a presidential candidate."

"Who are they?"

"A good-looking congresswoman from Texas, and two men, a Mr. Stackpull, I think, and a Secret Service agent named Flannery."

The two names fell like weights. Scenes flashed. Pete on the ground beside him, whispering into his ear. . . . Pete beside his stretcher. "Remember, Jim was driving." . . . Tail lights and a car trunk directly in front of the Continental . . . His foot slapping at the brake pedal and his hands pulling the wheel. Tension gripped him like a vise and his mouth felt dry. What had Pete said about the crash?

"Edna, could I please have some water?"

She handed him a glass and he drank greedily. "Do you know what happened to the people in the other car?"

"You're not going to worry your head about that now. You've got five stitches in it."

Eddie felt his scalp, exploring gingerly with his fingers, and came across the small taped pad. At that moment Dr. Inglis walked in, bid his patient a professionally cheery good morning, asked a few questions and began his examination while Edna took Eddie's blood pressure. Inglis's tests duplicated many performed the night before. Eddie spent an anxious ten minutes, his mind oscillating between concern for his body, the campaign and this other thing, this heavy weight.

"You appear sound enough except for that scalp laceration," said Inglis when he finished. "Now I want you to carry on normally. Walk around, use the bathroom, see your visitors. If you begin to feel weak or tired, back in bed. I'll see you again this afternoon."

"How about breakfast?"

"Only liquids this morning, water, juice, coffee. Maybe something solid later in the day. We'll see."

"Doc, when can I get out of here? I feel pretty good."

"Let me explain," said Inglis as he stood beside the bed. "The X rays look fine. I think you're all right. But there's always a chance of a subdural hematoma when the head's been banged up. That's a blood leakage in the brain. We can't be sure you're free of that for twenty-four hours, and with you, I prefer thirty-six. That takes us into Sunday morning."

"Couldn't you cut that back to tonight? They start voting three days from now."

Inglis shook his head slowly. "You're a practical man, Mr. Quinn, so I'll be frank with you. If you were a regular patient, I might release you tonight and take my chances." Inglis paused. Opportunity opened wide before him. "Actually, if I were one of your so-called Community Medical Corpsmen," he said with a touch of acid, "I'd probably let you go right now and forget it."

"Easy, Doc." Eddie grinned. "You've got the drop on me."

"Yes. Well, the fact is that you're known to everyone in the country. If you walked out of here and then collapsed with a hematoma, it would be my neck as well. I understand you like to simplify. Well, it's as simple as that."

"Fair enough." Eddie respected this man. "What about the other car?"

"I thought you knew. There was only one person in it, a man about thirty. He was dead when they pulled him out of the wreck."

Dead. Another weight fell. Could he have avoided the crash if he had kept it under sixty? No way. That Caprice was there without warning.

"You're a lucky man, Mr. Candidate, to get away with a head bump against a car window. And how your driver escaped injury is a miracle. . . . Now don't overdo."

Your driver! As the door closed after Ward Inglis, the significance of the phrase loomed wide and high. Of course. Pete Stackpole would have done exactly that. He would have reckoned with death or serious injury in the other car, thought of the election and instantly decided that his candidate could not risk the odium of being even partially responsible for a fatal automobile crash. With the full realization, Eddie felt a quick vibration as though a loud alarm had sounded. He had to see Pete at once.

"Edna . . ."

But through the door came a girl in a white uniform bearing a breakfast tray and behind her walked, not Pete, but Kate Witherspoon.

"Hey, Kate. God, you look good."

She's extra beautiful today, thought Eddie, the easy stride, the warm, expectant smile, the wide green eyes, the shining black hair. Kate wore a beige jersey dress that hugged her figure beneath a dark leather belt. A matching leather handbag swung from her shoulder and she carried several newspapers. She came to the bed and kissed his forehead while the attendant stood by with the tray.

"We got the good news from the doctor," said Kate. "You're a lucky man, Eddie. Tough too, thank God."

He took her hand and felt the warm pressure on his fingers. He was lucky and it was fine to be alive in a sunlit room with Kate beside him. He was glad she'd come alone, without Pete and Jim.

The girl placed the tray of fruit juice and coffee on the bedside table and cranked up the bed. Eddie waited until she left the room, then pulled Kate to him. The newspapers spilled over the coverlet as they embraced.

"Eddie, I'm so thankful. . . . Last night . . . well, I couldn't bear the thought of you in pain."

"I never felt much. . . . Funny, right now I want you more than ever."

She tapped the tip of his nose. "They call that the life force. Very, very healthy for lovers and candidates." She straightened up, brushed at her hair, then pulled a chair close to the bed. "Both of your sons called, Al from Chicago and Eddie, Jr., from Philadelphia. They're worried about you."

"I'm glad. Those boys are all right. I'll call them back after a while."

"Eddie, you're alive and we're here and I'm crazy about you. I just hope you're as happy as I am."

The word "alive" broke the spell. "Is it true the guy in the other car is dead?" Eddie realized he sounded almost feverishly curious.

"Yes, but you can't take that guilt on yourself. Jim couldn't help it. The man cut right in front of him."

Eddie winced. "How are the others?"

"Pete and Jim are fine. They put Bake to bed with a mild case of shock, but he's up and around this morning. He'll be all right. How Jim escaped without a scratch, we'll never know."

She saw the look of instant pain on Eddie's face. "What's the matter?"

Ignoring the question, he asked brusquely: "The papers. What do the papers say?"

She gathered up the two morning papers and held up the front pages of the New York *Times* and the Newark *Star-Ledger*. Eddie dominated the headlines: QUINN HURT IN CAR COLLISION . . . EDDIE QUINN INJURED IN FATAL TURNPIKE CRASH. He skimmed through both stories.

"They say that Jim's driving skill saved us."

"Yes," said Kate. "He had to be good, being cut off like that."

"No!" Eddie slammed out the negative as though with a hammer.

Kate looked bewildered. "What do you . . . ?"

"It was me." He said it fiercely. "The other driver cut in front of *me*."

Kate stared at him, stunned.

"I was driving, Kate. I was doing better than seventy. Then this Caprice cut right into the center lane while I was trying to pass it. I can see that car trunk right here." He held a hand before his eyes. "Kate, I . . . Oh, Christ."

She thought that he might weep, but Eddie was too intent on recalling a critical moment of life to yield to tears. "When I came to, I was lying on the center shoulder and my first thought was, Jesus, what a place to get it, right near the spot where I was born. But then I knew I was alive because I could hear Pete talking to me." Eddie spoke slowly now, striving for accuracy of memory. "He said Jim was driving. I remember he told me to squeeze his hand if I understood. I did and the pressure felt like, well, like life itself, just as your hand felt a minute ago. I knew damn well what I was doing last night. I understood Pete's message. Clear, real clear . . . But this morning?" He halted suddenly.

Kate looked into his eyes, testing for the truth she already sensed. Eddie returned her gaze, then looked away. "Is a state trooper waiting?" he asked.

"Yes, but he's agreed to wait until you're ready. It's a pure formality for him. No one is questioning Pete's statement about Jim at the wheel?"

"Has Jim said anything?"

She shook her head. "He has a room on this floor. The newspapermen think he's still asleep. He and Pete want to talk to you first."

"I don't know." Eddie's head ached now and he could feel his stomach slowly churning. "God, I'm glad you're here, Kate. . . . I think I need some help."

She nodded at the tray. "The first thing is to get some juice and coffee in you. Then you can think about it."

Eddie downed the orange juice in several swallows. "Canned!" he said with distaste. "Not even a guy running for President rates fresh orange juice any more." He sipped at the coffee.

Kate watched his growing agitation. His face was flushed and his eyes moved restlessly. Propping himself upright, he squirmed against the pillows on the elevated bed. He pointed to the scattered newspapers.

"Who gave them the dope? Pete?"

"Yes. Pete briefed the press last night. He said Flannery did a beautiful job of keeping the car from turning over. Baker was beside Jim, he said. You hit your head against the left rear door window and were pulled out by Jim and Bake, then Pete helped. . . . Nobody doubts the story, Eddie. It hasn't occurred to anyone that you might have been driving. I must say it never entered my head."

"Good Christ, Kate. That puts it up to me. I . . ."

"Eddie, you're in no condition to agonize over that now."

"When else?" His voice shot up in pitch. "Either I speak up right now or I live with this goddamn thing forever."

"You're thinking seriously of changing the story?"

"I'm thinking that I feel like hell about it."

"Is this a moral bit with you, Eddie?"

"Moral? That's one of those—what did you say the other night?—one of those baggy words. You can dump anything into it. All I know is that I had to tell you the truth right away. How would you feel if you found out that I'd lied to you about it?"

"That's not quite the same," she said slowly.

"If I couldn't lie to you, how about everybody out there?" He swept his arm in an arc, encompassing nameless millions.

"I'm not everybody, Eddie."

"I know. But what about my friends? I couldn't tell them. And Eddie, Jr., and Al? And the people I work with? I don't know, Kate. I'm afraid it would hit me every time I talked into a TV camera and asked people to trust me on some issue or other. From here, that doesn't look easy to live with."

"A lot of things aren't easy to live with. Have you always told the truth?"

"No, I haven't. But I can't recall anything this big, either. Not this kind of a bind. I . . . What would you do, Kate?"

She took a sip of Eddie's coffee, fumbled for her cigarettes in the leather bag and lit one. She sat down, smoothed her skirt and thought as she smoked.

"I really don't know. And that's honest." She spoke slowly, thinking as she went. "I'm not you. I'm me. If I were in the same spot, knowing everything involved—it's only three days until Tuesday now . . ." She paused. "I suppose I'd ride with Pete's story. Since the crash was inevitable, I'd ask myself does it really matter who was driving? If I confessed I was driving, well, in a close election like this, I might very well lose the ball game. Speeding. A man killed. I'd taken the wheel away from a skilled driver. People would wonder why I didn't have more important things on my mind than driving a car. . . . Well, it would just be handing Pinholster a million votes or so, maybe more."

"I know that." Eddie was twisting the coverlet in his fist. "But look at the other side. This would be a secret known to five people, the four of us in that Mark IV and now you. Sooner or later one of five people has to talk. Also, how do we know somebody didn't see me driving? For instance, I took over the wheel at the Camden-Philly tollgate. Maybe one of the collectors saw me. Maybe there are some clues inside the Continental as to where we were sitting. Maybe Pete and Jim and Bake get their stories mixed. Maybe I would. Hell, there are a lot of maybes."

"I'd say all those are very long shots. But what's certain if you tell the truth now is that you'd make a liar out of Pete and probably get Jim and Bake fired."

"I realize that." His strained face reflected the inner churning.

"Big-shot Eddie. I had to get my hands on that Mark IV. A dumb truck driver is right."

Kate smoked without speaking for some time. Was she helping or confusing? Eddie's eyes played fitfully over the newspaper stories again.

"Whatever you do," she said at last, "I'm with you, President or also-ran."

"I know that."

"Oh, you do? Pretty damn sure of yourself for a man who's just cracked his skull."

Eddie managed a smile. "Well, that's the way I feel." But the smile evaporated as quickly as it appeared.

She watched his tensions build up again. "Eddie, the way you feel is important. Sometimes in tough spots, I find it best just to relax and let my body speak. How do I *feel?* It may not bring the answer other people want, but it does tell me what I want—and usually that's best for me."

"Just how would I do that?" He was suspicious.

"Close your eyes. Don't think. Just feel."

"Sounds kind of far out."

"Try it. You've nothing to lose. It might work."

He frowned, but then in a moment his eyelids closed. Soon his face relaxed and his hand released the coverlet. He lay without moving for perhaps a minute, then opened his eyes.

"And?"

His smile was thin, self-deprecatory. He hunched his shoulders slightly. "I feel, Kate, like I'd make a lousy liar."

"Oh?" But it was no surprise to her.

"Absolutely. One hundred per cent lousy."

"Then you have your answer. Any idea why?"

"Oh hell, yes. Ever since I was a kid, every time I'd try a big one, I'd goof it up. Little lies, okay. But anything that mattered, well, I don't know. It just didn't work. There was always some smart-ass around who could see through my story."

"That's not quite right, Eddie." She gentled her voice in demurral. "How about the night at Flannery's shack? In a way, we lied about that."

"It's not the same." Eddie looked troubled. "Women, men, sex, love. The rules are different somehow. And we didn't lie. We just kept it a secret that you were around. Even so, when Vince found out, I had to admit that you came up there."

"A thin line, if you ask me. . . . All truth is relative, Eddie. I understand how you feel and what you want to do. The question is: Is it worth it?"

"I'm not weighing things.. I figure I'm just reacting."

"Honesty is never absolute. Do you realize you're risking a very good chance to be President?"

"Yeah, I know. But you asked me to find out how I felt. Well, I feel I don't want to go through with this. Maybe it's because I'm afraid I'd be found out sooner or later. Maybe there's something more. I'm not sure what it is. It's just there."

She looked at him wordlessly until the silence became uncomfortable.

"That's good enough, Eddie," she said softly.

She reached out, grasped his hand, then quickly stood up. She suspected that this big, warm, troubled man might have just elected Hugh Pinholster President of the United States and she was not at all sure how she felt about that. She could sense a great surge of affection for Eddie, but there were other, conflicting emotions that would have to be sorted out later. Was his a private victory or a public surrender? A campaign that might have changed a nation, and Kate Witherspoon along with it, had all but collapsed. Her last remark that night in the Skirvin—"We're winners, you and I" —echoed in memory, a hollow sound.

Edna rapped on the door. "A state trooper wants to see you. He says it'll only take a few minutes."

"No," said Eddie. "Tell him to wait a bit longer. I have to see Mr. Stackpole and Mr. Flannery right away. Are they around?"

"Both of them are right down the hall, waiting with a Mr. Baker. Okay, now you walk around some, go to the bathroom if you have to. I'll send your friends in."

Eddie was sitting on the edge of the bed, Kate in the chair, when the three men entered. Baker looked pale, but Stackpole and Flannery brimmed with energy.

"You're looking good, Eddie," said Flannery. Stackpole and Baker added their own cheery appraisals.

"I hear you're all okay, thank God," said Eddie. "Jim, I'm going to owe you as long as I live. What you did after I blacked out, I don't know, but you sure must have hit that brake and grabbed the wheel from me in a hurry."

Stackpole threw a quick, worried glance at the door. It was closed. He looked at Kate, then at Eddie.

"You told Kate?"

Eddie nodded.

"Well, that's okay, I guess. But no more. Five is enough." Pete said it as though five were four too many. "And from now on, for God's sake, no more talk like that, even among ourselves. Any time talk of that crash comes up, we start with Flannery driving and you in the left rear. I hate to hit you fast like this, Eddie, but it's important. Important? Hell, it's crucial."

Eddie plucked at the shoulder of his rough hospital gown. "Crucial maybe, but not true."

"What does that mean?"

"I'm sorry, Pete. I know what this involves for all of us, but we're going to tell it like it was."

The three men looked at Eddie with blank expressions, obviously not fully comprehending.

"We're going to *what?*" Pete brushed at his thinning hair, his automatic reflex when disconcerted.

"I'm going to tell the press that I was the driver, just tell what happened."

Flannery looked as if he had been struck in the mouth. Baker gaped. Stackpole stood for a frozen moment, then wheeled on Kate.

"Did you have something to do with this?"

She shook her head. "No," she said in a low voice. "It's pure Quinn."

"I'll see that you three won't be hurt," said Eddie. "If I tell it right, people will understand that you were doing what you thought necessary to protect me."

"The hell with us for right now. . . . Why?" Pete's voice shook with sudden rage. "For God's sake, Eddie, why?"

"I'm not sure. I just can't go through with it. I'm no good at big lies like this."

Shock held the three men for moments that quickly became almost unbearable. Then Stackpole, with an effort at control, said in a flat tone: "You know that means you'll lose."

"I suppose so." Eddie slid from the bed, put his feet into paper slippers and walked slowly about, the hospital gown, loosely tied in the back, exposing his bare back and rump. "I thought about that. But I also faced what it would be like, living with this as a secret. It wouldn't be easy for any of you either. Sometime, a year from now, two years, somebody would let it slip. Might as well get rid of it this morning."

"Let's put this off for a couple of hours." Pete's speech, after his wave of anger, was clipped, admonitory. "You're still not yourself. You've got to take time, think it through carefully."

"No. Every hour that goes by will only make it worse."

Pete confronted Eddie, gripped his arms as he had Flannery's the night before near the Turnpike guard rail. "Goddamn it, think! You're throwing away a chance to be President! You're not running for mayor of some two-bit town. You're going for the presidency. That's different. The big time has its own rules. You play to win right down to the wire, no matter what."

"I know with my head how the game is played." He spoke as from a distant dell of regret. "But my gut tells me different. I just couldn't pull it off."

"Pull it off? You don't have to do anything except keep quiet."

"Awful quiet for a long, long time."

Pete let his hands fall. "You know something, Eddie?" His voice throbbed with rage again. "You talk about guts. Well, I don't think you have the guts for the job. You almost quit cold Sunday night in Oklahoma City. Now you've found a nice, safe way to chicken out—and let Pinholster have it." He glared at Eddie, their faces only inches apart. "Maybe you don't have what it takes for the White House."

Kate intervened. "Please, Pete. Let up. We don't know yet about head injury."

"There's nothing wrong with this man's head." Pete turned his anger toward her. "But there's plenty wrong with his heart, or spirit, or whatever the hell you call it that makes a fighter. You're mixed up with a loser, Kate."

Quinn caught him by the forearm. "That's enough, Pete." Eddie struggled for control, found that he was shaking. His grip on Pete became less a restraining gesture than a means of supporting himself. "But I don't think you mean it," he added limply. "You're under pressure."

Stackpole wrenched himself away. "So you're finally thinking about us? Me, who lied to keep you in the running. Because of you, I'm broke, through forever in the party. Jim and Bake will be out of jobs, you can bet your ass on that. First you sail down the Turnpike on your own private ego trip, acting like some goddamn teen-age hot-rodder instead of a candidate. Then, when we try to cover for you, bang, Mr. Morality appears. Full of noble decisions. Confess your sin to the world—and screw your friends while you're doing it."

Eddie shuffled back to the bed, his paper slippers and yawning gown robbing him of any façade of dignity. He faced them as he lowered himself into the bed.

"I know how you feel. It isn't easy for me to pull the rug from under you when it was me you thought of first. But the country won't hold it against you. People will understand that you wanted to shield me. As for the future, hell, if we stick together, there can be a lot of politics ahead. People forgive and forget in time."

"Is your mind made up?" asked Pete coldly.

"Yes." Eddie leaned back on the elevated pillows. "In a way, now that I think of it, it's like the night in Oklahoma City or going to Merton. There isn't any decision to be made. There's really no choice."

"Just winning or losing."

"Forget it, Pete. It's settled."

Stackpole stood rooted. When he spoke, there wasn't a ray of warmth in his voice. "In that case, I'm going out and cancel L.A. and Chicago—and about $600,000 worth of TV spots."

Eddie looked puzzled. "Why cancel the commercials?"

"Have you forgotten how your big 30-second spot goes?" Pete spat out the question. "You're going to run the chauffeur-driven executive limos off the exit ramps, so ordinary Americans can have a clear shot on the thruway of something, crap, something. That would sound great after your own crash at Exit Nine and a man killed."

"I guess you're right." Eddie plucked at his gown. "But we filmed some other spots. They're okay."

"Better you should give the money to some of those blue-collar families you've been bleeding for." Pete turned toward the door, a bitter set to his face.

"Are you quitting?"

"Me? Quit? Hell, no, Eddie. I'm no quitter." He walked to the door. "Take care of yourself. I'll see you tomorrow when they release you. . . . Good luck." There was a catch in his voice and he did not bang the door behind him.

Silence made its own sound. Then Kate became aware of the ticking of her watch.

"I'm sorry, Jim," said Eddie. "This isn't much of a down payment for saving my life. . . . You too, Bake. I'll do my best for you when I call your office."

"It's rough." Flannery stood bleakly with folded arms. "I can't pretend it makes me happy."

"It's rougher on Pete. He did the talking."

"Don't you believe it. I lied to the Chief last night. There's no way out of that."

"Jim, it was my fault from the minute I took over that wheel."

The agent looked steadily at Eddie without expression. "There's blame enough to go around." He said it as an epitaph for trust. "Take it easy. We'll see you later."

He and Baker left, unsmiling.

"Anything I can help with?" asked Kate. The room suddenly seemed too small for them.

"No, I guess you'd better go too. I'm going to send for Vince Anderson. I couldn't face a press conference."

She came over and kissed him lightly on the forehead. "I'm not sure what goes on in there, but I guess I love you, Eddie."

"I don't guess. I know." He put his arms around her in a tight, swift embrace. "I love you." And he realized with a start that it had been twenty-five years since he had said those three words.

"Well!" Kate arched her eyebrows in a manner reminiscent of George Dawson's habitual mock surprise. "Where do I get treated for shock around this hospital?"

Eddie's grin flickered, then vanished. "Do you think Pete understood what I was talking about?"

She tilted her head, thinking. "Yes. But did you understand Pete?"

"I think so. In his shoes, I might have been tempted to do the same thing."

"No, I mean about the presidency. In Pete's code, a man who can win the White House should be ready to sacrifice anything for it, even his personal scruples."

"You think so too?"

"I told you I'd probably let the story ride as was . . . But I'm not you, Eddie. And if we're going on together, the worst beginning is to try to make the other person over into an image of one's self. We're not the same. Vive la différence. End of sermon."

"It's cockeyed," he said, musing. "I decide to come clean with the truth and then I feel like a horse's ass for doing it."

She stood up and placed her hand on her breast like a Girl Scout salute. "We take our text from Jerome K. Jerome who said: 'It is always the best policy to speak the truth, unless of course you are an exceptionally good liar.'"

"That fits." This time he flashed a good, warm grin.

Kate swung her handbag from the chair to her shoulder, tossed a smile his way and walked to the door, then turned. "Love you, Eddie, but I hate those cars of yours. Hate. Hate."

Alone, Eddie found his thoughts grinding. Was Pete right? Did a refusal to go with the cover story mean that subconsciously he resisted the big job and its responsibility? Was he privately relieved that the truth probably would place the burden on Pinholster's shoulders while he sauntered away, a free man? Did even Kate think that he had ducked out? Round and round went the doubts, but then that feeling. All he knew was that when he returned to the feeling, then he knew he must tell it the way it was. Only then did the pressure ease and a kind of rueful comfort settle in. Not a bad deal, feeling comfortable with himself. But the others . . .

There was a rap on the door.

"Come in." His own voice surprised him. He actually sounded cheerful.

An officer walked in. He was a husky, broken-nosed man in the light blue uniform of the New Jersey state police. He carried a notebook.

"Hub Young, Mr. Quinn." He inclined his head in greeting. "We've met a couple of times around the Turnpike building."

"Oh, sure, Hub. How's it going?"

"Okay. You feel up to a few questions? Only take a couple of minutes."

"No problem. I feel okay. But look, I'd like to make it easy on all of us. I have to tell my version to the press too. Would you mind if we get Vince Anderson up here? You probably know him. He's out of the AP bureau in Trenton. That way, I only have to tell the story once."

"Sure. I guess that's all right."

Eddie picked up the bedside phone and asked the operator to page Phil Liccardo, probably with the newsmen in the lobby. Phil was on the line within a minute.

"Eddie," he said after inquiries about the candidate's condition, "we've got about a hundred characters milling around here, waiting to hear your version of the crash."

"I can imagine. But I'm not up to more than one interviewer. Find Vince Anderson and send him up with a tape recorder. He can borrow one from some radio guy."

"Right away?"

"Yeah, and tell the rest of the press that Vince will be pooling for all of them."

Three minutes later Vince Anderson walked in, carrying a compact recorder with attached microphone. The short, jug-eared reporter was as dogged and as intent as ever. He inquired politely about Eddie's health, said a businesslike hello to Young as he fussed with the microphone and made several trial runs, experimenting with the push buttons.

"Ready?" he asked. Eddie nodded.

"Commissioner Quinn, could you just give us your version of what happened on the Turnpike last night?" Vince passed the mike to Eddie, then settled into a chair with his pencil and note pad. Trooper Young pulled his chair closer to the bed.

"I'd be happy to, Vince." Eddie's voice was strong, steady. "First, I'd like to make some corrections and apologize to the press for letting an inaccurate report go on for so many hours. I think you'll understand how that happened as I go along. The most important change I want to make is this: I was driving the car at the time of the accident, not Agent James Flannery of the Secret Service."

Anderson and Young traded looks of astonishment. The reporter studied the candidate briefly, then made quick notes in his pad. The trooper looked at Eddie with quickened interest.

"I'll go over what happened in detail," Eddie continued, "but t I want to pay my respects to three good friends, Pete Stackpole, jim Flannery and Oscar Baker. What they did was out of loyalty to me and, I suspect, out of regard for a candidate for the presidency. If the situation was reversed, I might have done the same thing for any of them. Mr. Stackpole can take care of himself, but I hope that Secret Service headquarters will take a sympathetic view of Jim and Bake and their actions last night. They did their best to protect me in every way they knew how.

"So now for what happened. When I finished my last speech in Philadelphia early last night, I decided to drive instead of fly to New York. At the entrance to the New Jersey Turnpike . . ."

He told everything he could remember, in sequence to the best of his ability. While he did not divulge the thoughts whirling in his mind from the moment of renewed consciousness to the present—they were so numerous, fleeting and conflicting that an attempted orderly account could only confuse and falsify—he did recount every fact and scrap of conversation. Pete whispering to him on the ground . . . the stretcher . . . lying on the emergency table and failing to refute the story that he was in the back seat . . . the doctor's orders . . . discovery this morning that the other driver was dead. He ended with Dr. Inglis's morning examination.

"So that's it, as far as I know," he said. "Of course, I have my own opinion about the accident. I was exceeding the speed limit, true. But even if I had been under the limit, doing sixty or less, there would have been no way to avoid that crash. The other driver should have straightened away in the outside lane after entering. Instead he cut across into my center lane while I was about to make a routine passing. I deeply sympathize with his family, but I hope his wife and children can understand that there was no way of avoiding that collision. As for my violation of the speed limit, I'm ready to pay the penalty. . . . If either of you have any questions, fire away."

"You said the last time you looked at the speedometer, you were doing seventy-one or two," said Trooper Young. "Could you estimate how long before the accident that was?"

"Not long. Maybe two or three minutes. I'm pretty sure I didn't vary it. I tend to drive at a steady speed."

"Had you been drinking any alcoholic beverages?" asked Young.

"Haven't touched the stuff in twenty years, not even beer or wine. Ginger ale's my drink. Vince can vouch for that, or anyone who knows me."

Anderson took the microphone. "Why were you driving over the speed limit?"

Eddie hesitated. "Like many people, I often drive faster than the posted limit. Of course, I know the Turnpike like my own hand."

"Is it possible," Anderson asked, "that you were in shock in the emergency room, so that even if you sensed Stackpole's story wasn't right, you were too confused to do anything about it?"

"Could be. You'll have to ask Dr. Inglis for his medical opinion about that. All I know is that when I was on the examining table, I was aware of someone saying I had been pulled out of the back seat. I knew that wasn't right, but I didn't object."

"Why did you decide to come out with this today?" Anderson pursued.

Eddie thought while the tape ran. "I'm not sure. . . . Lying makes me feel bad. As soon as I decided to tell the truth, the tension went away. Oh hell, Vince, as I said to Kate Witherspoon, I'm no good at lying."

"I notice that one recent poll said that 67 per cent of the people distrust their national leadership in America. In making up your mind, were you considering those voters who trust you?"

"Not consciously. But since you brought it up, I'm glad that I won't be contributing to more national distrust."

"Do you think your actions last night disqualify you for the presidency?"

"No, I don't, Vince. Of course, I've just got one vote. The rest of you will have to decide that. In retrospect, I should have let Baker do his job at the wheel. I don't think he's a better driver than I am, but that's been his duty in this campaign, not mine. So that was a mistake in judgment maybe. I was eleven or twelve miles over the speed limit. Millions of Americans have been guilty of that. That doesn't excuse me, of course. I've learned my lesson. From now on, I drive below the limit. Still, if we said that any man or woman who took the wheel at the wrong time or who drove too fast was barred from being President, we'd have a hard time finding anyone to serve."

Eddie glanced questioningly at both men. They shook their heads and Anderson clicked off the recorder.

"That does it for me." Trooper Young snapped his notebook shut. "I appreciate the detail, Commissioner."

"What happens now legally?" asked Anderson.

"When there's an auto death," said Young, "we have to submit a report to the prosecutor, Middlesex County in this case. But there doesn't appear to be any 'willful and wanton' recklessness here, which is what the law requires for an auto-death charge. The Commissioner's subject to loss of points for speeding. But that's only a guess. You'll have to get it from the prosecutor."

After Young left, Anderson lit a cigarette and stood somewhat uncertainly near the bed. He eyed Eddie closely, then cleared his throat.

"What's the matter, Vince? Something troubling you?"

"Yes. What you didn't say."

"There's nothing else that I know of. You've got the best story of the campaign. That's not enough?"

"Look, Eddie. We both know something that the other newspapermen have only guessed at."

"What's that,"

"Kate Witherspoon."

"What about Kate?" asked Eddie sharply.

"You didn't mention her."

"What's she got to do with the accident? Kate was in New York."

"That's just the point." Anderson drew nervously on his cigarette. "Why does a man who's on the verge of maybe being elected President take the chance of nighttime speeding? One reason could be that he's on his way to see somebody, a woman maybe, and he wants to get there fast."

"You're fishing." Eddie experienced a sinking feeling.

"It's only logical speculation."

"You're getting into motives. That's murky stuff." Suddenly the truth became as complex as life.

"Look, Eddie. You had no speech to make, no political appointment to keep, yet you were doing seventy-plus in Friday night traffic. Any good reporter would speculate on his own. Some of them did when Rockefeller was courting Happy on the sly."

"Lots of people drive that fast at night." Eddie could hear his own voice sounding strained, remote. "I can't prevent you from speculating."

"No, you can't." Anderson toyed with the microphone. For once in his professional life zeroing in on a target held no thrill. "And some guys will keep pressing that angle until something cracks. When it does, you'll look worse than if you'd stuck to Stackpole's story."

"Kate's not involved," said Eddie stubbornly.

"I don't believe you." It was a flat, non-accusatory statement. "My bet is that if you didn't have a date with Mrs. Witherspoon in New York, you'd have kept it under sixty."

Memory seared. . . . Pete's crack about how his arithmetic stank, that Kate would return earlier to the Waldorf . . . Stepping on the gas to move up the speed . . . Jim cautioning him to take it easy, that he was over seventy . . . And he had done seventy or better all the way. The truth, the whole truth and nothing but the truth, so help him God, and now there was no comfort, only a dry, flicking menace.

"Why this bugging, Vince?"

"I'm doing my job." Dogged, thought Eddie, solemnly insistent, an enemy with jug ears. "On the tape, when I asked why you were over the limit, you got vague. I caught it. So will some other reporters."

"You're pressuring me by using what you know about that night at Flannery's shack."

"Sure I am. I'd be a fool if I didn't. You're not running for township committeeman, Eddie. You're running for President."

Stackpole's twin brother, mouthing almost the same words. Had they rehearsed their act? Answer, true or false.

"Quinn, you're a big story."

And you're a big boy now, Eddie. Tell Mommy Anderson the whole story. You'll feel better if you face up to it.

"I told you what happened," said Eddie with an edge of asperity. "Reasons, motives, hell, they get cloudy."

"You can't have it both ways." Anderson sounded like a solicitous friend, but he was an antagonist, Eddie thought, remember that. "You can't go collecting merit badges for telling the truth and then hold out the main part of the story. Well, you can, but they'll crucify you for it."

"You too?"

"We stick to facts on the AP. But I know the newspaper business. A lot of guys covering your campaign have been yakking about you and Kate. One of them is bound to speculate that you were driving fast because you were anxious to get to New York to see Kate. Once that first story breaks, and there's a shred of proof, then everybody rushes into the act."

Anderson was right, Eddie surmised, but not as right as Stackpole had been. Truth was a traitor. "Let's get this over with. What do you want?"

"I want to go back on the tape and ask you again why you were doing seventy plus in Friday night traffic."

"No." Eddie paused, then spoke slowly, choosing his words with care. "The point here is my responsibility. I told the truth about the accident. I was at the wheel and I was over the limit. The reason

I was speeding is immaterial. There are a dozen reasons why people speed, the main one being plain old habit."

Anderson shrugged. He clamped the microphone and extension cord into place on the recorder, then looked down at the big man on the bed. "I could kill you with a single question, Eddie." And for a single moment, Anderson loathed his job.

"What's that?"

" 'Mr. Quinn, did you intend to see Congresswoman Witherspoon when you arrived in New York Friday night?' . . . But I'm not going to ask it."

"Thanks."

"I wish I could help you, Eddie, but I'm afraid you've had it. Sooner or later, you'll be asked that question."

"I'll face it when it comes. . . . Vince, if Kate's out in the hall, ask her to come in, will you?"

"Sure . . . Good luck, Eddie."

This was the worst, thought Eddie. If only he'd let Bake keep the wheel. If, if, if . . .

Kate, swinging into the room, seemed to sense trouble at once. She halted, then walked slowly toward the bed, as if tuning to the new vibrations. Eddie told her of Anderson's prediction.

"Vince is probably right," he concluded. "We're trapped."

She thought at once of Susan, her daughter's face shadowed by a montage of headlines that stripped the candidate and the congresswoman.

"We can't outlaw speculation," said Kate bitterly.

"I didn't see this coming, Kate." The truth had a rancid taste. "The stories won't be pretty. I kill a man when I'm speeding, they'll say, to keep a late date with a married woman. If that happens, they'll smear your name over every news program and front page in the country."

"I can see it. So we lose together, me in Dallas and you in fifty states and the District of Columbia." She forced a laugh that emerged high and strained. "Then sometime in December, we'll make the women's pages. Nice feature about the two losers living in sin."

"Can you suggest a way out?" His head began to throb.

"Not now." She said it with flat resignation.

Eddie guessed at what she was thinking. If only he had let Pete Stackpole's story alone, they would face nothing but a nation's solicitude and wishes for the candidate's swift recovery. Now, thanks to his stubborn courtship of truth, they faced possible disaster.

"I'm sorry, Kate."

"Maybe Vince is wrong. Maybe . . ." Suddenly she bent down, kissed him roughly, blinked as though fighting back tears, fumbled in her shoulder bag.

"Eddie, I'm coming unglued. I've got to get out of here. I love you but . . ." She found a tissue, blew her nose like a trumpet. "But you're a lousy liar. And I'm a lousy loser."

"Kate . . ."

But she was already hurrying from the room.

Before joining his colleagues in the hospital lobby, Vince Anderson telephoned the Associated Press bureau in Newark from a corridor phone booth.

"Anderson at Middlesex General," he told the desk man who answered. "I just taped Eddie Quinn and I've got to pool it. But I can do a few graphs that will hold for maybe five minutes. Gimme dictation."

Ninety seconds later, while Eddie and Kate talked, bells rang on news room teleprinters around the nation. Keys clattered across paper lurching out of machines a line at a time.

New Brunswick (AP)—Presidential Candidate Edward N. Quinn said today that he was driving the car involved in a fatal crash last night on the New Jersey Turnpike.

Flatly contradicting the version given by his campaign manager, Peter D. Stackpole, eleven hours earlier, Quinn said that Secret Service Agent James Flannery, the reported driver, actually was sitting beside him.

Quinn, who blacked out at the moment of impact, credited Flannery's quick action on the brake and steering wheel for saving the lives of the four men in the candidate's limousine.

In a tape-recorded interview, Quinn conceded that he was driving slightly more than seventy miles an hour, breaking the sixty-mile Turnpike speed limit, on his way to New York City and a packed campaign schedule for today.

Asked why he decided to tell his version of the accident, Quinn, wearing a bandage on his lacerated scalp, said from his elevated hospital bed: "I'm no good at lying."

(more to come)

Anderson's unadorned account of his interview was duplicated in a variety of forms in a hundred stories filed from New Brunswick within the next hour.

But at 3 P.M. the tone altered radically when Sybil Jamieson went before television cameras in an office of the Middlesex General Hospital for her regular fifteen-minute Saturday afternoon program of political commentary.

"Eddie Quinn's remarkable bedside interview," she said after summarizing the facts, "sets some kind of record for frankness by an American politician, but one important question remains unanswered. Why was the presidential candidate exceeding the speed limit? When asked this question, Mr. Quinn said quote 'Like many people, I often drive faster than the posted limit.' Unquote. True enough, no doubt. But this was Friday night, with the normal heavy Turnpike traffic, and Mr. Quinn had no political appointments or meetings scheduled last night in New York City. He was registered at the Waldorf-Astoria as was one of his advisers, Congresswoman Kate Witherspoon of Texas. Mrs. Witherspoon flew from Dallas to New York last night to address a women's liberation rally on her candidate's behalf.

"Now it is no secret in the press corps covering the Quinn campaign that the candidate and the congresswoman are intimate friends. They have seen a great deal of each other along the campaign trail, not just in staff huddles, but as a twosome. I talked to Mrs. Witherspoon this noon in a corridor of the Middlesex General Hospital and asked her whether she had expected to see Mr. Quinn last night at the Waldorf. She answered that of course she had, that she was a member of the staff. I also learned from one of the hospital people that Kate Witherspoon was the first visitor to see Mr. Quinn this morning and that she saw him again after his interview with Anderson of the AP.

"Ordinarily I believe in treating a politician's private life as just that, but in this case, Mr. Quinn himself has opened up every aspect of his Turnpike accident by calling in the press and telling a version completely at variance with the story of his campaign manager. We take it for granted this afternoon that Mr. Quinn told the truth, but did he tell the whole truth? Was he speeding on the highway because of an appointment with Mrs. Witherspoon in New York? Several hours ago I sent in a note to Mr. Quinn with that question which, incidentally, most of the press corps is asking this afternoon. At show time, there has been no answer.

"Truth wears many faces, as we all know. We can applaud Mr. Quinn's courage in telling the truth with the presidential election only three days away. But we also have a duty as responsible journalists to question whether the whole truth has been told. Having taken the stand as a voluntary witness in his own case, Mr. Quinn cannot plead invasion of privacy when a question of personal motive is pressed."

Sybil Jamieson's comments swiftly unlocked the press's normal reticence on matters of sex and romance at high political levels. By nightfall the news wires and electronic outlets bubbled with speculation about the candidate and the congresswoman and whether the speed of the Lincoln Continental had been advanced in an effort to pare the time before Eddie met Kate at the Waldorf.

That Saturday night, when Governor Hugh Pinholster returned to the Detroit Hilton after a day of motorcading, he found a telegram awaiting him from his foremost staff adviser, Hutchens Boyington III:

YOU'RE IN LIKE QUINN. THE TRUTH HAS SET HIM FREE.

21

"It's all over, Charlie," said Ted Witherspoon. "The son-of-a-bitch has had it."

"Check," agreed Herron. "Pinholster will take it by ten million votes."

The oil operator in Dallas and the banker in Chicago were conferring by telephone Sunday evening forty-five hours after the New Jersey Turnpike crash that killed a telephone repairman named William F. Deitz and slashed the scalp and image of Presidential Candidate Edward Quinn.

"Sorry some of the mud hit you, Ted." Herron's sorrow did not sound so profound as to disable him. "I can't understand this change in Kate. I thought of her as a world away from Quinn's kind."

"She and I . . . well, for some time it's been all but a legal separation." Ted paused, then added acidly: "But I must say I didn't expect to become the first man cuckolded on all three networks simultaneously."

"They'll murder Quinn in Chicago and bury him downstate. What about Texas?"

"Same story. They may even beat Kate down here. All in all, considering the shape we were in three days ago, this looks like a right nice li'l ol' election, as they say in West Texas."

As Herron and Witherspoon exchanged good-bys, Poller Arnold Swensson and Candidate Hugh Pinholster were saying their hellos on a telephone connection between New York and Washington.

Politics in the United States has but one immutable rule: No stroke of fortune is so dazzling nor calamity so dreadful as to fail to profit the American Telephone & Telegraph Company.

"The numbers all add up to Pinholster tonight," said Swensson without enthusiasm. The boor, Quinn, had ruined a classic blue-line projection by a squalid motor mishap on one of those intolerable expressways and Swensson would never forgive him. "If you've got your pencil handy, we make it: A—537. B—420. C—43. D—53.7. E—42. F—4.3. And G—Minus .3."

"Quinn's still falling off then?" Pinholster made no effort to mask his delight when talking to a man who was being paid a minor fortune to chart the temperature of the voters. For the final days Swensson had doubled his interview staff and was using the WATS lines to contact one thousand most-likely-to-vote citizens every four hours.

"Yes, but it looks as if he's striking bottom now. After all, we've had a net switch from Quinn to you of about six voters in every hundred in the last twenty-four hours. That's a massive shift, Governor. Put it this way. Even if Quinn picks up all the undecideds, which he can't, you're still an easy winner."

"Do the depth interviews still show the same pattern of reaction to the accident?"

"About the same as I told you this afternoon." Swensson flicked his eyes over some numbers he had underlined on the computer print-out. "Quinn's hurting with women especially. They don't mind a candidate speeding. They're troubled, but not devastated, by the fact he was implicated in the death of another driver. They could even take him laying somebody else's wife. But put it all together and it's too much for them."

"Does anybody give Eddie points for telling the truth?" Ever since he heard the first radio flash of Eddie's interview from the hospital bed, Pinholster had been obsessed with that question. As a politician, he immediately assumed that Eddie acted under threat of exposure by someone, newsman, physician or policeman. But as time went on, Pinholster began to wonder whether the accident had wrought some deep psychological change in Eddie or even impaired his mental capacity.

"A few." Swensson skimmed more numbers. "Actually there's been a slight increase of those who applaud Quinn for the line he took. That's in the last four hours. The increase is too small to be statistically significant. I merely mention it . . . Of course, projections are out of the question after the input of this kind of variable." Swensson handled the word "variable" as though it were a deadly fungus. "We can only go by hunch and my hunch is that this evening's figures are about the way people will vote on Tuesday." And rob him of $19,000, he thought gloomily.

Eddie Quinn and his accident at Exit Nine utterly absorbed the nation that weekend. Never in political history had a late-hour incident so stunned, bewildered and fascinated the electorate. For an approximation of the impact, experts had to reach back almost a century to 1884. In that election's closing days a Presbyterian minister, the Reverend Samuel D. Burchard, branded the Democrats as the party of "Rum, Romanism and Rebellion." The charge boomeranged, incensed Irish voters and elected Grover Cleveland by a slim margin. But Eddie's case embraced not a mere slogan but a personal act and confession that turned millions of homes into ethical debating societies. In the United States people talked of little else. Abroad, thanks to instant satellite communications, Eddie Quinn, cars, death and adultery recast a lively but remote American election into a human drama that brushed the life of every man.

The American news industry observes an unwritten rule that the private lives of political figures shall be regarded as wholesome, uncomplicated and for the most part exemplary. Unlike actors and actresses, no politician is drunken, drug-ridden, churlish, faithless, scheming, sadistic, neurotic or satyric. Every mate of a politician, whether female or male, is deemed fit for sympathetic portrayal on the most prudish women's page or the most banal of television shows. The industry consigns deviations from this mythical norm to the realm of trade gossip. Thus reporters stagger through life like Mexican burros, burdened by the knowledge of secret liaisons, drinking bouts, oedipal manifestations and manic passions among the mighty. In Eddie Quinn's case, most communicators covering his campaign suspected his attachment to Kate Witherspoon—some even knew the numbers of hotel rooms—but not one word about it had reached print, tape or film.

The industry's unwritten rule cracks under three conditions: (1) court or police action, (2) revelation by the politician or a rival, (3) exclusive airing by a prominent organ of the communications fraternity. The Eddie Quinn story met all three conditions. His accident became a police matter, he himself revealed that he was driving over the speed limit and Sybil Jamieson all but charged that Kate Witherspoon's presence in New York accounted for the nighttime speed.

Only a declaration of war or the elopement of the Pope with a Vatican chambermaid could have shattered the news monopoly of Edward Quinn and Kate Witherspoon. Millions of spoken and written words rushed like a torrent from a broken dam. All major newspapers printed Eddie's tape-recorded interview in full in Sunday editions. Front pages carried the earlier photographs of Eddie driving the gleaming Continental away from the Pan American Union in Washington, D.C., with Flannery beside him and Teegee Churchill in the rear seat. Writers reviewed Kate Witherspoon's life since childhood and reporters made futile efforts to quiz husband Ted in Dallas and daughter Susan at Foxcroft. Newsmen interviewed Stackpole, Flannery, Baker, Dr. Inglis, Trooper Young, Vince Anderson, highway safety experts, marriage counselors, psychiatrists and politicians by the score. For the first time in memory, according to the ratings, more people watched TV political talk shows than the Sunday afternoon professional football games.

The widow of the hapless William Deitz appeared on television as did Eddie's estranged wife, Mabel Probst Quinn, the latter after a quiet word passed by Rich Cuthbert to a friend in a network news department. Mabel branded Eddie as an early philanderer who obviously had not mended his ways. Electronic journalists beat a path once more to the stationary trailer of Mrs. Annabelle Janiszewski Quinn Getz in the Crestview Haven Mobile Home Park near Orlando, Florida. Eddie's mother, charm bracelets ajangle, said that her son had been reared to revere the truth. She recalled that she had rewarded several lapses from reverence with sound trashings. As pictured by Mrs. Getz, the hallways of veracity seemed less like shining corridors than dim subterranean passages through a warren of torture chambers. As for "that woman from Texas," as Mrs. Getz referred to Congresswoman Witherspoon, she had no comment.

To reporters who cornered her at a rear entrance of the Middlesex General Hospital, Kate herself confessed a fondness for Eddie based upon "mutual interests," a phrase that inspired a dozen gags which began racing about the country like madcap children.

Newspapers sermonized on the automobile and sexual cultures, and in New York, *The Kingdom and the Power* dwelled on the irony of "a son of the highways, born at Exit Nine, who became a political casualty of the expressways."

Pinholster tacticians let the torrent roar unaided by tributary rivers from the opposition. Pinholster released a statement of regret as boneless as cotton while his aides observed Manager Jeff Smithers's injunction against "anybody else on this staff opening his damn mouth." But governors and senators filled the airways and columns with weighty prose and prophecy. Privately most politicians were appalled at Eddie's confession and could only conclude either that he was suffering from brain damage or that, as Pete Stackpole had privately charged in his fit of anger, Quinn had no heart for the job of President. They found it incomprehensible that Eddie, with the White House within sight, would not try to lie his way into it. In the creed of many politicians, any candidate under stress who yielded to truth as readily as Eddie did exposed a character so flawed as to call into question his conduct in such crises as nuclear confrontation or brawls over Supreme Court appointments.

While voter reaction splintered into a hundred strains, much of it fed on suspicion. In hundreds of thousands of conversations in homes, churches, restaurants, buses and planes, many people assumed that Eddie harbored some dark, unspoken reason for telling his version of the so-called truth. Someone had seen him driving . . . the congresswoman was pregnant . . . the accident rendered him temporarily insane . . . he had secretly bet $100,000 on Pinholster to win at the recent even-money odds . . . his astrologer had warned him he would die in the White House . . . he had been bribed by Pinholster supporters.

A few skeptics believed that Eddie had conspired with Stackpole and Flannery to hoax the public. The actual driver of the car was Flannery, they argued, and Eddie's "confession" was a lie designed to elicit sympathy, generate publicity and earn him a spurious reputation as a moral folk hero.

But the majority of people believed that Eddie told the truth. Many of these rejoiced that personal honesty had found a welcoming home at such a high political level. His interview refreshed and invigorated them like a cold shower on a torpid day. Others did not find the truth particularly elevating. Some people resented Eddie's refusing to hide the facts as they would have done. His veracity, in a sense, became a rebuke to their duplicity. Still others looked upon the truth as a personal burden which Eddie had partially shifted to their unwilling shoulders.

The truth, so experience taught, was a treacherous tool. Compulsive truth-tellers tampered with the delicate fabric of deception so skillfully and artfully woven on the long march through the centuries from savagery to civilization. Falsehood, it was assumed, preserved urbanity, protected the naked psyche from predators prowling the streets and bedrooms, provided a silky sheathing for the endless contacts between master and slave, boss and employee, parent and child, husband and wife, that might otherwise lead to mayhem. Truth was a vandal and if truth was the ally of Eddie, already suspect as to his social graces, then perhaps there were two barbarians at the gate.

In a phrase, the unexpected truth took a bit of getting used to.

Amid this national atmosphere of surprise, praise, doubt, suspicion, resentment and wavering judgment, Eddie appeared on the NBC television network at 9 P.M. EST, Sunday. Never before had a half-hour paid political broadcast attracted so many viewers. *Variety*, the entertainment trade journal, would headline: EXIT NINE THRILLER ROUTS GIGGLE, SPY MONARCHS OF RIVAL NETS," shorthand for Eddie's capture of the huge faithful audiences which normally watched comedy and espionage shows on the two other major networks at this hour. Rating services estimated that between 69,000,000 and 76,000,000 people watched Eddie being interrogated by three newsmen selected by Phil Liccardo.

Released from the hospital in mid-afternoon after Dr. Ward

Inglis pronounced him physically and mentally fit, Eddie rode to New York City in the bulletproof Electra 225. Photographers caught Flannery at the wheel, Baker beside him and Eddie sandwiched between Pete Stackpole and Phil Liccardo in the back seat. Kate flew back to Dallas Sunday noon in a last-ditch effort to rescue her district from the clutches of the suddenly menacing enemy.

Before the cameras in the Rockefeller Center studio, Eddie looked serious and concerned and yet at ease in the living-room set ordered by the media director Stackpole had hired a few days earlier. Eddie wore a dark suit with matching tie and he sat in a comfortable armchair across a coffee table from the three newsmen. The only sign of the fatal crash was the small bandage on the left side of his head. With his large shoulders, ruddy complexion and quiet, warm smile, Eddie gave an impression of relaxed self-control and comforting solidity. A pool of three reporters and the traveling staff, Stackpole, Liccardo, Margot Hicks, R Dan Fenelli and Frank Janiszewski, watched from a corner of the studio. The staffers tried to exude cheer, but succeeded only in etching their low spirits. They were here to applaud the last hurrah of a candidate on the rim of oblivion.

Under the prearranged format, the first ten minutes of questioning embraced the issues, the last twenty the accident. Newsmen were free to ask anything they wished and none of the queries and answers had been rehearsed. Eddie put on a low-key, steady but unremarkable performance for the most part, saying little that he had not told Vince Anderson the day before. He sympathized with the widow of William Deitz, resketched his thoughts and feelings while he lay on the Turnpike's center strip and again described the highlights of Friday night.

Watching journalists noted a number of newsworthy developments. When asked if the speculation about the reason for his Turnpike speeding was correct, Eddie replied that he normally drove about seventy on the expressway. Asked specifically if he had intended to see Kate Witherspoon at the Waldorf Friday night, Eddie responded with a single word: "Yes." Pressed as to the nature of his relationship with the congresswoman, Eddie said: "She's a fine politician and a fine woman. I admire her greatly." Asked if he cared to elaborate, Eddie had another one-word reply: "No."

Midway of the broadcast a taped bulletin, prepared by Liccardo, ran across the bottom of the screen: "Average of major polls taken since the accident show Pinholster 54 per cent, Quinn 42 per cent, Undecided 4 per cent." The newspapermen, who thought it odd that Quinn tacticians would advertise Pinholster's wide lead on a paid political show, questioned Liccardo about it.

"Why try to hide the truth?" he replied, fingering a new psyche-delic tie. "Truth is what this half-hour is all about."

The final item deemed especially newsworthy was Eddie's reply in the closing minutes when he was asked: "You were only inches away from death Friday night, Mr. Quinn. What impact, if any, has that had on you?"

Eddie said nothing for a few seconds as he gazed into the lens of a camera taking a close-in shot. "I can only call it a humbling experience. People call me a fast study. Maybe I am and maybe I'm not, but I know I've learned a great deal in the last two days and nights. For one thing, from now on I'm going to be a lot more cautious around automobiles. I'm a car buff, as you know, but now I realize from personal experience that cars are also killers that must be treated with the same respect and restraint as a gun or a missile.

"I also learned the value of life for each of us. I can't describe the emotion I felt when I woke up Saturday morning in that hospital bed and realized that I was a whole man who lived, breathed and talked. From now on, I'll think long and hard before making a judgment that might threaten any person's most precious possession, life."

Eddie paused, frowned, hunched forward. "But I guess the most important thing was a new feeling about what really counts in life —self-respect, friendship, love. None of the three mean much unless we're honest with ourselves and with each other. It was hard to tell the truth, but I did and I'm glad I did and I hope I always will. Maybe it sounds corny, but that realization means more to me than who wins on Tuesday." He paused again and this time he grinned. "Not that there seems to be much doubt any more who'll win. Thanks and good night."

Pete Stackpole was the first to shake Eddie's hand when the staff gathered about him after the show ended.

"Nice going, Eddie. I'd rather lose with you than win with Pinholster—and that's no lie." He laughed self-consciously. "If candidates get on a new truth kick because of you, I'm out of a job. But it hurts nice. I mean it." He withdrew his hand and turned away.

"Where you going?"

"Got to call my political barometer. Don't forget, Eddie. She's voted with the winner in every presidential election since Herbert Hoover in twenty-eight."

Stackpole used an NBC office phone to call his mother in Morgantown, West Virginia. The familiar voice, thin, firm, a trifle testy, came on the line.

"Hi, Mom."

"I knew it was you, Peter, when I heard the ring. Always Sunday night before an election."

"So who're you voting for Tuesday?"

"Eddie Quinn," said Anna Lou Stackpole promptly. "Not because he's your man either. I was going to vote for that Pinholster, but I changed my mind after watching Eddie just now on television. First politician I ever heard of who told the truth. I didn't like them dragging that poor congresswoman"—Pete winced at the adjective —"into it like those newspaper people did, but that's not Eddie's fault. He faced the music. I like his cut. He looks you in the eye. Wish I could say the same about some of those other men you've worked for. . . . And don't forget my check from that fellow."

"Do me a favor, Ma. Call five or six of your friends and see how they're going to vote. I'm at the Waldorf. Call me back collect, will you?"

An hour later when Anna Lou Stackpole called back with the information that six of her friends were splitting three and three on the election, the staff assembled in Eddie's suite at the Waldorf already had decided that reports of their candidate's political demise, to misquote Mark Twain, were a trifle exaggerated. As the nation pondered the new face of truth—monster or angel?—the news funneling into the suite over three telephones bore the healthy tint of resuscitation.

Some of the politicians who had remained faithful to Eddie throughout the campaign reported that the telecast had rekindled interest in him. Teegee Churchill and Joe Kuzyk, calling from Washington, said favorable calls were beginning to bombard the headquarters' switchboard. Shelby Ewing, the vice-presidential candidate, phoned from Seattle to congratulate Eddie on "making the best of a messy situation." Coming from Ewing, who would not judge his own wife's hemline until he had consulted a wide slice of feminine opinion, this was seen as an indication of renascent public approval. The early edition of *The Kingdom and the Power* gave Eddie good marks for his television performance in a lead editorial which nevertheless restated the newspaper's conviction that the best interests of the nation would be served by the election of Governor Pinholster, a man of mature judgment, balanced intellect and lengthy experience in the craft of governing. Kate called from Dallas to say that Eddie had struck just the right note in his final minutes on TV. Whether or not they intended to vote for him, most people felt he was telling the truth. In summary, a plus for Eddie.

Phil Liccardo, who repaired to a Lexington Avenue bar to confer with publicists for various candidates on the party's New York ticket, returned to report one of the millions of political conversations in the United States that night. As recalled by Phil, the overheard dialogue went like this:

First Bar Patron: You see Eddie on the tube?

Bartender: Yeah. He looked okay for a guy they got by the short hairs. Eddie's all right. He's got my vote.

Second Patron: Me too. He's half Polish.

Bartender: Half Polack, but mostly Mick. I voted for Jack Kennedy and we done all right while he was in.

First Patron: Eddie won't take no lip from the big money. You know, I wouldn't put it past the sons-of-bitches to have paid that fellow Deitz to try to knock Eddie off on the Turnpike.

Second Patron: Yeah. Eddie was lucky to get out of it alive.

The staff stayed up late, discussing tactics for the final day. Liccardo wanted to use a clip from Quinn's TV soliloquy as a two-minute commercial. Stackpole vetoed the idea, arguing it would give the misleading impression that the candidate had rehearsed his lines. Eddie upheld the veto. No special action on Monday, he ruled. Let the voters think it over in peace save for a five-second spot already prepared by the media director.

They were drinking coffee and speculating on the vagaries and mysteries of the voting animal when the pro-Quinn employee called from Swensson's polling mill with his smuggled tabulation. Of one thousand people polled following the TV program, 516 said they would vote for Pinholster, 447 for Quinn and 37 undecided, a gain for Quinn in the last four hours of 2.7 per cent, his first upturn since disaster struck Friday night. Depth interviews revealed heavy support for Eddie among young voters.

A few minutes later Pete Stackpole turned from a phone conversation with a wry smile.

"That was Arnold Swensson."

"Swensson?" asked Eddie with surprise. "What did he want?"

"Oh, didn't I ever tell you, Eddie? We've got a thing the last three elections ever since somebody told him about my mother's record. He calls me the final Sunday night to find out how she's going to vote.

"Do you tell him?"

"Yeah. First I say I'll trade him for his results and he says they'll cost me twenty-eight thousand dollars. Then I ask how much he pays for one interview and he says fourteen dollars. So I tell him and he mails me a check that I endorse over to Anna Lou."

"How'd he take the news tonight?"

"He says between the Beckdale Arms and Exit Nine, you're the worst damn disaster since the invention of statistics."

At 2 A.M. Monday, with the opening of the first voting booths only twenty-eight hours away, Candidate Eddie Quinn was alive and well and living at the Waldorf.

At 10 A.M. Monday the prosecutor of Middlesex County announced that he was citing Edward N. Quinn under the New Jersey death-by-auto statute and would present the police report on

Friday's crash to the county grand jury, probably sometime in December.

The statute provided a thousand-dollar fine and/or imprisonment up to three years for those convicted of driving "carelessly and heedlessly, with willful and wanton disregard of the rights or safety of others" when an automobile fatality occurred.

The prosecutor said that while he personally believed the late Mr. Deitz bore the greater guilt in the collision, Commissioner Quinn's admission of nighttime speeding left the case in doubt. In view of the nationwide attention focused on the accident, he said, he felt it proper to air the facts before the twenty-three members of the grand jury.

At 1 P.M. Monday Senator Stanley Framingham of California, one of the Quinn kingmakers, announced in Washington that he would "reluctantly and regretfully" vote for Governor Pinholster because of the "weekend developments involving Mr. Quinn." This was the first time in his life, he noted, that he had deserted the presidential nominee of his party. Framingham failed to mention his earlier secret gift of three thousand dollars in cash to the Pinholster campaign fund. The virus of honesty, R Dan Fenelli observed, had not proved dangerously contagious.

Shortly after 2 o'clock Monday afternoon Arnold Swensson, still suffering from abdominal and statistical indigestion, reported by phone to Governor Pinholster that a new trend toward Quinn appeared to be building. "The damn trend line has acted like a roller coaster in the last week," he complained. The 1000 voters polled in the last four hours split 502 for Pinholster, 469 for Quinn and 29 undecided, a total gain for Eddie of 4.9 per cent since his nadir Sunday afternoon. "The depths show that a lot of people are having second thoughts," said Swensson. "Some are telling the interviewers that Quinn's the first politician they ever knew who told the truth about something that mattered. As for the congresswoman angle, many people blame Sybil Jamieson and the press for bringing it up at all. They seem to think that Quinn handled his affair with Mrs. Witherspoon just right, answering honestly when questioned but not involving her when he didn't have to." Pinholster's visceral reaction was his customary one when buffeted by bad news. "Oof!"

In early evening Monday a UPI exclusive out of the White House reported that Russell Bishop was privately quoting the President as having said: "It'll be a damn disgrace if that adulterer and reckless driver isn't buried under a landslide."

At 11:59 P.M. Pinholster concluded a two-hour network telethon in which he fielded questions from carefully screened voters around the country and incidentally spent almost the last of the $28,750,000 collected for his campaign through the primaries, convention and general election.

At midnight Monday the last Quinn commercial appeared on television screens in scattered metropolitan areas. It was a five-second shot of Eddie standing on the rear of a flat-bed truck, thrusting his right arm upward and outward in the familiar gesture while a feminine voice-over, gentle but insistent, asked: "Want honesty in the White House and a fair shake in Washington? Vote for Eddie Quinn."

At 12:01 A.M. Tuesday the polls opened in Hart's Location, New Hampshire, and five minutes later results of the entire voting population of six persons were flashed to a waiting world: Pinholster 4, Quinn 2.

The two candidates voted in midmorning, Hugh Pinholster in Hartford, Connecticut, and Eddie in New Brunswick, New Jersey. Sandwiched between Flannery and Baker, Eddie walked out of the polling place in the gymnasium of an elementary school into the bright sunlight and crisp, still air. Spiraling vapor stacks marked the spot on the sidewalk where a dozen waiting newsmen chatted.

"Who did you vote for, Commissioner?"

"Me."

"What's your prediction?" asked Vince Anderson.

"The country can't lose." Eddie grinned. "Either it elects me—or it won't have to listen to another of my speeches for six months."

And then, suddenly, it was all over but the counting. At Pinholster headquarters on Jackson Place in Washington, Jeff Smithers's college-boy assistant toted eighteen cases of champagne into the room where a huge blackboard and a battery of phones awaited the returns. The shipment arriving at Quinn headquarters on the fifth floor of 1140 Connecticut Avenue contained less festive merchandise, whisky, beer and a six-pack of ginger ale.

22

Eddie and Kate walked together into campaign headquarters shortly before 8 o'clock election night. "We might as well," she said. "We're a public affair now."

Kate had voted in Dallas, then flown to Washington and had dinner with Eddie and Pete Stackpole in Eddie's suite at the Hay-Adams. They had talked in low, muted tones as politicians often do in the shadow of the voters' decision. They made a three-way election bet of ten dollars, the winner to be whoever came closest to Eddie's electoral count. Out of the total 538 electoral votes, Eddie gave himself a scant 121, Pete estimated 189 and Kate 226, all far short of the majority of 270 needed for victory.

Eddie's arrival at 1140 Connecticut Avenue set off more than applause from the two hundred campaign workers in the long, open room with its clutter of desks and file cabinets. In a far corner someone set off a string of small firecrackers. They crackled busily, but the last one went pff-t.

Eddie waved to the volunteers. "I hope that last sound wasn't trying to tell us something. No speeches. You all know that if we win it's a miracle. But however this election comes out, I want to thank every one of you for the tremendous effort. You've been great."

Nothing quite matches the suspense and exhilaration of election night for those with a stake in it. A presidential count, especially, resembles a huge church wedding in which no one is sure whether the groom will show up. Or, at the other end of the metaphoric scale, it might be likened to a prolonged funeral, the mourners deciding by secret ballot which of two possible dignitaries will have the honor of serving as the corpse. Tonight it was amazing that Eddie's followers had any emotional reserve left to draw upon. They had seen their man climb from obscurity to the edge of triumph, only to nose-dive after a fateful collision. Now there was once again a chance, slim but intriguing, and headquarters buzzed with the small, nervous sounds of anticipation, laughter, a clink of glasses, the ringing of phones, the scrape of chairs, shouts, orders, a constant tread of feet hurrying about on a variety of largely useless errands.

Eddie and Kate settled down before a television set in a glass-paneled office that commanded a view of the long room and the big board where state-by-state final returns would be chalked. Gathered round them were members of the original inner staff, Pete, R Dan Fenelli, Hunk Janiszewski, Margot Hicks, Teegee Churchill, Joe Kuzyk and Phil Liccardo.

Teegee was dressed for victory in a flowered shirt and black leather miniskirt, but early scattered returns, showing Pinholster in the lead, depressed her. If Teegee had no faith in the system, she had even less in those she considered yoked to it. R Danny, as restless and optimistic as ever, bobbed about the room, drinking a scotch-and-water and plucking at his heavy brows. Hunk didn't like the looks of things. Besides, his war-splintered shin was aching, an omen, he thought. Margot, Pete and Joe were prepared for the worst, but anxious to be proved wrong in their foreboding. Phil, wearing a mint-colored jacket and a circus-poster tie, bit off the end of a cigar and contemplated his future, White House press secretary or Turnpike flack, without anxiety. Take it as it comes and enjoy yourself was still Phil's motto.

At this moment, actually, the decision had been made. Tens of millions of Americans, in single, silent acts, had picked who would govern them for the next four years. Except for the West Coast, Alaska and Hawaii, the polls already had closed across the nation. In schools, town halls, fire stations and armories, workers were unlocking voting machines, counting paper ballots and phoning results to district and county election commissions. All over the nation numbers, numbers and more numbers whistled over the wires. An army of

125,000 politicians, volunteers and paid spotters passed the figures up through an elaborate pyramidal structure from precincts to Rockefeller Plaza in New York. Two slaving computers, hired by the News Election Service, the co-operative of networks and news agencies, digested the figures and spewed out comprehensible totals under a program that required 10,000 man-hours to devise.

American presidential election returns sweep across the land like an autumn thunderstorm. First comes a sprinkling of results from isolated hamlets where the polls close early, in New Hampshire, Maine, Kansas, Kentucky, Tennessee. Next falls a patter of votes in swifter cadence from towns and cities along the eastern seaboard. If an epic victory is in the making, such as Lyndon Johnson's in 1964, it assumes its shape by sundown on the Atlantic Coast even though less than one per cent of the national head count has been recorded. Then comes the first cloudburst—Connecticut—at about 8 P.M. eastern time, followed quickly by a clap of thunder—Maryland. From then on, the storm spreads through the east, rolls south and west, gathering speed as it races through the time zones toward the Pacific, cheered and cursed by millions of citizens who have gathered in parlor and office, drinks in hand, to salute the renewal or transfer of power with a fervor or apprehension transcending a dozen New Year's Eves.

This night the early returns gave no hint of a possible partisan deluge. Although Pinholster took the lead in the total count, a potpourri of townships, villages and rural boxes from New Hampshire to Kansas, no trend shaped for either candidate. Volunteers and staffers shifted and fidgeted like theatergoers awaiting a late curtain. On the television screen Connecticut now held center stage. The first votes from the state began to fall, some for Eddie and some for Pinholster. The total grew by hundreds, then by thousands. Soon, like a downpour, the votes came down in great sheets, faster, faster. The state was going for Pinholster . . . no, for Eddie . . . no, for Pinholster.

Then, almost before the watchers were aware that the long night of counting had begun in earnest, the first cloudburst exhausted itself. Connecticut's total flashed on the screen. Quinn campaign workers in the long room groaned. Teegee uttered a fashionable obscenity. But Pete Stackpole let out a low whistle of surprise. Although Pinholster went on the board for the first solid count, eight electoral votes, he took Connecticut by less than 35,000 popular votes, 683,742 to 648,891.

"Hey, Eddie," said Pete, "we might be in business. A man only takes his home state by a sneeze, he's in trouble."

Almost immediately the heavens opened again and down fell Maryland—for Pinholster. He had now scored a total of eighteen electoral votes, but he won Maryland's ten by an even smaller margin, 27,000 votes out of more than 1,400,000 cast. A precinct captain in Baltimore promptly charged Pinholster election workers with fraud.

"I got lots of friends, it looks like," said Eddie, "but not quite enough to outpunch my enemies." He moved restlessly about in his chair, then reached for the six-pack and his first bottle of ginger ale.

"More friends than ol' Pinpooper," said Hunk. "I bet half the people on his side are really just votin' against you."

"How's that again, Hunk?" asked Margot Hicks.

"Never mind." Janiszewski's reproving glance swept upward from Margot's purple hose to her Afro-styled hair. "You worry about bringing Georgia in."

"We got no worries in Bee Branch," she retorted. "With Eddie's stand on busing, there's a Bee Branch landslide building up."

Hunk's ragged smile was a crafty one. "Folks in Arkansas got some sense." He and Margot were still cementing their friendship, block by block, with the mortar of insult.

Massachusetts, next to disgorge its commitment, had been delayed. People were still lined up to vote in Boston—a good sign for a Quinn, said Pete—and could not be denied under the law. At last the state came in, a clear 260,000-vote victory for Eddie.

A roar went up from the headquarters workers and this time a string of firecrackers banged away without a dud. On the television screen, portraying a network election center where people scurried purposefully about behind a silver-haired commentator who practiced composure under pressure, the popular vote now read: Pinholster 4,139,088, Quinn 3,872,615. Electoral vote: Pinholster 18, Quinn 14.

"I knew I had Massachusetts." Eddie said it with pride.

"Watch it, Eddie," said R Danny. "Remember, you're the man who's supposed to be our model of honesty."

"Well, I hoped for it anyway." Eddie's quick disclaimer did not match his mood. The fact that a large state, Massachusetts, actually had delivered its fourteen electoral votes to him seemed an event of surpassing wonder. Voters of a whole state, some 2,500,000 of them, had filed to the polls and turned their secret personal decisions into a mass choice—Eddie Quinn for President of the United States.

For a few seconds he experienced the same sinking sensation that mired him for so long in Oklahoma City, but he quickly rallied. This was the world of election night and in this world a hell of a lot of Americans thought he was the stuff of Presidents. Well, by God, he was, not like Lincoln or F.D.R. perhaps, but surely of the cut of Harry Truman and certainly more geared for action and change than Ike had been. A warm, vital feeling, part pride, part confidence, suffused him. He'd come a long way in nineteen days, Eddie had, since that sulphurous dawn in Houston when he went to the Astroworld without his socks. Learned a lot of things, about the country and about himself, and now he knew the core of truth: he wanted to be President. He wanted the challenge, the fame, the influence, the power. The feeling budded, swelled, towered, became a vast shaft of energy. He understood Kate's hunger now and he realized, with great clarity, why Pete's first instinct after the crash had been to try to lie Eddie out of a driver's responsibility.

Pete, sitting beside him, was adding a column of figures in a note pad and throwing quick glances at the TV screen. Eddie put his arm around Pete's thin shoulders and hugged him.

"What's that for?" Pete flicked his eyes to Eddie, then back toward the television set as if seeking an explanation in the ever-changing numbers.

"That's for my favorite manager. I'll make you a deal. I'll run for President any year you'll manage me."

"You're a tough one to handle, but I guess, damn it, you're worth it." What Pete could not handle for the moment was Eddie's display of affection.

"I just want to say thanks, Pete," said Eddie in a lower voice, "for what you tried to do on the Turnpike." He squeezed Pete's shoulders once more before taking his arm away.

"Yeah. Well, it's beginning to look as if you knew more about voter psychology than I did." Pete pointed to the screen where mounting returns showed Quinn and Pinholster running elbow to elbow in Texas, North Dakota, Arizona and Minnesota.

Rhode Island fell to Eddie. The candidates were running almost a dead heat in both popular and electoral count. Electors: Pinholster 18, Quinn 18. National total from all precincts reporting: Pinholster 6,781,500, Quinn, 6,778,372. Computer projection of the winner: Too close to call.

Then Pinholster captured South Carolina after a seesaw struggle and jumped ahead in the vital electoral column, 26 to 18. But Eddie was running ahead in two big industrial states, New Jersey and Pennsylvania.

Two hundred voices roared like a single explosion.

New York!

The second-largest state in the Union, forty-one electoral votes, went for Quinn. The margin was narrow, a plurality for Eddie of only 0.6 per cent out of 7,500,000 votes cast. Two minor candidates collected some 60,000 votes. Eddie took the city, Pinholster upstate, but Eddie ran better inside New York City than Pinholster ran outside. Now the electoral total read: Quinn 59, Pinholster 26.

Kate sprang from her chair, rushed across the room and threw her arms around the candidate. "Oh, Eddie!" She could say no more.

Eddie kissed her. "How about that! New York!"

Photographers and newsmen bunched in the doorway of the staff room. Phil Liccardo and R Dan Fenelli clinked glasses. Joe Kuzyk and Pete Stackpole slapped each other on the back. Margot Hicks grabbed Hunk Janiszewski's hand. "Come on, ol' man." The startled Hunk found himself dancing on his game leg, half jig, half jive. For the first time in his seventy-seven years his partner was a black woman.

"You're wearing socks, Eddie," said Teegee Churchill. "That's bad luck. You ought to take them off."

Someone began to chant: "Eddie, take your socks off. Eddie, take your socks off." The staff joined in, chanting and clapping in rhythm. Soon the whole headquarters echoed with the choral pleas. Teegee began unlacing his shoes and Eddie gravely complied, removing the black square-toed footgear, peeling off the socks. He stood barefoot for a moment and then put the shoes back on and exhibited his sockless ankles. Photographers snapped while newsmen jotted notes as frantically as though they were covering a summit conference.

The numbers continued clicking upward on the screen. Eddie took the lead for the first time since the count began on fragmentary returns in late afternoon. Popular: Quinn 11, 528, 144, Pinholster 11,-369,824. Eddie took his home state of New Jersey, but not by much, 46,000 votes out of more than three million. Pinholster won larger Pennsylvania, also narrowly, after Eddie had threatened by taking Philadelphia. The electoral count stood, Quinn 76, Pinholster 53, but as the national total passed 25,000,000 votes, Pinholster edged into the popular lead again. The computers stubbornly declined to predict a winner.

Election night buffs would have found something missing at Quinn headquarters. People moved, chalked, counted, drank, phoned, cursed, cheered and traded astute observations on the trend of the vote. But the atmosphere was strangely different from that of other presidential headquarters on election nights in the modern era. The missing element, which one would have found at once at Pinholster's election center, was a special reporting team. No battery of specialists manned telephones to receive confidential reports on key precincts and counties over the nation. Such an effort relies on a well-knit organization and Eddie had rent the party's fabric to a degree unknown in this century. After his split with the kingmakers, the bitter dispute over money and then his caustic attack on the interests which had been financing his predecessor, Senator Hudson, Eddie found himself a man without a party. His campaign had been aimed less at Pinholster than at the men who nominated him at Houston.

There was other evidence of the difference. Only three state chairmen had called Pete Stackpole since the counting began. No wealthy contributors appeared in black tie and evening gowns to shake the candidate's hand on their way to a victory dance. Few county chairmen or courthouse hacks heckled the switchboard to speak to Pete or Dan or Joe or Kate or indeed anyone connected with the candidate. In fact, the few reports that Stackpole did receive were disturbing. In some areas of the country vengeful local party officials had failed to provide proper quotas of poll watchers and challengers. As a result Pinholster swept some machine-controlled city wards where Eddie's populist stance should have earned him at least an even break.

At 10:45 P.M., when Eddie and Pinholster were running almost even in both electoral and popular votes, the dean of commentators sought to explain a phenomenon for patrons of the box. He was a lean, elderly man, gray of hair and face, ravaged by disillusion and pain of the world, yet holding wearily to his theme of tolerance and hope as a drowning man clings to a drifting spar.

"No computer, and certainly no man, can name the next President of the United States at this hour," he said in a voice that might have lit funeral pyres along the Ganges, "but one thing is now indelibly engraved on the nation's political edifice—the name and personality of Edward Nicholas Quinn. Whoever wins the presidency in this close and confusing election, Eddie Quinn already has won an immense personal victory. The way the count is running, something more than 37,000,000 voters today have expressed their confidence in Eddie Quinn, the man who came from the highways of nowhere to challenge first Governor Pinholster and then the leaders of his own party for the right to govern the country. He overcame tremendous handicaps, this unknown from Room Nineteen in the Buccaneer Motor Lodge. No public name, no money, no organization, then faced with unwanted responsibility during a frightening riot in his home state. And finally, the tragic fatal accident on his own Turnpike when Eddie tested his moral fiber with a candor unmatched by any politician of our time. His style? Simplicity. His prescription for what ails us? A fair shake for everyone. He is a true phenomenon, this Eddie Quinn and, win or lose, you'll hear his name for many years to come."

The commentator took a sip of water, eyed the clock and continued in his tone of brighter doomsdays to come. "There seems to be no fixed pattern to Eddie's big race in which he is running far ahead of his party's candidates for Senate and House and the governorships. Is he winning a good share of the female vote as predicted? Nobody can tell. Is he sweeping the working-class districts? Well, yes and no. Is his a city vote? Partially, but he has shown surprising strength in the rural areas.

"Only two things are definite so far. Quinn, despite his opposition to busing, that racial code issue, has done better with black voters than any nominee of his party since pre-New Deal days. In Harlem he tripled the vote his party's candidate usually gets there. He did even better in black neighborhoods of Newark and Philadelphia. In one black district in Merton, the New Jersey city where Eddie negotiated a settlement with black militants after the killing of his friend, George Dawson, Quinn actually won a majority. The other fact is that Eddie did better on the eastern seaboard than he is doing now in the Midwest. He's running strong in America's center, but not quite as strong as in the East. The Far West may well tell the story in this very, very close election which is duplicating 1960 and 1968 all over again. As to why Eddie racked up such a huge vote, we'll have to wait for tomorrow's analysts. All we can say right now, along with the remark dropped just a few minutes ago by Governor Pinholster at his headquarters, is: 'Eddie is going into the far turn with an awful lot of horsepower.'"

Eddie squinted at the screen. "He said that so nice, you'd think my wake had already started."

"The only thing he knows about the outcome of this election is that he doesn't know anything," said Stackpole. He mixed himself another drink, then stood gazing at Eddie as he shook the ice in his glass.

"What are you looking at me like that for?"

"I don't know. I guess you are a phenomenon. Here you are with a fifty-fifty chance to win and, by God, Eddie, I don't understand it."

"You call it fifty-fifty now?"

"Hell, yes. This thing is going right down to the wire. All the numbers point that way. I guess what I was thinking was that maybe three or four hours from now, we won't be calling you Eddie any more—but Mr. President."

Mr. President. Eddie savored the title, in imagination letting it roll back and forth on his tongue. Mr. President. God, how he wanted it now. So bad he could taste it? You bet.

The two men continued to stare at each other, soberly but affectionately. It was a strange moment, one in which a new, intangible bond was shaped. Then Eddie became aware that Kate was watching them with a bemused expression. She understood. She too knew that something indefinable had happened to him, to all of them.

Without a word, Eddie retrieved his black socks from under his chair, slowly removed his shoes, put the socks back on and relaced the square-toed oxfords. Neither Kate nor Pete smiled.

Soon the commentator was proved wrong about the Midwest. As the count rolled to the Mississippi River, Quinn and Pinholster fought for every city and county. Eddie took Indiana, Michigan and Wisconsin. Pinholster won Ohio. Illinois, with its rich twenty-six electoral votes, wobbled uncertainly. A number of Cook County precincts failed to come in while the count progressed downstate.

Now the South was all in. Pinholster won Florida with its bag of seventeen electoral votes, but Eddie earned an even split in the South after he took Louisiana easily and Arkansas by a whisker. Since Eddie also clinched Georgia, Margot and Hunk celebrated by breaking open a new bottle of bourbon.

Across the Plains States and into the Rocky Mountains swept the returns, Eddie and Pinholster racing toward the Pacific like two equally matched Indian runners who gained in stamina and power the longer they ran. But Pinholster carried new colors now, those of three states west of the Mississippi River, Minnesota, Iowa and Nebraska, a total of twenty-three electoral votes.

Then came a bolt of lightning out of the Southwest.

Texas! The huge state of oil and cattle, football and chauvinism, li'l ol' boys and astronauts, skyscrapers and tumbleweed, the nation within a nation, went for Edward Nicholas Quinn. Twenty-six glory-bound electoral votes.

A wild, throaty burst of sound shivered the partitions of Quinn headquarters as a near-hysterical girl volunteer from American University chalked the number 26 opposite Texas and under "Eddie" on the big board. The name Quinn was unknown and unsung to-night among his zealots. A long table stood in front of the board, enabling chalkers to reach the topmost "A" states, Alabama, Alaska, Arizona and Arkansas. Teegee Churchill, barefoot and long blond hair trailing like vapor, jumped on the table, cupped her hands at her mouth and shouted: "Quiet! Quiet!" Her audience hooted and protested, but finally obeyed.

"Announcement," she called. "We have another Texas winner with us. Kate Witherspoon has just been re-elected to a third term from the Fifth Congressional District."

The popping of firecrackers nailed the booming cheer to the ceiling. Kate and Eddie walked to the doorway of the glass-paneled office and waved to the workers. Eddie kissed Kate and the young crowd roared again, not alone for a pair of Texas victors, but for a muddle of abstractions, unconventional love, candor, false propriety shunned, the new freedom.

Photographers snapped candidate and congresswoman and then the rejoicing throng as every partisan added his private footnotes to the scene. With a thin, tight smile, Pete Stackpole thought of the $25,000 Ted Witherspoon had sent to Pinholster and of the $10,000 Kate had given Eddie's campaign fund from the joint Witherspoon account. Jim Flannery's thoughts, edged with anxiety, centered on a week from today when he and Baker faced a showdown at Secret Service offices over the Turnpike episode. R Dan Fenelli wondered whether Texas's vote, and all of the night's long, close count signaled a new era of politics. Had Eddie whetted a long dormant appetite for public frankness in America? No staffer or volunteer mentioned the word that had so obsessed Puritan New England and such chroniclers of its stern moral code as Nathaniel Hawthorne.

But a newspaperman did. A tall, balding columnist who peered down on humanity like a hovering marsh hawk, turned to Vince Anderson beside him. "Did you ever think you'd live to see the day when Texas would bless adultery with a 130,000-vote majority?"

"It looks like the whole country doesn't care much one way or the other," said Vince.

Based on data from Texas, including a phoned analysis by Kate's aide in Dallas, Art Rankin, it appeared that Texas made up its mind on the issues of jobs, pay and shelter, not sexual behavior. With few exceptions, Eddie took the black, Mexican-American and Anglo working districts, Pinholster the rich, professional and upper-middle-class residential areas. "Draw a line at fifteen grand a year," Rankin reported, "and you've about got it." Kate won handily, although by a reduced majority from two years earlier.

While still giddy from Texas, the Quinn fans absorbed a sobering blow. The last Chicago precincts, apparently withheld by the mayor's organization until all of downstate Illinois was in, fell into place. Pinholster won the twenty-six electoral votes of Illinois by a small majority.

Now the returns rushed westward across the wheatlands into the Rockies and over the Continental Divide. States fell like ripe grain into one basket or another, Eddie's or Pinholster's, only a few by sizable margins. Pinholster held the popular vote lead, 35,175,000 to Eddie's 34,940,000, but Eddie was outpointing Pinholster in the vital electoral count, 241 to 230.

Eddie needed but twenty-nine more electoral votes to become the next President. Pinholster had to have forty.

Now only five states, all lapped by the Pacific, were still out: California, Oregon, Washington, Alaska and Hawaii. The final question mark of the election loomed for all to see. Between them, the four states of Oregon, Washington, Alaska and Hawaii, had but twenty-two electoral votes. California boasted forty-five, largest in the nation. Suddenly, the four minor states lost all significance. They could disappear under a tidal wave without causing a ripple in the presidential outcome. To win the White House now, either man had to have California.

So now, at last, it all came down to California. California: its tawny hills ruffling like lions' manes, its John Birchers and its strident leftists, its freeways and its rich Imperial Valley, its Zen Buddhists, sunshine, chartreuse trousers, freaks, holy men, engineers, swinging scholars, grape pickers, film brokers, think tanks, Chicanos, retired farmers and grocers, Satan cultists, isolated housewives, yachtsmen and toy villages. California, the tanned, troubled, dubious face of all our tomorrows, socially chaotic, economically fragile and politically volatile.

A few California votes began trickling toward the computer shortly after 11 o'clock according to the timepieces in Quinn headquarters. Eddie leaned toward the television set. He was taut now, oblivious of his friends and even of Kate. He wanted to win, desperately. Never again thoughts of a loser. He was a winner and out there, 2800 miles away by highway but only a few milliseconds by electronics, stood the big, gilded prize. Huge armies of Californians had voted—estimates said 8,000,000—in the long state which stretched from the Oregon line to the Mexican border. Outwardly Eddie appeared calm. His tie was loosened, one arm thrown casually over the back of his chair, his legs stretched out. He had consumed but two bottles in the six-pack of ginger ale. But he could feel the creep of tension on his skin and within him his stomach knotted.

Eddie took a quick lead in the swiftly growing numbers on the electronic counter devoted to California in the network's election center. At 11:28 the figures read, Quinn 67,212, Pinholster 64,817. At 11:35 the clicking counter read Quinn 73,411, Pinholster 70,003. At 11:50 the count stood Quinn 101,628, Pinholster 97,539.

At midnight EST the silver-haired anchor man of the network election team adjusted his glasses, studied a slip of paper, cleared his throat.

"With slightly less than three per cent of the California vote in," he said, "the computer has projected a winner. We emphasize that this is not official in any way and the election team has nothing to do with it. This is a projection made by a non-partisan mechanical brain that . . ."

Get to it, get to it, thought Eddie. He could feel the sweat dampening his shirt.

". . . that has made no election bets. On the basis of three per cent of the vote, the computer forecasts that California will be won by Edward Quinn."

My God, thought Eddie, I'm President-elect of the United States.

Kate gasped, a quick intake of breath. Pete slapped Eddie's knee so hard his hand smarted. A great victory cry, more howl than cheer, vaulted from the long room where the volunteers milled. A bottle crashed against the wall and some loyal Southerner let out a piercing, oddly misplaced rebel yell.

"I could feel it comin'," said Hunk.

"It had to be," said Margot.

Eddie leaned forward, placing his forearms on his knees and clasping his hands tightly. To Kate he looked like a man apart.

"Hold it," said Pete.

On the screen, fellow election specialists could be seen waving and shouting frantically at the anchor man. A look of bewilderment came over his face, then one of slowly mounting pain as though he had just been stricken. He glanced at the paper again.

"I'm sorry," he said. "I've made an unpardonable error. The projected winner is not Eddie Quinn, but Hugh Pinholster. I repeat, the computer on the basis of three per cent of the tallied vote projects Governor Hugh Pinholster as the winner in California—and therefore, if the projection holds up, as the next President. . . . I apologize once more. I don't know what happened. I assure you it wasn't a Freudian slip, at least I don't think so. . . ."

"Oh, Christ!" said Kate. "Shut up . . . please."

Eddie could feel his muscles go limp. Then he experienced a nervous, rattling sensation as if part of him wanted to run away from the rest of his body. He stood up, used a nearby bottle opener to uncap another half-pint of ginger ale.

"How reliable are those computer projections for California, Pete?" he asked. He could not bear to look at the others in the room. "Three per cent doesn't seem like much."

"Depends." Pete glared bitterly at the screen. "I remember it was off in some big primary out there, but not in presidential elections. Still, I want to see that final vote. God damn it, we're that close." He held up his thumb and forefinger with a sliver of air between them. "If only we could have showed just one day and night in California."

An angry buzz replaced the echo of cheering in the long, hall-like room. On the screen the clicking numbers under the California legend seemed to belie the computer's prophecy. The count now read Quinn 178,202, Pinholster 173,867. Ten minutes later the gap was even wider, Quinn 289,904, Pinholster 281,664. Yet the name in the projected winner slot remained the same: PINHOLSTER.

Eddie began to hate the numbers even as Pinholster had once despised the figures that marched inexorably upward on the Quinn trend line in Swensson's poll. Eddie felt victimized by a faceless, hidden machine and he found it hard to realize that the ever-swelling digits were but the shadows of millions of citizens who had gone to the polls that day in California.

"Hey, look!" R Danny pointed at the screen.

In the slot below the legend, "Projected Winner," where Pinholster's name had resided beside an X, only a blank space now showed. The anchor man was in whispered conference with a young messenger who wore an election symbol on his dark blazer. The announcer nodded and addressed his unseen millions.

"It seems that both machines and humans are making errors tonight." His smile indicated relief that a computer now shared his culpability. "What happened was this. The model eight-two-eight, or 'Archie' as we call him, suddenly projected Governor Pinholster's winning margin in California as 168 per cent of the vote. Since not even the Almighty could win with more than 100 per cent, the technicians have pulled Archie down to see if they can find out what's wrong with him. I sincerely hope they're able to debug him, or we could be here until dawn before we know the name of the next President."

"Oh me." Teegee's lament was one of acute distress. "I may have to faint." She hid her eyes from the screen, then half staggered to the doorway of the glass-paneled office as though in need of air. But once there, she surveyed the outer room with a cool, practiced eye. Some student out there, she was sure, had an extra joint in his pocket.

"I don't trust them fellows," said Hunk, wagging a finger at the television set.

"Do you suppose that means the Pinholster projection was all wrong in the first place?" asked Kate of nobody in particular. Her inner vow of early evening to watch the intake of nicotine had been forgotten. A mound of cigarette stubs rested in the ash tray beside her.

Stackpole, roving the room with a glass of scotch in hand, stepped to the set and switched to another channel. A similar scene appeared. Men and women wearing headphones like earmuffs prowled three tiers of an elaborately decorated electronic workshop while an announcer speculated on the nature of the computer's malady. Pete switched again. The third network vacillated between apology and jokes about repairmen earning golden time. The same computer served all networks and wire services. Pete flipped back to the original channel, then telephoned the Los Angeles county chairman, a Quinn supporter, who said his information lagged behind the network's. "Whoever takes this state will do it by an eyelash," said the California politician. "I can't blame the computer for worrying itself sick."

Fenelli, who like Stackpole found it impossible to remain seated more than momentarily, paced the floor. "Oh Lord, you made the night too long. Much more of this and I'll need a stomach pump."

Phil Liccardo, wrapped in cigar smoke, suddenly decided that he no longer cared to take it as it came. He yearned for the White House, could see himself sitting at the press secretary's desk, dealing out copies of Eddie's State of the Union message to eager newsmen.

Eddie stared silently at the screen. He tried to think himself into a state of suspension, weightless, floating, as if lack of contact with his surroundings might somehow influence the computer to break all ties with Pinholster. It did not work. Into his mind flashed the scene at the Turnpike guard rail, he on the ground, wondering how he had died and why someone with the shape and voice of Pete Stackpole was whispering to him.

On the screen, the anchor man was talking again. "The projection trouble does not affect the running totals in California. As you can see, the votes continue to pile up while the experts tinker with Archie."

The totals read: Quinn 457,862, Pinholster 454,905.

"Somebody please start praying," said Joe Kuzyk.

The seconds ticked by, became minutes. The California numbers leaped upward by ten and twenty thousand at a clip now, moved past the million mark with Eddie holding a hairline lead. Then they swept beyond 1,300,000 votes. At 12:45 A.M. the count read: Quinn 681,900, Pinholster 679,949.

"Ah, now we have it," said the anchor man as he cocked his head, listening with his earphones. "The error has been discovered. Archie is back in working order. Actually, as usual, it wasn't the machine's fault. Let's see. . . ." He turned to face the board behind him.

Into the slot below "Projected Winner" dropped an X, then a name: PINHOLSTER.

"Yes, that's it," continued the commentator, radiating good will. The world was safe again. "With 16 per cent of California now in, the computer projects a definite percentage for Pinholster's victory in the state. It will be extremely narrow, says Archie. He gives the Connecticut governor 50.4 per cent of the final California vote and Quinn 49.5 per cent, the other one tenth going to several minor candidates."

There was silence before the television set, broken at last by a long sigh from Stackpole. Kate reached blindly for Eddie's hand.

A few minutes later, as if responding to the projection, Pinholster overtook Eddie for the first time in the actual California count, 1,107,720 to 1,105,093.

From that moment, 1:01 A.M. EST, it was all downhill at Quinn headquarters.

Eddie, unable to sit still, wandered through the long, cluttered room, shaking hands with volunteers, braving the half-hearted forecasts of eventual victory, struggling to stir a numbness within him, nipping at his ginger ale. Papers littered the floor and desks, a stale odor of whisky filled the air and in one side office, a girl leaned against a file cabinet and wept. Only an occasional phone rang, a dispirited signal like that in a rear outpost of a retreating army.

Pinholster's California lead increased as the total went over 5,000,000. Pinholster 2,592,435, Quinn 2,561,081.

One final modest cheer arose when the girl student proudly marked the electoral votes of three more states under the Quinn column: Alaska 3, Hawaii 4, Washington 9. But Pinholster won Oregon's six electoral votes and the final electoral count, assuming that California finished as projected, would stand:

Pinholster 281.

Quinn 257.

Pinholster ran far behind his party, which gained four seats in the Senate and twenty-two in the House and added five new governors to its list. But Eddie's star performance on the vanquished team brought scant solace to 1140 Connecticut Avenue.

The crowd began to thin, the young volunteers slipping away quietly by twos and threes. Eddie shook hands with some at the door. Then he returned to the glass-paneled office, put on his jacket and straightened his tie.

Shortly before 2 o'clock he went before the television cameras he had managed to avoid through most of the night. Some thirty newspapermen ringed the fallen candidate.

"I concede the election to Governor Pinholster," he said. "I congratulate him and pledge him my support through the transition period. After that, it depends on how he runs the country. It was a good, hard, clean fight and our new President-elect never once stooped to questionable tactics. He has nothing to regret. As for me, I regret losing. Actually, it's worse than that. I regret it like hell.

"I want to thank everyone who worked and voted for me. We lost, yes, but we piled up almost 40,000,000 votes and that should serve as a solid warning to the special interests in this country that it's time for a fair shake."

Eddie paused and shoved his jaw forward a fraction of an inch.

"I'll say this. If we don't get that fair shake soon, we'll be back . . . and back . . . and back." He thrust his right arm upward and outward in the familiar campaign gesture. "That's a promise. Good night, everyone."

The shrunken band of volunteers raised a final ragged cheer, then moved toward the door. The television crews packed their cases. Newsmen straggled toward the elevator.

Joe Kuzyk poured half a glass of blended whisky and downed it in three swallows. Margot Hicks dabbed at her eyes with a handkerchief. R Dan Fenelli led most of the staff members past the deserted switchboard into the corridor.

The television set, still running, showed a frantic, festive scene at Pinholster headquarters on Jackson Place. The governor, wearing his lucky wide belt with the brass dolphin at the buckle, spread his arms wide in a victory salute. His wife lifted a champagne glass. Hutchens Boyington III looked smugly happy. The audio carried elated voices, shouts and the popping of champagne corks. Pete Stackpole switched off the set.

A squad of cleaning women appeared at the entrance with mops, pails and a huge refuse cart. One dumpling of a woman hoisted her mop like a baton.

"Eddie! Eddie! Eddie Quinn!"

The chant of the five women fled to the vacant walls, then died as quickly as it was born. Pete Stackpole coughed, a lone sound in the silent room.

"Thanks, ladies," said Eddie. ". . . Well, that's it. Time to leave."

"Ma finally missed one," said Pete. Anna Lou Stackpole had voted for a presidential loser for the first time in half a century.

Eddie walked toward the elevator between Kate and Pete with Flannery and Baker on the flanks.

"You guys still with us?" Eddie asked Flannery. "They don't pay you to guard a Turnpike commissioner, do they?" His voice choked. He could not look at the agents.

"No," said Jim, "but we thought we'd drive you to the hotel on our own time."

"No car," said Eddie. "I've had enough cars for a while. I think we'll just hoof it back to the Hay-Adams."

No one spoke. The elevator dropped in a hush.

Eddie halted in the lobby. "Pete, we owe Kate some money. She came closest on the electoral vote."

They each took ten-dollar bills from their wallets and handed them to Kate.

"Some night," said Eddie. "You win your election and the money. Me, I'm a two-time loser."

"Same old world," said Pete. "The rich get richer."

And they walked into the cold night.

23

A chill rain, driven by a wind sweeping down from the north, pelted New York City the Thursday night after the election. Braving the dismal weather, a band of men and women trooped into a building on Fifth Avenue, shook their raincoats, stamped water from umbrellas and filed, damp but expectant, into the office of Arnold Swensson.

Political reporters, electronic journalists and a smattering of sociologists and political scientists answered the pollster's summons to an 8:30 P.M. press conference bearing on the nation's ballot decision on Tuesday.

As solemn as the myth of transubstantiation, his bald head glowing like an altar fire, the high priest of American polling faced some fifty rain-moistened believers and skeptics and asked permission to read a few words. Before anyone could object, Swensson adjusted his reading glasses, snapped a paper at the crease and began:

"At the request of a consortium of university political study centers, headed by the Woodrow Wilson school at Princeton, I have today polled six thousand voters in all fifty states and the District of Columbia. Our objective: to find out how the United States would have voted for President had the election been held today instead of two days ago.

"Like all my polls, this one was carefully weighted to provide an accurate picture of the electoral vote status. The polling was conducted from 7 A.M. to 7 P.M. EST today by skilled interviewers, most of whom worked for me during the recent campaign. Every fourth person polled was interviewed in depth. Based on the results, I can state with conviction that had the election been held today, it would have produced this outcome:

"Electoral vote: Edward Quinn 307, Hugh Pinholster 231.

"Popular vote rounded off: Quinn 41,500,000, Pinholster 40,000,-000, minor candidates 300,000.

"This contrasts with the actual election results Tuesday of Pinholster's 281 electoral votes to Quinn's 257 and Pinholster's 40,971,000 popular votes to Quinn's 40,525,000. So had the election been held today, our President-elect tonight would be Edward Quinn." Swensson smiled wistfully. "Of course, for a poller, the election is never today, but always tomorrow or yesterday."

"That's just the point, Mr. Swensson," said Vince Anderson. "Why conduct a poll for a nonexistent election?"

Swensson nodded to Anderson as though he were a bright pupil of enormous potential. "Yes. Well, my sponsors and I were intrigued by the impact on the election of Commissioner Quinn's unusual candor after his traffic accident. My poll had shown Quinn on a rising trend, perhaps enough to win, up until the time of his crash Friday. He then dropped off sharply, but on Sunday night a new trend toward Quinn set in. My depth interviews indicated this was caused by people who, on sober second thought, were impressed by what they considered to be Quinn's veracity. This Quinn trend continued right up until the voting started."

"How do you know today's poll isn't distorted by the soreheads who bet money on Quinn and don't like to be proved wrong?"

Swensson flinched at the mention of losing wagerers. "Because our depth interviews were devised to eliminate that factor among others. Also today's results fit perfectly with the late Quinn trend which began Sunday night after his TV appearance. Today's numbers sit on that trend line as nicely as sparrows on a wire."

"Are you saying that a major vote trend takes a few days to get up steam?"

"Exactly."

"How would California have gone if the election had been today?" asked Vince Anderson.

"All details are being withheld until the political scientists analyze the figures. I understand a paper will be issued in the spring with all the data. It should be very interesting."

"Won't this announcement just upset the country some more?" asked Sybil Jamieson.

"No. I don't think so." No upset, thought Swensson, could quite equal that of surrendering $19,000 in gambling winnings, still the best hunch bet of his career. "We put out the total because we knew you news hounds would sniff them out in a day or so anyway. No, the country will take these new numbers in stride."

But Swensson was wrong for the second time in his predictions. Hard losers swooped down on the numbers like vultures after fresh carrion. Arguments and post-mortems raged in home, factory and office. Brawls broke out in neighborhood bars. In Wilkes-Barre, Pennsylvania, a Pinholster partisan was stabbed to death. A dozen high schools adjourned classes Friday because of corridor rampages by warring Quinn and Pinholster factions. In some urban areas, fanatic followers raised Eddie to a quasi-martyr status as though he had been assassinated instead of merely defeated. A record company prepared to rush out an album of highway ballads, with new political lyrics to such songs as "Route 66" and "The Sailor on a Concrete Sea," under the title, *Epitaph to President Eddie*.

The inevitable demands for recounts erupted like acne. Quinn enthusiasts leveled allegations of fraud in Chicago, where the mayor's organization squeezed out a Pinholster triumph after holding back several precincts until downstate Illinois appeared safe. Pinholster carried Illinois by only 19,000 votes out of 5,000,000 cast. Had Eddie taken Illinois, he would have won the election without California. But recounts cost money and the Quinn non-organization could barely pay its TV and radio bills.

Thousands of college students believed that Eddie had been robbed. The university campuses, heavily pro-Quinn ever since his proposal to limit military service to men over fifty, were especially tender over Eddie's defeat and seized on Swensson's figures with glee.

Early Saturday morning the news wires carried an unusual item from Salt Lake City. A Pinholster elector with an unbelievable name, Ezekiel H. Thornquest, announced that when the Utah electors met on Monday, December 13, he would cast his ballot for Quinn instead of Pinholster. Thornquest reasoned that although Pinholster had carried Utah by the width of a knife blade, the state's sentiment was now Quinnish by a sizable margin. Citing Swensson's Thursday poll to show that the feeling was nationwide, he said he intended to vote for the man the people wanted regardless of his own commitment as a Pinholster elector.

Several hours later another Pinholster elector residing in Murfreesboro, Tennessee, said that he would follow Thornquest's lead. While Pinholster won Tennessee on a close vote, he said, it was now obvious that Tennessee wanted Eddie Quinn for President. When electors met in mid-December, he intended to bolt his party pledge and vote "the popular will."

In late afternoon a third elector, this one from Pennsylvania, announced that he too would desert Pinholster for Quinn. The name of the third defector made news. He was an able young lawyer named Ben Smithers, a cousin of Jeff Smithers, Pinholster's campaign manager. Ben Smithers said that under the Constitution electors were entitled to exercise independent judgment and that they had many options other than that of maintaining party loyalty.

"One of these options," said Smithers, "I call Exit Nine, that is the obligation to leave the highway of custom and vote for the other major candidate when there is clear and open evidence that the nation wants that candidate as its next President. In December therefore, I intend to take Exit Nine."

The phrase struck the fancy of communicators and within an hour "to take Exit Nine" was hammered into the national vocabulary as descriptive of the act of switching from Pinholster to Quinn in the Electoral College. Contacted in Salt Lake City, Ezekiel Thornquest gave his blessing to the designation. "Eddie Quinn broke with tradition to tell the truth about Exit Nine," he said, "and in that same spirit of facing facts as they are I plan to take Exit Nine next month."

The triple defection dominated the Saturday evening news shows. Was a trend under way that would reverse the election results? Baffled announcers noted that a shift of only thirteen Pinholster electors would throw the presidency to Quinn. Senator Framingham, the Quinn kingmaker who had bolted to Pinholster, charged that "a conspiracy to thwart the will of the people" had been hatched. The head of the American Bar Association warned of chaos and possible bloodshed should more electors repudiate party pledges. As if to underline his prognosis, two men exchanged gunfire on a Chicago street to climax a political quarrel and the Quinn zealot suffered a flesh wound. All over the country newsmen dug into the files for facts on the antiquated Electoral College process. Earlier defectors were named, including one in 1968, Dr. Lloyd W. Bailey of Rocky Mount, North Carolina, who voted for George Wallace instead of the candidate, Richard Nixon, who carried North Carolina.

Sunday morning, with the election now five days behind, Pinholster's right to become President on the basis of his paper-thin majority threatened to divide the nation once more. Preachers took the Electoral College for the text of sermons, prayed for sanity. Newspaper editorials, led by the solemn voice of *The Kingdom and the Power* in New York, pleaded with politicians to preserve Tuesday's results untarnished. Editorial writers pointed out that a post-election switch to Quinn would yield but questionable political profit anyway since Pinholster's party had swept the Congress and state legislatures. Hutchens Boyington III proposed that any elector deserting Pinholster be barred forever from any post, no matter how modest, in the party hierarchy. In Pennsylvania, Sam Shadowitz, one of the Quinn kingmakers, said that he and a group of citizens would sue in the courts to force Elector Smithers to honor his original pledge to Pinholster. The irony of a Quinn kingmaker now resorting to litigation to nail down the election of Eddie's opponent was but little noted in the general turmoil.

That Sunday morning Ted Witherspoon paced the book-lined den of his home in Highland Park, the Dallas enclave famous for the profusion of its springtime azalea blooms and the all-weather altitude of its incomes. Ted was raging. He had not spoken to Kate since she and that rabble-rousing swordsman from the Buccaneer Motor Lodge had turned him into a national joke. When Kate called from Washington the day after the election, Ted ordered his secretary to refer Mrs. Witherspoon to the law firm of Albright, Dodge & Kastenhood. His long-distance chats with Susan had been painful ordeals, especially since his daughter seemed less concerned about the family name than in the fact that her mother had been re-elected despite the scandal. Susan's tone hinted that she thought Dallas voters had been eminently reasonable and she sounded a shade patronizing when she said: "Don't worry, Dad. It'll all work out." Damn if he understood the cool sophistication of today's sixteen-year-olds.

And just now, as he leafed through the canceled checks in the October bank statement, he had found it. Of all the goddamned gall! A check for $10,000 made out to the "Eddie Quinn Campaign" and signed by Kate. From the joint checking account, sure, but most of that money had been deposited by him. My God, they were even liable for a gift tax on any contribution above $3000. He glanced at the date. October 20, the same day, wasn't it, that he met with Charlie and Rich at the Chicago Club? The worst of it was that he could imagine Kate's unruffled voice replying should he accuse her of trying to humiliate him by writing the check. "Humiliate?" she'd ask with that patina of innocence. "Why, Eddie was your candidate. You helped pick him. Don't you remember?"

The hell with Kate. What mattered now was that son-of-a-bitch Quinn. Ted glanced again at the headlines in the Sunday papers spread over the desk, then dialed Rich Cuthbert's home number in Grosse Pointe outside Detroit. When the publisher answered, the two dethroned kingmakers made short work of the opening pleasantries.

"This Exit Nine mania could get serious," said Ted.

"You're telling me," said Rich. "I just talked to Charlie in Chicago and he says one of the Illinois electors is threatening to jump to Quinn."

"I'm for a backfire. Let's start putting the heat on our own—I mean Quinn's—line-up. Same thing we talked over that day in Chicago."

"We're ahead of you. Charlie and I decided to go to work. He'd already lined up eight or nine Quinn electors around the country just in case. Matter of fact, I was just starting on my list when you

called. My first is Bob Schaffran in St. Louis. He's the one I
mentioned, the minority interest in our TV station. I've got some
others."

"I'll get on it. Are we going to co-ordinate or what?"

"Yeah," said Rich, "let's aim at a conference call at one this
afternoon to see how we're doing. Charlie and I think some
Quinn electors ought to announce right now their intention to
jump. That might discourage wavering Pinholster people."

"He's right. A good quick backfire will burn this thing out."

That Sunday afternoon three Quinn electors in states carried by
Eddie, Missouri, Michigan and Texas, made public their intention to
vote for Pinholster when electors met in state capitals on the date set
by law, the first Monday after the second Wednesday in December.
One of them, Robert Schaffran of St. Louis, said he decided on the
shift only as a means of counterbalancing the defecting Pinholster
electors who "would made a mockery of the integrity of the ballot in
this country." The Texas elector, David Cooper, commented in
similar vein.

Ted Witherspoon's prediction that a quick backfire would consume
the fires of rebellion in Pinholster's electoral ranks proved to be one
of the few accurate election forecasts since Eddie Quinn's bizarre
nomination in Houston less than four weeks before. Having suffered
through the trauma of the death of one presidential candidate, the
involvement of his replacement in a fatal motor accident, a hairline
election and then a pollster's estimate that the country actually had
voted against its own wishes, the nation was in no mood for another
cliff-hanger in the antiquated, little-understood Electoral College.
Accustomed to accept even close election results as philosophically
as they did unwanted football scores, the losers in Tuesday's elections decided to take Pinholster's victory in stride. The country,
they knew through experience, would survive. For most people there
was an air of unreality about the switching of the electors, obscure
persons whose strange voices reverberated hollowly in a well of
anonymity.

But leaders were taking no chances. Nothing congeals the arteries
of commerce more swiftly than uncertainty and men of means and
influence did not want more defecting electors to disturb the marts

of trade when the country returned to work Monday morning.
Striving for a common front to preserve Tuesday's election results
intact, members of the establishment sought one another out in
the ordered wilderness of the Bell System. As one sample of many
chain consultations Sunday afternoon, Albert Kunsler, president of
Empire Motors, called his good friend, the chairman of the board
of governors of the New York Stock Exchange, who called his good
friend, a senior vice-president of the Chase Manhattan Bank, who
telephoned his old and good friend, the President of the United
States, who, in turn, at 2 P.M. Sunday, called his close friend, the
Chief Justice of the United States.

"Stu, it's time to put an end to this Exit Nine insanity," said
the President.

"I agree, Mr. President," said the head of the Supreme Court.
"The idea of a bunch of political nobodies upsetting the people's
vote is absurd."

"I'm going to make a statement first thing in the morning, calling
upon all electors to stand by their party pledges. I think that will
end it, but just in case it doesn't, I wonder if you'd consider
saying something? I understand your delicate position, but there
are ways. . . ."

"Of course. I'll give it some thought. I can't believe it will be
necessary, but count on me for some reserve ammunition, Mr.
President."

"Thanks, Stu. But as I say, I doubt if we'll have to call on you."

As it turned out, neither the Chief Justice nor the President had
to say a word in public on the subject of fickle electors.

Eddie Quinn and Kate Witherspoon lazed in the hot Caribbean
sun that Sunday afternoon on St. Martin, the half-Dutch, half-
French island at the northern end of the gentle arc of the Leewards.
A friend of Kate's had lent them a stone house perched on a cliff
on the French side near the town of Marigot. Eddie, in swim
trunks, and Kate, wearing a white bikini, lounged in deck chairs at
the side of a pool carved from the mauve rocks. Sixty feet below, the
blue, creamy sea surged against the cliff with a rhythmic beat of
drums. Beyond the point, waves curled on a long, sloping beach of

gleaming sand. Several frigate birds wheeled effortlessly on languid updrafts. A soft breeze, moist and salty, riffled leaves of the yellow trumpet vines and crimson bougainvillea that draped the house like a brilliant scarf. In the distance the low, hazy profile of Anguilla Island lay beneath a lone cloud.

Eddie yawned. "If this is the life of the loser, maybe I ought to lose more often."

Kate opened one eye and smiled. She was stretched out on the blue pad of the deck chair, her black hair damp from a recent swim and her body beaded with shining drops of water. She had browned rapidly since they arrived two days ago.

"Remember our first night at the Apollo Motel in Houston?" she asked. "You said you'd like to make love on a high cliff, overlooking the sea, in bright sunlight. Well, here we are . . . but so are they." She motioned with her head toward the well-staffed house.

"That's the trouble with you rich. Too many little helpers."

"The election seems years away," she said lazily. "Wonder what people are saying about it today?"

They had not listened to the radio news nor seen a newspaper since early Saturday morning. Vince Anderson and three other reporters, the last remnants of the campaign brigade, were quartered in a Marigot hotel and had agreed not to bother Eddie until sundown today. But when Eddie and Kate returned from a beach stroll in late morning, the maid reported that a Mr. Anderson was anxious to reach Eddie on the phone. Eddie put it off. It was a day for blue sky, uncloaked sunshine and dozing by the pulsing sea.

"Let's try the three o'clock news," said Eddie. He reached down and switched on a portable radio resting on the flagstone deck.

The bolting electors completely dominated the fifteen-minute news program from the United States. Even discounting the pitch of frenzy the announcer sought to sustain from bulletin to bulletin, it was obvious that America was puzzled and disconcerted by some unknown figureheads called electors who threatened to confuse or even reverse last Tuesday's decision.

"What do you make of that?" asked Kate after he switched off the radio.

"It's nutty. There might be some excuse for it if I'd won the popular vote but got nosed out in the electoral count. But hell, I lost both ways."

Kate groped for a cigarette in the leather bag beside her lounge chair. "Ezekiel Thornquest! Of all the names. Did you ever hear of him?"

"Never. I wish I'd made a campaign pitch for abolishing the Electoral College. It makes no sense any more."

"Absolute nonsense. Suppose you'd been the winner and then your own electors tried to throw it to Pinholster. Say, I think I see Ted's fine hand in the counteroffensive. That Texas elector of yours, Dave Cooper, is a lawyer friend of Ted's."

"I think I ought to say something, Kate. If we just let this thing rock along, it might get out of hand."

"Right. I'd love you to be a winner, but not this way."

"I'd hate like hell to win the big one some day and then have a lot of party hacks steal it away from me on a technicality." Eddie heaved himself from the deck chair.

"You going to call Vince?"

"Yep. Won't take long." Eddie trotted up the stone steps to the clifftop house.

He worked with a pad and pencil for ten minutes at a metal mesh table on the sun-splashed patio, then put in a call for Vince Anderson at his hotel in Marigot. Anderson answered a few minutes later.

"I've got a statement for you," said Eddie. "If you want to come out at six, okay, but this is for use right away. Tell the other men, will you? . . . Ready? . . .

" 'While I appreciate the confidence in me as shown by some electors, I urge every Pinholster elector who has taken a so-called Exit Nine to cancel that intention and return to his original pledge. Furthermore, I urge all electors chosen on Tuesday to vote as the people of their states voted.

" 'If elected by a majority of the electors in December, as remote as that possibility may be, I would repudiate the designation of President-elect.

" 'If certified as the winner by Congress upon the opening of the elector ballots in the House of Representatives on January 6, I would refuse to serve as President. This is a fixed decision not subject to change under any conditions.

"'While I don't think either of these events will happen, I want to make my position clear right now before this unexpected switching of electors goes any further.

"'I wish I had been elected, but I was not. Last Tuesday the nation elected Governor Hugh Pinholster both by popular and electoral vote. To change the nation's decision after the fact, upon whatever pretext, would be to destroy a government of law and custom and substitute the whims of anarchy.'"

Eddie ended his slow dictation and waited until he heard Anderson stop typing. "You think that 'whims of anarchy' is too flowery, Vince?"

"No, it's okay. You don't usually talk that way, but this is special."

"Yeah." Eddie thought for a time. "Listen, Vince, I may be back on this high-speed lane someday, so do me a favor, huh?"

"What's that, Eddie?"

"When you write your story, put in there somewhere that when you asked me how I feel about losing such a close one, I just said: 'Well, I asked for a fair shake, and I'm still all shook up.' . . . Does that wrap it up, Vince?"

"No. There's another development. Senator Framingham has started a move to elect Rich Cuthbert chairman when the national committee meets next month. Framingham says the objective is to 'put the party back on the tracks of tradition and sanity after the recent aberration of Quinnism.' Any comment?"

"You're damn right. That's a move to keep the party in the hands of the same old clubby crowd of rich, self-interest, executive-suite boys. We'll fight 'em with everything we have. The next national chairman of this party is going to be Congressman Joe Kuzyk. The ordinary people showed their muscle last Tuesday and now, by God, they're going to start using it. From now on, this is the people's party."

"Is that for direct quotes?"

"Right. Just say Eddie Quinn is coming home fighting. We intend to change this party for good and the first step is the election of Joe Kuzyk as national chairman."

"What about governor of New Jersey, Eddie?"

"I'm not ready to announce yet, but I don't mind telling you off the record. Sure, I'm going for it—with Pete Stackpole as manager and Jim Flannery and Oscar Baker handling security. The people are on the move, Vince."

"You expect much opposition?"

"Opposition?" Eddie gazed through a window at Kate lounging on the pool deck below. The soft breeze stirred the trumpet vines and a frigate bird banked lazily above the sparkling sea.

"This fall I relearned a lesson from my old trucking days. There ain't no easy run."

Bestselling Thrillers — action-packed for a great read

___ $4.50 0-425-09138-4 **19 PURCHASE STREET**
Gerald A. Browne

___ $4.50 0-425-08383-7 **THE HUNT FOR RED OCTOBER**
Tom Clancy

___ $3.95 0-515-08415-8 **QUILLER** Adam Hall

___ $3.95 0-441-77812-7 **THE SPECIALIST** Gayle Rivers

___ $3.50 0-425-09104-X **RUSSIAN SPRING**
Dènnis Jones

___ $3.95 0-441-23422-4 **FIELD OF BLOOD**
Gerald Seymour

___ $3.95 0-441-58321-0 **NOCTURNE FOR THE GENERAL**
John Trenhaile

___ $3.95 0-425-09582-7 **THE LAST TRUMP**
John Gardner

___ $3.95 0-441-36934-0 **SILENT HUNTER**
Charles D. Taylor

___ $3.95 0-425-09558-4 **COLD SEA RISING**
Richard Moran

___ $4.50 0-425-09884-2 **STONE 588** Gerald A. Browne

___ $3.95 0-441-30598-9 **GULAG** Sean Flannery

___ $3.95 0-515-09178-2 **SKYFALL** Thomas H. Block